"I love it on so many levels, the immense feeling of place, the slow, irresistible sense of being drawn deep into the family and its story, and the strange hovering of menace somewhere in the idyll. Wonderful."
—Penny Vincenzi

"Spellbinding." —*Independent*

"Gripping." —*Irish Times*

"Gorgeous." —*Stylist*

"I can't remember the last time I was so enthralled." —*Red*

"Epic, absorbing…Full of intrigue and emotion." —*Fabulous*

"By turns painfully sad and heart-lifting, with characters that stay with you." —*Good Housekeeping*

"Authentic and satisfying. An immersive mystery." —*Woman & Home*

"A poignant tale." —*Woman*

"Fabulously gripping." —*Prima*

"Atmospheric and descriptive…Full of tragedy and hardship, love and redemption…Hugely enjoyable." —*Psychologies*

"I was blissfully carried away by this intelligent (she's as good as the great Rosamunde Pilcher), classy, and superbly executed family saga." —*Saga*

"A really superior modern saga, with utterly true-to-life characters." —*Sunday Mirror*

"The reader becomes deeply immersed in this charismatic family's fortunes. The result is that rare and lovely thing, an all-engaging and all-consuming drama." —*Daily Mail*

By Harriet Evans

THE
BELOVED
GIRLS

Praise for

The Beloved Girls
and the novels of Harriet Evans

"A gorgeous epic…It's slightly gothic, wholly absorbing—I adored it."   —Marian Keyes

"This sweeping, absorbing story is a treat."   —Adele Parks

"Bewitching, beguiling, and utterly beautiful, THE BELOVED GIRLS will pull you into their mysterious and enchanted world and never let you go. With a cast of compelling characters and a labyrinthine plot, it's a page-turner of the most luxurious kind—a real escape."   —Veronica Henry

"Comfort reading of the highest order."   —India Knight

"A sweeping novel you won't put down."   —Katie Fforde

"Richly layered…Unforgettable…This is a story to get truly lost in."   —Isabelle Broom

"This is the most gripping, atmospheric book, heavy with mystery and intriguing right till the end. I loved it."

—Sophie Kinsella

"She reels you in and then you're hooked, right to the last page."

—Patricia Scanlan

"Atmospheric and altogether wonderful."   —Lesley Pearse

THE
BELOVED

GIRLS

Harriet Evans

GC

GRAND CENTRAL
PUBLISHING

New York   Boston

Copyright © 2021 by Venetia Books
Reading group guide copyright © 2022 by Venetia Books and Hachette Book Group, Inc.
"Beloved Rituals" copyright © 2022 by Venetia Books

Cover design by Kathleen Lynch/Black Kat Design.
Cover images: door © Benjamin Harte/Arcangel; bronze bee © Miguel Sobreira; ivy and live bees from Getty; shadow figure from Shutterstock.
Cover copyright © 2022 by Hachette Book Group, Inc.

Grand Central Publishing
Hachette Book Group
1290 Avenue of the Americas, New York, NY 10104
grandcentralpublishing.com
twitter.com/grandcentralpub

First published in 2021 by Headline Review, an imprint of Headline Publishing Group, in the Great Britain.

First Edition: May 2022

Grand Central Publishing is a division of Hachette Book Group, Inc. The Grand Central Publishing name and logo is a trademark of Hachette Book Group, Inc.

The publisher is not responsible for websites (or their content) that are not owned by the publisher.

Library of Congress Control Number: 2021950106

ISBNs: 9781538722176 (trade pbk.), 9781538722183 (ebook)

Printed in the United States of America

LSC-C

Printing 1, 2022

This book is for anyone who needs it, with my love

The twelve hunters are locals. Eleven lepers will die in Christ if they accept the sacrament. The ten commandments are the word of God and must be obeyed even in this pagan place. Nine bright shiners are the diamonds in the family ring which Sylvia wore and Kitty would have inherited. Eight go into the hives in April for the spring harvest. Seven stars make up the Plow and when it is low in the sky that means August is here and we can collect. Six sides of the chapel, six sides of the cells. Five walkers walk with the hunters to the chapel every year. Four make the honey, the women's work. Three rivals are the men, it must be men, who stand to gain the most if the pact is broken. They must be watched. Two beloved girls dress in green and white and walk behind the procession; they symbolize purity.

And there is one alone, one outsider. They stand outside the chapel. They, like the lepers, are nothing, no one. They remind us inside how lucky we are.

I'll sing you twelve, O
Twelve come for the comb, O!
What are your twelve, O?
Twelve for the twelve new hunters
Eleven for the eleven who went to heaven,
Ten for the ten commandments,
Nine for the nine bright shiners,
Eight for the Spring Collectors,
Seven for the seven stars in the sky,
Six for the six-sides of the comb,
Five for the five proud walkers,
Four for the honey makers,
Three, three, the rivals,
Two, two, the beloved girls,
Clothed all in green, O,
One is one and all alone, and evermore shall be so.

Traditional Collecting Song, to the tune of
"Green Grow the Rushes, O"

Young women they run like hares on the mountains,
Young women they run like hares on the mountains
If I were but a young man, I'd soon go a hunting
To my right fol diddle dero, to my right fol diddle dee.

Young women they sing like birds in the bushes,
Young women they sing like birds in the bushes
If I were but a young man, I'd go and bang those bushes
To my right fol diddle dero, to my right fol diddle dee.

"Hares on the Mountain (First Version)"
Songs from Somerset, 1904, ed. Cecil Sharp

THE
BELOVED
GIRLS

Prologue

October 1983

I was twelve when I first went to Vanes. My mother had walked out on us the previous month, and I assume this is why we were invited. The postcard Sylvia sent my father asked us to *"please come for a few days, and bring Janey. Oh do come Simon, surely you'll come now?"* So Daddy and I drove down from London, insistent October rain following us all the way.

My father and I often took day trips out from the suburbs into the English countryside. To Windsor Castle or the Chilterns; or to Stonehenge, when I was only five, when you were still permitted to scramble about the vast, lichen-covered stones. Daddy made these trips magical for me, peppering the day with jokes, talk of ancient kings, natural phenomena, songs, and excellent sandwiches. "All shall be well, little one!" he'd say, if we hit traffic, or when a seagull on Lyme Regis beach stole my Nutella sandwich. "And all shall be well and all manner of things shall be well." It's Julian of Norwich. After he died, I found it in his wallet, torn from a library copy of *Revelations of Divine Love*. I hadn't realized it was a quote from someone else until then.

It's strange to say it but I didn't really miss my mother. I think I knew she didn't belong with us. She made the house a dark, anxious place—she so obviously disliked my father, and could not engage at all with his mad schemes, his living in the future, his avoidance of his past. So the drive to Vanes, our first trip since she'd left, was exciting. Our shabby mock-Tudor semi-detached house was, as ever, in chaos and it was good to be going away, Daddy kept saying. He had picked me up from school early, so we left in good time. "She has corns," he'd airily informed my teacher, as I packed my pencil case, watched with envy by Claire and Ems, and the rest of the class. "Dreadful corns."

Miss Linton had smiled as we left. My father had that effect on people. "Goodbye, Mr. Lestrange," she'd called. "Hope you feel better, Jane dear."

We laughed about it, in the car, eating Opal Fruits. I was designated DJ—we fought a little over that, since Daddy always wanted jazz, and I wanted pop music, but we were always able to compromise. Eventually, we settled on Kate Bush.

"Kitty and Joss have exeats this weekend," he told me. "So they'll be home from school. They're the same age as you."

I didn't know what exeats meant but I nodded. I was with Daddy, and everything was all right.

For most of the rest of the journey he was happy, singing old jazz standards, asking for coffee from the Thermos. But as we left the motorway and drove further west, through that thin strip of Somerset coastline above Exmoor bordering Devon where the countryside becomes dense, hilly woodland, peppered with ancient castles and grand remote houses, my father grew silent.

"I haven't seen them for so long," he said, a few times. "This feels very strange."

Eddies of swirling leaves rose and fell in front of us on the twisting lanes; periodically the green sea of the Bristol Channel flashed before our eyes, fringed by trees, then disappeared.

"How do you know them?" I asked, at some point, shivering in the rickety old Ford, which was always rather touch and go on long journeys.

"Knew him in the war. I knew her mother in London" was all he said. He was quiet, for a long time.

Then, abruptly, he added: "Sylvia's wonderful. And I'm sure her children will be too. It's a funny old house, Janey. They have this ceremony every summer."

"What kind of ceremony?"

"There's a chapel, in the grounds of the house. Half derelict. The Hunters keep bees in there."

"Bees?!" I said, amused. I remember it really clearly. Bees, they were strange, alien creatures, and beekeeping was not something anyone I knew did.

"Every year, on the same day, they process across to the chapel. They open the combs, taste the honey. Take it back to the house. Half for them" —my father winced, as though he had bitten down on a sore tooth— "and half for us."

It was almost dark by the time we arrived, though it was not yet five, but the thick woodland behind the house seemed to cast all in front into gloom. I could hear a dog, barking frantically over the whistling wind as we trundled slowly up the driveway.

As we got out of the car, soft rain gently soaked us. The trees were darkest green and orange, and, above, the faintest sliver of a teal sky, gilded with silver and gold from the setting sun. A side door opened and a lantern overhead was switched on, throwing us into relief, like criminals caught in the act. We froze.

"Ah! Come in, dear Simon, out of the rain," called a woman's clear voice.

"Shall we, Janey?" said Daddy. He rubbed my arm. "Listen, old girl. They're a bit—well, they're different to us. But we go back an awfully long way. Sylvia's invited us and it means a great deal to me that she did. I have to make sure she's all right, you see."

The rain was coming down heavily now. Under the open trunk of the car, his face was cast into shadow, the light from the lantern an ugly, mustard color. He looked tired, and suddenly I knew he didn't want to be there.

We grabbed our luggage—my father's capacious Gladstone bag, which was like Mary Poppins's carpet bag, it could hold anything, and my nylon pastel backpack which my mother had bought me before she left (a symbolic present if ever there was one). We dashed through the side gate toward the light, and someone pulled me inside.

It's funny, that first visit to Vanes was mostly spent *in* the house. Years later, when I stayed for the summer, I was rarely inside. We existed outside: on the terrace, by the pool, scrambling along the steep, scented paths down to the beach, into the woods. And the chapel, and the bees.

I stood in the hallway, dripping wet, as Daddy took off his coat. The house smelled of woodsmoke, and a metallic, waxen, turpentine smell. Inside, sound had a curiously deadened quality. In the cramped hall was a strange wooden half-table-half-box on tall legs, carved all over with leaves and fruit and bees.

Above it was a portrait. It was of a youngish man, his body in profile, his head turning toward the viewer, as if caught in the act. The effect was odd, like a photograph, not a painting. I stared at him, his hooded eyes, the long, tapering, curiously white fingers. I didn't like it much. I shivered in the cold, as Daddy held out his hand.

"Hello, darling Sylvia," he said.

The woman who had pulled me inside and was now standing under the swinging lightbulb didn't shake hands. She flung herself at my father. "Come here, oh come here," she said, and he wrapped his arms around her, and patted her hair, and gave a deep, strange, heartbreaking sound I didn't understand. Not then, not for a long time.

"You're here," she whispered, looking up at him, when she finally released him. "Darling Simon. You're really here. And this must be Janey."

She came toward me, clasped my face in her thin, small hands. She was like a girl. In fact she'd only have been in her late thirties, but I was twelve and knew nothing. This was Sylvia Hunter.

"You're very like your dad," she said, stroking my face, and the warmth of her motherly touch was repulsive to me—I moved away.

"Joss! Merry! Kitty! *Kitty!* They're here," she called, with a brightness which I knew well. We were always going to houses where people didn't want us—Daddy misunderstanding invitations, or my mother not wanting to be there, and children who didn't want to say hello.

"What?" A voice came from a room further down the dark corridor, a door banging open.

"Sorry, darling," said Sylvia. "Look, Simon's here. With his daughter, Janey. Remember?"

A tall, handsome man with a thin face and brown brackets of

hair falling over his forehead peered round the door. His eyes narrowed when he saw Daddy.

"Charles," my father said, with an almost imperceptible nod back.

"Simon. I see. Look, just on the phone to a man about a dog. Catch up with you later."

His gaze rested on me for a second then flickered away. Sylvia nodded, still smiling. "We'll eat at about seven, OK, darling?"

"Seven on the dot, please." He gave a minuscule acknowledgment to Daddy again, then shut the door.

I thought this was rude, and turned to my father to see his reaction. He was watching the closed door, his expression seemingly blank.

I wished we were still at home then, for a split second, in the comfortable mess of our front room, with the battered old blue sofa and the piles of records and books stacked on the coir matting floor, packets of biscuits, discarded homework and various inventions of Daddy's scattered throughout the room. I wanted to feel safe. And yet I liked the spicy, warm smell of home cooking here, of woodsmoke, the thudding sounds of family. I wanted to explore.

"Children!" Sylvia called, with a note of hysteria. "Please come and say hello!"

She had to repeat herself before, from around the corner of the wood-paneled hallway, three faces appeared.

"These are the twins, this is Joss, and this is Kitty," said Sylvia. "And this is little Merry. She's only nine."

Joss, tousle-haired, in an outsized rugby shirt, politely shook Daddy's hand, and nodded at me. "Good evening." I tried not to show it but I was impressed; boys my age back in Greenford merely grunted. Merry jumped up and down, excited that we were here. She chewed a plait and hung on to her mum's arm. Then Kitty stepped forward. I felt my father pushing me toward her, until we met under the pool of golden light.

"Hi."

"Hi," I said.

"I'm Catherine Hunter," she said, formally. She was in fact quite shy; I didn't know then. I saw only how very beautiful she was. "But you can call me Kitty."

"I'm Janey Lestrange," I said.

She took my hand. I stared into her face, her dark gold hair spilling over her shoulders, her wide, generous mouth, her tall frame. "Come on," she said. She smiled, and I saw the gap in her crooked teeth, the kindness in her eyes. "We found a hedgehog this afternoon in the leaves, we nearly accidentally set him on fire. Rory's locked up because he keeps trying to eat him. Do you want to come and see?"

"Yes," I said.

"He's in the shed. I think he's a he." She rummaged in her pocket, and took out a battered thin white paper bag. "Dad took me and Merry in to Minehead after he picked us up from school. He let us choose sweets. I saved one for you."

It was a Black Jack. I can still feel the almost wet waxiness of the paper, the anxious sliding of the nail to open up the tiny parcel, the delicious sweet-sugar rush of glucose and aniseed on my tongue.

Sylvia came toward me, and put her arm round my shoulder. "Here," she said, and she handed me a little bear, from a side table. It was worn and puckered, but soft, the fur matted into rosettes, a bit like an old guinea pig. He had a battered, ragged blue ribbon round his neck, and a tiny gold pendant, engraved "Harrods."

"He was my bear when I was young—"

"Sylvia," my father said, in a strange voice. "No. That's very kind of you, but she doesn't need it."

She reached as though to take it away but I very slightly moved back, and she shrugged, helplessly. So I was left holding the bear. He was a dull ginger brown, so soft, and smelled delicious, of lavender and sandalwood, like the house itself.

"All right, then. Just for the stay," said Sylvia, tweaking his little ribbon and pendant, in a quick, birdlike, nervous gesture. "It's just something for her to hold on to at night, Simon." She smiled brightly at me. "He's called Wellington. Wellington Bear."

"Wellington?"

The noise of the barking dog increased to a frenzy. I heard Charles shout, and the door opened again. "Sylvia, tell that dog to shut—"

He paused, staring at me and Kitty.

"Two beloved girls," said Sylvia. "Look at them, Charles, darling."

"Excuse me," said Daddy. "Think I left something in the car."

He went outside, banging the door in the still-pouring rain.

I stayed where I was, feeling desperately awkward. Charles folded his arms, seemingly in no hurry this time. "Poor old Simon," he said, smiling. He nodded at me and Kitty, standing side by side. "'*Two, two, the beloved girls.*' Perhaps one day, eh? When they're fully grown. Now, I really do need to work."

He turned into his study and I heard a yowl, and a whack, and silence. "Now stay like that, damn you," he said, dragging the whimpering dog back out into the hall. "I'm not having him in here. Train him properly, he's your dog, Sylvia. Otherwise I'll get rid of him. I mean it. Beloved Girls. Hah. Yes, perhaps she'd do for the Collecting. It's a good idea."

"Just a silly thing we do at the end of summer," Sylvia said to me, as Charles's study door swung open again. She brushed away my hair and tucked the bear back into my arms. "Kitty can explain it later. Now, where's Simon?"

After a minute Daddy reappeared, his hands shunted deep into his pockets, bringing fresh air and scudding lemon-yellow leaves with him. "My apologies," he said. "Rather light-headed. Must be the long drive. Sorry, Sylvia. Just—it's wonderful to see you, my dear."

And they stared at each other again, unsmiling, and I thought it couldn't be true, whatever they said out loud.

We were there for four perfect days, and when we drove away back to London I cried as though my heart would break.

"Well, I'm glad you enjoyed yourself," said Daddy wryly, as I sobbed, staring out of the window.

It had been magical. I thought of the dried, dead fern leaves the color of flames that we had collected and I'd stored inside my Judy Blume book, the Wham! cassette that Kitty played non-stop and she and I and Merry danced to, to Joss's huge annoyance, because he was really into New Romantics. The feel of Kitty's soft hair against my cheek, trapped by my arms flung around her shoulders, as we hugged goodbye. "I'll miss you so much," she'd whispered. And, tucked inside my backpack along with the ferns, Wellington Bear. "Don't tell your father, but I want you to have him," Sylvia had told me quietly. "Charles hates him. He remembers him too, you see. Keep him safe, darling."

As I stood in the hall, slumping with tiredness and misery at the thought of going back to Greenford, to a house without a mother and to a life with a mother who didn't love me the way other mothers did, this curious, hurried gesture meant something.

But what meant the most was when Kitty appeared as I was being reluctantly pushed toward the car. My father was saying goodbye to Sylvia, whispering in her ear, as she gave him a tight, jerky hug.

"Here," said Kitty, quietly. She held out her hand, a tight fist. "It's for you. Please will you come back." It wasn't a question.

Slowly, she unfurled her hand. There lay a soft, dark-gold, dead honeybee. Its black wings were folded up, its stripes soft, the black segmented legs in angular shapes. The sting was slightly bent.

She tipped it into my open palm. "Don't worry, it won't sting." Her small voice hissed in my ear: "It just means now that when you see one, it'll remind you of here. And of me. So you'll never forget us."

I didn't go to Vanes again for over five years. In those intervening years I didn't forget. I was reminded of her every time I saw a dead bee on a window sill or a pavement or in a dusty corner of our house, and I'd stop and nod. I needed no reminder though, because I thought about Kitty every day. How kind she was to me. How beautiful. Her house, her gilded life, her air of confidence, as if everything was easy. I wanted to be her. I wanted to be one of them. More than anything, before or since, God help me.

Part One

2018

Chapter One

When did it begin to fall apart? Afterward, she would look back to this point in time: the arrival back home, though she never knew precisely when the moment itself came, the tipping point, so that the weight of what she carried grew heavier and heavier, and the scales simply could not be balanced anymore.

"We should have just got the train," said Tom, moodily pulling his backpack out of the trunk. "We'd have been home like, *hours* ago. Mum, next time, can you *please* make Dad take the train."

"It's nearly midnight, for God's sake," said his older sister, Carys, flicking through her phone as she stood on the front door-step, chewing gum. She jerked her head back, letting her hoodie slide away and revealing a pink forelock that Catherine, getting out of the car, mentally reminded herself would have to be dyed back to its original blond before the school term started.

"You know what Dad's like about the Eurotunnel," she said, hauling her own bag smartly out of the car. "I can't help you. You're related to him by blood. Take it up with him."

Tom laughed. Their father, Davide, paused, the front-door key in one hand, and then turned to address his bedraggled, exhausted family.

"The Eurotunnel," he proclaimed, raising the key as if it were a baton, "is a miracle of engineering. To drive one's car onto a train, and to be conveyed by that train into France, is a great privilege. It is the longest—"

"*Submerged tunnel in the world,*" Carys said, without looking up from her phone. "I know, Dad. But there's also the Eurostar. You get on this strange thing called a 'train' and it takes you to, oh, I don't know, about ten minutes from our own house without driving a carbon-polluting vehicle—"

"Irrelevant," said Davide, inserting the key in the lock.

"And you don't have to—oh, I don't know," said Tom, joining in with glee, "queue up for hours at Calais and dodge desperate refugees trying to cling on to your car and then drive for hours on the other end in almost solid traffic."

"You cannot drive in solid traffic," said Davide, his handsome face splitting into a smile. "Haha! There. A fact."

"Oh my God. *Mum*," yelled Tom.

Catherine just laughed. Across the road, their neighbor Judith was putting out her recycling. Catherine waved briefly at her.

"Welcome back," Judith said. "Hope you had a wonderful time in France?"

"We did, thanks," said Catherine.

Judith stood up and Catherine saw her face wore a frown of concern. "And did you relax, Catherine? Have a proper break after that awful trial?" She put her head on one side. "I hope you ignored the newspapers."

Catherine smiled.

"I made her," said Davide, intervening. "I took her phone away, we went on long walks, we ate and we drank. Good Burgundy will solve everything."

"Oh, how nice," said Judith. She fluttered her eyelashes at Davide, who gave her a polite nod and turned to go inside.

Stupid woman. Catherine smiled. "It was good to get away. It's been fairly full on, as you say. Anyway—see you later." She raised her hand.

Carys pushed past her father and went inside first, turning on the hall light. "I'm going out, I promised Lily I'd drop off the memory stick for her. Mum? Where shall I put these letters?"

"On the hall table, but Carys—"

"OK. I need to grab an envelope for it from your study. Mum, there's a letter for you, on the top. Mum?"

But Catherine wasn't listening. Pausing just a moment on the doorstep, she breathed in the evening air. It was that time of year when spring crept in on you suddenly, without warning, the scent of fresh-foul bulbs bursting through the wet, black earth.

Paperwhite narcissi and grape hyacinths dotted their tiny front garden. She could smell new growth, perhaps even the first mown grass from Mr. Lebeniah's neat rectangle, the spicy scent of box next door. Boscastle Road was quiet; a few peach-gold lights glowing in rooms along the black silhouetted street, with the not-quite-dark deep clear sky in relief behind it all.

It was good to be home.

The ice storm the papers had feverishly christened the "Beast from the East" had lingered well into March, and Catherine's usually brisk walk into chambers in Holborn had been hampered for weeks now with frost and slushy brown snow. It seemed they were always in the hallway, struggling into layers of clothing. It had been a rotten Easter, freezing, sleeting weather.

But a few days into April the weather became deliciously warm. Waking up at her beloved in-laws' house in Albi, in southern France, the sound of doves cooing in the dovecote in the garden, the fragile pale-blue skies carved up only with the occasional swallow heading back north, Catherine would check her phone, to see what it was like back in London, wondering why every morning she felt such dread at the prospect of going home again. Usually she loved spring. Not summer. Never summer.

They'd been visiting Davide's family for just over a week and she hoped that a new chapter could begin now after their return. A new school term, the end of a long, brutal winter. The end of the Doyle case.

She shook her head, thoughts crowding in on her, the image of an inbox, filling up again. First, getting back into the swing of work, normal cases again. The prospect of visiting Grant Doyle in prison, not a welcome one. Then a visit to the care home. Then getting Carys to do some work for her exams.

"Catherine," said Davide, as their daughter stomped upstairs. "Come inside, my love. Pour me a drink. I will bring in the rest of the bags from the car."

"It's all done," said Catherine, briefly, smiling at him. She stepped over the threshold, inside the house, inhaling the old smell of home. Furniture polish and wood. The faintest scent of spicy sandalwood from a carved box on the mantelpiece in the sitting room, bought during their twentieth-anniversary trip to Marrakech.

"You confound me, woman," said Davide. He gave her a small kiss. "Are you glad to be back?"

"Sort of."

"Are you glad we went away?"

"Yes. Very."

He stroked her hair, his dark eyes holding hers. "Well, *I* am glad."

She caught hold of him for a moment. "Couldn't we—just move to Albi, Davide? Wouldn't it be nice?" He laughed, faintly uneasy.

"My love, live in the same place as my parents? And Sandrine? I don't think so. What has brought this on?"

"The—being back in it all." She let her shoulders slump. "What's to come. Oh, I'm just being silly."

"No, you have holiday withdrawal." He kissed her forehead. "We discussed, didn't we, the possibility of the weekend break, Catrine."

She edged away from him, and took off her shoes. "Yes...but—"

And suddenly from upstairs there came a scream. "What the— oh fuck. Mum! Oh fuck. Someone's broken in! They've been in your study!"

Catherine and Davide raced up the stairs to the study, a tiny room at the back of the house in between floors. Carys was standing just inside, her face white.

"The door was locked. I wanted an envelope so I unlocked it." She was gabbling. "There's glass all over the roof."

"My God." Davide pushed his daughter aside. "Have they been anywhere—else?"

"They must have come in and gone out through the window. The study was locked, Dad. I unlocked it. They couldn't have got to the rest of the house."

"They smashed the window?" Davide said, gazing round. "Oh no."

Every surface was covered with papers. Years of work, diaries, memos. Someone had sliced into box files and taken them out. While most of the glass was on the roof outside, a couple of pieces of glass rested on the window sill, glinting in the evening light. A glossy magazine, the pages torn out, was scattered on the floor. One page was scrunched up into a ball, resting on the keyboard.

Catherine stared, her hands pressed to her mouth.

"Let me—" Carys said, moving toward the piles of handwritten documents, the balled-up piece of paper.

"No," Catherine said, sharply. "There'll be glass. Get away, darling."

"Almost all the glass is outside actually, Mum. On the flat roof," Carys said.

"Have they—been anywhere else?"

Davide was looking through the rest of the house, the top floor, the kitchen. "I don't see anything," he called up to her, after a minute. "I'm phoning the police."

"No—" Catherine called down. "No, please don't."

"But of course, Catherine. They climbed in—"

Catherine put her hand on the desk, to steady herself. "Darling, do please get out of the way. Just in case."

But Carys bent down and started picking books and papers and stationery off the floor. "I'm going to get a dustpan from downstairs," she said, practically.

"Davide. Please. *Please* don't call them," Catherine said. "I mean it."

Her husband appeared on the landing, the phone in his hand, and stared at her in surprise. "Why on earth not?"

"I know who it was."

"What?"

Tom was at the bottom of the stairs. They were all watching her, the post-holiday bonhomie gone. She felt it, the ground shifting beneath her.

She thought of the article in the newspaper, found on the ferry back. How she had only seen it because she'd turned the page to avoid reading about Grant Doyle.

"It's to do with Grant. It's his sister. Or some friend. I know it is."

"What?" said Tom.

"Catrine. Why?"

"He's eighteen and he's in prison, probably for most of the rest of his life," said Catherine. "And he hates me. He sent some pal of his round to do it. Look. With the kitchen extension roof you can see how they'd get in. They climbed the wall on the street onto the roof and then it's easy." She was still staring round the room.

"Look what they did, though."

Catherine paused, stepping out of the moment, as she had taught herself to do using one of those mindfulness apps. She breathed deeply. They mustn't see how exposed she was. She gestured to the documents, the bundles of papers, scattered on the floor. "I know. I—maybe we should call the police. But I'd just rather not. Look. I'm going to see him soon. I'll talk to him."

"That sounds like a great plan, Mum," said Tom. "Definitely, like, just ask a guy who's been convicted of stabbing his pal to death with a kitchen knife…to stop it? Plan. Purrr-lan." He swallowed, though, his eyes flicking from his mother to his father.

"This is not acceptable," said Davide. "You must do something. If you don't, I'll call the police. Or Ashok, is that the lawyer? Get a cease and desist, you call it?" Their eyes met; a spring breeze, sharp and bold, rushed through the open window behind her, ruffling the papers, making the hairs on Catherine's arms stand up. "You must act. Catrine."

"Yes," she said. "Yes, definitely—yes. I'm sorry."

Davide's voice was terse. "What are you sorry for?"

"Everything."

Tom came up the stairs, gesturing to go into the study, and Catherine stepped past him out onto the tiny landing. But she underestimated the width of the door frame and stumbled slightly, hitting the side of her foot hard against the door. She had no shoes on and the pain of her little toe against the edge of the wood was greater than she'd have imagined.

"Jesus," she said, shaking her head. "Jesus effing Christ, that hurts. What next?"

"Are you OK?"

"It's fine. Banged my toe." In fact she had felt a tiny *crrack* on impact, but she didn't say anything—Davide was, in a very Gallic way, a great lover of a health complaint and would insist on her calling 999. Instantly the toe throbbed, as hot pain seemed to glow through her feet, up into her chest. She felt sick with the pain, then shook it away again. A toe! A tiny toe.

Behind her, she could hear Carys, talking to Tom. She was whispering something.

"Why wasn't the glass all over the study? Why is it on the roof? If you break a window from the outside it goes inside, right?"

"What?" Tom was saying, still dazed, and she saw him glancing at her.

"Talk to Grant Doyle," said Davide, shortly, turning and walking downstairs. "Promise me, my love." She nodded, still wincing. "It isn't right."

Catherine looked back in at the study. She gazed down the stairs, into the warm light of the hallway, the collection of shoes, the photographs lining the walls, the notices on the cork board. She closed her eyes, then opened them again. When she did, everything had changed.

Chapter Two

The café windows were steamed up with the heat from warm workers' bodies. April rain streamed along the narrow lane outside which, at lunchtime, was rammed with Central London workers in black and gray, buying noodles and tacos and phos.

"What can I get you, *bella*?"

"The soup, please, Frankie."

"*Certo.* One soup coming up. That foot, it is still painful? *Franco! Una zuppa, pronto!*"

Catherine gave a faint nodding smile and shifted the weight off her feet. The rain drummed down ceaselessly, and she frowned. Her colleague Jake Ellis, who had done his training the same time as her, twenty-five years ago now, was known to come in and cajole her, protesting, out into the fresh air for lunch.

"You'll turn gray if you stay here, Catherine. No one else works this hard. Get a life."

"I don't want a life. I like this life," Catherine would say, resisting him, sometimes seriously. But some days, today, she would come with him to buy sweet-and-sour noodles, or fried chicken, and sometimes they would walk down through Aldwych toward the river, the same walk they had done for decades now, feeling the pumping rhythm of the city, its fumes, its gray pavements and buildings, and every time she was reminded, just a little, of why she loved it here, never wanted to live anywhere else.

Fulton Chambers, where she and Jake worked, was in a tall Georgian building on Lincoln's Inn Fields, the Gothic fairy tale bulk of the Old Hall of Lincoln's Inn itself in the background, Narnia-like lamp posts on the corner. Catherine's narrow office, on the third floor, had one tiny window looking out over Lincoln's Inn Fields, a public park with a café, a tennis court and views of lounging tourists, lawyers and lunch-break workers, whatever the weather.

Catherine had probably spent more time in that close little office than anywhere else, working till 2 a.m. before she had the children, poring over papers, taking notes, on the phone, then later gathering up box files and dashing out to make it home for tea and a bath after the children. She had been there on Sundays, birthdays and several times on New Year's Day.

The humid warmth of the café was soporific. Jake was further down the lane now, queuing for pho, but Catherine had wanted soup, something comforting. She blinked, feeling she could just fall asleep here, in the warm fug. Her toe throbbed with a hot, urgent kind of pain. She imagined she could feel it growing, swelling inside her sneaker. Briskly, Catherine took out her phone and scrolled through her emails.

St. Hugh's School
Notice for parents on upcoming school trip to Swanage
Boden
Enjoy 25% off this weekend with offer code G4G8!
Jenny Timms Cello Academy
Overdue invoice
Christophe, Davide
Weekend away?
Boden
Enjoy 45% off! Offer code H5H7!
Anna Murphy
invoicing Herbert Smith
Jake Ellis
Lunch old bean?
Anna Murphy
HMP/YOI Tavistock visit to Grant Doyle—PLS review ASAP
Boden
75% off this weekend only with exclusive offer code BUMS!

It was three days since they'd got back and her toe hurt most of the time. Catherine had strapped it up with some washi tape from Carys's scrapbooking phase, and she'd iced it, and wore sneakers, but it was getting worse, not better. Thank God she wasn't in court that week; no way could she have worn her black heels. She couldn't walk in to work so she had to take the Tube, and was tired of the manspreading, the tinny music, the crowds. She was tired of it, most of all tired of the pain. It was embarrassing and silly. It was a *toe*, not an eye, or an ovary. It wasn't important. She knew she ought to do something about it, and yet she didn't.

The door of the café opened, the bell jangling, and Jake Ellis stuck his head in.

"Catherine? Hey! *Catherine Christophe!* You ready?"

Catherine's eyes snapped open. "Oh."

Jake came into the café. "Were you…asleep?" he said, mock-horrified.

"No! I was closing my eyes. Bit tired."

"Why?"

Catherine rubbed her eyes. "Oh…nothing much. Stuff."

"Tell me about it," said Jake, with an exaggerated shrug. "I was at dinner last night with this woman…honestly, Cat, it was a tasting menu and it went on for hours. I didn't get to bed till about two."

"You poor man," said Catherine, easing herself off the stool.

Single Jake was the same age as her and lived ten minutes away from her in Camden, but his life seemed wildly different to hers. His was a bachelor existence, where he fell madly in love with unattainable women who wore long, multi-layered skirts and silver jewelry. Usually, they abandoned him to live with wild horses in Patagonia. For a while Jake had been a little in love with Catherine, which had been awkward for both of them, until he'd fallen for a Russian countess called Sasha and gone back to coming into her office with a long, mooning face. "She said she loves me," he'd told her once. "But then she said seeing the Plain of Jars in Laos was more important. I don't know what to think."

Now Jake looked at her in concern. "Are you OK to walk on that foot?"

"God, the fuss. I'm fine. Just a bit stiff."

"One soup, here you go," Frankie said. "Hey! Sir! Get her to see a doctor about that toe. Crazy woman," he muttered under his breath, with a wink at her as she left.

Rage prickled across Catherine's scalp, the rage she kept tamped down all the time. She smiled at them both. "Let's go."

They walked slowly back. She didn't need to over-explain things to Jake; they'd known each other so long now. There were children who'd been born and graduated from university in the years since she'd joined Fulton.

Two years ago Jake had "taken silk" and been made a Queen's Counsel or QC, which meant one was a senior lawyer with all the prestige and rewards that entails. "When for you?" Davide had said, furious on her behalf; he was outraged when Catherine was passed over but never liked to consider it might be sexism for that was all lies, he said, lies to make women angry and demean men and women together. Davide believed in love, he said, not hatred. How easy it must be, she'd think sometimes, being a man. Being Davide. When she had also taken silk the following year he had been so proud, but she noted he was also relieved—as if he didn't have to worry about the idea that sexism might exist. As if all was well ordered in his life again.

"Want to sit in the square?"

"I ought to get on," Catherine said, and, as she spoke, heavy dots of unpredictable April rain splattered the paving stones and they both laughed.

"How did you do it?"

"What?"

"The toe."

"Oh. The frame of our bed sticks out. I wasn't wearing socks and I hit it against the edge. So annoying."

"Is it broken?"

"Hardly. I'm sure it's not. It's just bruised."

"Shouldn't you get it looked at?" said Jake, in a tone she found patronizing.

"I will. How's the Turleigh case coming along?"

"Pre-trial hearing next week," said Jake.

"Who's the judge?"

"Wilkinson. Not hopeful."

"Wilkinson's all right," said Catherine. "Don't smarm, that's all. He can spot it a mile away. Hide your deference. And he's very hot on trial by jury, the role of the juror in democracy and all that. So don't disparage the jury, even if some of them make you want to throw your chair at the bench."

"Mm," said Jake. He was silent, then said: "How's your last client, by the way?"

"Grant Doyle? I'm supposed to be fixing up a visit." She screwed up her nose. "I don't want to go."

"Will he appeal?"

"Unlikely. I just don't think he has grounds."

"Why are you going to see him, then?"

Catherine shrugged. "He's eighteen. He's in prison for murder. I couldn't get him off. He asked to see me—Ashok rang me last week," she said, trying to sound cool about it, "and it's a day trip to Rochester, isn't it?"

"I think the judge misdirected, Cat," said Jake. "I'm sure you have grounds. Self-defense. He was a punchbag for that group of boys. Hammersley, was that the name of the victim? He sounds like a thug."

"He was."

"Arrogant little shit with a millionaire dad who thinks he can buy his way out of anything."

"He couldn't buy his way out of his son being murdered, to be fair."

"Didn't they say he locked Grant Doyle in a cupboard overnight at school, with a rat?"

"They did. Hammersley paid someone to catch the rat for him. He really did spend a lot of time thinking about how to terrorize him. But—" She narrowed her eyes, thinking of the days in windowless rooms spent with Grant, staring at her, never blinking, just smirking slightly. His mother's whining voice, his sweet, furious younger sister's anger. *You were useless. Anyone else would have got the jury to understand what they did to him. What it was like for him.* She grimaced. "Let's not talk about it."

"Look," said Jake, at his most patronizing now. "I'm just saying, ignore what you read about it. And if you want me to—"

Her phone rang, shockingly loud. With some relief, Catherine answered it.

"Hello?"

"My *chérie*. How are you? How is the toe?"

Catherine raised an apologetic finger at Jake and moved under a portico out of the rain. "Fine. I'm just with Jake. What do you want, Davide?"

"Want? Oh, my. First—"

"I'm busy, darling—"

"Sorry." She knew what he'd be doing—making a dramatic facial expression to one of his co-workers, for he had carefully curated the brand of Catherine to them, his fearsome, sexy, world-striding, ball-breaking English lawyer wife. Davide worked for an insurance company that specialized in transporting valuable works of art across the world: Banksys hewn from youth club walls and flown to Miami, gigantic equestrian portraits of Renaissance European kings precisely installed on white gleaming walls in desert palaces in Saudi Arabia. "Our discussion the other day leads me to ask you, Catrine: are we doing anything over the bank holiday weekend?"

"Bank holiday? Nothing. Why?"

"*Ah bien.* Are you available to go away that weekend, Mrs. Christophe? Just you and me? An early anniversary present?"

Jake was leaning against a newsagent's window, studiously staring at his phone. "Oh…I'm…not sure. We've just got back, it's only a couple of weeks away…Leaving the kids so close to exams—"

"*Bof.* Those children must learn self-discipline. They will cope for a weekend. Cousin François can visit and check all is well."

"Well, we can discuss that." Catherine's mind began whirring with what would need to be organized if she left them for a weekend. "And…I was going to go to the care home for a visit then. I can't go the previous week or the week after."

"This Eileen." Davide made a dismissive sound. "You have done enough for her already, Catrine."

"She's Janey's mother, Davide. She's on her own. There's no one else."

"You brought her back from Spain, *chérie.* You found her the home. Her stepchildren don't email you once to ask how she is. Besides, she doesn't even remember her own daughter, let alone you. It is…unforgivable."

A jab of pain began between Catherine's eyes as the rain started again, the pavement suddenly swelling with people walking faster, running. She pulled at the front of her hairline, a habit she had had as a child, and one which left behind a little baby-fluff fringe of dark hair. The truth was, Eileen probably wouldn't notice if she didn't come on a Friday. She wouldn't notice if she never visited her again. "She doesn't have anyone else."

"But it's not your responsibility."

Catherine looked down at her feet in the neon sneakers, at the cooling soup in the soggy bag, the pockmarked newspaper. She closed her eyes as Davide said softly:

"A weekend away. Just us two. We will walk hand in hand. Feel some warmth on our shoulders. Drink a glass of crisp white Burgundy. Sit in a square, smell lavender, cigarette smoke, other places. Eat steak, *ma chérie*, chargrilled, rare steak, without Carys shouting at us about the baby cows."

Imagine if she just relaxed, if she just gave in to it, for once?

"You have been working so hard this year. Up all night, in the study, scribbling away."

"I've had a lot going on."

"I know that," he said, as if she thought he was an idiot. "I know the case was thrown into your lap, my love. Have you contacted his lawyer yet? Warned him to leave you alone?"

"No, Davide—"

His voice was soft, insistent. "You talk in your sleep, you know. Nursery rhymes. The same one, only I can never remember it in the morning. Do you know?"

"I'm asleep when I'm doing it, Davide."

There was silence, both of them not sure what to say. Catherine looked out over the square, at the huge red cranes, building yet more gleaming skyscrapers. She smiled at Jake, hovering a little way ahead, not wanting to listen. Davide said:

"I have been worried about you." His voice came closer to the phone. She heard his hesitation. "You—ah. You must know you're— you've not been yourself. A little, Catrine."

She bit her lip. "It's fine."

"It's not fine."

He knew her. Sometimes, it made her feel warm, waves of calm emanating from her. Sometimes it was being trapped, and she could not catch her breath when she thought about what he did not know. Sometimes she told herself it was nothing. That if he knew he'd understand.

She had met him when they were both aged eighteen, in another country, in another life. He had been standing in a town square, arms folded, quizzical expression, watching as two of his friends played football with a screwed-up paper bag. It was late October, an early autumn evening in Toulouse. She had run away from her life in England, from tragedy, from the summer she lost all her family, her home and her best friend; he lived there. And he had looked up and said, in a voice of surprise: "Hello."

She'd asked him later. "Why did you say hello? How did you know I was English?"

"I knew you," he had said. And that was all.

"You should drink Armagnac here, not cider, mademoiselle," he'd said, and she'd told him not to be ridiculous, that she was enjoying her cider, and he'd laughed.

"OK," she said now. "Let's do it. You're lovely. Where will we go?"

"Wait and see," Davide said, and his voice was lighter, and she knew he was pleased. "Don't worry. It's a place that's OK for you. Will you try to look forward to it?"

Even in the midst of the rising panic she felt, she managed to smile at the idea the destination might be a mystery. It would be Paris, which was more than OK with her, but it was a family joke Davide never wanted to holiday anywhere except France. "Yes. I will."

"Liar."

Catherine laughed, and peered out of the portico again. It had stopped raining. She looked around her, but Jake had gone. A lump formed in her throat, unexpectedly. "I'd better go," she said.

The lashing spring rain had suddenly eased, and a shaft of watery sunlight was hovering above the square, sewing silver seams onto the rainclouds. She was by the steps up to Fulton Chambers. Catherine stopped to check her phone again, to see if Grant Doyle's solicitor had been in touch. (The solicitor was the lawyer who had handled the case for the client from the beginning, and who hired, or instructed, the lawyer known as the barrister—in this instance Catherine—who argued the case in court.)

There was a faint hum in the air, like an engine running. It grew louder and then louder.

She jumped, but not quickly enough. A bee, flying straight for her. First time this year. It was loud—it was always very loud.

Catherine's head swam. The stairs up to the front door were narrow. Someone brushed past her; she jumped back. There was a charge in the air, suddenly.

Afterward she realized her body had understood it before her eyes had seen it. She looked back, staring across the road toward Lincoln's Inn Fields, and there she was.

A woman, standing on the edge of the freshly green lawn a few meters away, surrounded by the red and pink primula beds. She was staring at Catherine, patiently. As if she knew Catherine would eventually spot her. When their eyes met, she walked toward Catherine, and she smiled. It was a slow, curious smile.

"Hello there," she said.

Her slender shoulders were enveloped by long hair, which hung around her like dull gold ropes, softly shining. Her eyes—oh God. Those eyes, unchanged through almost thirty years. Bright blue-green, sea-glass.

She wore a long floral dress, and biker boots. She wore these things, she looked normal. She was real.

Catherine couldn't say anything. She just stared.

"I thought I'd come back." She folded her arms and smiled. She had a ring through her lip. "I wrote you a note. Did you get it? Are you pleased to see me, Catherine?"

Catherine blinked, pressing the palms of her hands into her eye sockets, buying time and then, eyes still closed, she fumbled with one hand for her lanyard in her pocket. Slowly, dragging her foot, she turned and climbed up the steps of the old Georgian mansion that housed the chambers—still she couldn't look behind her, across to the square.

At the top she held the card up and as the door unlocked, she turned around, blinking as the pain from the toe washed over her.

The woman had gone. Catherine breathed out. She lifted her

foot, rotating the ankle, breathing heavily, then put her hand on the door.

Then a slight rustle below her. Catherine looked at the pavement at the bottom of the steps. There she was again, and this time she was staring up.

"I said hello." The voice was the same, a little cracked and lower, but still that lyrical, upper-class cadence. She smiled, turning her face up toward Catherine.

Closer up, Catherine could see her once-dewy teenage skin was freckled and lined, weather-beaten. Her teeth were yellowed. She was not the beauty she had been.

"H-hello," Catherine said, softly, her voice breaking.

"Catherine!" From across the square came the sound of Jake's voice, calling her. "Sorry, Cat. I wandered off. It's quite nice now, are you sure you don't want to—"

He was hurrying toward the steps. Catherine looked down.

"Catherine." Another slow smile. "That's what you answer to, then? It's been nearly thirty years. Is that all you've got to say? 'Hello'?" She put her hand up to the iron staircase. "I saw you on the TV, that boy's murder trial. Aren't you—"

Jake had almost reached the steps. "I'm sorry," said Catherine, clutching her handbag and soup close to her body. "I have to go now."

This was the wrong thing to say. The peacock-blue-green eyes shone, almost too brightly. The stripes on her top were waves, as Catherine's vision swam. Catherine watched her swallow, and blink rapidly, as if she'd been slapped.

"I know you got the letter, Catherine. Weren't you pleased to hear from me? After all these years? Shouldn't we do something?"

"I have to go now," Catherine said again, and as she turned abruptly to jab her security pass on the reader, she felt a jolt of pain. She slipped, her foot folding underneath her like it was suddenly made of rubber, her head hitting the railings. Jake, the girl in the square on her phone and the security guard by the museum all stared at her: Catherine realized she must have screamed, but when she came to, lying on the ground, her foot burning with red-hot pain, and looked down the steps again, there was no one there.

Chapter Three

"Look, I'm fine," said Catherine, as Jake frogmarched her, carefully but firmly, into the doctor's practice. (*She banged her head on the railings. She fainted. She was screaming.*)

"I'm absolutely fine," she told them as they helped her into the waiting room.

"I'm completely fine," she repeated, shaking her head with firm embarrassment as the receptionist nodded, unmoved, and checked her details onscreen. "Doctor Jellicoe can see Mrs. Christophe in ten minutes, if she'd care to wait. He's with someone at the moment."

"Really, I'm fine. It's just a problem with—"

"She's broken her toe," Jake interjected, dramatically. "It's been getting worse and now she can hardly walk. I think it might be infected. I think she's hallucinating."

The receptionist did not react but Catherine saw her eyes flicker up toward her.

It's not a broken toe. It's not a head injury. I think I just saw a dead woman.

It was a plush, quiet practice, for private patients, as Catherine and Jake both had ludicrous health insurance. This was provided for by their chambers. Most barristers, though self-employed, belonged to their own chambers, an independent practice that housed their offices, dealt with admin, and handed out cases. They both resented paying for the health insurance but it entitled them to register at this doctor just around the corner, where rich Arabs, perfectly-turned-out ladies who lunch and plump, striped-suited businessmen made loud phone calls in reception. And where you could walk in when you wanted. Every time Catherine complained at a chambers meeting about the cost of the scheme she'd instantly find reason in the next couple of weeks to be glad of it, ridiculous though it was. It was very dark—dark wood, dark lighting, heavy scented candles. Catherine's children, who were registered at the local GP in Kentish Town, where everyone and anyone went, found it hilarious that their mother went here for gold-standard cervical smears and other medical procedures and where a man in the waiting room had once tried to advise Catherine on the danger of installing marble staircases in her home. "My friend Prince Alberto Gonzaga slipped on his own marble staircase, my dear. He broke his back in three places. Don't get one, I implore you. I'm telling everyone I know."

"I'll be fine, thanks, now," Catherine said to Jake. She spoke too loudly, and the other patients in the waiting room looked up. She glanced at all of them, trying to breathe, trying to tell herself it was nothing.

But it couldn't be dismissed. Because either way it was bad. The Devil was in the world again. Which was worse: that it was *her*, that she'd come back, or that she'd imagined her?

She hadn't imagined her.

Damned Jake. She liked him, loved him like a brother, but now he'd seen too much. Coming to, babbling nonsense with him kneeling over her, his face had been above hers, and it was the first thing she'd thought. "It's OK, Catherine," he'd said, flapping away other onlookers. "She's fine. Look, C, we're blocking the door. Anna, can you call Gray's Inn Surgery? Tell them I'm bringing Catherine Christophe over, she's banged her head. Yes, thank you."

He'd been so kind, that was the thing, and it was mortifying.

Now, as they sat on the slippery leather sofa together, in the heavy silence, he nudged Catherine. "This place is hilarious. Look."

How to Spend It, the *Financial Times* supplement, was on the coffee table in front of them, and someone had inserted Post-its in various pages. Jake flicked through it. "You can buy a Chaumet Mier something watch for only twelve thousand," he said. "Not on a criminal barrister's salary. Maybe if you're a negligence barrister. I wouldn't know." He nudged her, to show he'd made a joke.

Catherine smiled, but it hurt her cheeks. Her neck hurt too. All of her did.

"What did I say?" she said, after a pause.

"When?"

"When I was out cold."

"Say? Oh, you were babbling. It didn't really make much sense."

"Sorry."

"You were singing, actually. That old nursery rhyme." And Jake started singing. "'Green Grow the Rushes, O'—is that it? Can't remember the chorus…" He glanced at her and saw her face, and then, after a moment's pause, said: "So look, Cat, I'd better go. Anything I can do for you back at the office?"

"No worries." Catherine shook her head. "Tell Jenny I'll be back as soon as possible. I'm feeling much better actually." She tried to meet his eyes, but couldn't, quite. "I'm fine. This is silly."

The heavy leather-backed door shut quietly behind Jake, utter silence filling the scented waiting room again. Catherine's vision was cloudy, her head ached. She took out her phone to do some emails but found the words were blurry, and besides, she wasn't up to discussing Grant Doyle's appeal, or his prison visit, or reply-ing to the solicitor on the new marine insurance fraud case she was taking on, a trial lasting several weeks, if not months, involv-ing a vessel that had, the insurers claimed, been deliberately scuttled off the coast near Yemen.

She'd been looking forward to this next trial. She thrived on presenting good work, on long hours, on immersing herself in a case so deeply nothing could surprise her in court. When, ten years ago, she had made the switch away from the underfunded, unpredictable nature of criminal law to the calmer, lucrative waters of fraud and negligence, specializing in marine insurance, she had gone to Greek conversation classes above a pastry shop in Bayswater every Tuesday, so she could talk to the Greek ship-ping companies directly. Jake had laughed at her, but that was Catherine: it was about control, she knew that, and that was fine.

Catherine leaned forward, as if to quieten her mind. Her head throbbed again. She tried to sift through the story, how she would explain it all to the doctor, but as if in protest her vision grew more cloudy, air escaping from her lungs, her chest. Desperately, she scanned the magazines in front of her, pushing *How to Spend It* out of the way in irritation and picking up *Country Life*.

She had not read *Country Life* for years, since a misrepresentation case where she'd acted for a billionaire who had bought, unseen, a Scottish estate he'd spotted in *Country Life* while he was in the waiting room of his doctor's practice. Catherine smiled, wondering if it was this doctor's practice.

It had been an enjoyable case: inside, the house the billionaire had bought was not the ancient, wood-paneled manor evoked in the description but a badly built, Edwardian mock-Elizabethan hunting lodge that more resembled Skyfall after the shoot-out, riddled with dry rot. There was no salmon fishing; it was advertised as being "on the banks of the River Spey," which in fact was twenty miles away. The fact of the house apparently being grand enough to be advertised in *Country Life* formed the basis of Catherine's argument of fraud, and she and the pupil working with her had spent many hours thumbing through back issues, comparing like for like. Catherine had emerged with a stronger than ever distaste for the idle rich, but a secret addiction to property porn. She'd won the case, of course.

Someone she had been at Cambridge with was something to do with *Country Life*. What was his name? Tompkins. Gosh, she hadn't thought about him for a while. A name from the past, swimming out of her fragmented memory. He was an ex-public school boy, a member of the Pitt Club, not her crowd.

"Mrs. Mimi Caterina Bibby?"

A woman in huge sunglasses, a giant patterned scarf tied around her face, got up. The scent of her perfume—old-fashioned, heavy—washed over Catherine, tickling her senses. There was a very, very slight breeze, brushing the nape of her bare neck. The adrenaline of the past hour, the fear, the pain, was fading.

Hugo Tompkins. He had been at the Chelsea Flower Show one year and she'd quite literally bumped into him. "Good God," he'd said, looking at her in disbelief as she'd pushed herself away from him. "What the hell are *you* doing here?"

She was a serious person, but she always enjoyed telling that story. The gasp the listeners always gave. Because it was a reasonable question. She'd been taken to Chelsea as a guest of the head of chambers, Quentin Holyoake, and his wife, Bella. And, of course, she hadn't thought through how much she would hate it, surrounded by flowers. The bees seemed to follow her every-where and, eventually, she had had to make an early escape, citing a sudden migraine to Quentin and Bella: mortified, because she was so fond of them both.

The telephone rang in reception; Catherine's head tingled. It was Quentin who was the reason she'd taken on, and lost so badly, the Grant Doyle case. She could still hear Graeme, the clerk at Fulton Chambers, informing her the case was hers, the Friday a week away from the trial, in late February.

"Mr. Holyoake's out of intensive care, but he's not coming back to chambers, not for a while," he had said, rubbing his hands. "He's asked for you to take over."

"Not Jake?"

"No, Mrs. Christophe. Not Jake," Graeme had said, with relish.

"I'm not a criminal barrister."

"Oh but you are, Mrs. Christophe. In fact I have a whole file of cases to prove it. Here." He had jabbed at the ancient filing cabinet beside him.

"Not anymore—"

"I'll ring the hospital and tell Mr. Holyoake you said no then, shall I?"

Not for the first time, Catherine felt deep rage toward this red-faced bully of a man who held such sway in chambers. Like all clerks, his position was central to the chambers, and seemingly like all clerks he relished lording it over everyone. He would say it was irrespective of age, sex, position—Catherine and the other female barristers, especially the less experienced ones, knew that was rubbish.

But she had taken the case for Quentin—kind, flamboyant, cha-otic Quentin, whose ground-floor office was part of the character of the whole place, stuffed with various different busts of Beethoven, ancient copies of *The Times*, an old record player, framed photo-graphs and newspaper headlines. He was one of a dying breed, the old-school, prestigious criminal barrister. Younger barristers weren't interested in criminal practice. It was depressing, back-breaking work, decimated by legal aid cuts, often dealing with people who had no hope. A grammar school boy from York who'd won a scholarship to Cambridge and been in Footlights with Stephen Fry and Hugh Laurie, Quentin believed passionately in justice and representation for all. He remembered what it was like not to be accepted because of your accent and class.

He and Bella had no children. When Catherine had first started at Fulton he had taken her under his wing, and as she was living alone in Primrose Hill, working late most nights, he would often scoop her up and bring her back for dinner with Bella at their messy, rambling house on Lloyd Baker Street.

He had had a stroke, six weeks ago, a week before the trial was due to start, and was only now back at home. Catherine had been to see him. The warm, wood-paneled house, filled with photographs and vases of dried flowers and green and orange Penguin paperbacks in piles everywhere, seemed to have lost its spark, its charm. It was dirty and dark, Bella, totally at sea, aged ten years in only a few weeks, and Quentin still not able to speak. Catherine blinked at the memory, guilt sluicing her. Poor Quentin. She must visit him.

The list of obligations, of people she had to visit. Quentin in his rumpled bed. Grant Doyle, in prison. Eileen, in her care home.

As if from another lifetime she remembered the conversation with Davide, only an hour earlier. She was working too hard. He was taking her away.

Catherine sat up. And then the magazine slid open on the first page and there it was. And it wasn't the falling over, it wasn't losing the trial and Grant Doyle's mother saying to her: "They said you were the best, and you couldn't even remember my boy's name." It wasn't her study, all smashed up, it wasn't Carys, about to turn eighteen. She'd known what she'd find when she turned the page. She'd known it because she'd seen it already, in a discarded newspaper at the Eurotunnel café, and before that, on a news website, late at night before they left for France. The sale of Vanes was newsworthy.

Suddenly she was back in the café, the smell of coffee and greasy pastries catching in her throat, making her nauseous. Her fingertips gingerly gripping the edge of the newspaper, as if it were contaminated. *I thought I'd dealt with this already*, she'd said to herself. She had shoved the newspaper in the bin. Pushing the whole thing down, down, away, away.

But they were crowding around her, the ghosts, pressing closer and closer. She had no gatekeeper. There was no one. Catherine blinked, wondering if you could faint while sitting down, thinking she might just melt into nothing. *Aren't you pleased to see me?* she had said. *Aren't you?*

VANES, LARCOMBE, SOMERSET
6-BEDROOM 18TH CENTURY DETACHED MANSE ON THE
MARKET FOR THE FIRST TIME IN TWO HUNDRED YEARS

**A MOST UNUSUAL AND UNIQUE PROPERTY WHICH REQUIRES
SOME UPDATING TO BECOME THE PERFECT FAMILY HOME.**

AT THE EDGE OF EXMOOR, SITUATED IN AN IDYLLIC
POSITION ABOVE PRIVATE WOODLAND TUMBLING TOWARD
THE SEA, GRADE II* LISTED VANES IS AN EIGHTEENTH-
CENTURY HOUSE OF HISTORIC IMPORTANCE WHICH HAS BEEN
IN THE SAME FAMILY SINCE 1830. COMPRISING THREE
FLOORS AND TWO ACRES OF LAND, IT COMES WITH ITS OWN
TWO BEDROOMED LISTED GATEHOUSE WHICH COULD EASILY
BE ADAPTED FOR HOLIDAY LETS (SUBJECT TO THE USUAL
PERMISSIONS AND APPROVAL), OPEN AIR SWIMMING POOL
AND ANCIENT CHAPEL OUTSIDE THE GROUNDS, PARTIALLY
DEMOLISHED BUT OF GREAT HISTORIC INTEREST.
SIR JOSS HUNTER, WHOSE FAMILY HAS LIVED AT VANES FOR
FIVE GENERATIONS, SAYS: "IT IS TIME FOR VANES TO BE
ENJOYED BY ANOTHER FAMILY."

"Mrs. Christophe? Mrs. Christophe?" The receptionist stood up, a few minutes later, looking around her. "Where's she gone? Did anyone see her? Mrs. Christophe? Oh dear. How vexing."

Chapter Four

Catherine paused at the bottom of the steps and then climbed slowly up, holding her pass to the door. Her head still ached where she had banged it, and her foot was still agonizing, but she had managed to walk back without falling over.

"You don't need a doctor for a broken toe," she'd been told firmly. Having hobbled out of the doctor's office she'd rung the physical therapist she'd had several years ago when she'd broken a wrist skiing. "You need proper tape, and proper anti-inflammatories, and you need to rest it, and it'll be absolutely fine. Any other side effects?"

"No," Catherine had said. "None."

"Right. Well, just make sure you bind it up. Go back to the doctor if it doesn't get better. And for God's sake rest it," Shelagh said again. "I remember what you're like."

"I will," said Catherine. She smiled. Shelagh's no-nonsense manner was what she needed. Shelagh, she knew, didn't see dead people. Catherine had limped to Boots and bought everything Shelagh recommended, then gone back to chambers.

She stood there for a moment, looking out over the square. The thought crossed her mind: *Would it be so bad, if she really was back?*

"Anyone call for me?" she asked Jenny, the cyborg-like receptionist.

Jenny looked blank for a moment, then her face cleared.

"Yes," she said. "Oh yes, in fact." Her eyes widened slightly. "Grant Doyle, from Tarnmoor. He wants to know when you're coming to pay him a visit. He has something he needs to discuss with you urgently. That was the message."

"OK. Thanks."

"Fine." There was a pause. "He's a nasty piece of work, if you ask me," said Jenny, a spot of pink burning on each cheek.

Catherine was about to rebuke her, when she saw Jenny's face. She knew how the conversation would have gone.

"I'm so sorry, Jenny. He shouldn't talk to you like that. He's— well, he's in prison for at least the next decade, if it's any consolation. Thanks to my best efforts."

"Yes, thanks," said Jenny, with an attempt at a smile.

"Hm," said Catherine. Climbing the rickety stairs, clutching her purchases and a replacement soup, she opened the door into her small, thin office with its view of the square, where in the distance a game of erratic tennis had begun, and the last of the daffodils drooped under the plane trees. It had stopped raining. She was alone now, at last, and so she shut the door, trying to breathe, trying not to give in to panic. Breathe in-two-three-four-five. Hold-two-three-four-five. Breathe out-two-three-four-five. Carefully, she drew something out of her bag. The balled-up page from the magazine. She set it down on the desk, smoothing it carefully out from the center to the corners.

After a time, she was able to eat her soup, staring at the house.

She had not seen it for so long. She never looked it up. Never googled herself, though she had, once, heard someone in a pub talking about the Vanes tragedy, and knew then that people must know about it. And she let herself drink in the picture, and the three pictures in tiles below it, of the grounds, the small cozy sitting room and the chapel, looking out to sea. How long she sat there she wasn't sure. But the door handle shook suddenly, and as she started, violently, a voice said: "Sorry, Catherine, wrong room," shaking her back into the present.

I was just looking at a picture of my childhood home, she'd have told whoever it was, if they'd asked what she was doing. *The gables are shaped like beehives. No, I don't know why.*

It's called Vanes. There's a weathervane, of a stooped Father Time, and it spins and creaks in the wind. Does it still?

There's a pool, where we used to spend all day in the summer, and the water glows a strange green-blue, especially at night.

That's the sitting room where Sylvia had her studio. Her own private space, where she worked, away from children, away from her husband.

That's the chapel. That's where the bees lived. I don't like bees.

There were three children—Joss Hunter, Kitty Hunter and little Merry Hunter. So Joss is still there.

It was a beautiful place to grow up. There's a path down to the sea, a pool, a garden so big you can't see the edges. The Hunters have been important people in the area for centuries.

After it happened I became Catherine. Kitty Hunter was a different person. Very different. She was bold, imaginative, fierce, she did what she wanted.

And for the past twenty-nine years I have tried to do the same. I have tried, and in part it's worked, but lately it doesn't work anymore. I am timid, frightened, always frightened. I can't breathe, for a lot of the time. I wake up and can't breathe. And the more I try the worse it gets. I have these dreams, when I'm back there again, in the middle of it all, and I'm trying to replay it, and it always ends the same way.

The door of her office was heavy and soundproofed, as were the windows. Catherine sat with these thoughts, hearing the breath that fluttered in her throat. She touched the back of her head, where she'd banged it as she fell. She swallowed the painkillers, taped up her toe firmly, not too firmly, watching a YouTube video that explained how best to do it. She opened the window, just a crack. She could hear traffic, talking, music—London sounds, which soothed her. She paid the bill for Tom's cello lessons, amended an Ocado order, messaged a mother of a friend in Carys's class about some party at the weekend. "I don't have a problem with them hanging out on the Heath. They can walk back afterward," she wrote to the woman, who was a self-designated Anxious Mother. "If we don't let them they'll go anyway," she added, disobeying every instinct she had, which was that Carys should stay indoors chained to the kitchen table and never leave the house except for school.

With every action she felt the painkillers kicking in, her throbbing head easing. She could do it. She screwed the magazine page up and put it in the bin, opened her emails and started to work, sinking into it, into detail and legal minutiae as if into a long, hot bath.

"Here," called Davide, when he heard her arrive back that evening. He appeared by the stairs in the hall and tapped at his screen. "Look. I will book the Eurostar, for Friday, the fourth of May. OK? Look, I'm pressing 'book tickets,' *chérie*—look—Oh, my goodness. What happened?"

Tom was helping his mother in. "She finally got a crutch for her toe. About time, Mum."

"I fell over today," said Catherine, kissing Tom on the cheek and hobbling to the kitchen island. "Hit my head—no, it's fine, honestly."

"*Mon dieu*," muttered her husband. He put his iPad down and came toward her. "It takes this to make you see a doctor?"

"I didn't, actually." She smiled at him, then started to laugh in horror at his expression. "Don't worry! It's fine! Jake marched me to the doctor's office and I waited for a while, but then I got so sick of being in there I left, called Shelagh—you remember the nice physical therapist whose daughter was at school with Tom? She talked me through what I needed to get, so I went to Boots, took some painkillers, taped it up, grabbed a crutch out of Quentin's office and I'm right as rain. Listen. I've been thinking," she said, gripping her husband's hands, as he guided her gently into the sitting room and sat her down on the sofa. "I feel so much better. Better than I have in ages. It's that case, I'm sure."

"That case," he repeated.

"The murder trial. Grant Doyle." She still didn't like saying Grant's name. He was eighteen, smaller than Tom, but he haunted her.

"Ah," said Davide, his face clearing.

She leaned back against the cushions, her eyes heavy. "Shelagh says I should rest. I might not go into the office tomorrow, I'll work from home." She gave him a huge smile.

Davide grinned back at her. "OK. What painkillers are you on?"

"Combined ibuprofen and codeine. It's good. It feels good."

She closed her eyes and waited until Davide, who paused for a moment, looking at her, got up. Catherine opened her eyes, slowly. "Davide..."

"Yes? Can I get you anything?"

"Book the Eurostar. Book it now."

He was looking down at her, the expression in his eyes painful, because she knew how much he loved her. "Wonderful."

She heard him gently shutting the door and saying to someone outside: "She's just having a rest. The toe."

"But Mum's literally never ill," came Carys's voice.

"Exactly," said Davide. "So let her rest."

The first time they'd met, that evening in October, in a bar on a rose-pink stone square in southern France, she'd told him the truth. "I've run away from home," she'd said.

"Why?"

"My family," she'd told him.

"Again," he'd said, signaling for another *bière blonde*. "I must ask you, why?"

She'd sucked on her cherry-red paper straw, drawing up the last of her cider. Her bangs were growing out and tickled her eyelashes as she looked up at him.

She could remember the smell of the Place du Capitole, of cigarettes and grilled meats, of a fresh, autumn wind. The perfume of other diners.

Catherine was doing what she normally did when she arrived in a new town. Eating a *croque-monsieur*, which, because she'd been to the Dôme a couple of times, was the only item she knew how to order in French. It was almost two months since she'd run away, leaving them all behind. Her French was getting better every day; she'd immersed herself in it, doing nothing but speaking it whenever she could. (It was a project; she liked a project.) She had picked up bar work here and there, at a club in the suburbs, then at a beach bar on the Dordogne, while she waited to hear whether her place at Cambridge had been deferred for a year. She had asked for letters to be forwarded to the post office in Toulouse, *poste restante*, so she always knew she'd end up there.

She grew her short, tufted hair into a bob, like Betty Boo, learned to smoke, and listened to Kirsty MacColl, over and over again. She was getting used to being this girl now, the one who knew how to keep moving, how to deal with unfriendly hostel owners and French bureaucracy. It gave her confidence—not the wise-cracking, I-wanna-shout-it-from-the-rooftops kind of confidence, but in her own decisions, her own wisdom. She knew when a guy was dodgy, and that she should feel fine about ignoring him, and when he was lonely and probably OK. She knew that the bar owner in the Dordogne despised her—because she was a girl? She wasn't sure why, just that he did, and stopped wasting her time trying to get him to like her.

Summer was coming to an end and she wasn't worried about winter, exactly, more curious to see how it panned out. Since leaving Vanes, she didn't care much what happened to her. So when she noticed a dark-haired boy with a quizzical, confident manner watching her, she had smiled at him, briefly, but ignored him and got on with eating. After she'd finished—and this was typical of Davide, something she would remember after she had gone back to England—only after she'd finished, he got up, and sat down in front of her.

When he started asking about where she'd come from and why she'd left, she'd leaned over and stubbed out her cigarette.

"Look, I don't want to lie to you, so how about you don't ask me and I won't tell you why."

"Hm. OK." He'd shrugged. She could see his eyes, flickering over her, very quickly.

"I just don't want to talk about it." And she'd looked up at him from under her lashes, warily.

He'd swallowed. "What can you tell me?" he'd said. "Why don't you tell me what you can. Just don't lie to me, Catrine."

So she told him she'd run away from home. That she couldn't go back.

"Are you wanted by the police?" he'd said, laughing.

"Probably not," she'd said, with a flicker of a smile, and he'd nodded, suddenly seeing she was serious. She handed him a newspaper cutting she'd been keeping folded inside her book. The newspaper had been left on the seat of a touristy restaurant in Albi, folded open at that page. She had looked around, terrified, searching for someone watching her.

"Kitty Hunter," he'd said, handing her back the cutting, with a whistle.

"I'm Catherine now," she'd said.

"You think that is a disguise that will conceal you from the police?"

"They've called off the search," she'd said. "I read it yesterday in the paper."

"Why?"

"My family knows why we left."

"But…are you missing, or aren't you?" he'd said, and she liked the lilt in his voice, the rasp at the edge of his tone, his stubble, his smooth skin.

"I'm not," she'd said.

"And Janey? Janey Lestrange, your best friend?"

"Oh, she's dead," she told him, and it was true, then. She believed it, for the first time.

Catherine slept on the sofa in the small, warm sitting room for a couple of hours. When she awoke, it was totally dark, the only light from the golden-yellow of the street lamp outside. The pills had worn off; her head ached, and her toe was throbbing. For a second, she had no idea where, or who, she was. It was terrifying.

"Davide!" she cried out. "Davide? Where are you?" He was there, of course. He turned on the overhead light and she blinked up at him from the depths of the sofa.

"She is awake. Well, well," he said, and he came over and kissed her forehead. "I thought you were out for the night. Those painkillers are quite strong."

"I'll take some more before bed," she said, wiggling her toes, gingerly. "If I can just have a good night's sleep…I'm sorry to zonk out."

"You needed it."

"Where are the kids?"

"Tom is at Oscar's, Carys is upstairs. She has watched ten episodes of *Friends* in a row, she just informed me. She says it's very historically interesting."

"That girl makes me feel very old." Catherine swung her legs round, onto the floor, and stood up, leaning on her husband. She looked out into the street, thinking she saw someone. But it was only shadows, moving in the wind. She went upstairs. Passing the study with the flapping tarpaulin, she said: "Davide, you said your guy was going to fix that today."

"He is!"

Catherine frowned. "What, at ten thirty in the evening?"

"He is coming tomorrow. He is very apologetic." Davide was competitive with Catherine about tradespeople. If she found a good plumber, he always wanted to trump her with a plumber who was cheaper and superior in all ways. If they were French, so much the better. "He is a busy man."

"It's been a week." Catherine turned her head away from the open door. She didn't want to be reminded of the study. Of the papers in there she hadn't sorted through, the years of work. Of the moment the window was smashed, crumpling in on itself, the hatred required to do it.

"It will be fixed, Catrine. Go to sleep."

Catherine acquiesced. She fell into bed with relief, without even washing her face and brushing her hair, almost a first for her.

At 3 a.m. she woke up and knew something was wrong. Padding gingerly downstairs, Catherine saw, in the yellowing light from the street lamp, a letter on the floor, past the doormat, on the tiles themselves. Her name, written in outsized letters: "CATHERINE."

I have to pick it up now and read it, she told herself. *That's the game.* Crouched down in the hallway, cold and alone, she opened the folded piece of paper.

> *It was nice, seeing you today. But you didn't seem very pleased to see me. It takes a lot for me to come to your work and stand there waiting for you. And you ignored me, you swept past me up the stairs like you thought you were better than me.*
>
> *Old Kitty was like that, but I hoped Catherine wouldn't be.*
>
> *I've been thinking back, lately. Have you?*
>
> *I want to go and see the house again, don't you? One more time? Are you angry they don't know where you are? Kitty was born before Joss,*

she should inherit, shouldn't she? And what about your best friend, the one you made all your promises to, what about Janey? I miss her. I wonder if you do. I wonder if you're glad she's gone.

Let's go back. Let's go and see Joss. Tell him you deserve a share of the house, even if you don't need it. Let's smash it wide open and tell everyone the truth. What they did, what really happened to us.

I'll come to you and explain how, and when. Just be ready. Be ready to steal away. Because your husband doesn't know, does he? Your children don't know. Your colleagues, your neighbors—that nice old man Mr. Lebeniah who's lived next door to you for twenty years, that nosy Judith across the road, they don't know, do they, that we planned it all, that we left them for dead.

I know you'll make excuses. But I think you should see if you remember the words to the song. It's time the Beloved Girls went collecting again.

Chapter Five

The late April morning sun shot through the house at this time of year, sliding through the heavy bedroom curtains, hitting her in the eyes. Coming downstairs into the cool of the teal-blue iron and glass kitchen, Catherine found Davide, already sitting at the breakfast bar, flicking through the newspaper.

He didn't hear her and she had the luxury of watching him for a moment. His tousled dark hair, shot through with lead gray, his small tortoiseshell glasses, the stubble on his chiseled chin, still tanned after his two weeks in February, skiing in the Pyrenees. The same two weeks, every year, the same group of friends.

He shook out the paper and took another sip of coffee from the green porcelain cup she had given him twelve years ago which he had deemed "extremely acceptable, Catrine." Davide was a creature of habit. He had always read *The Times,* because he was an Arsenal fan and he liked their football coverage. He drank only coffee made with his Jura S8 and was horrified when people offered him a Nespresso or, God forbid, as a parent at a kid's birthday party had said to him a couple of years ago: "I'm just popping to Starbucks for a pumpkin latte, Dave. Do you want anything?"

He did all their cooking, and clearing away, and he liked folding laundry. He ironed his own shirts. Not hers. "I am not your servant, woman." He was tirelessly tidy—Catherine was tidy, but he took it to new levels. He loathed Sarkozy with a passion that surprised Catherine—really, how could one person be that bad? He had that Gallic contradictory combination she had never found with her own people, a formality and appreciation of the good things mixed with an almost frightening anarchism. "Yes, yes, they should riot, and some will die, but they will have stood up to the erosion of liberty!" he'd said once of the rail workers who were striking over proposed changes to their already—in Catherine's opinion extremely cushy—pension. He was so easy to live with. He said what he meant. He never, ever played games.

"Tell me what you can," he'd said to her, that first time. "Just don't lie to me, Catrine."

And all she had done was lie to him.

The glass door to the garden was slightly open; she could hear birdsong from outside. She cleared her throat slightly—still he did not stir.

"Morning, my love."

"Catrine. Good morning." He glanced up and raised his coffee cup to her. "I'll shut the door."

"No, it's fine ajar like that. I like the birds."

"You did not sleep well." It wasn't a question.

"I'm sorry. Did I wake you?"

"Only a little. Is it the new case? Or that young man who is so angry with you he smashes in windows? Or were you writing one of your histories again?"

"All three." She opened the fridge, took out the orange juice, and poured some into a glass. Her hand wobbled slightly.

"How does it go?"

She had always liked discussing her work with him. "It's interesting, actually. Some Yemeni pirates are supposed to have scuttled a ship, but the Piraeus guys think it was an insurance job." The fridge door was open, humming. She stood gazing at nothing, orange juice in hand.

Davide put down his cup and pushed away his plate. "I didn't mean the new case. I meant Grant Doyle. Whether you had uncovered why he is breaking into your house at night."

"I'm sure it was just a one-off," Catherine said.

"Nonetheless," said Davide, smoothing out his paper. "Did you speak to his solicitor?"

"You haven't said anything to anyone about it, have you?"

Davide shook his head, then stretched his hand over and clasped hers. "Only a few days to go, *chérie*. This time next week you'll be on a train, with me, sipping champagne, we will eat together, just the two of us, no malodorous teenagers crouched—like this—over their screens, growling for money or food. And you will sleep, we will walk hand in hand through—ah, I'll say no more, I don't want to ruin the surprise…" He raised his hand now so the palm was pressing against her palm, and pushed their hands upward. She smelled lavender, musk, citrus, his smell. He kissed her, gently. "All these things, my love. You work too hard. And you remember too much. Try to forget."

His taste, and the orange juice on an empty stomach, was like thick, gritty acid in her throat, her gullet.

She gave a small, tight smile. "Forget what?" She saw him hesitate.

"Your old life—who you were." They were still.

Catherine swallowed, and looked at him, as the warmth from his dry palm flowed into her, into her aching arm. "It'll be over soon," she said.

He squeezed her fingers one more time and dropped his hands, brushing everything away. "It will. Now. I have been talking to Claude. He wants to know if we want their place on the Île d'Oléron at the end of the summer, for a week. Do you think—"

"Yes," she said, immediately.

"The children? Really?"

Claude was Davide's cousin. His son, a romantic, languorous youth named François, was studying English in London for the year and they'd taken him under their wing. Carys and Tom loved him. He smoked, alone among virtually all other London teens. It gave him enormous novelty value and cemented his reputation with the children as a genuine eccentric. "The guy…he smokes. It's absolutely wild," Carys told her friends. It was so unlike Catherine's adolescence when if you smoked you were, just, without question, cool and that was that.

Catherine had helped him with his English, and with a troublesome landlord who gave way immediately on the points of property law he'd claimed were true when contacted by Davide's fearsome barrister wife, thus earning her François' undying adoration. "*Tante Catrine*," he'd call her, batting his long black lashes at her. "I am so grateful. Thank you."

"Will François be there? And Claude and Aurélie?"

"Yes, all summer. They've asked us for a week, they want to thank us for looking after François."

August—it was a lifetime away. She felt, for the first time, a sinking, dreadful, terrifying feeling. Black obscured her vision.

In the ensuing darkness she saw they would not go on that holiday, that it was all ending.

But she said brightly: "Definitely, I'd love to."

"It's France again," he said. "You don't mind?"

"I like France." She smiled at him and took her hand away, to smooth his hair. "And I like having plans in place. Sweet François."

"He's in love with you, that boy."

"François? He's twenty."

"I don't bring it up to find out if his age is the obstacle to you, *chérie*. It's a statement of fact."

Catherine rolled her eyes and turned the coffee machine on. "Will you make sure there's food in the fridge for them for the weekend?"

"He told Claude. He said you were a pearl." Davide was smiling. "Claude said to him: *When we first met her, at Davide's parents', we called her the English Mystery, the girl who appeared from nowhere, who survived a plague of bees.* This has fanned his ardor even more."

"It was a long time ago," Catherine said, pouring herself some cereal, sliding the paper toward her.

And then it started. A faint buzzing sound came suddenly toward them, growing louder all the time. A tiny thud.

"It's OK," Davide said, as his wife immediately slid from her stool, backing away. He stood up and strode toward the door. "It's fine, *chérie*. I see them. I've got it. OK?"

"Get—get it out. Please."

It was a spring bumblebee, lurching toward her in a zig-zag. It was not a worker bee. It juddered angrily around the glass kitchen, flinging itself furiously against the panes.

The sound. It was always so much louder than one believed it possibly could be.

Catherine's throat contracted, her eyes scratchy, her mouth dry. She backed herself up against the kitchen cupboards, flattening herself, palms digging into the handles. She stared ahead—she had learned closing her eyes made it worse.

"I have it, Catherine. It's outside. OK? It's outside."

"Yes."

She shut her eyes then, as he released the bee out of the cup. He closed the door and said quietly: "I shouldn't have opened the door."

"It's fine." She had to stand still for a moment, as the orange juice threatened to force itself up out of her throat.

"I'm sorry, *chérie*."

"Davide, forget it. It's my fault."

Every summer ended with him begging her to get the extension demolished, replaced with brick walls and windows. And yet she always said no.

Sounds thundered overhead; Tom, lumbering down the corridor to the bathroom, growling at his sister, a high-pitched scream of outrage at something. Davide's face was pale under the tan. These moments hit him hard; her vulnerability terrified him. She caught his hand again, clutching it so her knuckles were white, and there was a moment of silence between them, as their gazes locked. The great old diamond, Davide's grandmother's ring, flashed on her left hand: it seemed to catch and hold the morning light.

"I wish I could stop it for you" was all he said, and his kind face was etched with the pain of loving her.

Catherine shook her head, her mouth set in a firm line, unable to speak. He sat down again, glancing up at her once, the two of them wreathed in their own private misery, the old routes. "I'm fine," she managed to say.

She had to force herself to eat the cereal, force her hand upward, force the food, which formed into a hard bolus at the roof of her mouth, down her throat, force herself to keep chewing, swallowing, so that he stopped watching her, so that he could believe it might, just might be OK. All the time she was bargaining with herself.

It's just been rather rocky lately. You're not looking forward to today. She's not real, Catherine. She's not come back.

Afterward, she went upstairs and threw up her breakfast, and felt much better.

An hour and a half later, Catherine swung the heavy front door shut behind her. Getting the kids to the bus stop was always a rushed panic during which Davide mysteriously vanished, leaving her to chivvy them out of the door and onto the bus. She was a little late, a little too hot, convinced her dress was on back to front, that a streak of foundation lay on the bridge of her nose. Carys, stomping out of the house ahead of her, turned and looked down at her mother's feet.

"Oh Mum," she said, in what Tom called her Help the Aged voice. "Those sneakers again? They're blue and fluorescent yellow. You look like a reject from a K-Pop band."

"I have to wear the sneakers till my toe's all better. It's fine."

She inhaled deeply as they passed Mr. Lebeniah's garden. "May is almost here, darlings." They stared at her. She thought of what lay ahead that day, what she had to do, and shook her head, willing the subject away. "Speed up, come on. Now, just to recap. Remember, Dad and I are going away next week, for *three* nights. It's the bank holiday."

They had almost reached the bottom of the road. Tom stopped, dropping his rucksack to the ground. "What?"

Catherine ignored him. "Judith's going to pop over on Friday and make sure you're OK. Saturday and Sunday François is coming to stay. I'll leave money for a pizza."

Carys had stopped walking too, and both of them stared at her with that look of teenage horror mixed with bemusement and some pity, once again, as though she was doing something utterly outlandish, licking the brickwork or playing a flamingo.

"What do you mean, you're *going away next week*?" said Carys, eventually. "Where? *Where are you going?*"

"Judith's checking up on us? I'm not a child, Mother."

Catherine kept walking. "You'll miss the bus, both of you. I am going away with your father. I don't know where—"

"Although it's clearly Paris," Tom said, *sotto voce*, unable to resist the family joke. "But still," he said, returning to the theme. "Ohmigod."

Catherine said: "I've told you this before. Twice."

"Um, Mum," said Tom. "No, you haven't."

Catherine wondered sometimes if she appeared in the

morning and talked in a made-up language from morning till night whether they'd notice. "I have, several times. Tom, remember you have an extra cello lesson *tomorrow* afternoon and Miss Talbot is coming at six—"

"Miss Talbot's a thief! If you're not in the house—"

"She's not a thief."

"She bloody is. She swiped ten pounds off the hall table. And the silver photo frame, you know, the one that had that photo of you when you were younger that went missing—I'm sure I saw her. Anyway, I thought we'd all hang out—"

"Yeah, hang out together, do family stuff—"

"That was my idea—"

"Shut up, Tom, you're such a suck."

"You shut up."

"You two are unbelievable, honestly," said Catherine, trying not to smile. "You never want to spend a minute of free time with me and Dad normally." A woman walked past, on the other side of the street, and Catherine looked up and around at her.

"Who's that?"

"No one. Here we are." She stared up at the bus stop display board. "Yes. Three, three…"

Three, three.

Three, three, the rivals,
Two, two, the beloved girls,
Clothed all in green, O,
One is one and all alone and evermore shall be so.

She shivered. The children had not moved on. "One more reason you can't go, Mum, is—"

Catherine said sharply: "Look, it's your father's idea. Not mine. Take it up with him. It's an early anniversary present. Dad thinks I need a break—" They stared at her, horrified. "Oh, never mind."

"Is it that Grant weirdo?" said Tom, behind her. "Is it him, Mum? He sounds dodgy, I'd be careful."

"Sort of," said Catherine. She patted his arm, unexpectedly touched.

"Someone at school knew him," said Tom. "Remember my friend

Ali at school?" said Tom. "He was talking about him yesterday. He said he boasted about stabbing that guy he killed. Dan? Hammersley? He was going around, like, bragging about it?"

"Really?" The road was busier, more pedestrians. Suddenly Catherine knew someone was watching her, could feel their eyes on her back. She looked around again, at another woman passing on the street: old, Chinese, pulling a shopping cart, and felt fury, an impotent, all-consuming anger. With herself. None of these women were her. She was ridiculous.

"Listen," she said. "You shouldn't be telling me this. We shouldn't really be talking about it. Especially if he's going to appeal. I'd rather not know."

"But," said Tom, "Ali, he said he'd seen him—"

"Tom! Just be quiet. I said, don't tell me."

They were both scared, she could see. "All I meant was he doesn't sound very nice, Mum," said Tom in a small voice. "I don't want you to…" He trailed off.

He's not. He's not nice at all and you are. She looked up—*up*, for her baby boy, who had been born three weeks early and only weighed five pounds, was taller than her now—into her son's eyes. Then, again, always again, over his shoulder, at someone walking past. Always looking. Looking around.

It occurred to her, as she came back to the moment to find both her children staring at her that something had shifted inside her, something had irreparably broken and perhaps it would always be like this. She gazed at their faces in turn: Tom's unformed, craggy angularity, his rugby-player's frame, his soft hair and kind gray eyes—they were her dad's. Carys, fluffy-haired, doe-eyed and Gallic, so like Davide, a sweet, true arrow, a disrupter, a force of nature. Nearly eighteen. "I have to do what I have to do," she'd been famous for saying as a determined three-year-old trying to leave daycare to walk back home, where she thought her mum was. "I HAVE TO DO WHAT I HAVE TO DO."

The life they thought they'd had, the traditions she had built so carefully, the safe little world she had created for them, so, so gently. The babies she had cuddled, their warm backs pressing

into her body as they sat in her lap, cross-legged on the floor at
music classes, the smell of their hair, their faces as they slept... all
the love she had given them, poured into them, trying to fill them
with as much of it as she could, while she could, the horror all the
time that at any time, it might be taken away.

"Mum?" said Carys.

"Sorry. Just remembered something for work."

They turned to each other and rolled their eyes and she kissed
them both, glad of the sensation of physical contact, luxuriating
in the smell of them. For now, she could hug them, feel their
bodies, hold her daughter's hand and tut at her bitten nails, stroke
Tom's hair—quickly—squeeze his arm.

"Dad says you're up for the Île d'Oléron this summer," said
Tom, disentangling himself from his mother.

"I'll book the train tickets. We can stop over in Paris for the
night."

"Maybe the place you're going to with Dad will give you a dis-
count for rebooking so soon."

They all laughed, Catherine too loudly. "Don't be mean about
your father."

"*Chérie*," said Carys, a perfect imitation of her father. "I have
booked for you a romantic weekend in Berlin. They speak no
French there at all."

Another bus went past. Suddenly Catherine was gripped with a
wild desire to say: *Why don't we bunk off for the day? Let's go and get a
picnic and sit on the Heath, and then catch a movie, and have ice cream, and
then go into town and dance and eat tapas. Let's just... not bother with
school, or work, my darlings. Let's just hang out.*

Catherine said: "You know, when Dad finished at school, he
went traveling, do you know where he went?

"No," they said, their eyes lighting up—they loved stories of
their parents' childhoods, all too rare on her side. They knew
about her being an unhappy child, and leaving when she was
eighteen. About having long golden hair, not the mouse-brown
crop she had now, and loving the hard gray waves, and the fresh
air, and the woods that rose up to Exmoor and became vast,
heather-covered plains studded with ancient cairns and beacons
and windswept trees. She gave them enough information for

them to know where she was from and made sure the family they knew was Davide's large, warm, kind family in Albi, who were welcoming but formal in their curiosity, never prying too deeply. She had once tried to explain Exmoor and had hopelessly con-fused Davide's father, Albert. She found out afterward he had told his relatives Catherine came from the birthplace of Peter Rabbit.

Tom nudged her out of her reverie. "Where did Dad go then?"

"He went to the Canal du Midi. Up and down in a boat."

"How far from Toulouse?"

"About an hour away."

"What about you, Mum?"

"Me? I went—all over."

"After your exams?"

Catherine nodded. "After I got my results. I left and I never went back. Get your stuff ready, darlings, the bus'll be here any moment. Oh yes. I drove through France to Spain, then I got the train back, went to Italy—Rome. Naples. Then—oh, I went all round and ended up back in France. I worked there for a bit."

"And that's where you met Dad?"

She nodded, a small smile playing round her lips. "Yes." The cool spring air was delicious on her face. "Yes, in a café in Toulouse."

"You were on your own?"

"I was. And do you know what he said to me?"

"*You should drink Armagnac here, not cider, mademoiselle,*" the kids chorused in unison.

"Ah, and he bought you a drink. It's so romantic."

"It was."

"Look!" Tom cried, glad to change the subject away from his parents' romance. "The bus."

"Your parents, though," Carys said, suddenly. "Didn't they ever meet Dad? Did you ever take him back there?"

"No," said Catherine. "Never."

There was a pause. "What was the house called, where you grew up?" said Carys.

"Do you know, I can't remember," said Catherine. "Isn't that dreadful?"

"You can't remember the name of the house where you grew up?"

"Well, it was changed. When we moved there it was called something else. And we changed the name back to the original one, but I can't for the life of me tell you what it was." She glanced ahead. A woman, walking toward her. "We should go there, some time. Go to Exmoor. Get in touch with my roots. All we hear about is Daddy's family. You'd like to know more about mine, I expect."

"Yes," said Carys. "I would. Just—I have loads of questions." She blinked. "Sure, it's your right to not talk about it, but…And you've never really told us why you left."

"I know. I know. Now's not the time." There was a crack in her voice; she hid it. "I've always thought we'd have to have a talk about it. Just not at the bus stop at eight ten in the morning."

"Fair enough," said Carys, nodding at her. Tom shrugged.

"I love you both, my darlings," she said, dread at the day ahead flooding her, fearful now of everything, her empty stomach clenching with acid. "Have a—good day. I'll be back late tonight."

"I hope it rains all weekend in pissing Paris," Carys said, cheerfully, as the bus drew up. "When you come back and we are literally starving to death and the house has burned down." She paused. "Where are you going today?" she said, with actual, genuine curiosity.

I'm going to see a murderer.

"Work," she said. "Boring insurance cases again. I love you! Bye!" called Catherine, smiling, then turning so they couldn't see her expression. She arranged her face, then looked back. She saw them climb up onto the top deck as they did every morning, to be greeted by their friends, Carys at the back, Tom at the front. Which was strange given they were allegedly the only people at the whole damn school to get the bus.

The moment the bus pulled away her expression collapsed, the muscles in her face falling slackly back into place. *You're Catherine Christophe. You're forty-seven. You're married to Davide, you have two children. You are a barrister.*

All of this is true in the eyes of the law. No one can say it isn't.

On the other side of the road stood a woman. Catherine told

herself not to look; that it would be bad either way, feeding the beast. She'd read up on OCD once for a case, that you keep throwing the ball for the puppy, and the puppy keeps bringing it back, and you have to train yourself not to throw the ball in the first place.

She'd thought that was rubbish; the puppy needed to have the ball thrown, now and then. And she needed to experience these terrors she had, the weight of concealment that was sometimes, on a morning like this, too hard to bear.

So she looked.

And she was there. Standing, watching.

Catherine noted the way her hair was worn like a younger woman's, long and flowing, pinned back with those round tortoise-shell hairclips she'd worn as a girl.

She had the same dress on—was it the same? Or was it darker? The boots were the same.

"Hey, Catherine!" she said, in a perfectly normal voice. She didn't yell, or draw attention to herself. "Can't we talk? Why don't you want to see me? It's me, Catherine. It's me."

The boots had mud on them.

Her eyes, her beautiful, huge eyes. She was so lovely.

"When are we going back, Catherine? Don't you think we should talk about it?"

More than anything, Catherine wanted to cross the road. To hold her. Smell her. Lean on her. To say: *You understand. No one else does. And I'm sorry. I'm so so sorry.* That idea, of putting her head on her shoulder, of feeling the embrace of the only other person in the world who understood.

But she couldn't do it. So she kept on walking and, when she could, picked up the pace, though, even a couple of weeks on, the damned toe caused her to hobble very slightly. She darted down a narrow alleyway, which led up to the Heath, where she could, if necessary, hide until she was sure danger was past. It did not occur to her that this was not normal.

Chapter Six

Grant Doyle was in Tarnmoor, a Category A prison and Young Offenders' Institute an hour's train ride from London, just outside Rochester. Catherine had been there before but not for years, and it was pleasant to arrive somewhere else, to walk from the train station through the pretty Kentish town with its gabled shops on the high street, to peer into Satis House, where Miss Havisham had lived in *Great Expectations*, to stare up at the castle, lowering and bleak on this strangely cloudy April day.

At the prison, Catherine requested a locker for her phone and laptop, and her jewelry. She stood motionless as they patted her down, as a dog came out to sniff her.

"Sorry, ma'am," the prison guard said. "Won't take long."

He said it in a chummy, we're-on-the-same-side way.

The dog was an Alsatian. Catherine closed her eyes, hearing its snuffling, hot breath moving over her. "You all right?" said one of the prison officers, who was waiting by.

"I don't like dogs," she told them.

She was wearing a shift dress with a collar and pockets, and a navy jacket, as smart as possible to offset the sneakers. How stupid she'd been, she'd tell everyone who commented. Just a silly toe, ridiculous letting it get so bad. "It was the bump on the head," she'd joked to Jake, who kept popping in to see how she was, and to whom she kept having to say, with the appearance of regret, that she was so sorry but she couldn't come for lunch.

At work Catherine felt more and more like a ghost. She crept in and out of the building, hoping to move unseen. But every time she left and arrived she'd pause in the spot at the top of the stairs where she'd seen her first of all. Checking Lincoln's Inn Fields, checking down, on the ground below the stairs. Checking.

They walked her through the Victorian, warren-like building, eerily quiet. Rain from last night dripped through iron girders onto the floor just past the entrance. She was with two other women, one small, slight with lank hair in a straight central parting and drooping shoulders, dressed in sweat pants and a crop top, not meeting anyone's eye, and an older woman, handbag under her arm, in a smart jacket and sturdy black shoes, back straight, nodding at everyone.

In the month since the trial Catherine had often wondered where she'd gone wrong with Grant Doyle. Early on in her career she'd have got him off, no question. She was able to get inside the jury's heads, to make them see what she wanted and ignore what was inconvenient. She never troubled herself with the ethics of whether keeping a guilty person out of jail was the right thing to do. People asked for her by name. On the earliest version of the Fulton Chambers website, she'd been on the top fold. She'd won Barrister of the Year but had turned it down. She didn't want publicity.

Then they'd moved, to a larger house, when Tom was born, and there were holidays and things like new boilers and new shoes and it all added up, and when she decided to specialize in fraud and negligence instead her income doubled, and she wasn't dealing with the depth of human misery she'd had to wade through, nor the nagging fear when, as once happened, she successfully prosecuted the son of an Islington gangster for assault, and the father had pointed at her in court. "I'm coming for you, love," he'd said, the finger like an arrow. "I know where you live."

She'd reported it, and apparently he'd been spoken to, but she was terrified, not for herself, but for these blameless people who depended on her, Davide and Carys and Tom. Defending Grant had reminded her how much she disliked criminal practice, and yet how much she craved the thrill of it, the sense of justice being served at its sharpest point. Winning cases for these indolent shipping magnates and sharp-eyed insurers, the billionaires who needed hand-holding and flattery, was not her purpose in life, but it was safe. It had to be.

As she walked into the visiting room and saw him waiting for her, Catherine remembered with a jolt how small Grant Doyle was. He didn't look like the boy one tabloid had called "the most dangerous teenager in Britain."

In March, he had been sentenced to twelve years. Twelve was the longest term he'd get, though he'd be on license for the rest of his life and his sentence could be extended if it was deemed necessary. He had been seventeen when he was arrested, and he might not get out till he was thirty. His peers would have careers, relationships, lives with clear blue water between them and school. Not him.

Grant Doyle had been a scholarship pupil at Jolyons, the highly competitive and exclusive public school in South London. Grant had fallen in with a crowd of rich boys, sons of bankers, record executives, a celebrity chef, a Russian oligarch. The king of this crowd was Dan Hammersley, whose father was a hedge fund manager with a large stake in a football club. From Dan Hammersley's Instagram feed you could see the combination of money, access to footballers and a swaggering sense of entitlement which, mixed with—Catherine thought—a staggering lack of self-awareness, had made him a peculiarly unpleasant kind of schoolfellow.

Everyone agreed Dan had it in for Grant from the moment Grant started at Jolyons, aged thirteen. What was disputed was the extent to which his victimization of Grant and his exhortations to his friends to do the same ultimately led to his own death, the previous year, at a summer house party.

"Flushing my head down the toilet," Grant had told Catherine, the first time they'd met. "Three, five times in a row, I had to go to the hospital once. Check with the school. Punching me, over and over, every time they passed me in the corridor. Leaving shit on my front doorstep. My sister stepped in it. My sister's twelve. Tai, he was Dan's best friend, he sends messages to me, to Poppy, my mum, my friends. Pictures of aborted fetuses. *That's what should have happened to you.* That's what they say."

"I know—"

"Telling everyone in the school I lived on an estate. Them all believing that's something bad. Instead of something to be proud of. Telling everyone my dad was a postman. Like that's something bad too. Dan's girlfriend Talia, do you know what her dad does? Do you?"

"N-no." She remembered the name from the list of witnesses.

"Her dad's a millionaire from towing cars. He owns those trucks that go around taking them off the street so you have to pay, like, three hundred quid to get it back. Imagine that. Would you be proud of making money from that? None of you know what it's like." He had raised his head again and looked at her and Ashok, the solicitor. "You're living with it every single day. And if you call it out then they've won."

In court, Catherine had, slowly but surely, built up a picture of Grant—a shy boy, not great at making friends, bullied by classmates at his primary school for working too hard, close to his mother and sister. The pride in the family when he went for, and was offered, a scholarship at such a good school. The piece in the local paper about it. (Catherine mentally noted, with irony, the chance remark by the headmaster that Grant lived closer to the school than any of the other boys, who were ferried across South London by their mothers in vast black Range Rovers and Mercedes SUVs every day.) She had appealed to the jury, going over and over the treatment meted out by Dan and his mates. The danger Grant felt all the time. How he'd stopped sleeping. How the school had called it "high jinks" and refused to bring in Dan Hammersley's parents, Catherine managing to hint this might be because they didn't want to offend one of their most lucrative donors.

But the jury hadn't liked Grant Doyle. They'd heard it all and taken it all in and they'd found him guilty. And she knew why. It was more comforting to believe that the handsome, rich, blond boy wasn't bad, and that the poor boy, who throughout the trial stared unnervingly at each of them in turn, and who'd stabbed someone to death, was.

"How are you, Grant?" Catherine said, sitting down in the brightly lit, chilly room. At the other end of the room, the lank-haired, sad woman looked up as a huge bear of a man about three times her age appeared. He was almost too big for the door frame. "Morning," he said, too loudly, too cheerfully. "All right, love?"

The woman waiting for him didn't say anything, just shrugged. He sat down. In the far corner, a small, slight, elderly man was brought in, and was greeted by his wife, the dignified one with the handbag. Who were all these people? Catherine found herself thinking, as ever. What were their stories?

"I'm OK, thanks, Catherine," said Grant, meeting her eye, and he smiled. He looked like a Botticelli angel when he smiled. His dark blond hair, his large, guileless green eyes. "Thanks for coming to see me."

Catherine nodded at him. "I always try to."

"Does this happen to you a lot then, Catherine? Your client gets found guilty?"

"No."

Grant leaned forward, and the prison officer behind, her hands on the back of another chair, said sharply: "Keep a distance, Doyle."

"Has your mum been in?"

Grant looked around, nodding, smiling at the officer. "No, Catherine, she hasn't. She finds it too upsetting. Poppy can't visit, she's too young. My dad's been, but he wasn't really very well equipped to handle having a son in prison. He couldn't make eye contact with me, Catherine. Imagine that." His huge eyes held her gaze.

"I've got the papers through on the appeal," said Catherine. "I think there's grounds for it. I'm going to discuss it with Ashok and then get back to you. See what the situation is, test the lay of the land."

"Would you handle me again, Catherine?"

"I—would," she lied. "All being well."

"I hope so. That'd be great, Catherine." She looked up, unsure whether he was mocking her or not.

He had a light, crisp voice, with a little hiss at the edge of some words. It reminded her of Ka, in *The Jungle Book*. Always slightly self-conscious: a kid, playing at being a criminal mastermind. She glanced at the tall, Gothic windows covered with double glazing and bars. The windows faced an inner courtyard into which no light seemed to permeate.

"How are you settling in? Have you gotten to know anyone yet?"

"This isn't a nice posh boarding school like the one you went to, Catherine. You're making it sound like Hogwarts. It's not, is it?" He turned to the prison officer and smiled.

"Shut up, Doyle. I won't tell you again. Ten minutes."

She had a baton dangling off her belt loop. Catherine wondered if she'd ever hit anyone with it. What it was like. If it made her feel safer. When Catherine had once been incredibly angry about something, when the children were small and she was very tired, and she had been passed over for a case by Graeme, the head clerk, she'd gone into her office, shut the door and kicked the filing cabinets, really hard, and the harder she kicked the more she wanted to carry on doing it. She'd picked up a mug and thrown it across the room, but it wasn't the same—it bounced onto the floor, a slime of cold black coffee dregs leaking out as the mug rolled on the plastic carpet tiles. She remembered the violence of the metal drawers, crashing into the frame, the astonishing rush of release, the rage that was so near the surface. Barbara Fiennes, the older, well-respected barrister next door, had banged loudly on the door. "Good Lord, what's happening in there? You all right?"

"Stuck drawer," Catherine had called, looking at the dented, crumpled front of the liver-colored metal. "Sorry for the noise."

She had told herself she would never do it again. But she had known it would happen again. The cortisol and adrenaline meeting, coursing through her body.

"Anyway, no, I haven't made any friends, Catherine. As you may recall, I wasn't very good at it at school, so I don't see myself palling up with a nice gang here, either. Thanks for your concern. How have you been? How is Tom, your son? Do you remember, I know someone who knows him? And Carys, your daughter? And this reminds me, Catherine!" He clapped his hands together, gently. "How could I forget? I had a letter from someone who knows you."

"What?"

Grant folded his arms, looking amused. "It was sent via Ashok.

Asking me to cease and desist from harassment of you and your family. Which I thought was rather unfair. Very embarrassing, in front of my new boarding school chums, Catherine."

His voice was too loud and the couple on the other side of the room paused their silent misery, turning round together to stare at him.

"What did you say? A cease and desist?"

"Sent from your husband, I believe."

"I—I don't know what you mean," said Catherine. But she was remembering the conversation in the kitchen, the other morning, Davide's anger. "That can't be right."

"Oh but it is." The angelic eyes lit up, he had seen a weakness, a crack. "So you didn't know? That's funny. It says I got someone to come and smash up your study. Me."

He leaned toward her, and the officer stirred again.

"Who's been coming into your house and doing something horrible like that? 'Cause it wasn't me, Catherine. I had nothing to do with it." He narrowed his eyes, his calculating brain getting to work as he scanned her face. "Oh, this *is* good. So you didn't report it to the police. Why? Because you didn't want them to investigate. But…" He lowered his voice, staring off into the distance. "OK, I get it. You didn't tell your husband. You want him to believe it was me. So you know who did it, because if you didn't you'd want it cleared up too. I'm right, aren't I?"

Catherine had her hands in her pockets. She squeezed them, patting her jacket, but of course she had no phone, nothing. Her possessions were in the locker. (*You may bring a pen and paper, your purse, a snack [but no tin foil, please.]*) "Look, Grant, I'm sorry that happened to you. I'll talk to my husband. He shouldn't have—"

"I'm enjoying this. So you didn't know he was going to stick his nose in. But I think you do know who broke into the study and smashed it up." He leaned forward. "Because I know you, Catherine. I know you're hiding something. You're the same as me."

Catherine almost laughed: it was so overdramatic, a scene from a TV drama when the newly freed criminal reveals some extra layer of guilt to the unsuspecting lawyer. Grant, she knew, had watched endless police procedurals, fancied himself something of an expert on points of law—frequently he had interrupted her when she was running through some detail with him and Ash.

But this boy was in jail, and she was free. She said this to herself, twice, flexing her fingers, keeping her breathing steady.

"Rest assured this will be sorted out. I'll explain it to him."

His lips twitched, like he was trying not to laugh. "Well, well. What will you explain, though? And who's Kitty?"

Catherine said: "What? What do you mean by that?"

"I'm asking the questions." He glanced at the guard, but she didn't notice. "All right. When I came to meet you, that first time. You had a letter on the desk. From someone called Kitty. Writing just like your handwriting."

"How the hell did you know what my handwriting was like?"

"I like noticing things. So Ash had a note from you, after that old guy got ill. It was on top of all the papers. And I noticed it 'cause your writing is nice." He nodded at her. "You've got very nice handwriting, Catherine. So that first meeting, we came in, and there's this letter on the desk, and it's in your handwriting. You snatched it away, as we were sitting down. You snatched it away and shoved it in a drawer. I noticed all of it. It's my hobby." He was pleased with himself, tapping his head. "And I thought to myself then, what's she doing? I picked it out of the drawer, when you went to the bathroom."

Catherine folded her arms, then wished she hadn't. "Your mum was there, wasn't she? What did she say about you rifling through my stuff?"

He shrugged, looking up from under his lashes. "Mum lets me do what I like. It was important."

Mrs. Doyle was a faux-vintage kind of woman: hair pinned up, tight skirt and stilettos, and she was certain of two things: one, Grant was a lovely boy, and two, she had been wronged by virtually everyone and everything. Catherine had felt a cold, deep rage toward her, as the trial date grew closer, and any work Catherine and Ash did to get Grant to appear more contrite and vulnerable to the jury was undone by Grant's mother telling him he just had to be himself and forget about the haters.

Her son had stabbed someone four times, including once in the eye. He'd left the body down the side passage of the house where the party was. Then he'd gone back to the party for an hour. This was the detail the jury couldn't get past, Catherine heard afterward. Privately, she didn't blame them.

"I'm Kitty," she heard herself say. "It's a nickname. I write—I write up notes. About things that happened to me. To my family. It's helpful, it's my way of working through things." She couldn't even remember the letter. Had it been left on her desk? Had she written it? "Listen, Grant. I know what it's like to be an outsider. I know what it's like to be totally alone. Believe me." She sat up straight, pushed her short bobbed hair out of her face and cleared her throat. "Look, I'll get my husband to retract the letter. I know it wasn't you."

"Of course you do." And Grant Doyle shifted just slightly in his seat. He smiled. "I think you know exactly who did it. You're hiding something." He inhaled, quickly, with a hiss, excited. "Ah, yes, mate. I can tell. We're the same, you and me. I knew it from the moment you got put on my case." His eyes moved over her, but his body was utterly still. "You're a liar. You're lying about everything."

"I'm sorry to disappoint you, but I'm not."

But his smile stretched wider and wider. The room was too hot. Catherine gave him a crisp smile. She pushed the chair back and stood up in one swift movement.

"Ash said you hadn't been well."

"I'm fine."

He clicked his fingers. "Truth. He said you hurt yourself. Banged your head or something."

"To repeat: I'm fine. Look, I'm going now, Grant. I'll check in on the paperwork."

He leaned further back in the creaking plastic chair, nodding. "You don't want them to know. You're scared. Kitty, Kitty. You know why I killed Dan Hammersley?" Grant said. He put his hands behind his head. "Because he thought brute force was what counted. He thought he could bully me, terrorize me, and he'd win. But he never won. I won."

Slowly, Catherine said: "But you didn't win. You're in here. And you used brute force to kill him, Grant."

"But you don't understand. I'm the winner, 'cause I'm free. I'm

totally free 'cause I'm still here and he's not and that's why I won."
He jerked his thumb behind him at the guard. "I have someone to
open doors for me, Catherine. You can't change that. Forgetting
even how shit you were at defending me. You deserve to be pun-
ished for that, you know."

Catherine paused. She knew she ought to write some of this
down, to feed the notes of the conversation back to Ash, no matter how difficult.

But the rage was rising inside her again. And she couldn't, and
wouldn't. Instead, she leaned over the table toward him. The officer stood up. Catherine raised her hand, as if to say, *It's OK, I
promise.*

"Grant," she said, softly. "Do you remember the day the start of
the trial was delayed? The judge was ill?"

He nodded, waggling his fingers at her, like she was dust,
brushing her away. "So?"

"Good. Do you remember you couldn't find me? You said I was
a stupid bitch for keeping you waiting, do you remember?"

The couple behind them had run out of conversation. She
knew they were listening, the bulky man hunched over his slender
wife, the shadow of their outline exaggeratedly cast onto the
white wall behind.

"I wouldn't have used words like that, Catherine."

"Anyway. Do you remember?"

He shrugged.

"I'd been for a stroll." She inhaled, adrenaline coursing through
her. "Do you know what Dead Man's Walk is?"

The prison officer behind her shifted. Catherine glanced at her,
saw the flicker of recognition in her face.

"No, I don't know," said Grant, but she heard a small intake
of breath. "I wonder if I can persuade you to tell me though,
Catherine."

Her voice was still soft. "They built it hundreds of years ago,
when it was still Newgate Prison. It's the walk the condemned
man takes to the gallows, Grant." She cleared her throat, which
was tacky with saliva. "They built it for murderers. Like you. It's in
the basement of the Old Bailey. So far below everything else it
doesn't get any light." She leaned in. "There's seven or eight doors,

from the cell to the drop, and each door gets smaller, and smaller. The sign your life is getting smaller and smaller. The last door is tiny, because on the other side of it is the hangman. Because the next door is death. Every trial I have at the Old Bailey I walk that walk. Just to remind me. We're all going that way; some of us don't get to choose. It's taken from us." She moved a fraction closer; she could see two blackheads shining on his pale skin. "You're in here now, Grant. So don't threaten me."

He laughed, but she suddenly knew she'd unnerved him. *He's not a criminal mastermind. He's no one. He knows it.*

"I'll be out one day, though, and I'll find you. So stop trying to scare me with stories about shrinking doors, Kitty Kitty. You lost my case. You're a fucking liar, mate, and you're bad at your job. You're hiding something. It doesn't take a genius to see your husband is trying to protect you. He thinks it's me, that I'm the danger. But he's got it wrong, hasn't he? I'm not the one you need protecting from."

Catherine didn't move for a moment. Then she spread her hands across the table and closed her eyes. When she opened them she was smiling. She spoke so quietly no one else could hear, her voice a thin thread of steel.

"Listen to me. I left someone to die once. I walked away and left her to die, *Grant.* And no one ever found out. You have no idea what I've done, the things I've seen." She saw his eyes widen, his mouth part; she didn't think he had ever reacted spontaneously to anything she'd said until then. "I'd do it to you, in a heartbeat. And you know, don't you, they won't believe you, they'll believe me. So don't even think about reporting me, or my family. Do you understand?"

He clenched his jaw, shrugging. One leg scuffed the plastic coated table leg, like a bored schoolchild.

"I said do you understand?"

"Yes."

"So. Don't think about me again. I'm not a person in your life now. You have no idea what you're getting into. Just leave me alone and I'll leave you alone. OK?"

There was a pause.

"I'll have to get out of here," he said, his voice small. "You don't understand. I can't do it. I can't stay here."

Catherine stood up. "Justice." She shrugged. She pulled down the front of her jacket, raised her chin and smiled. She didn't look at him, but she could see, in her peripheral vision, his huddled, small form, frozen for a short time, then leaning back in the plastic chair, which creaked, and unclipped itself from its frame.

This was no one. This was a case she had lost, a not very pleasant person found guilty of killing another not very pleasant person. He was just a child. She had done her best by him, and it hadn't been enough, and it was time to move on. Keep on moving on. That was what her father always said, it was what she'd said to herself the day of the Collecting twenty-nine years ago. It was what she lived by.

"I'm ready to go now," she said to the guard, who stood up, nodding politely at her.

Chapter Seven

The knock on the door was so faint at first she almost didn't hear it. She was always hearing sounds, real or imagined, kept thinking she saw figures in the periphery of her vision, real or imagined. Probably it wasn't real. Catherine carried on working.

Toc, toc, toc

"Hello?" she said, after a second's silence. "Who is it?"

"Hi, Mum." The door opened a crack, and Carys's head—framed by her short, blond, still very slightly pink hair—appeared in the blackness of the dark staircase.

Catherine tried not to let the relief in her face show. "It's so late, darling. Why aren't you asleep?"

"I woke up." Carys came in, slowly, looking around her. "I came for a glass of water and I saw your light was on."

Catherine looked at her computer. It was 1 a.m. She glanced at her daughter, who was standing awkwardly in the tiny space, holding one arm, shoulder slumped. Plump, dark shadows bloomed under her eyes.

"Sit down," said Catherine, moving some box files perched on an old IKEA stool out of the way.

Carys edged in and sat, glancing around her, almost furtively. She looked at the files on the floor.

"*Liability denied…Question tariff imports,*" she read.

"My new case."

"Is it interesting?"

"Not compared to Grant Doyle. But I prefer this kind of work."

"Why?"

"Oh. Well…it's like being a worker bee."

"You hate bees, Mum."

"Not all the time. You have to be diligent. Just keep going through the papers. Keep working away, filling your brain with information. Going out and collecting evidence, bringing it back, sorting it into what's useful, what isn't." She was smiling. "You see, I don't hate them."

"Mum…" Carys shivered in the chill, pulling at the ragged cuffs of her old woolen cardigan that had been Catherine's. She chewed on one for a moment. Catherine watched her.

"Yes, darling?"

"Mum, can I ask you about some stuff?"

"Now?" she said, and then saw her daughter's face.

"It's just… I can't sleep, lately, that's all. Thinking about things."

"Of course. I promised you, last week, didn't I?"

"I didn't know if you meant it." Carys tried to make it sound like a joke. "You see, you always manage to get out of talking about you and I never noticed till recently. Till…"

Catherine put down her pen, staring at the desk while she gave herself a couple of seconds. "I've let Dad take center stage. Partly it's because I love his family, and partly because I don't really have much of a family."

Carys hesitated, pulling at the cuffs of her cardigan again, and Catherine followed her daughter's eyes as they ranged around the room. All was back in order, nothing out of place save for the box files on the floor. The putty from the mended window hadn't been painted over yet. It was finger-colored. There was an imprint from the glazier's thumb on the bottom of the frame. Carys looked up at her mother, the front lock of her hair falling in her eyes, and smiled, sadly. "You're doing it now, Mum."

Catherine stared at her daughter, hungrily. She remembered how she had never smiled when she was a tiny baby. How she'd lie in bed with her, looking at her small, round face with its huge dark eyes, and wonder with the obsessive curiosity of the first-time mother if her daughter was sad. She wasn't. She was just thoughtful. Always had been. And then baby Tom, holding him and realizing how different he was with his unblinking gaze and huge grin, how she'd got her first child wrong and needed to have another one to see it. She wondered suddenly how she'd let it get to this, where any way forward now was going to hurt them.

"How do you mean?"

"You never talk about your childhood, Mum. Don't pretend. You know you don't."

"Well, children aren't interested in old family histories, are they?"

"That's not true. You think we've only just noticed. But we've always noticed. We just knew not to ask, that's all. I don't know how but we did. And then I realized you wriggle out of it when I do ask. Every time. Who else was a lawyer in your family? I asked you that once. You answered me but it was an answer about how you loved some program about lawyers in LA when you were little. And so I feel I've had an answer but I haven't."

There was silence, and the heavy quiet of the rest of the house seemed to flood into the room. Catherine nodded. She said, simply: "I know."

"Dad always says you just don't like talking about your family."

"It's true." Catherine paused, cupped her hands under her chin and looked at her daughter. The tips of her fingers were ice-cold. "I don't talk about it because it wasn't a very happy childhood. I left home the day of my eighteenth birthday. And I thought I'd never make it, quite often. I thought no one was on my side. My family wasn't a—a good family."

"How?"

She chose her words carefully. "How. You know the mums' race?"

Carys nodded. This was the story of how Carys, aged seven, had begged her mother to enter the mothers' race at their school sports day, and by some fluke and a great expending of energy Catherine had won. Walking back across Hampstead Heath, the four of them, Catherine flushed and with her arm flung round Davide for support, holding on to Carys's hand with her other hand. A little boy called Reuben had watched Carys and her family drawing closer to him. Biting his thumbnail, looking furious, he'd said as they passed: "I wish I was in your family."

Tom had waited till they ducked down into the woods before he polished an imaginary medal on his chest. "Well, would you believe it," he'd said. "People want to be like us," and his tone of utter bemusement, the sheer unlikeliness of this idea, seemed hilarious to them all.

But Catherine thought of that little boy every day. She

understood him. She had wanted to crouch down in front of him, grip his thin shoulders and say: *Listen, I was like you. I wanted it so desperately. And I was wrong. Totally wrong. Don't worry, little one. You are enough as you are. I promise.*

"I really felt for Reuben, after the mums' race. I was like him. I was always on the edge, looking in." She took a deep breath. "OK. The summer it all happened, a girl came to stay. Janey Lestrange. She'd lost her father, only four months earlier. Simon. And her mother, Eileen, she was—oh, she was gone. Hopeless." Catherine gazed out of the window.

"Is Eileen the one you visit, in the care home?"

"Absolutely." She nodded at her daughter, with a sad smile. "Eileen Lestrange."

"I don't understand why you bother with her, Mum."

Catherine said gently: "She's Janey's mother, lovey. She went off to Spain when Jane was a child. She's got dementia now. Her second husband died and the house wasn't hers, and her stepchildren aren't interested, so I found her a place in a care home here and brought her back."

"Yeah, but I suppose I'm saying why do you need to? She's not your mum."

"Look," said Catherine. "We made a pact, Janey and I. That we'd always take care of each other. So, the summer Janey came to stay, it was also the summer everything was coming to a head. Vanes wasn't a great place to grow up."

"Vanes. You said before you couldn't remember what it was called, Mum."

"I didn't want you to have any details about it." Catherine screwed her eyes shut. "I lied, darling. Because I want to protect you from…it all. That's why. It was wrong. But you'll find out someday. It's beautiful, a huge place overlooking the sea, it's got a pool, space to run around, filled with antiques, but really—" She breathed in. "It was rotten. Had been for years. Charles, my father, wasn't a good person. My poor mother—well, she never stood a chance."

Carys's face was pale. "How? Did he—hit her?"

"No, it wasn't like that." Catherine smiled into her daughter's eyes. "We didn't understand them, what had gone on between them, not till it was too late. This is why I don't talk about it, darling. It's hard to explain. Janey was—well, it wasn't before, but now it's so clear to me," said Catherine, and her expression was sad. "Janey was cool. She'd had a terrible time. Lost her dad, and her mum really—she just wasn't interested in her—and she was mousy and looked quiet, but she was a disrupter, you know? Liked to shake things up. Couldn't stand injustice, or hypocrisy. What we call cancel culture—you know, I disagree with your opinion so I'm going to silence you. That kind of thing really wound her up. She was—a fish out of water in Vanes."

She looked away, out of the window into the dark night.

"Vanes is one of those English country places that hadn't changed in years, I see that now. It was full of antiques, furniture that had been there for centuries, possessions from other people's houses that were sold on for money—everything was old, everything was about the past, about preserving that past. Any change to anything appalled them. And they—the Hunters—they never went anywhere else. Anywhere."

Carys settled herself on the seat. "Where is it, Mum?"

"It's near Exmoor. Somerset, but it's almost Devon. It's buried away, really hard to get to. The hills and the woods cut you off. You know, every time you looked out of the window toward the sea there was a different view. Even rain was exciting." She closed her eyes. She could hear it. The smell of rain, metallic and clean, on the hot flagstones, the noise muffling the sound of screams. "It's surrounded by these ancient woods that had all these myths associated with them. There were families there with names going back hundreds of years. They'd have been smugglers, or wreckers; they'd wait for ships to founder on the rocks and collect the cargo. They'd rob dying men of the coins in their pockets." She saw Carys shiver. "And up at the chapel just beyond the house, where the ceremony took place, that's where they'd come to repent of these sins…" She was silent, trying to sound calm. "The house…I wonder what it's like now, what state he's kept it in."

"Who?"

Catherine said after a pause: "Sir Joss Hunter. There were three of us. Jocelyn Raverat Hunter. Catherine Lestrange Hunter. Melissa Hester Hunter."

"You had a brother? A sister too?"

"We called her Merry." Catherine stopped, in her tracks. "Her birthday was the twenty-fifth of April, you know. Tomorrow. I think about her in particular on her birthday. She loved celebrations. She loved the Collecting…" She was silent for a moment, watching as Carys reached for her phone in her pocket. "But they're just not the kind of people to reveal much of themselves online. You google them yourself, you'll see. When I'm researching clients or prosecution cases, I go onto Companies House, local council planning sites, to see what tax schemes they're involved in, what illegal extensions they've applied for. But Joss doesn't need to do any of that. There's nothing about him, nothing at all. I don't even know if he's married."

Catherine shivered, jumping violently, the taste of him in her mouth. A moist, peppery taste, his tongue hard. Cigarette smoke. The feel of his skull underneath his long, flopping hair, the bones moving as her fingers traced the shape of him.

"OK," said Carys, tapping at her phone. "What the hell is the Collecting then? Loads of stuff's come up about some ceremony and some bees."

Catherine said: "It's another long story. But they don't get it right. Don't read the internet, Carys, not if you're searching for answers. I look it up sometimes and, trust me, they don't know what happened that day." She pushed her daughter's phone down onto the surface of the desk. "Look up—OK, google Kitty Hunter Vanes, now."

Her daughter turned the phone round, the screen alight with rows of pictures. "There," Catherine said. "That's not me, is it? And that's not even the house. I don't know where that is. This is why the internet doesn't work when what's gone before has lasted for centuries. They've got the wrong people. It's Aunt Rosalind, not Rosamund. They don't know why the bees attacked. Or who died. No one does, unless they were there. Even if they were still alive these people wouldn't have the first interest in publicizing themselves. Not the locals, not even the holidaymakers who rent the thatched cottages on the harbor and buy into it all. Least of all my family."

Carys was watching her, amazed. "I don't believe it."

"You don't have to, my love. I'm just saying, if you want the truth, don't clog your mind up with the three or four conspiracy theory sites that are interested in it. Because they don't know what they're talking about." She cleared her throat. "Truth is stranger than fiction, isn't that what they say? Don't I see that in action every day?" Carys shrugged. Catherine watched her and then cleared her throat. "This is the truth. Every August at Vanes there was a ceremony called the Collecting. We'd process across the grounds to the chapel on the outside of the boundary of the house, and we'd sing an ancient folk song."

"You did what?"

"Yep. A version of 'Green Grow the Rushes, O!,' only this version is called the 'Collecting Carol.' It's not found anywhere else."

"I did 'Green Grow the Rushes, O!' at primary school."

"I remember," said Catherine. She nodded at her. She wouldn't tell her what having to sit there listening to rows of little children sing that song had been like. The prickling along her neck, in her eyes, the primary urge to just get up and run run run away from what was coming. "So for the Collecting everyone has a role. There's five bells, they're rung by the Walkers, three spoons carried by the Rivals for collecting the honey. Is this on Google?" Carys shook her head, eyes bulging. "Exactly. Two Beloved Girls are picked each year to walk with the procession. They have to be pure. They wear greenery in their hair. The Hunters go into the chapel and collect the honey from the hives inside the tombs that are stacked up on each side of the altar, in recesses."

Carys rubbed her eyes, her head down, staring at the floor. "This is—weird."

"Well." Catherine spoke softly. "Oh darling. I know. So there are bees in the unused tombs, where there weren't any coffins. They've been there for centuries." She watched her daughter, whose hands were pressed on each side of the stool. More than anything else, she longed to reach out, to take her in her arms, there in the still, quiet night, to say she was making it all up, to go downstairs with her, heat up some of the leftover soup, snuggle on the sofa and watch two episodes of *Brooklyn Nine-Nine* until she was falling asleep and could stumble upstairs again. To say, we're normal. This isn't in your life. It's not going to hurt you.

"There are different myths about how the bees got there, which we won't get into. But, long ago, there was a priest, who came to live in the house, and people say he made a pact with the Devil. He invented the ceremony. He promised the bees he'd only take half and leave them half for winter."

"Why?"

Catherine looked at her daughter. "You have to leave them some honey for winter," she said. "If you take too much, they'll starve. They collect nectar all spring and summer, to store up food for winter, and they pollinate everything at the same time. Pollinating crops is pretty important to the survival of the planet."

"Well—I know that. I just didn't ever think much about what they do all winter. So is that why bees make honey then? Kind of like all the ready meals in our freezer."

They both laughed, slightly too loudly. "I see now the result of letting you grow up in central London with a father who can't name a single flower and thinks the only growing thing that matters is the coffee bean," Catherine said.

Carys smiled. Then she said: "But, um . . . so, why did you leave, Mum?"

Catherine took a deep breath. She looked down at the desk, the whorls of her fingers tracing patterns on the whorls of the wood. The silence hummed in her ears.

"There was an accident. At the end of that summer. Janey and I—we had to leave. Things had happened. We'd found out some bad stuff about the family. Darling, I don't talk about it much because it's painful to remember, and a lot of it is jumbled up now. I don't understand a lot of it myself." She opened her mouth to say more, to say all of it, and she couldn't. She shook her head. "Sorry."

"That's OK. That's fine." She jumped, as Carys put her hand lightly on hers. "Do you know what happened to Janey, Mum?"

"She's dead. Yeah." She nodded, convincing herself of it for the umpteenth time. "She's dead. I left her."

"You left her?"

"Look," Catherine said. Already she was struggling to see clearly. Too well she knew the fluttering, light feeling in her chest and stomach that meant she had stopped breathing with any depth, that meant soon her vision would go, her head would swim. "It

75

didn't pan out how we'd expected. We'd planned to get away that day, but she changed…she changed her mind. So—Janey stayed behind, and I—I left. I drove away from there and went to Europe. I worked in a few bars, traveled through France, and that's where I met Dad."

"That's what saved you."

Catherine shook her head. "Saved me? No. What saved me was going to Cambridge." Carys laughed. "No. I'm serious. I wanted to study. I wanted to learn. I wasn't supposed to go. I was a girl, they did everything to prevent me from going, they wanted Kitty Hunter to be…decorative, beautiful, compliant." She had to stop herself shivering. "I arrived at Cambridge this mess of a girl, half formed, unsure about everything. I'd had a good education, but, boy, by the time I left three years later, my brain had been squeezed and pummeled and I'd learned—oh, how to concentrate, to really drill down, to question, to be scrupulous—all these things that are so important and that more and more don't matter to politicians and companies and people who push rubbish on social media and call it a job…" Carys rolled her eyes. "But I knew it was the only thing that mattered, Carys. We all deserve the same. It saved me. I was shy, I hated myself, I had no place in the world, and when I left I knew how to beat the most arrogant, self-assured prick on the bench, how to cut his arguments down to size, line by line, point by point." She realized she couldn't catch a breath. She put her hand on her breastbone. "I'm sorry. It's hard to talk about." Carys was thumbing a scrap of paper, smoothing it out like one of the red-tailed Chinese fortune-telling fish she'd always put in their Christmas stockings.

"It's OK," she said, shyly. She put her hand on her mother's knee. Catherine looked down, wrapping her fingers around her daughter's, squeezing so tight she felt the bones move.

"Sorry."

Carys shook her head. "It's fine. So your mother, your sister, the others—are they still alive? And you don't want to see them?"

Catherine shook her head.

"My grandmother?" Carys rubbed her forehead. "Mum—they're your family—our family."

"But they're not, to me, not anymore." Catherine blinked, steadily. She had to stay calm.

Carys said, very quietly: "Mum. Did they abuse you?"

Catherine took her free hand. "No, my love. Not how you think. I need you to understand. This is in the past. It was an unhappy house. It all culminated in a strange, dreadful summer. I had to get away. They weren't like me. I should have seen it earlier. Some people have to leave their families, leave them far behind, cut off all contact. Do you understand?"

"Sure." Carys patted her mother's knee, very lightly. "Claudia in my year, her mum doesn't see any of her family. Something about when her dad died. And Mr. Lebeniah."

"Well, exactly." Mr. Lebeniah had a brother who periodically turned up, ranting and screaming about money that was owed him when the family had come to London. The children had found it terrifying, when they were small, and latterly had lost interest, though it was always quite a spectacle. He had a walking stick, which he used to shake, like a villain in a cartoon. "He's crazy," the kind, otherwise unflappable Mr. Lebeniah would say of his brother, drawing back the curtains, unlocking the front door after he was sure he'd gone. "I hate that fucking idiot. I don't ever want to be near him again, until I can spit on his grave."

Catherine looked down at Carys's piece of paper, the one she had been smoothing with her fingers. "What's that?" she said, sharply.

Carys held it out. She looked scared. "I found it on the floor, the night of the break-in. When everything was all in chaos. I kept it." And she handed it to her mother, wordlessly. It was a teardrop-shaped piece of paper, torn from a glossy magazine.

The Most Beloved Girl: Kitty Hunter, 17, already known as "the most sought-after beauty in the South West" on holiday from boarding school Letham's at Giles Leigh-Smith's lavish 18th birthday party ball, with best friends the Hon. Polly Baring and Lucy Calthorpe. Beautiful Kitty Hunter, says admirer Nico Alexis, son of billionaire shipping magnate Aristides Alexis, is "the girl the boys are all after." Kitty's family, the Hunters, long established in Exmoor, hold a famed ceremony every year to collect honey from their ancient hives at Vanes, near Larcombe. Kitty and her twin, Joss, turn 18 next August. Kitty is looking for a pal to be the "Beloved Girl" with her in this year's ceremony. "It's very arcane, but I rather love it," says Kitty, who says her interests include "history, law, walking Rory our family dog and planning my travels."

"*Harpers & Queen*, April 1989," Carys read at the very bottom of the scrap of paper, in tiny lettering. "Mum—Mum, really? You were...oh my God. You were a posh Sloane Ranger!"

Catherine shook her head. "None of that was me. And when Janey came, ah, well. It all changed."

She looked into her daughter's eyes. Carys's pupils were huge, her nail-bitten fingers flexing and unflexing. Catherine took her hand. Neither of them said anything for a while.

"Oh, Mum." Carys pulled her hand away. Her voice trembled. "It's very good. It's almost all there. There's just one thing that keeps bothering me."

"What's that, darling?"

"The window. I can't explain the window."

"What window?" Catherine didn't understand for a moment, her mind back at Vanes. Gabled windows against a clear blue sky, the tiny window in the chapel. The roaring of a swarm, like a crashing wave. But then Carys pointed.

"This window." She stood up, biting her thumb, and Catherine felt the thudding, fluttering feeling in her chest start up again. "The glass was all over the extension ceiling. Not on the floor here. If someone had broken in, like you said, they'd have smashed in from *outside*. The glass would have fallen *in*. And there was no glass in the room at all, apart from one or two shards. I don't know, I-I think you're lying."

"About what?"

"About this—" Carys gestured around the small room.

"Why do you think I'm lying?"

"Because...because...something about how you're downplaying it all doesn't make sense. Is it Grant Doyle? Are you trying to protect him?"

"No!" Catherine reached out to her, but Carys shook her head.

"Then who broke in? Did you let them in? And what's it got to do with... all this?" She pointed to the cutting. "Why are you telling me about it all now?"

"Darling, you asked me about it! And can't you see how hard it is for me to talk about it?"

Carys nodded. "I suppose—that description, those Sloaney rich people. That really doesn't sound like you."

"It wasn't. I don't like talking about my family, Carys." She hated the indignation in her own voice, as if Carys wasn't allowed to ask. She paused, taking a moment to collect her thoughts.

"Were they really posh?"

"Not really posh, no. They liked to play up to it. My father was an antiques dealer. Charles Hunter Antiques. He had a card printed, in curly writing. He did the whole dodgy act up and down Portobello Road and Chelsea in the late fifties and sixties, scouring the place for bargains. And he'd charm old people into believing their heirlooms were worthless, buy them for a shilling and sell them for five times the price. He had an eye, I'll give him that." She was silent. "Janey's dad, Simon, used to say there was no better metaphor for Charles Hunter than his antiques business." She was smiling. "I'm trying to tell you as much as I can. I find it difficult to say it out loud after all these years."

"I understand," Carys said. Her voice was hoarse, her small lips wrinkled together because she was trying not to cry. "I want to believe you."

"Good. Look, about the break-in—I'm sure it probably wasn't Grant. I think it was just—one of those things. No harm came of it, did it?" She raised her voice, slightly, almost daring Carys to challenge her.

But Carys shook her head. "Mum—don't you ever think about going back? Confronting the past?"

"It was rotten, all of it." Catherine pressed her hands to her face. "The honeycombs... Some years, we'd crack open one hive and they'd all have died, disease or predators or the cold, and you'd have no idea until you looked inside. Blackened, dried out, the honey gone. That was the Hunters. And I got away." She jabbed at the torn piece of paper. "Kitty Hunter, she escaped. She's free." She felt the tension in her jaw, the ache. "You have to understand, my own beloved girl. I don't want you to ever be a part of it. I wanted to keep you, and Tom, and Dad, away from it all and I did."

Catherine breathed out, trying to smile at her daughter. But as she looked at Carys's face, and saw her eyes flicker away from her mother, toward the fresh putty on the window, only then did she understand that she had failed.

Chapter Eight

Catherine had just picked up her wheelie suitcase to leave the office at lunchtime, propping open the door with her foot, when the phone rang. She was halfway out of the door; she debated whether to ignore it or not.

"Hello?"

"Catherine? It's Ash. Ashok Sengupta. Grant's solicitor."

Catherine leaned the handle of the case against the bookshelf and slid back into her chair. "Hi, Ash. How are you?"

She gazed out over the square. It was a beautiful day, only May 4, but there was heat in the air. The building next to their chambers had a wisteria in full bloom; the scent, as she arrived and left, was heady. She always longed to open the window, to let the smell of it in. Scanning the ground, she could see nothing of interest. Nothing at all.

"Catherine. Have you heard?" Ash had a mildly scolding tone. He'd had it throughout the trial. As if she were at fault, all the time.

"Heard what?"

"About Grant."

"No—I saw him the other day. He was fine."

"He's not fine." Ash's voice rose. "He's tried to kill himself. Last night. They found him this morning, unconscious, in his cell. He managed to get hold of the blade from a razor, somehow."

A couple stood under the spreading plane tree below; one of them laying out a blanket. "Is he alive?"

"He is. He's been transferred to St. Thomas's. He lost a lot of blood. But he did it the right way—up the vein, you know."

"Don't," she started to say, and then cleared her throat, turning away from the square. "OK. I'm so sorry, Ash. I'll phone his mother."

"No," said Ash, flatly. "His mother called me to tell me. She asked me to let you know. She's saying it's your fault. You upset him so much last week, that nonsense about the cease and desist from your family, she's saying you made threats against him. What the hell happened?"

"I did no such thing, Ash. That's simply not true." Her hand holding the phone was slick with moisture.

"Isn't it? Well. OK."

Catherine spun back toward her desk, the familiar swooping, arcing feeling of freefalling swamping her again, and this time it didn't, wouldn't stop, as she raised her eyes to the view in front of her.

There she was, in the middle of Lincoln's Inn Fields, waving up at Catherine. Her long hair shone in the hot May sun. Yes, it was spring, but a spring day that is like summer, and summer was her time, it always had been.

She was in a different outfit, a variation on the same long floral dress and leggings. Catherine knew she could see her. Her eyes— piercing, unblinking, fixed on her office, as though through crosshairs.

I want it to stop.

Catherine tried to listen to Ash, who was at his most pompous. She knew she should listen, she should take care, that she should care more about this boy whom she had failed. But she didn't care. She knew Grant had killed someone else and been glad of it, and he was a bad person, and the jury had understood that and that she'd have never got him off. Sometimes, it was as simple as good and bad, and she saw it now. He was not a good person. But he was a boy. The same age as Tom. He had slit his own wrists, and she didn't care.

She sat there and nodded and agreed to be investigated and to hand over files and papers and talk to the police and all the time she watched her, from the window, watched her shadow, moving slightly now and then, watched as she took out a phone and played with it, made gestures up toward Catherine's window. Waving, smiling, tapping.

Catherine put the phone down and turned her back on the window, bent over, head between her legs, holding her face, her skull, tightly. She stayed like that for a few seconds, and when she stood up, and looked out again, there was no one there. The small room seemed to be closing in on her.

The bus wheezed slowly up Kentish Town Road. It was too hot inside already, the air conditioning in the new busses already malfunctioning though it was only May.

It was two hours until she had to meet her husband at St. Pancras—four hours until the Eurostar left, but Davide loved being early for everything. The last thing she wanted to do before the weekend away was visit the home. Even as she got on the Tube that would take her toward North London she'd told herself that she could go another time. She wanted to pull the shades down and sit in her quiet, safe office where she could work for a few hours uninterrupted on the marine insurance fraud case and read through her briefing notes on a new case, an overstretched hospital, a stand-in doctor's botched cesarean section. She should have been grateful that, after Doyle, her old work was piling up. The familiar grind, defensive NHS management, distressed families, money in play and she, Catherine, swimming calmly through it all, establishing the facts, building a case, attaining consensus. She could be—she had been—so good at it.

On the bus she had time to think. As the woman next to her muttered under her breath, fanning herself ostentatiously with a thin, flapping piece of paper, Catherine tried to breathe herself, to calm herself. She had rung Grant's mother, who had put the phone down on her, then Poppy, his sister, who'd told her that she knew she'd threatened him and he was still a child. "I know," said Catherine, blankly. "I know he is." Poppy had put the phone down on her, too.

What is good and bad. What bad means. For some reason she found herself thinking of Tom. When he was twelve, he'd gone through a phase of being awful—kicking Carys, swearing, being rude to Mr. Lebeniah—he'd spat at Catherine, when she told him he had to tidy his room and had gone in herself with a black bin bag. At the same time, money kept disappearing out of her purse and coat—one-pound, two-pound coins she knew she kept hold of for parking and for tea and coffee machines. She'd seen Tom taking coins out of her coat pocket, putting them in his, but she had not said anything, waiting to tackle him about it, knowing if she told Davide, he would have Tom sent off to the Foreign Legion, or marched him to the police station. The next day, when she walked him to the bus stop, Catherine pretended to disappear around the corner again then lingered behind a curved old wall, to watch him for a time. She saw him bend down, give the money to a young man outside the Overground station, who had a decrepit Staffie covered in bald patches, curled peacefully next to him. Tom fondled the dog's ears while he was chatting to the young man. That was what she remembered.

She talked to him about it that evening.

"It's wrong to take without asking, darling, you know that, don't you?"

He'd nodded. "I—I didn't want to tell you about it."

"Why?"

He'd scratched the back of his head, suddenly grown-up.

"Some stuff makes you sad."

They were climbing up past the Heath, past her own house. She felt her eyes fill with painful tears which she blinked back. Come on, she told herself. It's been twenty-nine years, you've done it for this long, you can carry on doing it.

She shook her head, faster and faster. Only a few hours until she'd be on the train with Davide and all would be well...She would admit to everything with Grant, she would take whatever punishment was on offer. She had been wrong. If she could just get away, get a reset, just her and Davide...it was still in her control to keep this all going. She swallowed down a sour taste in her mouth.

Driftwood was the name of Eileen Lestrange's retirement home: it was a tall, Gothic, turreted building that seemed to have been stretched upward to fit into the tiny plot of land it occupied beside Hampstead Heath. It always reminded her of Jan Pienkowski castles in books she'd read to the children.

Since January she had come here once a fortnight. She hated it. Hated the distant muffled screams down corridors and the smell of antiseptic and urine and Katalina, the buxom nurse who wore terrible foundation like stage pancake makeup and pushed the residents in wheelchairs up and down the corridor too fast as some of them cried out, obviously terrified.

Most of all she hated Eileen's bare, sad, dark room. Three pictures on the wall, a cushion in a garish sixties orange and pink paisley print, jarringly out of place in the fawn and beige of the home—Catherine had no idea where it had come from. Every time she left she dared to tell herself perhaps she wouldn't go again. It was too much. Eileen had no idea who she was. And somehow, every time, ten days would pass and she'd know she had to go and see her. Just in case she said something, told her something more.

"They're poisoning my tea," Eileen said as Catherine walked in.

Catherine stood her suitcase by the wall and took her jacket off. It was always hot inside. A vase of magenta and orange parrot tulips stood next to the bed, indecently frilly, bent and warped in their last stages. She moved them along the Formica table out of the bright sunshine. Several petals fell onto the carpet.

"I'm sorry to hear that. Hello—Eileen. These are nice flowers. How are you?"

Eileen's hair was lank, her cashmere cardigan rather dirty, but otherwise she looked OK. The room was close and smelled sweet, of something rotten. Catherine stooped and kissed her soft cheek. She put the tin of chocolate biscuits from Fortnum & Mason down and then went to open the window.

"Who are you? Have you been to see me before?"

Catherine yanked the window open, drinking in the fresh air, then shut it so it was only open a crack. "I'm Janey's friend. Catherine. Yes, I come every other week or so, to see how you're settling in."

"Ah." The gray eyes blinked, quite intelligently. "You know Janey."

"Yes."

"My husband, Martin, he'll be here soon. He's in Spain."

Catherine always hated this bit. "Yes."

"I had to come back, you see. His children didn't like me. They were stealing from me. He's still there. Isn't he?"

"I'm not sure, Eileen."

"I'll wait here, anyway. They're putting poison in my tea. I told them to stop yesterday."

"What makes you think they're doing that, Eileen?"

"Mrs. Caraway Seeds to you, thank you very much."

"I—"

"I can taste it in the tea. It tastes of—" She stopped and looked at the spongy brown carpet, the small, delicate hands clutched tight in her lap. "I don't remember. Caraway seeds?"

They chatted for a time in the usual desultory fashion: someone new in the room across the corridor who was very loud. How when she'd lived in Spain she'd had excellent TV reception, all the UK channels. How there was a different presenter on *Cash in the Attic* and Eileen didn't care for her, she was rather brash. Whether Kate Middleton was too thin or not. They were poisoning her tea. As always Catherine found herself staring at Eileen's hands. The nails, beautifully shaped, always kept trimmed. Did she do it? The thin gold band, so slender it might crack, with a tiny cluster of pearls. And what had puzzled her, since Eileen had been brought back from Spain late last year after a combination of factors (the death of Martin, her second husband, Brexit—"They hate us, the Spanish. They're waiting to steal our houses and all our possessions"—and after her dementia had advanced rapidly): why did she wear her first husband's ring? She'd left him years ago, when her daughter was twelve, to run off with Martin.

Catherine's phone buzzed in her bag. She rubbed her eyes and found the older woman staring at her with an expressionless gaze. She stared down at the ring on her finger, then at Catherine again.

"I don't know why I'm here," she said, conversationally.

Catherine tried to update her once a visit. She didn't like doing it more than once though. "You moved back. From Spain. Martin died. Your husband. Do you remember?"

"Martin, my husband." Eileen looked totally blank. "Simon was my husband, dear. Catherine, is it?"

"Simon was your husband, then you left him and married Martin. He was a surveyor for Greenford Council? Do you remember?" Eileen shook her head. "His children were Jeanette and Adam?"

"Oh, *them*," said Eileen, bitterly. "Promised me I could stay in Murcia. Swore blind. Lied, both of them. They lied! Sold the house from under me! Liars! It was my house!"

A visitor, walking past the open door, looked in with alarm at this last dramatic declaration. *Who are you visiting?* Catherine wanted to ask her. *Who are they? Do you care? Is it horrible?*

"It was their father's house," she said instead, patiently, although she had sympathy with Eileen's anger, since soon after Martin had died it had been revealed she had no claim whatsoever to the house she'd lived in for thirty years or more. Her second husband's children had moved brutally fast and the house was sold weeks later—Eileen's stepchildren perhaps exacting a cold revenge for the removal of their father from their lives as children.

It had been Catherine whom they contacted, and it was Catherine who found her a home, got her settled and, of course, paid the bills. But she did it. She had to—what choice did she have?

"You're crazy," Davide had said, when she'd told him what she was planning, back in October. "She's a terrible woman. You've always said so."

"Her stepchildren have abandoned her. She's got no money, no friends in Spain—"

"After years there? Nothing to show for it at all? Catherine, this woman is not your problem."

Davide had a way of simplifying things that was sometimes extremely comforting, sometimes not. Catherine sighed.

"I'll use my money. You won't notice. Listen. I have to take care of her. She's my responsibility."

For once she saw him look almost angry, and that sliver of phosphorescent tension that sometimes sparked up between them, threatening to grow into something bigger, flickered for a second. But then he shrugged. "You must do what you must do, *chérie*," he'd said, paraphrasing Carys, and she'd smiled. "I won't ask." But sometimes she wished he would ask.

"My mother was Italian," Eileen said now. She lifted her eyes up, looking out of the window at the blue sky and the Heath beyond. Very, very far away, there was a kite. "From Italy, this ring is. Like me."

"I didn't know that—that's lovely," Catherine said, as her phone buzzed again. She never wanted to ask questions—she was afraid of the answers, but something made her say: "It's a beautiful ring."

"Well, Simon gave it to me. Janey's father. Did you know him?"

"Yes, I did."

Eileen nodded, pleased. "He was in love with her, you know, but he married me. I was a dull old thing. I don't know why he chose me but he did. He came back from his job up North one day, and he just walked back into the shop and put that ring on my finger himself."

"Did he bring it back... from Italy specially for you?"

"Don't be silly. I was thirteen when the war ended. He'd have been arrested for going with me when I was thirteen. *He* wasn't like that. He was an old father, my Simon! Yes, he used to joke about it. They both were." Her eyes were bright. "Do you know, it's a funny thing. I was so busy wanting him to take me away from my dull old life, Mother, me, one room in Clerkenwell, only mixing with other Italian widows, evenings sewing, and he seemed so glamorous. So full of ..." She stared out over the Heath, at the glorious new green on the trees. "So full of *life*. And it wasn't till long afterward, you see. I realized something."

"What did you realize?"

"Oh, I didn't love him. I didn't really like him, actually. All his... castle in the sky ways."

Catherine nodded—she knew better than to engage any further. She had tried it before and it upset Eileen. And herself.

"My ring," said Eileen proudly, to herself, as if the whole conversation had never happened.

Catherine said, as calmly as she could: "So he bought the ring out in Naples during the war, then. He saw it and thought it was the perfect ring."

"How do you know he was in Naples in the war?" The voice was suspicious, the mild demeanor suddenly gone.

"You've told me before. He was there in the war. Those tulips, Eileen—"

"He was there, yes, he was there. It was dreadful."

"You said. Who brought you these flowers, Eileen?"

"He went out after it had been destroyed. 1944, Janey. Whole of Naples was rubble. Children starving in the streets. Some already dead. Rows of women waiting in warehouses every afternoon. You could go in and choose which one would sit herself down on you and you'd do it to her—" The older woman wrinkled her nose, as if it was distasteful for her to have to tell her all this, as if she didn't want to. "Then you'd—ahm—and afterward, you'd give her your rations—as payment. He told me all this. He couldn't stop his men going off there. Women tearing hair out of each other for chunks of bread. Selling themselves, their families. A little boy—I won't tell you what they did to him. Simon found him."

Catherine felt an icy trickle of water start at the nape of her neck. "Eileen—"

Eileen's eyes were alight, her face mobile for once. "Well. The Germans had abandoned the place and left them all to die. Simon was trying to help them. The Eye-Ties, they called them. But it broke him, you know. He wasn't able to get through it, after-ward...That's what Sylvia used to say, anyway." She stopped again and stared at her ring once more. The hum of the cooling units on the wall outside filled the empty room. "Oh well. Do you remember him? My darling Simon?"

"Yes—yes, of course I do."

"Very difficult man. But he was. Drove me to distraction. I couldn't bear it anymore. Waking up screaming, sometimes. Saying he'd done wrong. Writing these letters he never sent. He felt such guilt about it all. About abandoning *her*. And he didn't love me! And his daughter. I mean she's my child too, but she never loved me. The two of them, off in everything together, exploring, reading, making things—hah! Leaving *me* out of it!" The slight Cockney tinge to her accent increased. "That was it, you see. Martin and me, we were very comfortable, and he had a nice place in Malaga. Very nice it was. Simon wasn't interested in going to Spain, or anywhere like that. He had no ambition for himself. Big dreams, oh yes, but putting it into practice? You must be joking! Martin pointed it out, you know. And your father, he let you do what you liked, Janey! Meeting that Black girl every morning on the bridge, even when you was so little. Claire, was it? The mother was totally mad. Hah. *She has to learn to stand on her own two feet, Eileen!* That's what he'd say to me. He'd *say* that."

"Eileen—"

"You never ask about him, when you come here. Claire, what's she up to, these days?"

"No—I'm not Janey." Her hand had left a sweaty print on the nylon-velvet chair. The phone buzzed again. "I'm Catherine. Simon was Janey's father."

Eileen's dark gray eyes rested on her for a moment, considering. "You two, you ran away, didn't you? The house. Vanes. Now you remember the house, don't you? They looked after those bees." Eileen twisted her wedding ring around her finger, round and round. Every time, the stones caught on the sagging webbing between her middle and ring finger. "So you're one of them? One of the Hunters?" Her voice was rising. "She was no good, that girl. Or the mother!"

The door burst open, causing Catherine to leap out of her chair in shock. "Hello, girls," said Jonathan, the home's director of entertainment. "Just giving you a leaflet about the show later on in the Trafalgar Suite. Four p.m. Brian and Julie's Latin Lounge Time. A little tea dance for all our lovely ladies and gents, chance to trip the light fantastic, will you be there?" His eyes twinkled encouragingly at Eileen, who paused and said flatly:

"No."

"Oh, come on, Eileen." The joke passed without mention, neither Jonathan nor Eileen seeming to notice it. "You'd enjoy it. Katalina said you should give it a try. How about you, madam, will you be able to stay?"

Catherine and Eileen jointly said:

"No."

"She can't go. She's too busy, she's a—what's your job? She's busy, anyway."

Jonathan stared at Catherine. "You're her daughter? Oh my days!"

"No, I—"

He beamed at Eileen. "I never knew she had any family, poor dear. I've never seen you before."

"I'm not her daughter," Catherine told him. "I come every other week. I was a friend of her daughter. She's dead."

"Well that's sad, isn't it? How it is." Jonathan put his head on one side. "What happened?"

"What's she saying?" Eileen gave Catherine a nasty look. "Is she lying to you? She's a liar. You're a liar, aren't you?"

Instantly Jonathan said brightly: "Well, I'd best be off, know how it is! You two will want to catch up. I'll hope to see you ladies later!"

He almost ran out of the room. Silence fell, and Catherine resisted the urge to look at her phone. She gazed at the tulips again. Who had brought her such opulent flowers? What did she think about, alone in bed at night, did she know the truth? As she came to, Eileen was staring at her, her head turned toward her, eyes, mouth open, as if greedily waiting to gobble her up.

"She's dead. You make a fool of me. Coming here. You think I don't remember? I've got all the time in the world to remember. I said this to her last week when she brought the flowers. I told her all about it and she laughed. She said I should ask you about it. Because you're mine."

Catherine looked down; her hands were shaking. "Who brought the flowers?"

I am mad. I'm in it, right now. It's taking me over and I don't—I don't know how to get out of it.

"I raised you. I didn't want to, but I did. And you—you never came to me. You only wanted Daddy." She said it in a mocking tone.

"Who brought those pink and red tulips, Eileen? It's about a week ago, they're dying, who was it?"

And Eileen said: "A lady from the church. She knew it was my birthday. She's from the church. She remembered my birthday. You didn't even bother."

Catherine breathed out. "I'm sorry. I'm so sorry I forgot your birthday, Eileen. I've been—" She looked at her hands, still shaking. "I've been busy."

"My own daughter, and you didn't remember."

This had happened before, once before: Eileen had spent the entire afternoon asking her how Janey had died, where she'd gone.

She had begun to remember. About that summer, and going up to Cambridge, and Kitty. Begun was the wrong word for it. More as though snow swirled almost ceaselessly across her thoughts but occasionally, just occasionally, the storm lulled and she saw a little clearly.

Catherine stood up. "I'd better go. I have to catch a train. Goodbye—bye, Eileen." Her throat swelled up tight, and she bent down and kissed the older woman. As ever, she wondered if this would be the last time.

"Thanks for coming," Eileen said, as if nothing had happened. She pulled at the top button of her cardigan, suddenly looking very tired, and gazed into space. "She's dead, isn't she, Catherine? She is, isn't she?"

"Yes. She is."

She began fumbling for the remote. "I thought so. All the villagers ran. No one stayed to help. Isn't that sad?" She gave a little chuckle, pleased. "And the daughter. What was she called?"

"Kitty. Catherine. Me. I'm Catherine."

There was a silence.

"But you're not the daughter." The eyes were watchful. "I know you're not. You say this, every time. But you're not."

"I can show you my passport. It says Catherine Christophe on it, and my date of birth," said Catherine with an attempt at humor, and that, at least, was the truth.

Chapter Nine

Dragging the suitcase through the automatic doors, waving goodbye to the receptionist, a glum man with a drooping mustache behind a glass partition, Catherine stood still for a moment, drinking in the open air.

She looked up at a faint sound and ran, spotting a black cab in the distance down the wide empty road. She ran as fast as she was able to, the suitcase bumping over cracked paving stones. All the time, just saying to herself. *Just get there. Davide will be there. Just get there. Walk toward him. Don't look for anyone else.*

"St. Pancras, Eurostar, please," she said, settling into the back seat and reaching for her phone. She tried to answer some emails. There was a text from Jake.

U OK hun? Heard about Doyle. LMK if I can help.

It was shocking how easy it had been to let go of Jake, to put him aside.

She scrolled through old photos of the children: Carys on her tenth birthday, so adorable in her sundress. Tom on his first day of big school, hair slicked down, tanned cheeks from a summer in France with her in-laws, and she felt again the tide wash across her. She started deleting photos, selecting whole days, months, years at a time. Wiping out scores of memories.

The phone froze with the effort, and in the end she just stared out of the cab window as she rolled down the road toward St. Pancras Old Church. Thomas Hardy had dug up graves in the graveyard there to make way for the railway line in the nineteenth century. Joss had told her that—he had been a surprising mine of information, always picking up new things. What had happened to the bodies? She hadn't known. Joss hadn't, either.

Now she had thought about it all anyway, she allowed herself the pain of recalling his handsome face, the cowlick of blond hair, the flush across the cheeks, the hazel-gray eyes. The fingers, clumsily strumming a guitar. Studying Sylvia at her drawing board. Watching Merry, idly playing with Rory, a remote control in her other hand. Watching PF as he polished things, and timed things, and ordered people about. Pater familias. Poor Joss. He never stood a chance.

They were closer than ever now. She could feel the swooping, awful giddy feeling, worse than ever. She tried to shut it out, to focus on getting past this moment, then the next, then the next. She told herself if she got past it then she'd be OK.

It's not real.

Davide is real. He's waiting for you.

Forget about Grant. Leave him behind, for now. That and the house being for sale. That's why. There's reasons for all of this.

It made such complete sense, almost immediate was the release in tension. She blinked, breathing slowly, drumming her fingers up and down the back of her skull, a habit she had developed as a way of releasing pent-up anxiety. The cab driver paid her no attention, thankfully. She carried on doing it.

She had run away from Eileen before the usual hour and so Catherine was twenty minutes early to meet Davide. She wandered up and down the bustling concourse of shops in St. Pancras, idly fingering baby clothes she did not need and books she would not read, all the time trying to ignore the feeling in her head, in her throat, the one that said *Get out. Get out now.* She paused in front of the small Fortnum & Mason concession shop in the station, remembering the paltry packet of biscuits, and Eileen's face again as she stared at her.

She went into Marks and Spencer, to buy some snacks for the train—when the Eurostar had first opened, in Waterloo, and she had been able to go over and visit him, she had always brought Davide something from M&S. As she was reaching for a plastic tub of pineapple chunks she felt an arm slide around her waist and a low, gently wry voice say in her ear:

"Madame, by any chance are you free at all this weekend?"

His hands turned her slim frame around so she was pressed against him and she stared into her husband's face, drinking him in with joy. Joy that she loved him and still found him so savagely attractive. She could feel him very slightly pressing against her, and loved that—demure, controlled, urbane Davide in his beautifully pressed suit and gabardine trench coat, growing hard for his wife of twenty years, there in the fruit and deli aisle of Marks and Spencer.

"I can't wait for this weekend," he said, and he kissed her neck, and she felt as she always did at the end of the day the infinitesimal scrape of stubble, for he was beautifully clean-shaven. "I want you all to myself, my darling." He cupped her face in his hands. "I think you've guessed. And I'm sorry. Do you forgive me?"

"For what?"

"For taking you to Paris, not somewhere exotic?"

"Oh. Oh! Of course—" she said, and she told herself that it was OK, that she could feel all misery, anxiety, fear flowing away from her, far away—

She kissed him again and then stopped, her eyes closed. Somehow her body knew before her brain. A cold, metallic numbness, the beating drum in her head and throat. And she looked over his shoulder, and she knew he felt her stiffen.

"What is it?"

"That—"

She pointed, and he turned to look out of the shop at the Eurostar check-in, but then turned back. To him there was nothing, other than the usual stream of people queuing, passing through, saying goodbye. But there—at the front of the taped section. There she was.

A tall, blond woman in a white flowing top, fiddling with her backpack. It was red, rather tatty-looking, at odds with her glamorous appearance. She looked up and smiled at them both.

Davide smiled back, then stopped, as if he wasn't sure why he'd done it. "What?"

"Hello," the woman said. "It's time, Catherine. You know it is."

She walked on, toward a coffee shop on the corner, and paused for a second, before merging into the crowds. She looked over once, then disappeared. Davide had already turned away.

"The tattoo," Davide said. He nodded very slightly toward her and lowered his voice.

"What?"

"On her arm. Didn't you almost get one of those? When you were traveling?"

"What tattoo?" She was fumbling through her handbag, looking for something. "Oh no…please, no…"

"The bee tattoo. Thank God you didn't, eh? This age, with a tattoo, and bees as well—are you OK, *chérie*?"

Catherine straightened up. "Sorry. This is infuriating." She shook her head. "Don't be cross, Davide. I've left my passport in the safe at work."

"Catherine," Davide growled. "Good Lord, woman, why do you try to offend me, to thwart me all the time?"

She made herself look up, to play her part. "I do it to annoy you." She was shaking her head, smiling at him. His eyes were flinty gray with flecks of amber; it was one of the first things she had noticed about him when they'd met in that rose-gold square, all those years ago. She had fallen for him that very minute, and he had never doubted her, never not trusted her. "I can see it now, I can picture myself locking the safe. I had to take it in last month for a security check on the money-laundering case. I meant to remind myself this morning but I was in court…Oh shit. Darling, I'm so sorry."

He nodded, and flicked his wrist to look at his watch, and, she knew, to hide how irritated he was. She knew everything about him. "We will miss the train."

"Nonsense. I'll hop on the Tube, it's two stops to Holborn, I'll be back here in half an hour. We are always early, remember? We have lots of time." Her voice seemed to thicken, and she coughed.

"Lots of time?"

"Lots of time—I'm sorry, darling. I'm so sorry."

"But—"

The store was crowded; a man and an excited child pushed

them out of the way and they stepped back out onto the concourse together. "Stay here. I'll—I'll—"

She looked around wildly, then gave him one more kiss, a long, deep, intimate kiss only for him, and she breathed in deeply, as if inhaling his smell, and pressed his hand to her lips. They were still like that, for a moment, one more moment. She could see doubt, unease, flickering in his eyes.

"Is this all it is?"

"What do you mean?"

When the phone rang at six in the morning ten years ago, and she came down into the hallway to see him in his blue pajamas, ruffled hair, toes curling because of the cold Victorian tiles, on the phone, being told that his dear father had passed away in the night, Davide had had a smile on his face. A sad yet quizzical smile, as if he knew life was—what? A construct, a cage of spun sugar, a comb that could be smashed open at any time. He had that expression now.

He watched, as she pressed a square of paper into his hand.

"What's this?"

"You asked me about it, the other week." She looked up, a small smile playing on her pale, heart-shaped face. "The cutting. And Carys found it, online, too. It's not the wrong way round."

"What? Catherine—I don't care, *chérie*." She saw the panic mounting in his eyes.

"I'll be b-back in forty minutes." She could hardly speak. "I have—to, I have to go now. I love you." He was shaking his head. "I love the children. Tell them? Will you please make sure you tell them? Will you promise? I'm sorry."

And then she was gone.

Davide watched her go. He looked down at the flimsy square in his hand. It was a photograph from a newspaper of two girls. The one on the right was a young Catherine, with short, patchy hair, a big smile, huge eyes. There were so few photos of his wife as a young woman: as the hubbub in the station raged on, even as he knew she was walking away, he looked eagerly at the photo, but as he did so his frown deepened, his eyes widening, and then he put his hand to his mouth, frozen to the spot.

The Beloved Girls, missing after yesterday's tragedy: Left, Jane Lestrange, a family friend. Right, Catherine Hunter, daughter of Charles and Sylvia Hunter. Below, Catherine Hunter, as a young girl, with her parents and brother and sister.

Davide stared at the photos of Catherine Hunter.

"But that woman is not my wife," he said. He said it softly, then again, then again, louder each time. "That's not my wife." He was shouting it now, shouting into the emptiness of the crowded station. No one paid any attention. "That's not her!"

DAILY MAIL, 7 MAY 2018

Disappearance of top woman barrister "entirely out of character" says family

- **Third day since last sighting of Catherine Christophe, 47**
- **Mother-of-two left husband at London's St. Pancras station**
- **Top barrister had recently lost high-profile murder trial**

Police today were appealing for help in tracking the last known movements of London barrister Catherine Christophe, whose anniversary trip to Paris with her husband was abandoned after Mrs. Christophe left the Eurostar terminal to collect her passport.

But she never went back to her office and there is no sign of her passport either there or at her £2 million home in Dartmouth Park, North London. Friends and family say there is no reason for her sudden disappearance and, though she had been under pressure lately, she had not been acting out of character. Mrs. Christophe had recently unsuccessfully defended the high-profile Jolyons school Snapchat murder case; the 18-year-old Grant Doyle was found guilty and attempted suicide in prison last week.

Mrs. Christophe's credit cards have not been used, there are no phone records of her and, bafflingly after the initial CCTV of her leaving the ticket hall, there appears to be no further video evidence of her in the station. Her empty suitcase was found nearby.

"Any help the public can give as to the whereabouts of Mrs. Christophe would be greatly appreciated in reuniting this lady with her teenage children and husband who are understandably concerned for her safety," said Commander Sam O'Reilly of the Metropolitan Police.

Davide Christophe, her husband, insists he is frantic with worry. "She was so excited about the weekend. And then it's as if she changed. She said she'd forgotten the passport and she had to go and get it. But Catherine never forgets anything."

Yesterday it emerged that as a teenager Mrs. Christophe, then Catherine (Kitty) Hunter, was present at a notorious tragedy at her family home, Vanes, near Exmoor in Somerset, in August 1989. Several members of the Hunter family died during a secretive ancient ritual in a chapel in the grounds of the family home. At the time it was widely reported that Mrs. Christophe and her best friend, Janey Lestrange, had escaped the carnage. Police did not investigate further, at the family's behest. Mr. Christophe refused to comment.

Anyone with any relevant information is urged to contact the Metropolitan Police.

Part Two

1989

Extract from English Folklore, Fortescue, Millard, 1952, etc.

THE COLLECTING CAROL
TRADITIONAL, TO THE TUNE OF *GREEN GROW THE RUSHES, O!*

I'll sing you one, O,
One come for the comb, O!
What is your one, O?
One is one and all alone and evermore shall be so.

The origin of this bastardization of a traditional folk song is unclear, but while a great number of versions have been taken down and performed all over the West Country (see Baring-Gould & Sheppard, *Songs and Ballads of the West*, 1889) this version is sung only in an obscure corner of Somerset on the edge of Exmoor and thus entirely preserved as such is worthy of our attention.

Every year, in a ritual known as the Collecting dating back to the 18th century, the Hunter family in the parish of Larcombe invites the village to process through the woods (formerly inhabited by lepers) and beyond the boundary of the house to the ruined chapel of St. Dunstan where are kept and tended by the family many beehives. These bees, cultivated for over two centuries, are thought to inhabit some of the oldest hives in the country, perhaps the world (in Morocco, there is tell of hives extant for four centuries in an ancient monastery at the foot of the Atlas mountains). On St. Bartholomew's Day, the patron saint of bees and beekeepers, August 24, the ceremony must take place. The hives are opened, and half the comb cut away, to be eaten and enjoyed by the family and assembled throng "with some rapture." Then the honey is collected, to be sampled throughout the year, with the warning: "Half for us, half for them, else the Devil take us all," and the understanding that, if too much is taken from the bees, the inhabitants of Vanes and thus the Hunter family will fall.

The ceremony was instigated two hundred years ago by the incumbent priest of Vanes rectory, Caradoc Diver, about whom various stories are still told in the village. A short history by a junior member of the Hunter family, purporting to tell the true history of the Reverend Diver and the origins of the ceremony, is said to exist but has never been circulated beyond the family. Village rumor has it he made a pact with the Devil to conjure up a congregation to the church and secure the living. Some say accusations of a most grave nature against Diver are true. Unbelievable and scandalous as such claims may be, they are hard to disprove in a community almost entirely unchanged for centuries.

Chapter Ten

"Lestrange? Hey, are you Janey Lestrange?"

In my mind's eye I still see them all perfectly, not as they were that first visit when I was twelve, but as I did the summer of 1989. I was eighteen, and my father had died four months earlier.

I had taken the train to Taunton, then a bus to Minehead. There had been a rail strike the previous day and virtually no one was aboard the train out of London. Though I'd been to Vanes before I had no idea where I was going, nor where I was when I got to Taunton. I was directed to the bus by a "kindly guard" holding up a sign with my name on it.

He stared at me when I walked toward him, head down, too shy to make full eye contact. I knew he'd been expecting someone grown-up, glamorous; my surname does that. My mother hated it and gave me a plain name to offset it, which instead highlighted it. I should have been Jacquetta, or Hildegard or something. Mine and Daddy's favorite obscure fact had been that Ray Stanton Avery, the inventor of the sticky label, married a woman named Ernestine Onderdonk. Now that's a name. I never cared for my name at all, until it wasn't mine anymore.

"Are you Janey Lestrange?"

I nodded, only then looking up and glancing at him, defiantly. *Come on. Stare at me. I know I'm a freak.* I've always looked young, but that summer of 1989, for about four months by then, I had had no hair. One might wonder how my mother could have let me go away, but back then horrific things came to seem quite normal.

My summer job at Boots had come to an end prematurely and I was living alone in the family home, eating McDonald's or spaghetti hoops out of cans. Daddy had done all the cooking, and while my mother had come back from Spain a couple of weeks before to chivvy me along, and to sort out the house, she had left after ten days, the two of us more distant than ever, every evening spent in resentful, bemused silence. Salvation came in the form of the invitation to Vanes from Sylvia, who telephoned one evening while I happened to be out with my best friend, Claire. I got home to find my mother had accepted on my behalf. "Go and stay with them. It'll do you good to get out of the house, Janey. Have a change of scene."

There was no invitation to return to Spain with her. "I'd have you over, Janey, but Martin's children are there at the moment and it's difficult…"

I think she was afraid of my grief, of the horrendous pain I felt. I have sympathy. I was afraid of it, too. She left, exhorted me to tidy up, or think about sorting the house out so we could put it on the market. I did nothing about it. The night before I was due to leave, alone again, I sat in the house one last time. Impossible to quantify the feelings, the sense of the man still there, of my life drifting utterly away from me. I told myself I didn't really care. Before falling into bed, I piled a load of clothes into Daddy's Gladstone bag, any old thing. It's interesting to consider whether, if I had known I'd never go back, never return to that life again, would I have packed more carefully?

I wish I had a photograph of him. That's all.

The driver was kind, pointing out a seat by the front. "It's better up front, you don't feel so sick."

The ancient bus juddered as though it were a collection of springs held together by string, bouncing through narrow, winding roads toward Minehead, where at the bus station, on a side street, I climbed out along with my fellow passengers, looking around for someone to meet me. At the sight of my patchy head, a child in a pushchair dropped her ice-cream cone onto the ground, with a cartoonish splat. As the roars faded into the distance, and I stared around shivering slightly in the lengthening shadows and pulling the precious but unwieldy Gladstone bag closer toward me, a voice said:

"Aha. So you're the tragic waif and stray then, are you? Jane, isn't it? Hello again."

I looked up, and there was a boy, trapped in a shaft of sunlight, watching me with a quizzical, curious expression. Without doubt he was the most beautiful boy I'd ever seen, from the crown of his lustrous head to the pointed dark-plum Chelsea boots on his long, slender feet.

"I'm Janey," I said. My dad had always called me Janey. Never Jane.

He came forward, pushing his hair out of his eyes. "It's lovely to see you again, Janey Lestrange. I'm Joss Hunter."

"I remember," I said, awkwardly. He stared at me, as everyone did, but Joss was too well-mannered to do it for long.

"Mum's professional name," he said, smoothly. "Of course." I looked blank. "Sylvia Lestrange. PF loathes it. I'd forgotten it was your father's name she took."

Your father. He said it almost accusingly and my back stiffened. "Right." I shrugged, and then said, because I didn't know what else to say: "I don't know why you'd open with that as a greeting, to be honest."

His hair fell in his face again and he flicked it away, smiling with enjoyment. "Oh wow. Kitty said you were punchy." He held out a hand and I shook it, each of us summing the other up. "You're here now. I've come to take you home."

Daddy would have moved out of London, but for work, and my mother. His own mother, who died long before I was born, had grown up in one room in a tiny cottage in Dorset, and Daddy loved to tell the story of how as a young girl my grandmother had been given an apple by an ancient Thomas Hardy. He missed the countryside. He talked about it a lot. Curlews, and red campion, and tawny owls. Glow worms, and crickets, and the sound of a breeze in a wheat field just before harvest.

But apart from our holidays in Worthing every year, where we stayed in a small, prim hotel called Fairgreen with the same trifle for pudding every evening and the same sickly-sweet-smelling guests, where the sea was four streets away down narrow, chilly lanes, we did not really leave London, save for our snatched day trips here or there. My mother didn't like to. She was a townie, proudly so, she always said.

Those day trips were all the more precious, therefore. Every year, just before school started in September, Daddy would wake me early and we'd catch a train somewhere. Out to the Chilterns, to go walking—once we got lost and had to shelter from the rain in a pub near Checkers, and we saw Mrs. Thatcher's car drive past. We went to Bath, and Daddy took a photo of me, reading *Emma*, in front of the Royal Crescent. We went to Greenwich, by boat, and looked at the giant telescope and saw the spot in Greenwich Park where Flamsteed burned three hundred copies of his own star atlas, because it was full of inaccuracies and he had not wanted it published, but Halley and Newton had gone ahead anyway. (I simmered with the injustice of this for weeks.) We went to Cambridge and saw Trinity College, where Newton himself had been a valet to pay his way for his own studies. One year we decided to drive to Alton Towers but the car broke down, and Daddy got anxious, because we had no money for a new car, I think, and we couldn't go. Mummy had to go to Clerkenwell to collect Gran's Austin and fetch us from a service station on the motorway. She was silently furious the whole way home, Daddy dozing lightly, seat pushed all the way back to accommodate his long legs, arms folded, that gentle, amused smile draped across his face.

Mummy left a year or so after that. I used to call her Mummy, but when she left, I stopped really calling her anything. "My mother," I'd say to people, carelessly. "My mother's gone off with someone else."

So it was Daddy who showed me new places, horizons, people. He had always been out in the world. First, in Egypt, where my grandfather had worked his way up from the position of lowly bootboy to still-fairly-lowly colonial servant in Alexandria. This was where my father grew up, eating dates and figs, hearing of an England he'd never visited, building images in his mind. He was sent back to England for school, and then joined the army like his father, culminating in a posting to Naples at the end of the Second World War. That was how, indirectly, he came to meet my mother. And more directly it was how I came to be catching a train to Vanes, one summer morning, off on an adventure just like the ones he and I used to go on, only this time he was dead and I was being packed off to this strange family whom I barely remembered from one trip, over five years ago, and I had to keep getting up from my seat to go and be sick in the tiny, filthy British Rail lavatory.

Joss's car was parked almost diagonally on the windy Minehead seafront, a vast curving expanse of beach and promenade, with hills bookmarking each end. Waves crowned with frothy foam danced toward us; here and there people sat in thirties pastel-colored shelters, looking out to sea.

"Here you go," said Joss, throwing open the battered thin blue door of the Mini, covered in scrapes and pockmarks. He reached for my bag—I clung to it, for a second, as if he were trying to snatch it, and then released it. He stared down at it. "Unusual."

"It was D—It was my dad's," I said, and he nodded.

"Oh. Of course. Do get in. Listen, let's get on. Don't want to be late for supper. PF's funny about that sort of thing."

"I remember. How's Kitty? I brought a book of hers back."

I'd thought it would be a nice icebreaker, to return a copy of *The Dark Is Rising* to her, five years after taking it. I was looking forward to seeing her again very much; the first time since Daddy died, in fact, that I'd looked forward to something.

Joss looked rather surprised. "Kitty? She's the same, I suppose."

The car smelled of cigarettes, and mints, and the bloom of teenage body odors and aftershave. I shut the door and tugged at the seat belt. "Here," he said, and leaned over me, hand on my leg, quite casually, yanking it down and into the clip. I stiffened, but he sat back and drove off, quite heedless of the fact that this was the most physical contact I had had with anyone for weeks. My best friend Claire and I had hugged every morning on the bridge before school. But school was over, and Claire had gone to visit her family in Jamaica a couple of weeks ago.

"How long till we get there?"

"About twenty minutes, with a fair wind. Oh, look. Ha! Hey!" He beeped the horn loudly. "Muggers!" He wound down the window furiously. "Muggers! I say!"

A tall boy our age glanced around, but apparently didn't register Joss, for he carried on walking.

"Dammit," said Joss. "Didn't see me. He's a mate. Oh well. I can phone him later actually. I've got his phone number."

"Right."

He turned on the car radio. The tinny sound of Jason Donovan's latest hit crackled over the speakers. "Muggers lives nearby. Family has a huge place. He's got two tennis courts."

"Wow."

"Yep. He's friends with me, Giles, Nico and so forth. There's lots of people our age round here, but it's whether you've got a car or not."

"What about the bus?" I said, pointing at another bus trundling the other way.

Joss stared at me. "The bus? That's hilarious. Oh, of course, you got the bus, but that's OK, it was from the train. You'll meet the chaps at some point. Everyone's back now, before we all head off again. It's going to be a great summer."

I wished he'd stop talking. I wanted to sink down into the seat, not to look out of the window, because the landscape, vaguely familiar yet utterly alien, made me realize just how far away I was.

We were driving away from the sea through town, along the high street decked with begonias in hanging baskets and candy-striped plastic windbreakers rolled up outside shops. Children and adults shuffled along in jelly shoes, shoulders slumped. Away from the seafront it was hot—too hot, as it had been for weeks in London too, a cloudless heat seemingly draped over everything. We stopped at the lights. A child, being dragged along by its father, caught sight of me and started yelling. "Look at her! Dad Dad Dad! Look at her hair!!" I shut my eyes—I thought I might be sick in the car, and that would be unimaginable.

Joss glanced over at me and turned the radio off. "Here," he said, fumbling in the glove compartment and shoving a tape into the tape deck. "More restful."

It was classical music, I didn't know what, but it was rather nice. Joss lit a cigarette and offered me one. I shook my head.

"This is Bruch," he said. "I mean it's maybe the greatest piece of work for a violin ever written. It's really emotional. I just listen to it in my room and think."

"Right."

"Do you like classical music?"

"My dad loved it. He'd go to the Proms sometimes." He looked blank. "The concerts…they have them every summer at the Albert Hall? He used to take me…" I trailed off, unable to speak.

"OK. I love classical. It's just very poetic. I love house, too. House music? Acid. S'Express. Danny Rampling. Lil Louis. Do you like acid house?"

"Not really," I said. "Sorry."

"What music do you like then?"

"Um—all sorts. Transvision Vamp. Marvin Gaye, Gladys Knight, Kate Bush. And of course…" I put my hands together in prayer. "…of course, Madonna. I record the charts off the radio."

"Oh." He snorted. "Chart stuff. Bloody Jason Donovan, he's everywhere. Kylie. And Big Fun. Melissa loves them."

"Who?"

"My little sister. You remember Merry. She's trying to get us to call her Melissa, but it doesn't work."

"I do remember her. Of course," I said, defensively. I wanted to make out that I was entirely at home at their place, that this was all normal. "Does she like Madonna? *Like a Prayer* is my favorite album of hers. Have you got it?"

"Me?" Joss sounded horrified. "No."

"Oh." I shrugged. "That's OK. You can borrow my cassette if you want. And Soul II Soul. That album is amazing…My best friend Claire and I listen to it all the time." Claire had been given the Soul II Soul album by her dad. We almost wore it out on the record player in her cramped, cluttered bedroom, sitting on the bed with her pastel blue and peach duvet cover. I swallowed. "And Flanders and Swann. Tom Lehrer. Also, I really adore Liza Minnelli singing 'Losing My Mind.' My dad loves musicals." I corrected myself, briskly. "He loved musicals."

I could sense Joss struggling to put a label on this. Joss, for all his wild declarations of individuality, in his paisley shirt and black 501s and leather waistcoat and pendant silver crescent hanging from the leather thong and love of classical music, was as conformist as any number of public school boys. To be truly radical that summer for a boy like him would be to love Jason Donovan. "That's—sure."

"It's what I like," I said, shrugging.

He glanced at me. "Yeah, right, of course. Cool."

We were out of town now. Dense woods hugged the hills, a ribbon of slim otherland, somewhere caught between the moors and the sea. Memory came back to me. The winding roads. The wet, dripping orange and green. Kitty's friendly, kind face, in a sea of gloom. Dancing to Wham! Hiding from Merry and Joss. Laughing till we were sick.

"The Collecting is at the end of August," Joss said. "Will you be here then?"

"I don't know."

"You didn't bring much for six weeks, if that's the case."

"I'm not sure how long I'm staying," I said, wishing he'd shut up. I gazed out of the window.

"I am very sorry about your father," he said after a short silence, very formally, which was excruciating.

"It's fine."

He cleared his throat. "I—you're not at school with Kitty, are you?"

"I live in London."

"But it's a boarding school, Letham's."

"Still no," I said, nonplussed. "I went to St. Cecilia's School for Girls. In Greenford."

"Oh. I—I don't know anyone there."

I concealed a smile. "You don't know Donna Kingsley?"

"N-no—at least, has she been to any Gatecrasher balls?"

"No, she ran over her dad last year. It was on the six o'clock news. And Sarah Johnson—she had a baby in the lavatory. It made all the local papers."

"That's rather wild." He giggled nervously. "They don't do stuff like that at Kitty's school. They down a lot of vodka but—no"—he hunched over the steering wheel, as the car climbed a narrow, steep lane—"Letham's is the girls' version of my school. Farrars? You know?"

"I remember you talking about it last time. You were about to go there."

"Right." He nodded, modestly. "I'll miss the place. Proud to say I'm a Farrars man, although of course it's all a load of nonsense, isn't it?"

"Right," I said again. My mother had always had a rather un-savory obsession with "Jennifer's Diary" in *Harpers & Queen*, unsavory because she knew no one in it and used to pore over the pages, acidly commenting on people. After she moved in with Martin, and before they moved to Spain, I'd go round for tea every week and we'd discuss what was in the society pages. "The Duchess of Roxburghe, in that gown, look at her! Dreadful. He's handsome, that Edward Lamont Du—du-something. I don't know their names." (This was not true—she knew all of them. When Prince Andrew married Sarah Ferguson my mother recog-nized most of the congregation in Westminster Abbey.)

I wonder if she was first drawn to my father because of his name, which did indeed go back to one of the dukes who came over with William the Conqueror. Daddy was proud of this, of this idea of nobility which he endlessly tried to strive toward, be-fore ending up a rather older father in Greenford, with my mother's ferns matching mint-colored lounge furniture and a crest of the Lestranges in the downstairs lavatory as if humbly drawing attention to it. It made me feel uncomfortable that it mattered to him. I remember even then thinking how silly that was. Ironi-cally my mother's heritage was much richer, being half Scottish, half Sicilian. Now, I think this is much more interesting, and yet she spent her life trying to pretend she was something she wasn't.

"Farrars was founded in 1543," Joss was saying. "The year Henry VIII married Catherine Parr. It's forty miles away or so from here." I shrugged. "Four prime ministers went there, and a Prince of Wales. And a Maharajah—that was in Dad's time—quite a fellow. It's a very special place."

"Well, so was St. Cecilia's," I said, wondering whether to mention the time the police raided the lockers and found so much glue they declared the area a biohazard risk, or the daughter of an Afghan scientist who had arrived at the school having fled Kabul, and not speaking a word of English, and who had last year won a scholarship to Imperial College London.

"Where are you off to after exams? I'm going to agricultural college, if I get in."

"You'll enjoy being a secretary," my mother had said, when I hadn't got the offer from Oxford, because I'd screwed up the interview. It was a week after Daddy died. This talk of Oxford, prompted by my headteacher, Miss Minas, who had called Daddy in for a serious meeting about my future a year ago, had mortified my mother. She was, I knew, glad when it came to nothing.

"I'm going to be a secretary," I said, winding down the window, to let the sea air in, and breathing in deeply. "I'm enrolled on a course in Ealing, this September."

"Lucky you. Get a flat in London somewhere, find some fun flatmates, sounds bloody amazing. Kitty has to go to Cambridge if she gets the right exams, poor sod. She doesn't want to."

I had taken my exams, but as with the Oxford interview it was barely two months after Daddy died. I'd stopped working, couldn't concentrate, couldn't think straight, really. I was so certain I'd failed them I told myself I had very little interest in the process now. For one paper, history, I'd written out the track listing of *Like a Prayer*, very slowly, to make it look like I was doing something.

"Why not? I remember she was very clever."

He shrugged. "Kitty? Think she must be. But she says she wants to travel instead, get out of here. I don't know. I don't really understand what goes on inside her head these days."

"Aren't you twins?" I said, half joking.

"Not lately." He stubbed out the cigarette, deftly, on the frame of the car, then swerved alarmingly, only just avoiding another car. "Here we are." We turned into a driveway at the end of which was a tiny one-story cottage. "Aunt Ros, dear old thing," said Joss, and he nodded. I saw a curtain move in the front room, and a hand wave methodically, as though it had been waiting by the window for us to arrive.

"Who?"

"Oh, you'll see her at some point. Probably later tonight. She's Daddy's sister."

I didn't remember there being an aunt in a gatehouse before. But then I couldn't remember what was real and what wasn't from my previous trip, mythologized in my mind ever since.

"She's rather odd but there's no harm in her. We keep her around to add to the air of general mystery," he said carelessly. "Here we are. The others will be on the terrace."

He got out and quickly raced to the other side of the car to open my door, before I could protest. The idea that a boy that I knew in this day and age did such a thing made me want to laugh. "I'll just get your bag."

He picked up my Gladstone bag and gestured past the golden edifice of the old house, with the four curious scalloping, hive-shaped gables atop the two stories. There was a doorway, cut into a stone wall. I gasped, because it was so familiar, and yet because it was summer, and everything was green, and because light and heat suffused everything, it was utterly different, like seeing it for the first time. Joss put his hand on the heavy wooden door. "It's this way."

In the years since that summer sometimes a scent, or a sound, will creep up on me unawares, and the shock of it—how it is hard-wired into me, the role it has in my memory—jolts me from the present instantly back as if I'm there again, opening that gate, about to join the Hunters once more.

I think it is the smell that most of all has the power to transport me there. It was so very different to what I knew, from the acidic, petroleum smell of our dusty suburban road and the faint scents of fox and urine on the rusting iron footbridge where, for seven years every morning before school, I waited for Claire so we could walk in together, feet dragging, bag straps dangling, giggling, plotting.

The smell when I came to Vanes—ah. The smell of the sea and salt that reached out to us across the expanse of turf and meadow, the lightest, slightest wafts of it, always mixed with the heady honey scent of the white dots of alyssum, and the herbs left to sprawl along the slim bed in front of the house so that through the drafty windows the woody, luxuriant scent of thyme, bay and rosemary crept at all times. Otherwise there weren't many flowers close to the house. They didn't want to encourage swarming, I was to learn.

Beyond the terrace were four low wide steps. The stones grew hot in the summer sun. The scent of the herbs and alyssum, the heat rising from the stones, the mildew and wet sea spray against the heat—they all swirled together to form a most specific smell, one I have never encountered again. I remember that Joss slowly opened the heavy wooden door and we were on the other side. To the right, against a wall laced with a delicate, frowsy hydrangea, there was a table, around which sat the other Hunters. They were waiting for me, and I was being served up to them, on a plate, with honey.

Chapter Eleven

They were all there, with them an ancient, black, soft-eared dog who was shuffling slowly around them, like a guard. I couldn't remember his name.

"Ah," I heard an older, male voice say to the others. "She's here." The euphoria I had told myself I felt at my return suddenly vanished, like a trapdoor opening up beneath my feet. They all turned toward me, as if at some psychic signal.

The thing you have to understand about the Hunters is that they were all, every one in a different way, very beautiful. People don't talk about natural beauty, how it twists things. Sylvia had a heart-shaped face, expressive, with apple cheeks and a knot of thick black hair, shot through with silver, at the top of her head. She wore a dress in dusky rose-colored velvet covered with dark-pink and jade-green flowers, and a navy apron with huge pockets, exactly like the last time. Something about her felt too familiar. It made my skin prickle, my eyes water.

"Sylvia could have been the greatest designer of her generation if she'd wanted," Daddy had said on the way back from our visit, when I'd artlessly ventured that I wanted to be her when I grew up. "She didn't take the chance that was given her, Janey. Remember that."

Now I smiled at her, nervously. Her slim hands were pressed flat on the table, and she did not seem to see me, but to be staring past me.

Next to her was Merry, with her pale skin and dark hair and those huge expressive eyes. She was scraping at a stick with a penknife; shavings curled into a soft pile beside her, but as my gaze shifted away from her mother onto her she leaned forward, grinning at me eagerly, then, glancing at her sister, lounged back in her chair again. Much later on when I analyzed her welcome, I realized Merry alone had betrayed the others: I was an outsider. They wished I wasn't there.

Merry was gorgeous, but she would never have the aristocratic beauty of Joss, standing next to her, with his kind eyes and chiseled cheekbones, nor Charles their father, imperious even when sitting down. Charles was dashing in what I'd thought of as a TV series way; rather like Peter Bowles in my mother's favorite program, *To the Manor Born*. I didn't know anyone who dressed like him, in tweed and checks. He was handsome, like a statue, with a fine carved profile.

"Hello, Charles," I said, because he, at least, met my eyes. "Thank you for having me."

"Well hello—" he said, then stopped. As if he'd been about to say something else. "Terribly sorry about everything, Jane, what? Come and sit down. Oy, you." And he nudged the figure next to him. "Be polite, you fat oaf. Say hello to our guest."

At the end of the table a girl raised her face to look at me, blankly.

"Hi." Heavy, corn-colored shining hair fell about Kitty's face. She stared at me, then turned away, recrossing her tanned legs, which were resting on the wooden table. The dark green-blue eyes, fringed with heavy black lashes, were the same, but she herself was altered. Gone were the round cheeks; now she had a square, tomboyish jaw that gave her a wild, androgynous look. She wore denim cut-offs and a ruffled coral cotton top.

I took a deep breath, about to proffer my copy of *The Dark Is Rising*, then patted my pocket and sat down. No. Of course not. In the intervening years, I had grown into an idiosyncratic young woman; Kitty meanwhile had transformed into a goddess, or rather some kind of fallen angel.

"My darling Janey," said Sylvia, suddenly coming alive again. She leaped up from the chair and rushed toward me, followed by the ancient spaniel. *Rory*. That was his name. I groped for actual memories, still feeling as though I'd fallen into another world. "It is so lovely to see you. I am—we are so glad your mother allowed you to come to us. So glad, darling."

She looked at me properly then and I saw her eyes were full of tears. I glanced down, embarrassed, my gaze falling on the print of her dress and then I remembered: Daddy had had a handkerchief in the same material.

"Thanks," I said, uncomfortably.

Rory pushed against me and I staggered back. "Ignore Rory. He doesn't like outsiders, and he's blind and deaf. Aren't you, old boy?" She fondled his silky ears and muttered, quietly: "I'm so sorry about your father, my darling. I loved him so much. You know I did." One hand rubbed my elbow, the other my cheek. She straightened up and said more loudly: "You have wonderful bones, Janey. I must make you a headscarf, Hermès-style. Now, Charles is a stickler for timings—do you want to spend a penny before supper? It's chicken and ratatouille. I must quickly go and stir it."

I nodded, relieved, as very little of the rest of this made sense. I didn't know what she meant by a headscarf "Ermez" style. I wondered if she was mocking me. And ratatouille, well, I'd absolutely never heard of it, but it sounded awful. Homesickness, for a home I wanted but did not have, swamped me; my stomach contracted with acidic misery. I started as Sylvia reached over and swiftly touched my bare head. "When did you lose it?"

"A couple of weeks after." I closed my eyes. I didn't want to say more, trying not to flinch as she stroked my bare skin, her fingers flickering over my skull. She dropped a swift kiss on the scalp and then released me, vanishing into the kitchen.

"Dad," said Joss, who'd been silent through this beside me. "Shall I put the car away?"

"Well, welcome to Vanes once again, Jane," Charles said, as if Joss hadn't spoken. He gave me a brief smile. "It's a good summer for you to be here." There was a short silence in which he clearly expected me to speak. I didn't know how to reply to this. "Of course, you might not want to join in with the whole business, but I think you will. I shall be delighted to talk you through it all, and what we get up to, once you've settled in, what what?"

"I'd like that," I said, trying to sound polite, though I didn't really care.

"I never liked him," my mother had said when we'd spoken last. "Never understood why your father used to go around with him. But you won't have to bother with him much."

As I stood there wondering what my mother was up to now, whether she and Martin were enjoying a vodka and Coke on the gray concrete terrace of their flat, whether she ever, ever thought about me, a voice broke into my thoughts. "Why is your hair all patchy?" Merry asked.

I looked around, but Sylvia hadn't returned. Joss was talking to his father, in a low voice. Kitty had picked up a worn, fat paperback, facedown on the table, and was reading, apparently absorbed.

"I—it fell out."

Merry advanced toward me in a quick darting motion, like her mother, then stopped. "Did you have cancer?"

"No. I—I just wasn't very well. They say it'll grow back."

Her eyes grew huge. "Oh. Is it catching?"

She waited for me to say more and then, when I said nothing, she sat down again, turning back to her penknife and the stick she was holding, brushing her hair away from her face. A long, paper-thin shaving curled away from the wood and drifted like a feather to the floor.

My eyes ached. I wanted to be alone. I knew she wanted to touch it—the waxy smoothness of the bald patches, the gritty, bristly stubble of the new growth. It had got so patchy that Claire had shaved off what remained a couple of weeks ago. That'll teach the hair that's fallen out to grow back evenly again, she'd said, as if the absent hair, the hair that had fallen out in great clumps, lifting away from my scalp at night by the handful in the weeks after Daddy had died, merely needed to understand it was being silly and just needed to jump back onto my head again. I'd nodded.

The long day and the sleepless night before it were catching up with me now. Behind us, the horizon shimmered in the evening sun. Oh Claire. I missed her.

Charles looked up then. "Kitty, take Jo up and show her to her room. See she's settled in."

Kitty heaved herself up from the table, immediately, leaving the book open downward on the table. "Janey?"

"Yes, of course Janey. Do you understand?"

"Yes. But you called her Jo."

"I did no such thing."

Kitty raised her eyebrows. "Err...Well, you did, but it doesn't matter."

"Don't talk to me like that, you. Have some damned manners," said her father, sharply. He glanced around at the others, raising his eyebrows. *Can you believe this girl?* "Stand up, stop flashing your legs around. We don't want to see all that. Show our guest to her room, now. You understand me? I'm starving. You must be too, Jane. Kitty, tell your mother we'll want to eat a little earlier, about seven thirty."

Slowly, Kitty nodded. "Yes, PF."

Charles nudged Joss. "The bag."

"What, sir?"

Charles's thin, handsome face twitched. "The bag, you ass. Fetch your guest's bag, hand it to your sister."

"Of course." Joss handed Kitty the bag. They didn't look at each other. But she glanced down at the bag, and an unreadable expression flitted across her face. I followed her across the terrace, enviously drinking in her curved, willowy silhouette, the way the coral ruffles on her top filtered the evening sun, and the cut-offs that were just the right length—Claire and Ems, another girl from school, and I had cut ours off the previous summer and they'd been uneven, a disaster. Ems's mum had made her throw hers away, she said they were shorter than her underpants, which we found hilarious. Ems had stowed them in the back of her cupboard, like contraband vodka. She vowed she'd take them to university, wear them there.

Kitty's shorts were so short you could see the white fabric of the pockets on her bum, but somehow it worked. On her slender feet were electric-blue flat slip-ons with thin straps. I wanted them. I wanted everything she had.

I looked down. I was dressed in a velvet jacket and badly fitting Laura Ashley skirt I had bought at a thrift shop, and a shapeless T-shirt, much worn, once emblazoned with the legend "DIALTHETICS"—one of Daddy's many schemes that had promised untold wealth but had ended with him losing money and selling his car to pay his debts. The white symbol, with the slogan underneath ("Dial 01 993 5684 for FITNESS NOW") had almost faded to nothing. I liked wearing it, because though it didn't smell of him, it had been his. Before he died I wouldn't have been seen dead in it, as it were. The velvet jacket had been Daddy's too. "Must you wear that?" my mother had asked, on her last visit when we went out shopping. As if I was dressed in only a thong.

Kitty banged the back door open. "Mum," she yelled. "Daddy says let's eat at seven thirty, OK?"

"No shouting, Kitty," her father yelled back.

"Yes, Daddy." Under her breath she muttered: "Stinking hypocrite."

We stood in the blessed cool of the corridor, breathing slowly. My eyes fell on the carved oak coffer, a box on legs, in effect, the varnish black and so covered with pockmarks, holes, scratches, carved words that had then been varnished that it seemed tacky, like treacle, gleaming in the weak light. It was too large for the cool, narrow hallway.

Above it was the portrait, which I'd thought about often recently, I didn't know why. The odd young man, with the hooded eyes. I found myself staring at it, as Kitty stared at me with irritation. The man's long face was expressionless, thin lips pursed—actually his lips may not have been thin, it was the way his mouth was clamped shut.

"I can turn it on if you want." She pulled at a cord beside it and a light went on above the painting. I jumped. The man gleamed in the gloom and I stepped back.

THE REVEREND CARADOC DIVER,
RECTOR OF VANES, 1789

read the small black capitals carved or stamped into the frame at the bottom.

"Who was he again?"

She shrugged. "Hah. No one important, believe me. Come on." She pulled the cord and it twanged, the picture plunging into gloom again.

"I can take my bag up by myself, Catherine."

"It's still Kitty. Call me Kitty."

"Call me Jo," I said, trying to make a joke.

Suddenly she stopped and held out her hand to me. I shook it.

My bony, nail-bitten fingers rested on her cool, soft, white skin, her thumb pressing gently onto the back of my hand.

"That's the Bee box," she said, nodding as she saw me looking at the large box. "Do you remember what he keeps in there?"

"Bee box?"

"Things for the Collecting. This stupid ceremony. He keeps it locked. Don't bother looking."

Then she lowered her voice, her hand still in mine, tightening, hard, so her squeezing my bones was painful.

"Listen," she said, her eyes raking my face. "I don't want you here. You should leave."

I felt as though I'd been slapped. "I don't want to be here either, actually."

"Then why the hell did you come?" With every shake of her head, the shingling shimmer of hair rippled around her shoulders like a honey-colored cloak, protecting her. "You're a nobody. I don't care what they said to get you here, what they promised you. You don't belong here."

"It's none of your business" was the only pathetic reply I could think of. Girls were mean at my school, but it was the punching in the face, yanking your bag from behind kind of mean, not this sustained verbal knifing that left you tingling with pain.

Kitty's fingers tightened around mine.

"Oh, it *is* my business." She smiled, but she wasn't really smiling. "My advice to you is get out as soon as you can. Otherwise you'll see why."

She dropped my hand and turned, stomping upstairs, and I trailed behind her, casting one last glance at the unsmiling, angular white face in the curious frame. Up, up, two flights of winding wooden stairs cut into the heart of the strange old house till we emerged at the top and she led me down an uneven corridor.

"I'm there," she gestured to a shut door. "That's the linen cupboard. There's the bathroom. Joss is at the other end, you understand? This is your room. Mum says you had it last time." She opened the door, which had one of those iron latches, and dropped the unwieldy Gladstone bag on the floor. The old zip was coming away at the seams, and there was a battered old bear, one eye missing, poking out of the top, and the *Penguin Atlas of Europe*, about to fall out of the gap in the side. I saw her staring at them. *A teddy bear. An atlas. Weirdo.* "Supper's in half an hour, don't be late." And she left.

There was a view of the terrace, the garden, the wild clifftops beyond the boundary walls, and the sea in the distance. Just the other side of the wall was what I thought must be a pile of rubble, until I looked more closely and saw that most of it still stood. It was shaped like a hexagon, each side perfectly straight, but half the roof was missing, the stones piled up at the side. The contrast, between the heather-flecked wilderness one side of the stone wall and the pleasingly suburban stripes of the vast lawn, was jarring.

I sat down on the bed and rubbed my scalp.

I'd had friends from school who'd changed over the years. Maybe Kitty was just a nasty person. I began lifting out my paltry possessions: my books, my sundress, my notebook, my pad and paper to write to Claire and Ems, my address book, my Walkman, a few tapes, not many: *Like a Prayer*, Soul II Soul, a mix tape Claire had made me, a blank tape, a few T-shirts, my denim jacket, my penny loafers, some shorts, two skirts and a small bottle of vodka that I had taken from the drinks cupboard, last night. I'd lain in bed, with the bag packed beside me, eyes blinking in the dark, listening to the sound of the A40, and the barking dog down the road, and the hum—of life, going on around me. Inside, the almost-empty house was deadly quiet. It was the only home I'd ever known and yet I'd always known it wasn't my home, that it wasn't where I was meant to be. I can't explain it. Already, last night seemed ages ago, another life.

I took out Wellington Bear, still with the bedraggled Harrods ribbon around his neck, the pendant long gone. His soft fur was matted from years of my nuzzling him in bed, last thing at night. I didn't know if Sylvia would remember. I laid him on the bed, and he stared at me curiously. One ear was slightly wonky. It always had been, but it had fallen off soon after we'd returned home when Sylvia had given him to me. Dad had sewn the ear back on with black thread, not well, it has to be said, but I loved it.

"Well," I told him. "We're back again." I swallowed. "Yep." I looked down into the bag. The last item, Daddy's letter. I knew now that I was here I had to read it again, though I didn't want to.

"I came," I said to him quietly, looking around me. "So there."

I opened the envelope. The neat curls of his script, the fountain pen he'd had since the war. He'd put the letter in his breast pocket afterward, and it had been there when I found him in the garage. They always say "dangling." He wasn't dangling. He was perfectly still. The only movement was the other end of the rope, swinging in the breeze from the open door, and the liquid dripping from his heavy, lifeless body.

Darkness swooped across my vision, and the vise feeling gripped my forehead and neck. I opened the folded paper, gritting my teeth.

Darling Janey

I'm so sorry. I really can't face it all anymore. I thought there'd be a way out, for years, and now I see there isn't.

I am so proud of you!

Work hard. Do your best! Please take what chances you can.

I will always be by your side; you don't even need to look for me. I'll be there.

And remember what have I always told you:

"All shall be well, and all shall be well, and all manner of things shall be well."

I'm so very sorry. I wish I could stay. It hurts too much.

Daddy

And on the back, written in long, shaking letters that filled the whole page, landscape style:

RESCUE SYLVIA

My damp fingers pinched the thin paper, feeling the grooves of the pen strokes. His touch, his actions, him, the hands that squeezed my shoulders as we sat in bed reading together when I was little, the fingers that wriggled when I made him laugh, his whole body juddering in joy. I knew, had known since the funeral in an anonymous Victorian church next to the North Circular road, that I would never be happy now, couldn't feel that the way others did. I had made lots of promises to myself in the four months since his death. I would study harder, I would be organized, I would dye my hair blond, I would be bolder. I would write to prisoners, I would read more, watch less TV, see the world, change myself. As if by becoming a different person I could offset his suicide, even things out.

A movement above my window made me jump—I saw it was swifts, nesting in the eaves, but it was frightening, as though I was being watched. I stared at the birds, swooping and rising in the pale lemon-blue of the evening light, and my eye was drawn down to the terrace. The Hunters had regathered. They were sprawled around the table below. Once, Joss half looked up, then back down again.

I suppose it began then. I had spent the last few years thinking how nice it would be to be a Hunter. Now, I just wanted to stop being Janey Lestrange, to walk into this closed circle, this secretive, effortless, golden life, to become them, and not be me anymore.

Chapter Twelve

We sat outside, on the terrace. "A special meal for your arrival, what what?" Charles said. He looked different; I wondered if he'd brushed his hair, but as I looked around I realized all of them had changed for dinner. I had never done this in my life. People did in *Upstairs, Downstairs* (another favorite of my mother's), but here, now, in 1989 I was still in the sweaty and crumpled T-shirt and skirt I had worn in the train. Merry's plaits, which had been firmly bound up, were loosened, her hair around her shoulders. Joss was in a new patterned shirt and smelled delicious. When he leaned over toward his mother, his arm brushed my bare skin, and the contact was like a jolt.

A damask tablecloth was spread over the wooden table. There were tablemats, ancient maps of the area printed on them, edged in gold. The family crystal, cut-glass tumblers that caught the evening light, small and delicate glasses for the wine. Giant pink willow-patterned serving dishes and platters and dinner service, the pattern itself, I saw afterward, worn away, faded with thousands of gray square cracks across the delicate paintwork.

"We've had it for years, and Sylvia has to wash it by hand now, unfortunately," said Charles with a note of regret. "It was my mother's dowry. Along with the jewelry."

"She doesn't wash that," said Merry solemnly, and they all laughed, indulgently, as though Merry were a precocious four-year-old, not fourteen, and I laughed too.

Merry was the only one who seemed not to have altered. The others—this place—seemed so different from my only previous visit. Back then, I hadn't noticed the isolation, the sense of being on the edge of the world—it had been autumn, and rainy, and it was cozy to be there, I'd thought. I hadn't noticed how absent Sylvia was—she'd fall silent for long periods, eyes vacant, but in between she had chatted to Daddy, her face alight, laughing, asking me about school, cajoling the children, humming as she washed dishes. I hadn't noticed how much I didn't like Charles—Daddy had been there, Daddy, my buffer between me and the world, polishing it up, making it magical for me, and now I was alone.

We ate the ratatouille, which was not at all what I expected (what did I expect? Either a complicated pudding or, at the back of my mind, something rodent-based) but tomatoes and peppers, sweet, silky, tasting of herbs, garlic and warmth. It came with chicken sweetened with honey, in a wide, brightly colored dish, the caramelized sugary skin studded with scattered tart, plump shards of lemon and smoky oregano leaves. Sylvia's cooking was extremely good. Everything *tasted* of something—I know that sounds silly, but back then and in my world food was mass-produced, there were no farmer's markets, or organic produce, no interest in where it came from. That summer, I realized chicken had flavor—deep, brothy, silky, meaty flavor. And that potatoes could taste of earth and butter at the same time, and that a peach, plucked and eaten on exactly the right day, has the most softly luscious, raspingly sweet-sour taste imaginable.

The Hunters ate mostly in silence. I, not used to sitting at a table with others for months now, did the same. There was wine and I had a glass. Charles poured his son one too. Kitty, who appeared late and sat down, scraping her chair loudly on the flagstones, held out her glass after me.

"None for you, Kitty," Charles said, covering the neck with his hand as his daughter reached for it, then sat back, as if winded. "Here, Jane. Have a little more, come on. Good, isn't it? Hm?"

"Yes," I said, enjoying Kitty's look of fury, her gritted teeth and folded arms. "It's lovely. Fruity."

The wine was red and heavy, and it was much nicer than the last wine I'd drunk—a bottle of £2.99 "Italian Wine" from the Spar down the road which I had hastily necked down with Claire before our school ball, back at the beginning of July.

"Oh! Do you know a lot about wine then?" said Kitty, looking at me in amusement.

"Yeah, sure. There was a wine tasting at our school leavers' ball," I said, surprising myself with the fluency of the lie.

I didn't mind wine, actually, especially red wine. Daddy had let me have the odd glass. I hated white wine. And spirits. It was, however, true to say that the leavers' ball had been the last time I'd had anything to drink. I had utterly disgraced myself, and the next day had decided I had to go to Vanes, even if I didn't want to.

Claire and I had met in our usual place, the bridge. We'd exchanged presents—we hadn't agreed beforehand, but both of us knew it was the last time we'd meet there. That was one of the things I loved about her, that we thought the same way, just about small, unimportant things, that Rizzo was better than Sandy, that Wham! were better than Duran Duran, and that Golden Wonder were the best snacks. I gave her a hardback copy of *The Princess Bride*, which was a book based on our favorite film, and a purse embroidered with plastic beads like little dots of color I'd found in a flea market and which I knew she'd like. She gave me some White Musk perfume from the Body Shop and a mix tape.

Claire had given me someone to play with, to share my secrets with, someone to love unconditionally. I had given her my friendship, the quiet of my house. She had loved my dad too: Daddy had helped her with her university application forms. At the funeral, it was Claire who sat next to me.

After we'd unwrapped the presents, we hugged, tightly, on the bridge, and walked to the town hall, swigging our bottles of cheap white wine and feeling so grown-up, world-weary even. I had hopes of getting a boy I liked named Paul Rolles to notice me. He was a kind, gangly, shy youth who was in a jazz band at St. Luke's, the boys' school, and we'd smiled at each other a few times over the past year, but I was far too hopeless to do anything about it, and so, it seemed, was he. But I wanted to kiss Paul Rolles— badly—and so to give myself Dutch courage I carried on drinking the wine.

"Cutch dourage," I'd said as we got to the town hall, and Claire had looked at me in concern.

"That's the fourth time you've said that," she said, patting my cheeks. "You sure you're OK?"

"I'm OK!" I said. The wine was great—it made it seem like you were swimming away from everything.

I didn't do anything outrageous, like pulling down my dress or slapping a teacher—that would have been a badge of honor of sorts. No, I disgraced myself by sitting alone, having no one with me once Claire picked up Elliot, Paul's best friend, and retreated to a corner with him. All the other girls were resplendent in either tight-fitting black Lycra numbers that skimmed their skinny bodies, or pouf-balls of joy in flouncing fake or real Laura Ashley and *hair*, hair flowing everywhere, being tossed around, shimmering down backs, corn-rowed, sprayed into place, framing faces dripping with sweat. I was always cold, since mine had fallen out and been shaved off and so I sat and shivered there in my patchy hair and uncomfortable dull, claret-colored, ruched, fake-silk ball dress, bought from Next on a sale rack, the boning of which caused me to stoop forward slightly like a hook. I was left alone, the object of pity, of scorn, leaving me free to drink the two cups of wine I'd stowed under my chair. I knew by this stage anyway that people don't want to help someone in pain. It's easier if they can blame you in some way, for being ignored, shunned: it makes them feel better, of course, if they can shift the blame for a crap situation that upsets them back onto you. "Her dad was mad, Mum said," I'd heard Amy Shipman tell her best friend Cheryl the day we left school. "He never got over her mum dumping him, she always said he was a wrong 'un. Poor Janey. But you can't help wondering…"

I got up periodically and wandered round, stealing drinks out of people's glasses. At about ten thirty I realized I couldn't really see that much, and that tears were filling my eyes, running down my cheeks. I wanted to be at home—I hated home, where Daddy's clothes still hung in the wardrobe and where the absence of him was everywhere, but, still, anywhere was better than here. I walked through the bodies grinding to the Fine Young Cannibals—everyone the same, all in black, all conforming.

I walked home alone. Along a quiet side street a man walked behind me and asked me if I was all right. Daddy had taught me always to trust my instincts, and here blind instinct punched its way through my blind drunkenness. "If they make you feel bad for saying no," he'd say, "get away from them." I knew, from the way this man was too chatty, that I did not like him.

"I'm going to meet some friends," I lied. "Bye then."

"But I'm just being friendly," he said, with contempt, angrily scuffing at the ground. "I'm just trying to talk to you." Heaven knows what would have happened, but misery and hunger and, of course, the wine meant that I was then sick into a hedge, and when I turned around he was gone. I went home feeling rather lighter than at any point in the evening.

I thought of that walk home, of the smell of sick, the patches of it on my fake black suede pumps. I missed Claire already, with a gut-wrenching twist that made me think I might be sick again. She was going away the next week then right off to university. No doubt with Claire about whether she'd get the grades. She had no doubts, about anything. But I didn't know who I was anymore. As I stood on the bridge, our bridge, I tried to tell myself I could turn things around, make Daddy proud of me. Then I remembered—I must have blocked it out before—writing a joke on the empty page of my economics exam paper. Something about a crab. And the wine really hit me then, like falling into a pool. I staggered home: I lost a shoe on the way and didn't notice.

The worst part was that when I unlocked the front door I forgot, for a blessed, sweet split second, that Daddy was dead. I called out his name, softly, not to wake him, and then realized. I kicked off the remaining shoe, and I remember how alone I felt. And this feeling—there in that cold, tiled hall, in my empty childhood home—it was sad, and terrifying, but there was something curiously blank about the feeling. I was on my own now.

Charles poured the rest of the wine into his glass. He pushed his plate away, just an inch or so. "Very nice, Sylvia," he said and smiled at her. "Thank you." I looked over at her, hands sunk into the blue apron with the white stripes, jutting her jaw out to blow upward air to cool her flushed face, her bangs damp with the heat. She was smiling, not at him, at something far away.

"There's pudding," she said. "Kitty, hurry up and finish, darling."

Kitty was wearing a green-blue cotton dress, a vibrant, dazzling color that brought out the honey in her thick hair, the tan in her golden skin, the green in her eyes. A bee landed on my plate and I hesitated, but Joss laughed. "Go on, little friend." He let it crawl onto his knuckles. "Five more weeks for you to make hay."

"It's not *hay*," said Merry, with the pedantic tone of youth. "They don't make *hay*, Joss."

"I know, Benny, OK? It's an expression. Eat your tea."

"Don't call me Benny! It's *Melissa*!" Merry's face crumpled.

Joss flicked his hair and turned to me, knife and fork in hand. "Merry's pretty thick so we call her Benny, like Benny from *Crossroads*, you know?" This was a notoriously bumbling character in a terrible, amateurish soap opera at the time.

"I'm not thick."

"Daddy says she has to marry well. Kitty's the brains, aren't you, Kits?"

Kitty raised one shoulder, very slightly. "Shut up, Joss."

"You be quiet, Kitty," said her father, in a low voice, and she looked up.

"Sure, PF." I saw her face. She was—not scared of him, Kitty was never scared. But she was wary of him. She pressed her lips together, as if forcibly reminding herself to be quiet. When she caught me looking at her, she glared. *Yes?* her expression said. *What do you want, freak?*

"Daddy, make Joss say I'm not th—"

"Well, Jane, we'll have to show you around," Charles said, as if no one had spoken. Neatly, he speared the single remaining piece of chicken on the serving plate. "Walk you through the Collecting, explain a bit of our rather unusual history down here." He gave a chuckle. "Of course, to a townie like you, no doubt it'll all seem very odd. But if you're going to take part in the Collecting…"

"Is she?" said Merry, eyes wide. "Really? Will she still be here then?"

I saw the twins looking at each other. "Why not?" Charles said to me with a smile. "If we're stuck with you for the summer, we might as well make use of you, what? She could be the Outsider."

I gave an inane grin but I felt as though he'd punched me.

"Don't joke," said Sylvia. "Charles is joking, darling. He means

132

one of the Beloved Girls. That's what we always had in mind. Tradition has it they should be twins, but this is perfect." She was nodding at her husband, eagerly. "Yes? Two girls, the same age, same height—you two even look similar. Your father would have liked that, Janey, knowing you were taking part in it…"

I didn't want to talk about Daddy. I said as politely as I could: "I'm not that sure what the ceremony is, I'm afraid. Something to do with bees, isn't it?"

"Ah!" Charles laughed, as though delighted, but, as ever, his eyes weren't smiling. He struck his wineglass with a spoon. "It probably seems rather arcane to others, but it's important to us."

Sylvia began collecting the plates. "Kitty, Merry, help clear away, please. No, not you, Janey darling. Stay there, talk to Joss and Charles."

"Our little tradition," said Charles. I saw him glare at his wife, for interrupting him. "Here in this forgotten corner of the world. The locals like it, and we do, and that's all there is to it. This year it's later than normal, to celebrate the twins' eighteenth on August 31."

Then, I thought it was crazy that one old tradition could be the focal point of everyone's efforts for the best part of the summer. Then, of course, I knew absolutely nothing.

"What do I do?"

Charles gave an airy wave. "Ah, it's not for tonight. The main thing now is for you to relax and have a jolly nice holiday, before— what is it you're doing, in the autumn?"

"I'm going to secretarial college."

"I see. Very good idea, for a girl to get a sensible job. Lots of girls at Letham's with no idea for the future at all. Go back home and—what? Get under everyone's feet." I blinked, wondering what Miss Minas would say if she could hear this. "At least be a chalet girl, or learn to type, or finishing school, or *something*."

"Yes," said Kitty, nodding earnestly. "Polly Baring's going to Lucie Clayton. You learn how to get out of a car the right way. *And* you meet all sorts of suitable people."

"Ideal for BJ Baring," said Joss, with a snort.

"Catherine here is the brains in the family." Charles ignored them. "Her mother's sorted the whole thing out. Taken her round colleges, the lot. And good for her, she's got the offer, she's going, and we're very proud. Though I'm not sure if Cambridge isn't a bit of a waste of time, but anyway."

I stared at my wineglass, which had been refilled. I genuinely didn't understand. "Why would it be a waste of time?"

"Well. If you go, you ought to use what you learn. And if you spend the rest of your life—how does one put this—not *using* it, then aren't you, well, taking the place of a chap who'd *really* benefit?"

"He means women, Janey." Kitty's voice was silky smooth. "He thinks it's a waste if I'm going to marry someone rich for him and be a good wifey at home for the rest of my lifey."

"Oh!" I frowned. "Who are you marrying?"

Luckily, this was apparently such a silly question they both laughed.

"I'm not going, anyway, so it doesn't really matter," said Kitty. "I'm going traveling. I'm going to see the world and I'm never coming back."

She said this quite matter-of-factly, but what was stranger still was that her father did not appear to register that she'd spoken at all. "Go and help your mother," he said, smiling.

"I can't," she said. "I said I'd phone Giles."

Joss's head jerked up. I'd almost forgotten he was there. "Are you meeting up with Giles tonight?" he demanded.

Another bee now ambled onto Charles's cheese plate, possibly scenting the quince jelly. Charles lowered his thumb onto it, from the side, avoiding the sting at the base. I could see the wings, the soft velvet of the fur, the split second before he squashed it. There was a crackling sound, like cartilage tearing. Charles flicked the dead insect away. He stared at Kitty, his small eyes running over her, up and down her body.

"Go and help your mother. You little tart."

Kitty pushed away from the table. She stood behind her father and stared at him, from behind. The sight of her obvious loathing was so palpable it sharpened the taste of the wine in my mouth.

Joss continued, trying to keep it light. "Hey, Kitty, if you speak to him, to Giles, yeah? Can you—say hi from me. Tell him we

should grab a pint at the Leper soon. With the other chaps. Kitty?"
But Kitty had walked away, as though he hadn't spoken.

Charles muttered something under his breath. Joss cleared his
throat and said hurriedly: "Giles Leigh-Smith is my best mate.
From Farrars. The Leigh-Smiths are in the big house over there,
past Minehead. He's a great chap." He pushed the wine bottle toward me.

"Yes," I said. "You told me."

"Did I? Oh. Well, he is. Here," he said. "Have another glass.
Come on."

As I lifted the bottle, footsteps sounded on the gravel. Someone
singing. It was a reedy, determined voice, and even recalling it
now makes me nauseous—a swooping, terrifying nausea.

"I'll sing you one, O,
Green come for the comb, O!
What is your one, O?
One is one and all alone and evermore shall be so."

To my astonishment no one really seemed to react. A woman
appeared, marching in time really, swinging her arms. She wore
mud-caked wellingtons, had a bobbled, ancient tweed skirt on, a
shapeless pie-crust blouse, short, cropped, curly hair. Her eyes
were cast down—she did not look at them, nor make any effort to
greet them, but kept on singing.

"I'll sing you two, O,
Two come for the comb, O!"

Her hair was an indeterminate, dirty blond-gray and it was impossible, without seeing her face, to work out how old she was,
what kind of person she was, and then I saw her face, saw that it
was the eyes, not able to make contact with anyone, swooping and
whirling in their sockets, that gave everything away.

"Two, two, the beloved girls, clothed all in green—Oh!" She stopped
and looked up. "Charles, hello!"

"Hello there, old girl," said Charles, smiling that white-toothy
smile that never reached his eyes and which now turned my
stomach. "Have you eaten? Stay and take some tuck."

"I'm having a sort of midnight feast later, jolly good idea," said
this stranger, hitching up her skirt and standing, legs apart, hands

on hips. "Hello, Charles, hello, Joss, hello. Ah. I don't know you. I'm Rosalind Hunter. Charles's big sister."

"This is Jane Lestrange. One of Sylvia's lame ducks." Ros reached out her hand, but made no move toward me, and I stayed in my seat, unsure what to do. Her eyes ranged over us, the table, never quite resting on any one thing, and then she looked up and gazed out toward the cliffs. "Not long now, brother! Not long to wait! Do you remember the summer Father got the day wrong?"

"Yes, Lindy. I do."

"Out in the pouring rain, scrabbling about for comb, stung to bits, that boy with him who slipped!" She clapped her hands. "Comb everywhere, crushed on the floor, what a damned waste of honey, don't you think?"

Charles nodded. She gave a little shiver, then a smile. "Anyways, lovely to meet you, Jane. They've been looking forward to you coming. Give her the booklet, Charles, will you? Pammy's booklet. Think she'd like it. Read up on the history, what?"

Charles turned away from his sister, fiddling with the corkscrew. "Oh do shut up, Lindy. She's just got here."

"Right right, then. Now, must be off. Hello, Rory. Will you come with me?"

She looked down and fondled the dog, longingly, but Rory slunk away from the caress of her red, nail-bitten fingers.

"Leftover ratatouille, Lindy. In the kitchen."

"Oh." She stopped, at her brother's voice. "Yup, thanks, Charles." She stalked into the house through the back door, still singing. *"One is one and all alone and evermore shall be so."*

I could hear her talking to Sylvia. Low voices, the clatter of plates, then the singing starting up again, reverberating in the old house. Then more footsteps, the sound growing fainter, the front door slammed, and the noise was gone.

"Five weeks," said Sylvia, appearing a moment later with a tray and putting down glass bowls filled with dark-red strawberries topped with thick, yellow cream. "We'll have to plan what you're to do here, dear Janey. There's lots of places to see—interesting things like…" She waved her fork vaguely. "…the beach, and Larcombe castle, and Exmoor, and the railway…Here's Kitty, hello, darling!" she said, anxiously. Joss looked up at his sister.

"Did Giles say about band practice? Kitty?"

Kitty turned to her brother, watching him almost curiously. "He didn't mention it."

"But it's tomorrow. You are coming, aren't you?"

"I can't remember."

"Jesus, Kitty. He'll find another girl singer if you won't play ball." Joss turned to me. "I'm in a band. Kitty's doing some singing for us. My mate, Giles—oh, I just told you about him. Well, he has stables we can practice in. You should come some time. And there's a plan to go to the pub on the night of the A-level exam results, and you can watch some gigs, too. Don't worry, we'll show you a wonderful summer." He smiled at me with those lovely gray eyes that were almost like his sister's, his slim fingers pausing in the act of spearing a strawberry, and dipped it into the little bowl of honey at the center of the table. "Won't we? Gosh, Mum, this really is gorgeous."

I ate some more and nodded. When my mother left, I was almost thirteen. Daddy learned to cook, and the results were mixed, often wildly successful, often not. Certainly the kitchen was often a total mess, but he was good at cleaning up afterward. Once, not long after she'd gone, my mother turned up—some excuse about a handbag that could only be here. It's strange but having left, I think, she missed us. She let herself in at the back door, talking as she entered, and found us throwing noodles at the wall to see if they'd stick. She turned and went back to Martin. We just carried on.

We were finishing pudding when it happened. Rory gave a little growl from where he had collapsed at his mistress's feet, then started barking.

"Oh God," said Charles, rolling his eyes. "The dog's got ideas again."

Joss looked up, then followed his father's gaze. "Do you see?"

"Can't quite tell yet." Charles wiped his mouth with a napkin, still staring up, and put it down on the table. "Yes, look."

Rory's barks grew louder. There was a thin stream of black in the deepening blue sky, heading toward us. I breathed in and put my hands on my head—I know it sounds silly, but it was instinctive. I pressed my palms against my half-scratchy, half-soft scalp, and my eye caught Kitty's. She was staring up at the sky, a pulse beating in her throat, and she looked terrified.

"What is it?" I said.

"The bees are overcrowded. Sometimes, in the evening, when they've all come back for the day, a few of them will try to make a break for it, and it looks like they'll swarm. But they always turn back, at this time of year. It just can be rather a nuisance." Joss looked at his father. "Do you want me to deal with them, PF?"

"Go down and make sure they're all right," said Charles. "I've finished now." He drained his glass, took a toothpick from an ivory-and-silver case and was picking at his teeth. Kitty flicked her hair behind her shoulders, and took a deep breath.

"Charles," said Sylvia.

There was a small pause. I watched Joss, heading down the lawn to the chapel beyond, late sunlight glinting in his hair.

"Charles," Sylvia said again.

"A minute, Sylvia."

"I want to go upstairs now," said Sylvia suddenly.

"Good grief. Yes," Charles said briskly and stood up. I saw him glance at Kitty again.

"Come on. Good night," said Sylvia, to me. "You've got towels, and the bathroom—oh, and—but never mind. Kitty will show you everything. Won't you, Kitty? Keep her company? I hope you sleep well, darling—we'll talk properly tomorrow. The bees and everything."

"Joss?" Charles called. "Make sure the bolt is fastened."

"What?"

"I said, make sure the bolt is fastened," Charles repeated. "Are you going deaf?" He smiled at me, as if I was in on a joke with him. "I swear he's going bloody deaf, Jane."

Sylvia was smoothing down her skirt. She untied her apron, moving her hands over her hips, smoothing, polishing. "Charles. Now."

"Yes, yes." And she went into the house, Charles following her, their meal not quite finished, without another word.

"They were in a hurry," I said, more for something to say into the silence, but neither of the girls met my eye.

A minute later, I heard them in the bedroom, which was just above us, the arched windows open. They talked in low voices, then came a sigh and the sound of creaking furniture. There was silence for a while, as we ate the rest of the strawberries. The noises started, getting louder and louder and, as I realized what was going on, a terrible blush crept over me. The others didn't seem to notice. No, that's not true. Merry did. She was watching for my reaction, a blank expression on her face.

Sylvia's cries, like jagged sobs, floated down to us. The evening was very still. Joss approached from across the lawn and stood leaning on the table. He cleared his throat, obviously wishing he'd stayed down with the bees for longer. Kitty flicked something from her nail.

"Mummy gets in the mood after dinner, lately," said Merry, as we carried the plates into the messy kitchen to be left in a pile, presumably for Sylvia to wash later. "Most nights. You know? Daddy has to do it. It takes ages."

The sounds from the bedroom were louder than ever, and Sylvia sounded as if she was in pain. There was a huge roar from Charles.

"You know?" said Merry, again. "Do you know what I mean, Janey?"

"Yes," I said. I cleared my throat, humming as if occupied by something else. In the background, Kitty had put on a tape, clicked the deck shut. Prince's *Batman* began, "The Future," the first track, drowning out any background noise. She leaned against the dresser, arms folded, watching me. Merry was still babbling away.

"Everyone does it. Don't be prudish about it, will you? We're not. So—will you keep your hair short? Like Lisa Stansfield? You could grow some kiss curls. It might be cool."

Joss pressed my glass into my hand, refilled with wine. He and Merry sat down at the long kitchen table, and he gestured to me to sit, too. I honestly didn't know what to say. I thought it was my fault for finding it weird that my hosts should excuse themselves hastily after dinner to engage in loud copulation.

"No, I'm not like that." I took a long gulp from my wineglass. I reminded myself of my scheme to be a different person this summer, to change, shed my outer shell, to pupate into another butterfly. Daddy had chosen to leave me. I had left school, and I only had the summer before I was forced down another path not of my choosing. Let me be someone different, just for a short time. "Live and let live, I say."

"Good-oh," said Joss, and he smiled at me.

Chapter Thirteen

Vanes
Larcombe
Somerset
31 July 1989

Dear Mummy,
Thank you for your letter. I am sorry not to have replied sooner. I telephoned but it was call waiting and I had to go to dinner. You could call me. Or, perhaps write me a postcard with a time when I can call you if you don't mind me reversing the charges.

It is fine here. They are all nice. We have been outside a lot as it has been lovely weather. We've been swimming in the pool every day. Joss says the pool is old & made of the same stone as the house. It has been there for two hundred years. Everything is old here.

I hope you are enjoying being back in Spain. You said the apartment was nice and cool. I hope Martin is well.

Sylvia asked me to send you her love if I wrote to you. I like her so much. She has made me a sun dress and some scarves, and a lovely skirt. ~~She said~~ She showed me some of her designs—she works late at night and after lunch when Charles is dozing. She says Charles gets annoyed if she's lost in the clouds when he wants his tea!

There's a big thing they do here called the Collecting. They have these bees, in hives, in a chapel just beyond the house wall. I am to play a part in this year's ceremony when they collect the honey. There will be a big party because the twins turning 18 is a huge deal from a point of view of Joss coming of age. Charles is going to walk me round it all in a few days. There are two girls who accompany the procession, and Kitty and I are to do it together!

The twins' birthday is 31 August. Imagine that, the last day of summer. They must be the youngest in their year. Kitty doesn't seem that way, she seems older than everyone. I can't quite work her out. She has a place at Cambridge to study history, but she doesn't want to go. There are arguments about it, I don't see how it's going to end. I don't think she's the sort of person to change her mind about something. Joss is nice. He likes Tchaikovsky and Rachmaninov and poetry. He is going to agricultural college, which he is looking forward to. They have a sister, called Merry. She is 14 and she is really sweet.

Mummy, will you please reconsider about teacher training, or even university? I know we discussed it. But I have thought a lot about it since arriving at Vanes and I really don't want to go to secretarial college when I could study more instead. I know I've probably ruined my chances for university this autumn but I would try anything, I really would. Miss Minas said retaking exams is still possible. She has written to me here and she will contact you directly about it. I gave her your address, please don't be cross. Miss Minas says if I want to apply for a university place through the clearing scheme she will give me references and speak to admissions tutors herself about the circumstances of me taking the exams so soon after Daddy died. She says it is a shame I am not at least trying. Mummy, I know that you want me to have a proper job but if I go to university I'll be able to get a good job, won't I? I know what you said about Daddy and money. I promise I'm not like him in all the ways that annoyed you. He was only trying because he so wanted me to go. You know he did. Please Mummy, don't be cross when you read this letter, and will you think about it?

Love Janey

PPS The water in the pool is perfectly safe and I don't go in there when it's dark
PPPS—

I put down my pen, absent-mindedly stroking the lump on my middle finger which was still bulging after months of mock exams and revision, even before I gave up on it. All that training and learning that was, even now, seeping, running out of my brain, never to be used again. I looked down at the tight little lines in my cramped, difficult handwriting, which Claire used to say looked like spiders dancing. I wondered whether my mother would real-ize how much I wasn't telling her.

I didn't tell her about Charles and Sylvia: their loud, animal coupling most nights, and how after a week at Vanes it had come to seem normal. About how sweet Sylvia was, but totally vacant most of the time, as if she'd seen a ghost. I didn't say about Charles, and how she deferred to him about everything, but still didn't really seem that interested in what he said. I didn't tell her that Kitty barely appeared all day, except by the pool and at mealtimes, and that Merry and I had started a club where we rolled our eyes at each other, and smiled. I liked Merry, for all that she was a bit childish.

I didn't say that Rosalind Hunter popped up at the most unexpected times, humming that song—*"Twelve for the twelve new hunters"*—and it unsettled me, how absent her eyes were, like Sylvia's, only more so. I had started to dread the sound of feet on gravel, though the others barely registered her appearances. There was something about her lumbering tread that could have been amusingly, cartoonishly Frankenstein-like. But it wasn't amusing. The previous night it had rained so we hadn't heard her, and all four of us had jumped as the door banged and she walked through the living room, where we were sitting after dinner, listening to some violin concerto of Joss's: me reading, Merry drawing, Kitty curled up filing her nails, Joss staring at nothing—sometimes at me, but usually at nothing. Upstairs the usual sounds, audible over the rain and the music.

Ros had very solid hair. It never moved. She had pasty-colored skin across which were hundreds of tiny white bumps, like join the dots. Her eyes rarely fixed on anything, and yet there was purpose to what she did, the way she did it. I knew this. As she burst into the room Merry and I tried to ignore her, but Kitty jumped, and shrank against the wide corner seat.

"Oh go away, for God's sake, Aunty Ros. Why can't you just leave us alone!" Her voice cracked on alone.

Ros ignored her. She stood there with her hands on her hips, smiling that strangely grotesque smile.

"Got the Old Girls' newsletter today, Kits. Merry. Come here. I'll show it to you. Jacks Benson—top girl, jolly good sort. She's bloody gone and become an MP! Look! How bloody hilarious. Jackseat Benson, lording it in the House of Commons!"

"Wow," I said, impressed. I didn't know any MPs. "Was she a friend of yours?"

"No," said Ros, shortly. "Didn't play fair. In lacrosse. Wasn't nice to Daisy."

Daisy had been Ros's best friend, who was often mentioned but, according to the others, never seen. She had married a merchant banker and lived in Godalming. "And Aunty Ros was her bridesmaid and she keeps a photo of her by her bed but Daisy never even writes to her anymore. Her husband said Aunty Ros couldn't come in the house," Merry had informed me with relish, not long after my arrival. "He said she was a crackpot."

"How do you know?" I said, and they all looked at me.

"How do I know what?"

"Well—where's the proof? How do you know he said that? Who was there?"

"Well, I don't know," said Merry, with a shrug. But the photo of Daisy was on Ros's bedside table, along with a picture of Unity, Ros's pet King Charles Spaniel she'd had as a girl who'd been squashed by a tractor, almost, it seemed, to Charles's satisfaction.

"I told her she was mad to keep a dog like that by the main road. But that's Ros," he'd informed the table, several times now. "Adios Unity."

"Jackie Benson, MP, what a coup for Letham's, girls! Our first MP."

Ros smiled at her nieces, who registered no enthusiasm for this whatsoever. "Letham's prides itself on the quality of the education it gives its girls but also its all-round approach," said Aunty Ros to me.

"Well," I said. "It should, shouldn't it?"

"You can have a look at the book next time you're up at the gatehouse. *From Crumpets to Crenellations: One Hundred Years of Letham's Ladies' College*. It's awfully interesting, even if you didn't go there."

I nodded politely at her. "I'm sure it is," I said.

I didn't tell my mother they laughed at Aunty Ros, when their father wasn't present. Sylvia too. Rosalind was Charles's senior by five years. I knew Charles was older than most fathers, like Daddy had been, but to me Ros seemed to belong to a different generation entirely. I had been, with Merry, to her tiny little cottage, the gatehouse to Vanes, seen the stacked black-and-white photos of her schooldays on the damp walls, labeled in precise calligraphy by an unknown hand: "Letham's Ladies' College 1935–6" "Drama Group, LLC, 1938." "Kitty will miss the place frantically," she told me, munching her lips, her words, her eyes ranging over the photos, never meeting mine. "One never really leaves Letham's though. Kitty knows that too. And you, Merry!"

"Oh yes!" said Merry, clasping her hands together.

There was something guileless about her and perhaps I'd have liked Ros more if she ever showed any interest in anything else. She didn't once ask me about myself, for example, not that I wanted her to. I realized why, and came to dread her appearances. She was like a stuck record, with only two tunes: Letham's and the Collecting.

"I'll sing you one, O,
One come for the comb, O!
What is your one, O?
One is one and all alone and evermore shall be so."

I didn't tell my mother the rest of the business about the bees. It hadn't come up last time. It had been almost winter and they were inside keeping warm, or maybe I simply hadn't noticed, caught up in playing stupid games with Kitty, dancing, lying on her bed, chatting.

But I understood now that everything was about the bees. You were always aware of them, no matter where you were. Sometimes it was so faint you wondered if it was the sea. Out on the terrace, you could hear them everywhere, especially toward the chapel. Out in the long drive lined with flowerbeds that turned into hedgerow toward Rosalind's cottage, and on the other side into woodland, you could hear them constantly collecting, collecting as they darted from flower to flower. The strength of their wings when you got too close to them shocked me: the whirring, cold air. I never really got used to it, though I stopped jumping when one landed near me.

Thankfully the bees never appeared in a great number as they had done that first evening. "They're angry bees, this lot. Hungry. They give no end of trouble," Mrs. Red, the daily help who came up from the village, liked to say.

Most of all I didn't tell my mother about Joss. How his arm would, at supper, be next to mine: fine hairs and the faintest touch of skin were all that connected us, but it was like being stroked, repeatedly, kissed with fire, with a fluttering feeling in my heart and stomach. How we stayed close to each other anywhere we went, sometimes accidentally on purpose walking so our arms pressed together. How he touched my hand to ask me if I wanted more honey on my muesli at breakfast, or wine at dinner. How I never said no to him, but never looked at him. It is still hard for me to recall how ugly I believed myself to be, yet another difference between me and Kitty. Most days I wore a headscarf Sylvia had run up for me, in a pastel mint and apricot pattern, or Daddy's panama.

Once Joss passed me on the stairs and I brushed in front of him, my chest touching his. I felt my nipples, sharp as points, tingling to be touched, touched by him. I wanted him, and I was horrified by it, which is sad. I was eighteen, and full of life, and I should have been proud of my body, should have wanted to share it with someone else, to explore their body, too.

I didn't tell my mother about the house—the chaos of it, the broken china, the faint waft of manure that drifted over when the wind changed, and then the sea again, asserting its primacy. Mrs. Red, whose family had lived here for generations, liked to tell us bloodcurdling stories of yesteryear. "There were wolves in the woods, long ago, they'd eat the lepers, and the bones would be found, flush with flies, they'd have to burn them." (I sometimes tried to imagine hearing a sentence like that back in Greenford.) The bickering: when my mother was still there my home was icily still, confrontation never dreamed of, usually the only sound me and Daddy, chatting about something, or him, in the garage, whistling over his inventions, or some new plans. Afterward it was just the two of us, latterly quieter than ever as Daddy sat slumped at his desk, scribbling out plans, ideas, late into the night. And then it was just me.

Here, someone was always snarling at someone else, Merry at

Joss when he teased her about *Top of the Pops*, Charles at his eldest two children, Kitty at everyone. And the past: everything was about the past, nothing was new, apart from Merry's pop magazines and Kitty's Walkman. There was no computer, only two radios, one with a tape machine shared by Joss and Kitty, one in the kitchen. The TV had no remote control. It was color at least, a fact they all kept telling me as if it was something of which to be slightly ashamed. "I thought of getting a fax machine once, when I was really getting a lot of interest in my work," Sylvia had told me. "But Charles didn't think it was worth the money." The china had been here longer than any of the occupants, and the lichen on the stones, and the ancient spring flowing down from Exmoor behind us that fed the pool, winding its way past the chapel and down the cliffs to the sea.

There was plenty else I didn't tell my mother. I could not risk upsetting her anymore. I understood the reason she couldn't countenance letting me be anything else but a secretary. She wanted to make sure I didn't get ideas above my station. She was terrified I would turn out like my father, who had too many ideas, and lived entirely above his station.

I have sympathy for her. Daddy had loved my mother in his way, I know that. He'd loved how she sometimes smiled at him, her frowning gray eyes lighting up as he said something to strike the flint within her. He loved her calmness—she was always calm, though at what cost I don't know. She was never late to pick me up, and she listened to my concerns, if I had been unfairly treated or was concerned about something. I inherited my desire for justice from her, not him. I am grateful to her for that. But perhaps too many years working at the labyrinthine town hall in the Planning Department, months spent defusing neighborly tensions, mopping up tears, deciphering handwriting and soothing ruffled feathers, combined with being married to my father, had done something to her. She had started out as a shop girl selling gloves, and retrained to work for the council when I was old enough to go to daycare. I think of her now with more affection than when she was my mother. I see how hard it must have been for her, and that she was admirable, in many ways, not wanting to tie herself to the stove, to live the life prescribed for her. But I didn't really love her. I don't know if she loved my father. And I am certain she didn't love me. I'm not sure when I realized this—before she left, I think.

I pictured her now, sitting at the little white table of Martin's tiny apartment in Spain that looked out over the ziggurat-shaped apartment block opposite. There was acid-purple bougainvillea on a wall, but otherwise no view. You walked to a bar, filled with English people, and a supermarket, where they said *Hole-lar* and *Grassy-arse* to the cashier. There were things I liked about being there: the baby fried squid and the *patatas bravas*, and the smell of warmth, of cigarettes, of cooking, but I never really felt like I was abroad, let alone somewhere new, exciting.

I took a deep breath and wrote the final line.

PPS Please think again about university, Mum. Thank you so much. Hope you are having a wonderful summer and are glad to be back. Say hi to Martin. I miss you. Don't worry about me. I've settled in well and am really starting to feel at home with them all xxx

As with so much else in the letter, this wasn't true. The more I got to know the Hunters, the fuzzier they seemed to become, quite the reverse of normal people.

Chapter Fourteen

It was lovely to wake up in the little bedroom at the top of the house, cocooned inside a hive-shaped gable. The sun flooded into the warm, quiet room and I'd lie in bed smelling that salted, herb-scented air, feeling almost content. It was very different from the grief that swamped me at night, when I woke unable to breathe, my heart aching with longing for Daddy, for his crooked smile, his eyes brimful of laughter, the pain he must have been in... At night when I couldn't sleep, owls and nightjars called out loudly in the woods behind the house.

Ten days into my stay, it was Charles's birthday, and the day Sylvia came up with a new idea for her work, what would become the famous "Summer Rain" print.

There was a tiny harbor at Larcombe, where you could fish, or go crabbing, a pub—the Good Leper—a café, and a shop and post office. People kept boats in the harbor. Once, it had been an important port along the wild coast. Mostly it was a ridged channel of pebbles, a natural barricade against the sea salt marshes, stretching flat along from the harbor up to the hills, but there was a tiny stretch of shingle beach.

We walked down to Larcombe along the narrow track through the ancient oak woodland that curled gracefully against the curve of the land: dry leaves crackled underfoot. On the way down, we met several walkers: I hadn't seen anyone else other than Mrs. Red since I'd arrived. They stared at me, mouths open, aghast, taking no trouble to hide it. As if I wouldn't notice their expressions, as if my baldness rendered me blind, too, and as if, by being different, I deserved to be stared at. It stayed with me, that idea I'd first noticed after Daddy died, that if you are most in need you are often met not with compassion and help but hostility from others, as if your situation threatens their stability, their happiness. It's easier for white people to think I'm a bad or dangerous person than engage with how racist the world around them is, Claire's dad had said to me once, and I hadn't understood him. I'd been offended, even. I had no idea why he'd want to say that. She's a nutty Women's Libber, I'd heard Ems's dad say of my beady-eyed headmistress, Miss Minas, who had written a letter home about encouraging girls to try for a university education. The year after I left school Miss Minas left too, drummed out by the local Conservative MP, who said she was indoctrinating girls. Indoctrinating them into what? Happier lives? The governors fired her. It was easier to make her the problem.

I didn't know then what the walkers were saying was: I don't want to look at this sad-looking girl with no hair and lavender-ringed eyes. She can't be sad, or ill, because that would ruin my day. It's easier to think she must be difficult, a weirdo, must have brought it on herself.

As I fumbled in my pocket for my headscarf, Merry gave out a gushing "Hello, it's my dad's birthday today!" Sylvia, with Rory on a lead, smiled and nodded vaguely. The path was very narrow. As one couple passed me, I heard the woman, in a knitted green sweater, whisper:

"Poor thing. I do think she should wear a *hat*, if she's out and about."

"Good afternoon!" came a voice behind me. "Your shoes are on the wrong way round."

I turned, to see Kitty, pointing at the feet of a thin, tall man with knobbly ankles, the woman in green's husband. His wife, still gazing at me, backed into him, knocking him over. As we passed by, leaving the two of them wrestling awkwardly together on the uneven ground, I thought I heard Kitty snort, but I was sure I couldn't have. She didn't make noises like that.

We ate delicious fish and chips, sitting out on the wall before the pier, listening to the clanking boats, the cry of gulls, watching oystercatchers out on the marshes. It was discombobulating, being away from the house, seeing other houses and other people, and I realized with a start that, beyond walks on the cliffs, I had not left Vanes since my arrival.

It was a fresh day, bright sunshine mixed with splashy showers that rode in suddenly across the bay out of nowhere—one of the last days like that before the humid still heat of August set in. Joss was next to me, our bodies decorously separated, our legs studiously not touching, and the tension of that gap between us was intoxicating.

Last night, I had come out of my room to brush my teeth after I thought everyone else had gone to bed and had found him in the corridor, waiting for me.

"H-hello," he'd said, in a soft, husky voice. He was nervous, his eyes huge, something determined about his expression I found attractive. His hands had held my breasts, through my T-shirt, and he had kissed my neck, his lips fluttering over my skin, then my patchy, prickly head, nuzzling it, as I leaned against him, woozy at the softness and the firmness of his touch. Today we were like strangers. It was extremely exciting.

"Happy birthday, PF," Merry said at one point, leaning against her father and stealing a fry. He put his arm round her, squeezing her almost affectionately. "Little Mer," he said. She kissed his cheek, then popped the fry in her mouth and said, after she'd swallowed: "It's properly summer now that it's your birthday, PF. I thought that last year, too."

"Why, when was his birthday last year?" said Joss, faux-serious.

"Very funny. Come on, Joss," said Charles.

Next to Charles on his other side, Sylvia was banging her foot against the harbor wall, humming to herself, in another world as ever.

I often wondered whether Sylvia actually enjoyed her husband's company. One would say obviously she did, I heard them every night, her panting, mewling ecstasy. "Now," she'd say, frequently in fact. "Now, Charles, do it now." As if it—lust?—was an immediate requirement. But I didn't understand it. She was lovely, witty, bright, beloved by everyone, from the landlord of the Good Leper to the holidaymakers who came up to say hello to Mrs. Red and her children, to dogs and babies. Everyone smiled when Sylvia appeared.

The only way I can describe it is that she was mechanical around

Charles, whose glamour for me had dulled with familiarity, whose red veins on his nose and cheeks reminded me of the tiny cracked patterns on the china, who believed he was right about everything. He displayed no interest in anyone unless it related to the bees, or Farrars, or the local populace and land, and was virtually asleep after every meal before being roused by Sylvia and marched off to bed. Even the suspicion that he was the butt of a family joke could ruin a hitherto amicable evening. He, however, thought nothing of mocking his own wife and children, as often as possible. In particular Kitty.

"You'd better lay off the cream cakes, hadn't you, Kits?" he'd said the second night I was there, jabbing a long finger into his daughter's side as she sat at the table in a crop-top.

"Shut up, Joss, you tell a story once and it's fine and you get a reaction and then you ruin it by making everyone listen to it again. Pretty dull. Don't be dull, old boy."

"My wife?" he'd said, when I'd asked, tentatively, where she was, a few days into my stay. "Staring vacantly out of a window when she should be making lunch or doing something to help me, I expect. It's like living with Eeyore."

He was friendly to Merry. I didn't understand why at first, then I came to see it was because in his eyes she was still a young child. He preferred her to stay that way.

Charles liked people to believe he was a gentleman of leisure, but he sold antiques on the side. He'd got very lucky with a piece in the sixties: an oak sideboard which he'd found at a house clearance in Chelsea, and bought for five pounds. It turned out to have been early Tudor and he sold it on for over five thousand pounds, enhancing his reputation no end. He freely admitted this. "It's all luck of the draw really," he'd told me. "Right place, right time." And times were lean, when I stayed with the Hunters. Money was in short supply and there was a constant worry about school fees, and on Charles's part a rampant curiosity about other people's money. I remember seeing scores of statements, in piles around the study, and checks, which Sylvia scratched her head over, and sighed, and occasionally took in a plastic bag to the bank to pay in. It was Sylvia, I think, who paid for a lot of things—I remember her, silhouetted in the long hallway leading out to the back garden, handing her husband a check with an unintentional flourish, the paper wafting in the breeze. Him kissing her on top of her head, then patting her bottom. "Good girl."

I think it was her work that paid for the boarding schools, the repairs to the roof, Charles's suits, and of course money had to be found to pay Mrs. Red to come in to change the sheets and push a duster around. She paid for everything. Yet at Vanes her job wasn't ever talked about. You'd never hear it mentioned that Habitat had sold her prints for years. She designed cushions, and placemats, and children's clothing, but her first real love was textiles. She worked in the mornings, while Charles was in his study reading the paper and doing whatever work he did and while Mrs. Red bustled around the house, before Sylvia had to lay down her pen to start on lunch. It was all, always, squeezed into the demands of the day.

Last year, there was an exhibition of her work at the Textile Museum in London. I went to see it, though I was nervous throughout, wondering if I'd see anyone there.

Afterward, I sat out in a café on Bermondsey Street, still relishing this sense of freedom, thinking about Sylvia, about my own escape. I ate tiny pickles, and scraps of garlicky salami, and had a cold, malty lager, and I read the blurb from the catalog, the sun shining on my face.

Sylvia Lestrange: Stranger in her Own Land

The diminished reputation of Sylvia Lestrange should be a national scandal. One of our foremost post-war designers, famed of course for her best-known print, "The Hive," her eye for stark detail was doubtless fomented during her childhood, the daughter of a broken marriage, an alcoholic mother and a brutal, yet largely absent, army captain father. She grew up in fifties Chelsea, then a quiet bohemian backwater favored by artists and writers, before training at what was then the Central School of Art and Design, where her eye for simplicity and elegance was noted. Coming of age at the height of the Swinging Sixties before her early marriage, Lestrange was hugely influenced by the colorful bold prints of the Scandinavian designers such as Josef Frank. But Lestrange was very much her own woman, in the glorious tradition of other English visionaries and eccentrics from Blake and Morris to Vivienne Westwood and Alexander McQueen.

After witnessing the violent deaths of her parents in a horrific accident,* Lestrange was alone and almost entirely without support, relying on the income from her mother's boarding house until a family friend assumed the role of guardian, pushing her toward art college; she took his name professionally as a mark of gratitude. Sadly, however, her decision to marry cut short her degree. After her marriage she relocated to Vanes, her husband's family home in a remote corner of Somerset by the Bristol Channel, where for many years she was preoccupied by motherhood. She was able, when her children were older, to begin designing again, and produced some of her most famous prints, which endure to this day: "Rose at Dusk," "Lion," "Summer Rain" and, of course, "The Hive," often anonymously. She made all her own clothes, and those of her children, for years; her youngest daughter, Melissa Hunter, who supervised the loan of much of Lestrange's archive for this exhibition, remembers the cotton print smocked dresses they wore as children:

> they were better than Laura Ashley, which was rather old-fashioned for girls like me and my older sister, who wanted to roam the countryside, and didn't like ruffles. They were designed for girls and boys who liked climbing trees. They lasted ages—we always outgrew them. And then, later, she made us dresses. Even my sister Catherine, who, like most teenagers, wasn't easy to please, happily wore the dresses.

Sylvia Lestrange's career was curbed by her duties as a wife and mother and bookended by yet another terrible event: the tragedy that took place at Vanes in the summer of 1989, decimating the family. What is known is that she left behind a legacy that endures to this day, and a sense of potential unfulfilled.

* For more information on the accident at Harrods, and Lestrange's lucky escape, see notes on Room 3: "The Teddy Bear and the Gloves."

In Sylvia's messy, warm, bright study, off the hall on the other side of the kitchen, was an empty honeycomb—she showed it to me once. Joss, aged eight, had solemnly carried it up to the house after the Collecting one year, sliced it open and handed it to her. It gave her the idea for "The Hive," the rigid simplicity of the comb interior, but hand-drawn, giving it an imperfect tension. The bees, as drawn by her, were golden beads of light, crawling in and out of the cells. The skill of her draftsmanship meant she could convey the 3D nature of the hive. It was intricate, delicate, beautiful, but modern—after she released "The Hive," Conran called her the "William Morris of the Twentieth Century."

I didn't appreciate any of this when I stayed with her. Because she craved anonymity, at times she found herself selling many of her designs on to shops and manufacturers and losing her own copyright. If she'd been a man, someone else would have cooked, and taken care of the children. I used to think if she had been a different person, she would have been able to fight more for what she wanted. But now, knowing it all, I am not sure.

That day, down by Larcombe harbor, eating fish and chips and watching the weather fronts gather miles away over the Bristol Channel, feeling warm and secure, gave her the idea for "Summer Rain," a splashy, joyous print of long, diagonal, sketchy rods of rain set against scattering people and green hills.

The catalog continued, a better witness than I, even though I walked back up to the house with her that day:

She hurried back to the house, sketched out the basic idea and layout, before her husband asked about supper. Later that night, when Charles Hunter was asleep, his wife went downstairs and worked again on it, so that the next day, in the morning, she found an almost perfect rough waiting for her in her studio. She said this way of working was not ideal, but that it forced her to learn to distil the essence of a good idea as swiftly as possible.

"Now we have to start worrying about the Collecting," Merry said, screwing the remains of her fish and chips and the paper into a ball. She dropped it into the plastic bag at Sylvia's feet and tried to do an arabesque, there on the harbor wall.

"No we don't, Benny," said Kitty shortly. "Not yet."

"It's Melissa."

"Sure, Benny," said Joss, through a mouthful of fish.

"It'll be here before we know it. The sixth today, normally do it on St. Bartholomew's day, but it's a week later…yes, three and a bit weeks till the thirty-first," said Charles. "People have been asking me about it. The Culneys have said they can provide two hunters this year." He looked at me from under his brows. "Jane. One evening soon I should walk you round. Show you the bees, bring you up to speed. Not tonight, too thundery. And that reminds me. Where are the handbells?"

"They're in Mummy's study," said Merry promptly.

"How do you know that?" said Sylvia, sharply.

"I was looking for some Blu-tack in there yesterday."

"Oh, wow, how exciting. Is this for your Big Fun poster?" said Joss, imitating a kiss with a loud smacking sound.

"Rack *off*, Joss! I hate you!"

"The handbells?" Charles frowned. "They should be kept in the box in the hall, Sylvia." He turned to her, and I saw the pale eyes blazing in his red face. "You know the rules, Sylvia. Goddammit, can't you keep the place a bit tidier?"

"My study's out of bounds, sweetheart," said Sylvia, calmly, to Merry. She smiled. "I was polishing them, Charles. Didn't you ask me to?"

"Don't think so," said Charles, but he stood up abruptly, throwing his polystyrene carton away, and brushed off his trousers, then sat down again.

"St. Bartholomew was the patron saint of bees," Sylvia told me. "You'll have some honey to take home with you this year. Everyone gets some!" She clapped her hands, making it sound like a jolly day out. Pretending I hadn't been told this several times already, I smiled.

"Not this year, remember," said Merry. "It's ten days later, the twins' birthday."

"Yes…" Sylvia was frowning and I saw her dart a quick look at her husband. "I still think it's too late, Charles. They're restless already."

"Nonsense." Charles wiped his mouth, then crushed the paper napkin between his fingers. "The bees understand, as well as we do. Joss will take over the house, it's right we mark his eighteenth birthday."

"Happy birthday, PF," said Kitty, smiling sardonically at him. He looked mistrustfully at her.

"Thank you, Kitty," he said. "And thank you for my present. Mummy retrieved it. It looks rather good."

"My pleasure." I saw the reddening of her cheeks, how she rubbed her nose, awkwardly, suddenly a child again. I saw she wanted to love her father.

"She gave him a book she thought he'd like. Some politician's diaries. But he chucked it in the bin," Merry told me afterward. "Said it wasn't his sort of thing."

"Thank you for a delightful birthday feast," said Charles, standing up again. "Now, I must go and see a man about a dog."

He wandered away past the Good Leper pub, down toward the Harbor Master's office, with a casually raised hand, leaving us sitting on the wall. Sylvia clapped her hands. "Let's go back to the house," she said. "Rory is tired, aren't you, darling? I have things to do."

Merry had already finished, Joss too, and Kitty and I were left eating our fries. We hurriedly scarfed down some more and then, adding the rest to the bag that Joss was carrying, followed the others along the uneven cobbles out of the harbor and onto the groynes, and the vast expanse of flat marsh giving way to meadow that formed the bay.

Once we had left the beach, Joss dropped the bag of rubbish

in the lane, kicking it into a hedgerow. Some of the screwed-up wrapping fell onto the tarmac.

"It smells. I can't be bothered to carry it all the way back up," he said, with a rueful smile. Sylvia shrugged.

"Lazy boy," she said, unsmiling, and hurried in front of him.

It sounds so silly, but it was so shocking to me. I can feel the claggy taste of batter fat and acid in my mouth now, shame at myself for not picking up the bag.

"I don't understand about the bees," I said later that night.

"It's just always been something we do," Joss told me, as we sat outside on the terrace steps. We were holding hands, his thumb caressing my palm. "I know it sounds weird, but it's a big deal around here. It's about showing you're part of the land, respecting the traditions of it and the villagers and everything." He cleared his throat, too loudly in the darkness. "So, everyone comes. We process at dusk, 'cause they're more relaxed then. We light beeswax candles and we sing the song, and then we take the honey."

"You take their honey?"

"It's a tradition. We eat it all year, haven't you noticed? It's been that way since the old reverend first found the combs in the chapel."

"Who?"

"The Reverend Diver. The portrait. Hasn't Aunty Ros made you read the pamphlet about it yet?"

"No."

"Well, you should. Their other sister wrote it when she was a girl." He was silent.

"Their other sister," I prompted, after a moment.

"Oh. Yeah—it's good. She was into all that. Pammy, she was called. She'd go around collecting folk songs and the like. There's all these stories about Diver—we have some, the villagers have others."

"Like what?"

"Um…" Joss stroked my hand again. "Like he was—oh, someone special."

"You make him sound like the second coming." I laughed, but he turned to me, solemnly.

"No, seriously. Some people think he might have been."

I stared at him. "Joss. You don't believe that."

"Well, he cured the lepers. And there's other stuff too. Listen, there are other people who think he was a charlatan. But he made the bees come in the first place. By promising them they'd be safe here." His voice was soft in my ear now. "And, you know. He's dead, but they've stayed there for two hundred years. Why? Something obviously keeping them there. We have to respect that."

"Oh," I said, chastened.

I wanted to ask more, but I was aching as we sat there. I wanted him to do things to me; the thrill of huddling together there, unseen by the house, whose inhabitants were, I assumed, in bed asleep or at least inside—as so often at Vanes, much was left unsaid.

"Yes," said Joss, and there was a strange quality to his voice—uncertainty, or nerves. "You hear the song everyone sings, just once a year, and when you hear it, your neck starts to prickle... you know you're there, in that moment."

"A bit like Christmas carols."

"Maybe. But not really. It's only us, you see. Only us in the whole world. *The Times* wanted to do a piece on it once, Daddy said no, quite right too. It's our tradition. And it's not a big deal. It's just something we...we do."

"It's very interesting," I lied, and I nestled my head in his shoulder, gently pushing myself against him; he only needed the smallest of signals. His hands ran inside my bare thigh, up over my T-shirt; we kissed, gently, as we had done a couple of times.

"I want to do it to you," he murmured, his voice thick. "You're—you're so remote. I can't work you out. Like the guy says, *Full beautiful, a faery's child.*"

"Oh," I said, awfully pleased that what I believed to be my dull drabness was reclassed as some mysterious quality. It was thrilling, all of it.

"You'll love the Collecting, Janey," he said, and our fingers touched again, and I shivered, in the cool, starry night, unable to believe that I was living this, that it was me. "You'll see. It's something very special. It's what makes our family. And you're part of it, this year."

"I am?"

"You'll see," he said, and kissed me again, and I tried to forget everything else.

For a brief period I could, but I kept remembering the discarded rubbish bag of leftover fish and chips. How it would get caught on the brambles, how long it would take to decompose. Such a tiny thing.

And yet again I felt sick, as the oily taste of frying rose in my mouth. Suddenly all I could think about was Daddy's last birthday, how he and I had been to see *Indiana Jones* together, and got an ice cream, and sat outside. It was March, the first lovely spring day. "Everything's all right, when the sun shines, isn't it, darling?" Daddy kept saying. "Everything's all right." He'd reached over, and patted my hand. "We're all right, aren't we? Aren't we!"

He killed himself eight days later. So obviously not. But I know he was happy that day. We had a little cake in the evening—thirty candles, as many as I could cram onto the cake. I bought five flimsy little packets of striped candles from Woolworths, because I knew how much he loved them. And he had cards, as usual, from our neighbors, from old friends, even from Mum. Sylvia sent him a card, with a long message. I knew this because he propped it up on the mantelpiece, but he must have taken it down afterward; I couldn't find it after he'd died.

Later, turning around in bed, alive with the feeling of Joss's touch still on me, wired with the memory of that day, and Daddy's birthday, I couldn't sleep. It struck me how strange Charles's birthday was—no cake, no happy birthday, no cards. Daddy, on the verge of ending his life, had a better birthday, but then it didn't matter, made no difference.

Chapter Fifteen

A few days later, I met the bees.

I was by the pool, in the early evening, with Joss. Charles and Sylvia had eaten earlier than us and were upstairs, but we had gone to the pool with some sandwiches—it was still light. Merry was in the water, determinedly swimming up and down, singing loudly. I think she felt awkward.

"Do the Locomotion! The Locomotion!"

Joss and I were sitting close together, faces turned toward the setting sun. The outline of the old chapel was a black silhouette edged with flame. Our arms were almost touching. I was very aware of my body, in the bright peach bikini that Sylvia had made for me, of my pale limbs that were gradually turning golden after days in the sun. My face glowed in the evenings when I cleaned my teeth. My head had a soft regrowth of baby-fine light hair and it made me feel much better, as well as the headscarves, which I loved wearing, like I was a fifties heroine. As if I was assuming my own identity, playing a part of the person I wanted to be.

The space between me and Joss was nothing. I wanted to reach over, to kiss him, taste his lips. He was delicious, that Joss. He was unlike anyone else I had met—shy, handsome Paul Rolles and I had never got off the ground, much less got off with each other. But, with Joss, it felt as though anything, everything, could explode between us.

I felt my chest, rising and falling, at the thought of him, if he were to lean over now, his damp, cold skin fresh from the lime-green pool on my warm, dry body, his wet hair dripping onto me…

"The only way is UP! BAB—argh!"

Merry ran, and jumped into the pool, skidding slightly, tumbling in at the last moment and falling backward into the water. We looked up in alarm, and I gave a small cry of distress. "Joss—"

"She's fine," he said, but he stood up, though as he did so Merry reappeared, a minute later, black head moving toward us. "I'm OK!"

We smiled, adults together, as she turned back, swimming away from us.

"She'd always have been OK," murmured Joss, sitting back down, a little closer than before, and as there was no way she could see us, he turned toward me, putting one hand on the other side of my hips, so he was leaning over me. I sat up, a little, and we kissed again, and I held his head in my hands.

"Your hair is growing back much lighter," he said. "Look." He moved his hands up, toward my headscarf—I put them on my breasts, and he gave a small giggle.

"You're the only girl I know who'd rather I touched her tits than her head," he said, and he carried on kissing me.

"I'm self-conscious about it," I said.

"No one cares as much as you do," he murmured, squeezing my breasts, inexpertly, like they were oranges. I caught one hand, reshaping it over my left breast, showing him how I liked it. I didn't know how, only that this was what I wanted. The gate behind the little pool house jangled, and we sprang apart—I leaned back.

"Where's Kitty?" said Charles, a figure in shadow, as we squinted at him.

"She went into the village. Band practice."

"She walked?"

"Giles picked her up."

Charles clicked his tongue. I pulled my T-shirt dress over my head. "She should tell us when she goes out."

"You were busy," said Joss, flatly, and I noticed Merry stopped swimming, watching too. Joss never talked back to his father.

"She needs to plan her day. That's her trouble. Instead of lazing around reading and waiting for boys who don't call her." Charles was getting worked up. "She should be helping her mother in the kitchen, being polite to our guest." But he didn't look at me.

"I'll tell her, PF."

"Yes. Well, make sure you do. It's two weeks to go, after all, her last ceremony." He flicked his head almost imperceptibly toward me. "Ready?"

And he turned and left.

"He means you," said Joss. I scrambled into my flipflops, feeling Joss's hand on my wrist, pulling me down for one more kiss, and one more intense, supercharged stare into each other's eyes.

I felt wanton, loose, open, a creature of myth and mystery, as I scurried across the lawn, catching sight of my shadow against the grass. Kitty had said I would never belong here but she was wrong, I knew she was wrong. I was me, Janey Lestrange, in my short, clinging T-shirt dress, wet with the imprint of Joss's skin on mine, as I walked toward the bees.

The sun cast fire over the side of the chapel; it illuminated the curved wall of the boundary as I passed through the gate onto the other side.

"You should always visit them in the evening," Charles said. "They're calmer then. We all are."

It was a still evening, no wind. Above us, the sky was royal blue, the stars already out though it was still light. On the little path that wound down through the woods to Larcombe were the first blackberries, and early rose hips. The ivy along the boundary edge bloomed its pale-green flowers, and the once blowsy elderflowers were now tight, blood-red berries; Joss had pointed them all out to me, earlier that day. Summer was edging toward its close.

Suddenly I did not want to step outside the threshold of Vanes. I felt safe there, not here, on the edge of the darkness. I looked up at Charles, remembering how much my father disliked him.

Rescue Sylvia.

Charles couldn't work the lock, and had to wiggle the key several times. Eventually it opened, with a cracking sound, as if something was breaking. "Stupid thing," Charles said, viciously. He kicked the door open. "Come in, then."

I followed him in, unwillingly. The interior was dark, even though the roof was partially missing. The place smelled of damp and incense—why on earth, when no one used it as a place of worship, I didn't stop to consider. I could hear the roar of the sea, amplified in the silence of the echoing chamber.

Charles looked at his watch, then over at the furthest wall, where a stone stood. "The altar was there once. And behind that's the tombs." He paused. "They're awfully loud tonight. I don't think they want us here."

Something brushed past me in the gloom, with a puckish hissing in my ear. I jerked away, swatting my neck, and realized the roaring sound wasn't the sea, it was the bees, that they were inside here. A humming, intense sound, so close it was as though it was touching you, reverberating in your throat, your stomach. I looked around, carefully rubbing my short, soft hair. I realized that I was scared.

"Right," said Charles. "Now, listen. We won't stay long. It's good you want to participate in the Collecting. Very pleased."

"Of course I want to," I said, staunchly, trying to make out that I was the natural person to be asked. "Daddy and I used to talk about it. Wonder what it was about. It's lovely to be asked."

"Ah. Not quite sure what your father would make of you involving yourself in it." He smiled, teeth shining white in the gathering dusk.

"Really? Why?"

"Well. He loved a bit of folklore, didn't he, old Si? But on his own terms. Didn't like it here. He never came to visit Sylvia, except that one time, and he was supposed to be her guardian, wasn't he?"

"Oh," I said. "I don't know."

"Well anyway. I invited him, several times. Sylvia wanted me to. He never came."

"You invited Daddy to stay?"

"You too, Janey. Every summer after you'd been down. Sylvia was so keen for you and Kitty to be friends. You'd got on. But he was always busy."

I'd asked Daddy so many times when we'd go back. "Can't I see Kitty again? Can't we go and stay, just for a weekend?"

But he'd always shrugged, sadly. "I know. I've written to Sylvia saying the same. I'd love to, but we can't very well just turn up, can we?"

So someone was lying.

As my eyes adjusted to the gloom, I could see faint wall markings, barely visible to the naked eye, on each wall. There were four windows, two on each side, small, hive-shaped, like the gables of the house. In one side of the hexagon only there was an extra window. It was about two feet high, and only a hand's width, filled with algae-flecked glass. I peered at it.

"That's the leper squint," said Charles. "The Reverend Diver, that fellow in the hallway, put in a window, so they could watch the service. They'd come up from the woods on Sundays. The chap over at Larcombe wouldn't let them near his church. But everyone was welcome here. He left food out for them. Learned about the bees from them. That's what they say. My sister wrote a decent little pamphlet about the history of it." He stopped, and bit his lip. "She was a clever thing, you see, not like me and Ros. Bit purple in places, but adds to the suspense, what?"

"Was this..." I screwed my eyes shut, trying to remember what Joss had told me. "Pammy?"

"Yes." His face clouded over. "She died, young." He batted it away with his long fingers. "Don't, please. Where was I? Read the booklet, it's good stuff. You see, the Reds, and the Culneys, their families have been here for centuries. They know the stories. People remember what this place was like before he came."

"What was it like?"

Charles was leaning over a box in the corner of the chapel, taking out things. He held each one up to the light. I saw candlesticks, spoons, candles, cloths.

"You have to understand something, before I tell you," he said. "Listen. You come from London. You have a father who believes in noble deeds and heroic tales. Loved history, didn't he?"

"Yes," I said, watching as he held the candlesticks up and they glinted in the gloom of the chapel. "Me too. We used to have these days out..." I trailed off.

"Well, you see that's the trouble. He's like lots of people. Wants history to be a—what's it called?—a theme park, laid out for him to visit on a Sunday drive out of town. And a lot of it wasn't his business. He didn't understand it. Poking his nose in. I'd say to him: you can't explain everything that's happened in the past. It can't all be black and white, there's so much in between."

The interesting thing is Charles Hunter was right, and I came to agree with him. Not the nonsense about being from London, as if that gave me no nuance or insight into anything outside it, but the stuff about shades of gray. The joke, if it is a joke, is that he himself didn't believe it. He'd no more have left food out for starving lepers than he would have voted for the Green Party. He believed in self-preservation, first and foremost.

"This place has been handed down father to son, father to son, for over a hundred and fifty years. And that's because we've kept ourselves to ourselves, and we honor the countryside, and we respect dirty old Reverend Diver and his bees, what what."

"Dirty? What do you mean?"

"Oh, just rumor. It's beside the point," he said, sharply. "We leave them alone, but for this one day, when we take the honey off their hands. We come into the chapel, and we say: thank you. Half for you, half for me. We remember Diver, and how he asked God to send believers, and how the bees came, and people came too."

"But do you have to do the Collecting now? You don't—um." I didn't know how to say it. "You don't need worshippers now, do you?"

"We need to Collect every year, to keep the ritual going. When you don't, the whole edifice collapses."

"You—" I wanted to show him I got it. "You—lose the house and your way of life."

He came toward me. It was very quiet, all of a sudden, the only sound the low, constant static of the hum. A slight breeze caused the hairs on the back of my neck and on my arms to rise. I was afraid.

"It's not about winning, or losing. The ceremony is about our relationship with our surroundings. We need the bees to survive, and they need us to survive. Once you understand that, you understand the history of Vanes, you understand our family." He turned away, so I couldn't see his face. "It's not a game, Janey." His voice was soft, the edges of his words muffled, swallowed on the breeze. It was almost hypnotic and I shook myself, wanting to break out of this reverie. "It's more than that. The fabric of society. The foundations of the country. What we believe in."

I wanted to be one of them, to fit in, but I was also my father's daughter, I saw then, and that meant being allergic to notions of Empire and Country and all the things that bound Charles's life together and which Daddy had come to reject. Still. I swallowed, pushing these reservations aside.

"What do you want me to do?" I asked, quietly.

Charles was polishing some spoons with a soft cloth. He laid them on the altar and turned back to me. "Do you know it? The song we sing?"

I shook my head. "I've heard it. I don't know what any of it means."

Very softly, he began singing.

"I'll sing you twelve, O,
Twelve come for the comb, O!
What are your twelve, O?
Twelve for the twelve new hunters,
Eleven for the eleven who went to heaven,
Ten for the ten commandments,
Nine for the nine bright shiners,
Eight for the Spring Collectors,
Seven for the seven stars in the sky,
Six for the six-sides of the comb,
Five for the five proud walkers,
Four for the honey makers,
Three, three, the rivals,
Two, two, the beloved girls,
Clothed all in green, O,
One is one and all alone and evermore shall be so."

As he started singing, it was embarrassing. Then it was almost unbearable, his reedy, light voice, floating around the small space, ringing out, into the woods. His face cleared; it was totally without expression, turned toward the stacked tombs on either side of the altar. He was holding a candlestick and one of the spoons.

I had no idea what to do, where to look, but after a while I realized: he didn't care whether I was there or not. He was singing to himself. It ended, and he nodded. I raised my hands to clap, believe it or not, then let them drop.

"You ask what it means," he said. "The twelve hunters are locals. Eleven lepers will die in Christ if they accept the sacrament. The ten commandments are the word of God and must be obeyed even in this pagan place. Nine bright shiners are the diamonds in the family ring which Sylvia wears, and which Joss's wife will one day wear." Now he was counting them off on his fingers, going faster and faster. "Eight open the hives in April for the spring harvest. Seven stars make up the Plow, and when it is low in the sky that means August is here and we can collect. Six sides of the chapel, six sides of the cells. Five walkers walk with the hunters to the chapel every year. Four make the honey, that's the women's work. Three rivals are the men, it must be men, who stand to gain the most if the pact is broken. They must be watched. Two beloved girls, dressed in green and crowned with flowers, walk behind the procession. Now, they symbolize purity." He gave me an odd glance. "That's very important. They must be pure. Then— ah, then there's one alone, one outsider. They are the first to be invited in, they unlock the door. They, like the lepers, are nothing, no one. They remind us how lucky we are. That one day we will all be nothing again."

I knew he was quoting from something, but I didn't know what it was. I still don't.

He gestured behind the altar, to the stacked tombs behind him, and now my eyes were fully accustomed to the gloom I could see the bees, flying in and out of tiny holes and cracks in each tomb. I peered forward.

"They're—in there?"

Charles pointed. "There they are," he said, his voice thin and high. "And—up there."

He rocked on his heels, hands clasped tightly behind his back, as I stared up at the low ceiling, a third of which was missing. Wooden boards covered most of it. But a gap about five or six inches wide showed something. A row of yellow-gray, thick, plate-like shapes, like dough or something squashed or rolled out into a waxy, lipped circle, sticking out of the ceiling. At first I thought it was expanding foam, like the stuff Daddy used to get rid of mice. Then I looked again at the tiny crawling forms covering them. Combs. They were honeycombs.

Charles jerked his head over toward the furthest wall, into which were set five or six stone recesses: tombs, places of rest for the dead. The bottom two—about three feet wide—were shut. The others were shut too, but sealed up and over with something messy like clay, straw poking out of the mixture, and a hole about the size of a penny at the top of each one. In and out of these holes, and in the ceiling, bees flew, crawled, hovered. I could see only a few—probably about fifty. But the sound—I knew from the sound there were many, many more than that.

"In my grandfather's day we had trouble with the death's head hawkmoths. They'd come into the chapel, getting up into the ceiling. Then there were swifts, trying to build nests, bee-eaters—all kinds of birds. Some of them did a lot of damage. So we nudged them toward the tombs. Easier to keep a smaller entrance. But they still love the ceiling, too. They won't swarm, my girls. Oh, sometimes you think they're going to but they won't. They'll never leave. They know they're luckier than most bees."

"Why?"

"We look after them, they look after us. It's always been that way." He got closer to me, and I could feel his warm breath, the faint stench of wine and Sylvia's perfume on him. "This is what you have to understand. If we leave, they die. And vice versa."

We were both still. I did not move. I felt he wanted me to give way, submit, and I wasn't going to. And I was trying to digest whether he really believed this or not when suddenly, outside, far in the distance, came the sound of a horn, like a hunting cry.

"What the hell is that?" said Charles.

"I think it's a car horn," I said. It started, then stopped, then started again.

"Idiots," he said, irritated. "Where was I? Swarms, oh yes. If half your hive flies away you haven't taken care of them, and you deserve to lose them. You can tell when they're looking to swarm. They send out messengers, looking for pastures new. They start laying new queens. You check the hive. You uncover the mud, smoke them a bit, have a look in the comb—this slides out, you see." He gestured to the metallic shelves of the chapel's tombs.

And again, the sound of the horn came, more loudly than before, continuous now. "What the bloody hell *is* that?" he repeated. "Have a look for queen bee cells. Then you wait, and you look out for them, and when they swarm, you capture them. And you gently shove them back in here. Plenty of space for them, any-where in the chapel. All they need. The world is here, isn't it?" He spread his arms wide. "All the world is here."

For the first time I found myself wondering if he was a little mad. "Why don't you have—um, those hives like everyone else has?" I mimed "hive," making a sort of square shape with my hands.

Charles gave a barking laugh. "Force them to my will? Bees weren't made to be kept by men. They were made to build a hive the way they want. That's nature. They found this place them-selves. When they came to the Reverend all those years ago, he understood that. When my great-great-grandfather bought the house and chapel, he knew the history, he knew what had hap-pened here, he understood that too. You have to. We were from the area. We knew the stories. How they came here. What it means, you know. You can't hem them in. Listen, just read Pammy's little booklet. My parents weren't keen on it, oh no. That's why we don't share it around, you know. But it's good, if you look past some of the rubbish she's convinced about. She was only twelve."

I waited for him to expand. "Merry's got it. I'll get her to lend it to you. It's jolly interesting. She writes well. We always thought—anyway, lot better than a lot of these people you read about these days. Cartland, and so forth. Tells a damned good story."

"I'd like to read it," I said. My analytical brain wanted to take in some actual information. It was tired of this swirling uncertainty. "Thank you—"

The horn blared again, and this time I could hear car tires, the screeching scrape of rubber on gravel, and voices. "Jesus Christ," said Charles, forgetting where he was, all expansiveness gone. "I think it's troublemakers of some kind. Gypsies. I bet it's gypsies. We'd better go and see. Hurry up. Pick up that—no, not that." He gathered the spoons, and the candles, flipping them into the wooden box, locked it and almost pushed me out of the door. It was nearly dark outside.

"Thank you—" I began, but Charles was moving away.

"Sylvia's the Outsider, understand? She unlocks the place. Since you're one of the Beloved Girls, Merry can be a Hunter this year.

So Sylvia plays a role for once. And as Joss's mother, on his eighteenth birthday, it's only right, yes, it's right…" He paused for a second. "Yes. You and Kitty wait inside with the candles to light the way while we open the combs. Got it?" He squinted into the distance. "Now, one more thing," he said, and the horn blew again, and I could see something, moving across the lawn, stumbling.

"Look—" I said. "Over there—"

I gasped, as Charles grabbed my arm. Softly, he said: "I said one more thing, Jane. Listen, if you don't mind." He was pinching the soft flesh above my elbow. "Sylvia is glad you're here. She was fond of your father. But don't get ideas, do you hear me? The Collecting happens, and then it's time for you to move on. Wherever that is. Understand?"

"Oh yes," I said, staring blankly at him. "I understand."

Behind him, on the lawn, someone slumped to the grass, laughing loudly. I squinted, adjusting from the darkness of the chapel to the light outside to the shade again.

"Who's that?" I said, and I pulled away from him. From the house I could hear shouts. As we got closer, it looked like a pile of bright patterned colors, one of Sylvia's huge scarves. It moved. A slim, dirty foot encased in a leather thong poked out.

"Kitty?"

"Good God," said Charles, under his breath. He overtook me, reaching his daughter, jabbing her with his foot. I realized the laughter was hers.

She was slumped on one side, but she flopped over, onto her back, hair slipping over her face. I saw the mascara, smudged, the dim, unfocused eyes, the slack mouth.

"Well, hellooo," she said, and then she rolled onto her side again, and belched, loudly.

"Get up, Catherine," said her father, nudging her again with his foot. "Help her," he barked at me. "Now."

I slid my arm under hers, and tried to haul her up but she was like a dead weight. She smelled of Anaïs Anaïs, and cigarettes, and wine. Her breath was stale, like yogurt.

"Kitty!" Sylvia was calling, from an open window. "Oh goodness. *Kitty?*"

Aunty Ros stood on the terrace. "She woke me up, Charles. They drove at ninety, I'm sure. Those boys. She was screaming and crying. They had music on so loud, they just opened the door and she fell out. And the horn, Charles. So loud. I was frightened."

"Catherine, are you—are you drunk?" said Charles, though I should have thought that was obvious.

Kitty turned over, bum in the air, and I saw the back of her skirt was filthy with caked-on mud and dirt. She scrabbled to her feet: with anyone else it would have been a ridiculous, undignified sequence. She raised herself up to her full height, adjusting her sliding navy T-shirt, and putting her hat—a battered panama, tatty blue ribbon—on her golden head at a rakish angle. Her bare legs were dirty. Her eyes glittered.

"I'm drunk, oh yes I am, because I've been at the pub, with boys, doing lots of things I shouldn't be doing, and in two weeks' time I'll be eighteen, *Daddy*, and I can do what the hell I want." She was swaying, like a pendulum, almost in time, as she spoke.

"Get inside, have a bath. You're in a disgusting state."

"No."

"Did you hear, Charles! Kitty woke me up! She woke me up, Charles!" Ros was covering her ears, her too-short white embroidered nightdress riding up almost to her groin. In the yellow light from the kitchen, she looked much older than Charles; her sagging jaw, and the hands, swollen with arthritis, yet wrinkled, dotted with liver spots. Her eyes were blank.

Charles looked down at his daughter, thin lips white with fury. "You're making quite a name for yourself, Kitty, you realize that."

"Yes, Kitty. You are," said Ros, hands still over her ears.

Kitty turned away from her aunt, toward her father. "Brrrrrllllll." She flung her arms out, head back, waggling her tongue. She really was quite out of it. "They're Joss's friends. You don't have a problem with Joss going out and getting wasted with them. You *like* that. You want him to get in with Giles. You want his dad to buy those George something mamog- mahogany dining chairs off you."

"God's sake, Kitty. Don't you see why Mummy and I—" Charles's face screwed up into an extraordinary combination of rage and pain. "Be a good girl. Here—I'm talking to you. Don't walk away!"

"A good girl. You have no idea. I'm good. I'm *very* good," said Kitty, and she turned, and was walking away, the scarf trailing behind her across the lawn. She flung one hand up high. "Sorry I woke you, Aunty Ros."

Ros took her hands away from her ears. "Are the bees OK, Charles? Did you check the—Charles?"

But Charles wasn't listening. He was staring at his retreating daughter, hands scrunching and unscrunching at his side.

"Two weeks, Daddy-o! Two weeks to go! Then it's all over for you!"

Joss appeared at the pool gateway. He gestured to me. *Come here?*

But I didn't want to stick around. I didn't want to see anymore. I stalked past them, up the stairs, to my room, quietly shutting the door, putting a chair under the handle.

I lay on the bed, listening to the sobbing echoing through the house, the whispered fury. The lines from the song kept playing around and around in my head, the rest of that hot, still night.

Two, two, the beloved girls,
Clothed all in green, O,
One is one and all alone and evermore shall be so.

Chapter Sixteen

"Is there something wrong with Kitty?" I asked Merry, two days after Kitty's disgrace. We were walking through the garden toward the chapel, I slopping along in the too-big and tatty old wellingtons from the boot room which I wore rather proudly. There had been a heavy storm the previous night and my other shoes weren't suitable for the wet path down to the village. Merry, in a blue and green toweling playsuit and muddy sneakers, leaped nimbly ahead of me, a long switch of mallow in her hand to swipe flies, wasps and butterflies off the flowers, leaving them free for the bees.

I'd been at Vanes about three weeks and beyond the intermittent showers of Charles's birthday, this was the first time it had properly rained. That spring, and summer, there had been hardly any rain, only day after day of blazing sunshine. The TV news, on the rare occasions we saw it, showed people my age, in fluorescent acid colors, tripping and dancing to house music in fields bleached yellow. Back in London, the streets seamy and bone dry, I'd felt addled with heat.

The previous night's downpour reset everything. It was now sunny, but breezy, the wind challenging us, the weathervane for once pointing a different direction—west—the sky a bright, hard blue. Charles had gone to "meet a buyer." Sylvia was working—since Charles's birthday, she had been holed up in her study much more than usual, drafting and redrafting her new textile design, what would become "Summer Rain," Rory sleeping by her side. He seemed to have aged several years in the last week, and all he wanted to do, more than ever, was stick by Sylvia. I loved stroking his soft ears in the afternoons as we sat on the terrace shelling peas with Sylvia or in the kitchen helping her to wash up and I knew how he felt; she was the only member of the family I could be myself with, and she was the hardest to pin down.

"Kitty?" Merry said. She wrinkled her nose. "Dunno. She's just—a bit different these days."

"Why doesn't she want to go to Cambridge?"

"No idea. Maybe it's because she thinks she's not clever enough? I'm pretty sure Mummy got her a place, anyway."

"That can't be true," I said, shocked.

"She didn't even get called for an interview. All Joss's friends did, at Farrars, and Kitty's much cleverer than them. So Mummy rang up the history professor at King's College. Professor Lovibond, isn't that a great name?"

"Yes—"

"I love it. I want to write a novel about someone called Lovibond, one day, don't you—"

"What happened, Merry?"

"Oh. Fine. Sorry. Well, Mummy knew him from when she was growing up. He was her mum's lodger. Do you know about her mum? Never mind, anyway, he spoke to her history teacher at Letham's, they were old buddies too, Kitty got called in for an interview then given an offer. A and two Bs. It's not what you know, et cetera."

Those had been my predicted grades, in another world, another life. "That's not fair," I said.

"Why not? Kitty deserved a place." Merry sprang instantly to her sister's defense. "She's as good as anyone else. But, anyway, she's furious Mummy interfered, and I think she's nervous. Convinced she's not good enough, et cetera, et cetera."

"Your mum wouldn't do that," I said, definitely.

"Mummy organizes everything, you just don't see it. She makes out that she's away with the fairies. It's all an act."

"Oh." I was silent for a moment, wondering what to say next, as our tread fell in tandem, one with the other, and we crunched away from the house past the pool.

("No thanks, Merry," Kitty had said flatly when her little sister had run to the pool and asked her and Joss if they wanted to walk into Larcombe with us. She'd hardly been seen since the night of her disgrace two days ago. She'd spent the next day in bed, only emerging at lunchtime that day in sunglasses. "You two go ahead." And she'd slowly crossed one leg over the other, then turned back to reading *Emma*, pushing the sunglasses very slightly up her nose.

Joss stubbed out his cigarette and raised his eyebrows at me. "Have fun, you two.")

"Mummy's furious she doesn't want to go, and Mummy never really gets furious. But Daddy doesn't seem to care. I don't know."

"What will she do?"

"Giles Leigh-Smith says she should just carry on being backing singer in his rock group. Giles says they're going to be massive soon. They're called the Minotaurs. He says he's got some producer coming down from London who will definitely sign them up. But Kitty needs to be in it for people to have something to look at. She doesn't really sing, she just hums and la-la-las and wiggles in the back. I've heard she says she won't do that anymore either. She won't wear their clothes and do what Giles says."

"I'm surprised they even tried," I said, wondering at the person who would try to tell Kitty what to do.

"Giles is really pissed off. Everyone is with her at the moment."

"Giles is at school with Joss?"

Merry turned, and I saw her face was red. "He's the most popular boy in the year. His family is very rich. They just got a satellite dish, too." She looked at me, unsure whether I'd understand what a big deal this was. "It gets programs from a satellite up in space."

"Oh right." I didn't say Claire's TV-obsessed mother had got one last month, or that the Ghoshes down the road had had, for the last five years, a vast satellite dish which boomed Bollywood musicals and Indian soaps—"*Doordarshan* time!"—into their living room, which we used to watch, sitting on the living room floor, passing bowls of sesame sticks and Mrs. Ghosh's samosas to one another.

"Giles wants her to dress like that girl out of Shakespears Sister. They were on T-O-T-P"—Merry enunciated the letters of the immensely popular pop music show *Top of the Pops* carefully— "last week. Siobhan Fahey had a black bra on and black lacey top and a big floppy hat and a miniskirt. That's the sort of thing singers wear. But Kitty won't. He says she should because she's his girlfriend." Merry shrugged slightly, and I saw her expression. "Joss and Kitty had a big fight about it because Joss says Giles is his mate. Joss is like that."

"Like what?"

"Friends with everyone, friend to no one," said Merry, gnomi-cally, and she opened the gate that led toward the chapel.

In the golden light of day, not at dusk, I could look at the strange, half-ruined building more calmly. Before, I couldn't see that it had once been a beautiful building, and as Merry opened the door I spotted wild thyme and grasses, flourishing in the cracks on the an-cient stone floor, the walls bathed in afternoon light upon which were the carvings—naïve, other-worldly outlines. I could just make out a lion, jaw open, prone on the ground, and further along, a saint of some kind, with bees around his head, almost like a halo. Outside, around us, all was silent but for the distant, humming roar, quieter now than in the evening.

"We won't stay long," said Merry, authoritatively. "There's some-thing about them this summer. Aunty Ros says we're leaving it too late to collect. She says it's because they burned the field over at Smallcombe Farm last year. There was sedge and ragwort and sycamores, and ivy, and all sorts, now it's all gone. Less food for the bees, you see. They're having to work harder and they're cross. And it's thundery. They hate thunder."

"Why?"

"They pick up the static in the air, I think. Every time the work-ers come back to the hive they give the queen an electric shock. It makes her awfully bad-tempered and she passes it on to them."

"It's been very humid," I said, trying to show I understood. "They'll be glad the storm's over."

"More storms coming though. Aunty Ros says they were trying to swarm the other day, only they lost their nerve. She's the one who knows about them, really." Merry turned, raising her shoulders up around her ears, then dropping them. Her eyebrows were black hinges, her sweetly comic face alight with excitement. "I'm so glad you're going to be here! Kitty won't take it seriously, and Joss...oh, he takes it far, far too seriously but I don't think he actually cares about it that much. But honestly, Janey, it's quite something—you'll see. Oh, you'll see! Because you're one of the Beloved Girls!"

"Yes. I am."

"And Mummy's the Outsider! Which is very funny as she's not of course."

"Who does it normally?"

"The Outsider is on their own. They don't have to come from outside. They just have to be alone. Often it's Aunty Ros. So last year it was Mrs. Culney, she's a widow. Year before it was Kitty, actually. Daddy said it'd teach her a lesson. But I think he's making Mummy do it this year as a symbol."

"Of what?"

"Oh, that she's not from here. And of—the twins growing up, leaving home, all that." Merry shrugged. "It's a reminder that we're all alone."

This is what Charles had said, almost word for word. "I think that's a bit weird, if that's what it means."

"Mummy said she wanted to do it," Merry said instantly. "When Daddy told her, she agreed right away. She said it was a nice idea."

"What's this? Divers?" I said, changing the subject and patting a small, brown box. It was fixed on an outside wall, at about my stomach height, and I had not noticed it on my previous visit. Carved into it were the words DIVERS FUND.

"People pay into it. For good luck. First it was to help the lepers, then it became about paying to rescue the sailors who were washed up on the cliffs below. Now, Daddy empties it after the Collecting and he mails it off to the Lifeboat Institute."

"Were there *really* lepers?"

"Oh yes. They were driven into the woods. A whole load of tea pickers from somewhere? Far away, anyway. A really long time ago? They'd all become infected and they were taken off their ship by the captain and dumped in these woods. That was in the Reverend Diver's day. Most of them died. They find bones, occasionally."

We gazed down at the deep green woods, and I shivered.

"But the ones who didn't, they used to watch the service through that window." She tapped the glass slit at the side of the chapel. "So they didn't infect anyone."

"That's awful."

Merry looked uneasy. "I never thought about it. It's just the way it was. Then there was a colony of them. They made charcoal for the Earl of Larcombe. He put it in trust for them, built houses for them, but he died and his son was a bad one and embezzled the money." Her hands were running over the dark-gray stone, her eyes fixed on the woods behind us. "They were the first ones to keep the bees, they say. They used to put honey on their wounds."

"Did it work?"

Merry looked up. Her thin shoulders were hunched, her dark eyes unreadable. She gave me a small, sad smile, and she looked much older then.

"Course not. It's just honey."

I put a hand onto the cold surface; the humming swell seemed to roar louder as I touched it, and I leaped away, feeling as though things were crawling over me...

Merry laughed.

"Daddy said you were a bit freaked out."

"I wasn't. I liked it."

"It's hard for someone else, to understand how important it is. It's kind of weird. Let's go."

Someone else. They were like that, the Hunters, lavishing you with affection, then drawing back. I knew it, yet I kept dashing to the water's edge, hoping to see myself reflected in their depths.

"OK," I said. I gave a small shrug to show I understood, and turned my face away from her.

"Are you cross with me?"

"Of course not," I said.

There was a silence, the wind whipping around us. Merry gave a dramatic sigh.

"Ugh. Don't do that sad face. Kitty says it breaks her heart when you look like that. Close the door," Merry said.

"Oh, please don't," I said. "I don't like the idea. I'm—I'm not sure I can...I can help at the ceremony, not anymore."

I hadn't said this out loud, to anyone.

Merry's expression changed. She said: "Don't be afraid. There's nothing to be afraid of, honestly, Janey. You don't have to go in. The two Beloved Girls stand outside waiting until the combs are broken open. *I* go in, I'm one of the Walkers. I ring the handbells." She hugged herself. "Me, Daddy, Joss, Aunty Ros, Mrs. Red, I think. Daddy always does the comb business, breaking it apart. Half for us, half for them. But this year Joss will do it. For the first time."

"I—" I faltered. I gave a weak laugh, and shrugged. "It's—I don't know how to explain it." I didn't want to sound rude. I was eighteen, and unable to understand it wasn't my fault. I was out of my depth.

Merry clicked her tongue. "Stupid me. I forgot. I've got this booklet about it for you actually. Daddy asked me to give it to you. A kind of ... information leaflet." She pulled something out of her denim backpack.

"Your aunt wrote it, is that right? A sort of guide book?"

"My aunt? Oh, I see. Pammy. Dad's sister. She didn't do it to be a guide book. She wrote it as an essay at Letham's and showed it to some friends and she got into fearful trouble for it. Her head-mistress said it was immoral."

"Gosh," I said. "Now I do want to read it."

But Merry didn't laugh. "Aunty Ros got mixed up in it. She was all set to be head girl and after this they said Ros wasn't suitable, 'cause she was Pammy's sister and...My grandparents were called in to the school, it was a big fuss." She rolled her eyes. "They never talk about it. Dad once said she was a trouble-maker. I'm not sure what happened. I think the school thought he wasn't the sort of person a nice girl should be writing about. She was two years younger than me, after all."

"What's in it then?"

She handed me a thin booklet. "You'll see when you read it. He was an odd fellow, the Reverend Diver. Her spelling's not great. Some of it's pretty weird, to be honest." Her sweet dark eyes clouded over. "I kind of wish..." And she shrugged. "Doesn't matter. Come on, we'll be late."

I hesitated. "I'd love to read it."

"Now?"

"Sure." I shrugged, but my heart was racing. "Do you mind going into the village on your own?"

I thought she'd be pleased, that I wanted to know more. But I had upset her, and I couldn't understand why.

"Fine. Don't—oh I don't know."

"Don't what?"

"Well..." She squinted at me. "It's good to have someone else around. Someone who's not obsessed with it all. Don't...oh, don't get too drawn into it."

"I won't," I said, nodding at her, lips pressed together. "Promise."

I looked at the cover. Typed onto mildewed, folded paper was the cover, which read:

```
The History of the Reverend Diver and the Col-
lecting Ceremony by Sybilla Pamela Hunter
```

"This is Pammy, then?"

"PF and Ros's little sister. She died that summer. She was only twelve. She was very brilliant. Read at the age of three...she'd just started at Letham's when it happened."

"Really? I didn't know—"

"OK then, see you later," she said, and turned to go.

A typewritten cross had been attempted, only partially successfully, on the page.

The staples were rusting and the paper smelled gently of damp. On the inside, in precise printed letters:

```
The Property of Pamela Hunter
Lower Fourth
Davenant House
Letham's Ladies' College
Dolehill
Somerset
England
Great Britain
United Kingdom of Great Britain and Northern
  Ireland
The British Isles
```

Europe
The World
The Universe

Merry disappeared down the path and I sank onto the springy turf. And, as the harebells nodded beside me and the warm breeze washed over my bare legs, I read the history of my hosts and their house.

¶

A Short History of the Reverend Diver and the
Collecting Ceremony
by Sybilla Pamela Hunter of Vanes
12 years old
1938

A brief history of my family's house and the
ceromony which takes place every year.

...

I'll sing you twelve, O,
Twelve come for the comb, O!
What are your twelve, O?
Twelve for the twelve new hunters,
Eleven for the eleven who went to heaven,
Ten for the ten commandments,
Nine for the nine bright shiners,
Eight for the Spring Collectors,
Seven for the seven stars in the sky,
Six for the six-sides of the comb,
Five for the five proud walkers,
Four for the honey makers,
Three, three, the rivals,
Two, two, the beloved girls,
Clothed all in green, O,
One is one and all alone and evermore
shall be so.

There was a place of worship on this very spot over a thousand years ago. As you climb up to the cliffs, the ancient woodland winds like a ribbon between the village of Larcombe and the beginning of the moorland. Above these woods at the top of the cliffs someone built a chapel. No one knows quite how the building would have looked, but it was hexgonal, the same shape as a cell in a hive. At some point the building collapsed—it is not known how, but local legend said it was knocked down by a terrible storm one night, the greatest wave ever seen in England which crashed up and over the cliffs. The sea was angry, they said. Locals deserted the church—the lepers, hiding in the woods, had nowhere to go, their hives, on the edge of the wood, were all gone; the tiny rectory, set back from the cliffs, was destroyed too.

Soon after that, some time in the late eighteenth century Caradoc Diver came to the village. He had come across the country in answer to the call of the diocese for help.

In the hallway of our house, Vanes, there is a portrait of the Reverend C. Diver. We can see he was a tall, rangy man, with fierce pale-green eyes, their expresion intense, deep set within a protruding skull, against a black backdrop which has now faded to a deep kind of aubergine over the centuries. On the table next to him sit five handbells, his one long index finger resting on the middle one, as if he is about to pick it up and shake it.

From books and letters in the house and what the villagers have handed down about him we know various facts about Reverend Diver's early life. He had grown up in Pickering, by the North Yorkshire moors, the son of an apprentice glovemaker. The family was very poor, and as a child Diver sold scraps of kid at the market; this fear of poverty followed him through his life. His father violently opposed the "New Dissenters" and the visits John Wesley made to the town to spread his message of Nonconformism. I think this made an impresion on him. I think he saw what might be possible. Thanks to the aid of a rich local supporter who recognized the promise in the young man Diver studied at Trinity College, Oxford, where he sang in the choir, and become a keen apiarist which is someone who is a collector of different species of bee and their honey. I was unable to find out how he came to Somerset, how he heard of the living vacancy. But come he did, in the 1780s, and there he found a ruined church, no rectory, no incumbent for over a decade, no glebe farm.

The parish of Larcombe was rotten. For years no vicar could be found, and the Reverend Culney, vicar at Crowcombe, the neighboring parish, refused to perform the funerals of either the lepers living in the woods or the battered bodies thrown up onto the rocks by the sea, saying he did not know if they were Christian men or not. So many men lost their lives that way, and the number of services that had to be held was dreadfuly hard on the local inhabitants—watching the ship pitch and roll in the storm, knowing the poor souls on board were doomed but for a miracle, knowing the coast was too trecherous for them to attempt to land. This same vicar also declared he would not oppose any parishioners who burned the woods in an attempt to rid them of the leper colonies—at that time there was a particularly large one, men and women enslaved in Assam and shipwrecked many years earlier, driven into the woods, who would creep out at night and steal, the poor desparate souls.

Poverty in this wild harsh country was every-where, and a bad harvest meant certain starvation to some villagers and their families. A blind eye was turned to the foul habit of "wrecking," where men, women and children risked their own lives on the rocky, violent shoreline, scrab-bling for treasure from the shipwrecks. I myself find it disgraceful that such things occurred but they did I am sorry to say. The wreckers would rob dying men of their coins; they once found a heart, pierced on a rock, and one man fed it to his pig. The local landowner around these parts was then a dastardly fellow named Smythe, but he took no interest in the people and his own land, leeching from them to line his own pock-ets. All was as I say rotten, when Caradoc Diver arrived.

Partly to solve the problem, partly to make it go away, at Diver's entreaties the Bishop agreed a new parish could be formed, but in his records it was refered to as "a parish of the damned." Diver was given some modest rebuilding funds—no one to this day knows where the rest of the money came from, but later people said the Devil left a small bag of gold on the door of the chapel. He rebuilt the chapel around the ancient hexagonal floor (giving it the carved wall pan-els and the too-elaborate vaulted ceiling which later collapsed), and it was Reverend Diver for whom the house was built—a manse in size and scale comparable to a small Manor House rather than the more modest rectory in Larcombe, greatly to the disgust of the vicar of that parish. And while building went on, every day the Revered Diver (I typed Revered—that is quite appro-priate!) went to the farms and cottages, the huts and shacks thereabouts, trying to persuade people to come and worship in their own parish again, not to cross to Crowcombe or, which would be worse, to the Chapel at Winsford. He went to the woods, and talked to the lepers, and invited them to come and worship. The story goes that they gave him some of their honey, and that he carried it back to the house with him.

"We have built a chapel for lost souls," he said, and it is recorded in the diary of George Red, a farmer's son who became a great pamphleter and abolitionist in Bristol. "We have raised up a sanctury with money sent from the Lord."

But no one came. Every Sunday, Reverend Diver would wait at the door, the wind blowing in his face, and no one came. Six long months came and went and no one came—the warmest summer for many years fading into one of the finest autumns in men's memorys, with a rich harvest and much rejoicing, and then the storms began. And every month or so Diver would have to perform the funeral rites of a sailor lost at sea, would have to drag the bodies up from the rocks with only the help of the sexton, a local man called Ned Watchet, whose family had lived in the district for many generations. The villagers could not plunder shipwrecks any more, not when the vicar was so often down at Larcombe, keeping an eye on them. Ned Watchet told everyone the vicar was a strange one, who beleived things that weren't in the Bible, but a good 'un the same. He told them about the chapel, inlaid with carved stone panels showing scenes from the Bible, Samson breaking open the jaws of the lion and taking the honey from its corpse, St. Bartholomew, tending the bees, the leper squint window for those who could not come inside, who were shunned, to partake. He told them the vicar had given him, and his family, rost beef and plum pudding on Christmas

Day. But still no one came. And then it was winter, cruel and long, and more sailors died, more services were had, and Diver said nothing about his lot, but hauled the bodies up from the rocks himself, his tall frame ripling with sinew, thick hair growing longer. His funds, the mysterious money that had enabled him to build a grander house and chapel than he had ever been allotted money for, had dwindled to nothing. He received no tithe that autumn. Underneath the muscle he was thin. No one came.

And then they say one May morning, when the countryside was at the height of its beauty, when the swallows and swifts swung up and over him as he walked through the fields to the chapel, Reverend Diver found something had come. A vast swarm of bees had landed inside one of the tombs in the chapel that were tightly stacked like hives themselves.

Have you ever seen a swarm of bees, dear reader? One hundred and fifty thousand or more there can be of them. They are not yellow & gold. They are black, like a cloud, like a reptile, moving smoothly, acting as one. They understand each other, and we who have conquered the Earth and understand the skies—we still do not even understand how bees talk to each other, how they know what they know.

This swarm did not move, and the Reverend did not ask them to move. With the last of his money he bought from a friend of Ned Watchet's a skep, a hive made of willow reeds, coiled into the hive shape. He caked it with the salty mud from the flats on the beach. Then he kneeled down in the chapel and he said a prayer over them. Standing in the empty space, the sound of the gentle, menasing humming outside, he blessed the bees for finding him, for visiting him, and he asked them to stay. He made a pact with them, in fact.

I will protect you with this vow: if anyone tries to remove you, the Devil will remove them. If anyone takes more than his share of your honey, the Devil take them. If anyone comes here and lies to you, and does not tell you their secrets, the Devil will see his heart's desires and strike him down. Half for us and half for you, else the Devil take us all.

There are those who say he did not invoke the Devil, but it must be true, because of what happened.

That Sunday, and the following, still no one came. And he said the words again, and by now the bees were settled inside the tombs and inside the skep, which he set upon the ground outside the chapel and they did not like being disturbed. They were angry bees, and it remains true to this day.

Finally, he went into the village and bought a slab of sugar and set it upon the wall beside the chapel, and the bees were grateful, but still no one came.

A month went by and he waited at the chapel door to welcome his flock, but no one came, and now Reverend Diver grew angry. He was brown from summer sun. "I wish I hadn't helped you," he screamed at the bees, and only Watchet heard him, and he was used to his madness by then.

Then it was the end of summer, 24th August, feast day of St. Bartholomew, patron saint of bees and glovemakers, and Reverend Diver came early to the church, his eyes downcast, sunken in their sockets. He stood by the door, waiting.

And then he felt a hand on his arm, and up he jumped, almost out of his wits. There was Ned

Watchet and his wife Lily, and their two children. "We thought we'd worship with you today," he said. "Seeing as how the Reverend Culney's been taken ill."

And as he was seating them inside the small space, he heard a cough, and there was young Amabel Turleigh, the fresh young governess over at the Hall, with Augusta Dawson, the formidable housekeeper, and Amabel could not meet his eye, for she was desperately shy, but Mrs. Dawson told him she'd risen that morning with a sudden desire to worship the Lord.

"Come, Mrs. Dawson," he said, kindly. "Come in and be seated. God is here."

"Come child," Mrs. Dawson said briskly to Amabel, who raised her eyes to his, blushing furiously, and the Reverend chucked her under the chin.

"You are safe here, my dear," he said, his finger resting underneath her jaw for a moment. "Be not afraid."

"Yes, sir," she said, and Mrs. Dawson watched, approvingly, but old Ned saw this, and was troubled.

And more behind them, the Locksleys over at Larcombe Hall, for the curate had been taken ill there too, paralyzed in the night they said, and then Pauly Goddard and his family, they'd walked all the way from Tors Head, and more and more until the tiny chapel was full, then finally out of the woods the lepers came, and they stood at the window, and the others watched them with respect, and said nothing, everyone listening to Caradoc Diver preach. He found he had to shout to be heard over the sound of the bees.

"Today a miracle has happened," he called, to them all. "You came, in faith, to worship our

Lord, to stand together, on this last summer day, you came in love, to show him your devotion, and you came because I—I asked it."

There was a fresh honeycomb inside one of the tombs. He reached inside and tore off some of the paper-thin comb, and ate it. The sugar burned his tongue, the back of his mouth, and he gave some to old Ned, who closed his eyes.

"'Tis good honey," the older man said, nodding.

The Reverend Diver thought suddenly of the bees, and the pact he had made, but then brushed it aside. He stared instead at the faces of the congregation, packed so tight in, staring at him. He had them. He had them now. "Come, take some. Here, and here." Glancing at Mrs. Locksley's scandilized expression he said: "It is not the communion, Mrs. Locksley. It is an honest declaration of thanks for what God has provided. For does not Milton say: *Let us with a gladsome mind*?"

And he tore of a small piece of the comb, and handed it to her, and when she tasted it, her eyes were lit from within with golden fire, and she smiled.

The Reverend Culney over at Larcombe never recovered from what had ailed him that morning. He was found dead outside his cottage, face down in a rose bush. So those from Larcombe stayed with Reverend Diver. They had tasted the honey, and rumors soon began to abound about its properties. Some said there was magic in it, or a madness, that it made you invincible, that it sent you crazy. But still the congregation swelled. They came, and others joined them.

Reverend Diver was grateful. He reaped the benefit of the bees. He called the chapel St. Bees, though it had been dedicated to St.

Dunstan, an abbot who had apparently several times defeated the Devil. His congregation swelled. It was rumored that he had cured the lepers in the woods. But this was a rumor I believe was set about by him, the lying Devil.

Smart people, Lord and Lady Lowther and so forth, started to come.

The Reverend I think wanted to be part of history. That is why he set up the ceremony he called the Collecting, to give thanks for the resurrection of the parish and the saving of lost souls, every year at the end of the summer, on St. Bartholomew's Day. No one needed to wreck any more. The crops did not fail. The harvest was always good. But there were no more lost souls rescued from the sea, as the Reverend had been begged by Lady Lowther not to risk his own body down there. So the bodies lay pinned on dark spikes through winter and summer, visible from the cliffs above, cut to ribbons by the storms as the months went by.

At the end of summer every year on St. Bartholomew's day came the procession of villagers, holding beeswax candles. They came up from the old, now-abandoned church in Larcombe through the winding lanes and paths through the wood, high up onto the cairn called the Vane Stones up on the hill where they had lit a beacon to warn of the approaching Spanish Armada over two hundred years ago, then through the garden down to the chapel. The villagers sang, softly, and people who heard it always said it sounded like angels, walking toward you through the old pathways. My own grandmother tells of how as a girl she came across the procession, in the lanes, and the sound of it drove her to follow up, up onto the plain where stood the chapel, and it is there she first saw my grandfather.

Those who were there report that they felt the presence of God, laying His light on them, that they felt His touch upon their shoulders. And then to the chapel, where the Reverend removed the combs from the recesses in the walls, giving the honey that came from them to the assembled guests—some say the ceremony took on a certain Bacchanelian aspect at this point, and madness ensued, others say that is greatly exaggerated. They certainly used the silver spoons Lady Lowther had had commissioned for Caradoc Diver as a gift. But still, some whispered it was sacriligeous, like a taking of communion.

The Reverend Diver was well-known, and if the shameful business with the young governness who went missing and who was found up by the Vane Stones was of interest to some and if Lady Lowther's absence from the home for six months was remarked upon by no one but noticed by all and if he had a temper and ego that grew through the years, well, people were grateful enough for the miracle of God's presence and the effects of the honey they felt to say nothing more of it. I myself know what both those events were about and leave it to the reader to draw his own conclusions. Everyone who was present at the Collecting when Diver presided over it claims extraordinary events took place. That the Reverend called up the Holy Spirit, that He was there, he answered them, he held them close, they felt all worry and hunger and illness disappear, all because of Reverend Diver.

And then one day, without word to anyone, he hanged himself in the church.

Ned Watchet found him, but he never revealed what was in the note he left behind. As Ned was cutting him down, he was found by the churchwarden, who fainted clean away at the expression on the dead man's face.

They said, in the village, and in the surrounding countryside, that he had been seen muttering to himself out in the lanes and up on the moor late at night in the long summer twilight. They said that he lured the bees using dark magic. That he took too much of their honey, for if you don't leave enough for winter they have nothing to live on, for why else do they make it if not for themselves? Wasn't that the pact he'd made with them, and with the Devil, to leave them their honey?

I am sorry to say some said the little governess had been in an "interesting condition" when they found her. They said the bees drove Diver mad, that their droning bored into his brain and helped him lose his senses. The five handbells were scattered at his feet. Ned gathered them up, and polished them, and put them back in the bible box of his old master, and the candlesticks and the spoons, and left them in the house.

As a suicide, the Reverend could not be buried in the churchyard. At Ned's suggestion the remains were taken up onto Exmoor, to the Vane Stones high up overlooking the sea, and buried there.

There was often trouble at the village after his death. Larcombe became a black place, where the Good Leper Inn was notorious along the coast and smuggling and all sorts were rife. Reverend Diver's name became sanctified. He was not to be insulted. Vicars would not stay up at Vanes. The house was too lonely, too cold, too wild, but mainly far too grand—how had he persuaded the Church to build such a palace! Still, the bees came back every year, some in greater years than others.

In the end the Church of England was glad to sell it off. My family, the Hunters, had some connection with the house. My great-grandfather Hunter was a beekeeper of some renown and had made money in the mines in Somerset. His father had taken part in the Collecting ceremonies as a boy and had often talked about them with wonder. Great-grandfather Hunter wished to out-do his father, and could find no greater solution than to buy this house. When another bad storm, as bad as the Great Wave before it, destroyed the roof of the chapel, a month after he bought Vanes he did not take it personally. He kept the tradition of the Collecting going, preserved the house, fitting it out with Victorian flourishes. By the time Charles Hunter, my brother, was born in 1925, the ceremony was long re-established. This summer I will, along with my sister Rosalind, take the part of one of The Beloved Girls who process at the rear of the procession, symbolizing the purity of our mission, of the honey, of our lives here. It is our honor and duty to keep it going. I myself am happy to do so only as long as we Hunters understand the rules: half for us and half for them, else the Devil take us all.

Sybilla Pamela Hunter

Vanes, Somerset, 1938

¶

Chapter Seventeen

When Merry returned from Larcombe she found me there, among the stones, staring at the pamphlet, legs stretched out to catch the sun, and she laughed at my serious face. "Don't believe everything in it," she said, but I knew she didn't mean it. I was shaken by it, in a way I couldn't explain. I wanted to ask her: Don't you feel trapped by it? By the history?

But I didn't. We talked for a while as Merry pottered about picking up stray stalks and dead bees inside the chapel, sweeping them up onto an old piece of stiff card, then flinging them aside, about what she'd bought at the village, about what we'd eat that night, about whether we'd watch *Cagney and Lacey* or a repeat of *The Paul Daniels Magic Show*.

When she had finished tidying she kissed the stone wall, and I felt most strongly then her connection to the landscape, and the chapel, and this piece of earth upon which we stood, and the fact I was an outsider here, was not like them. A tall bronze candlestick was propped outside the door. Charles had forgotten to put it away.

"I'll leave it there, and we'll collect it later," Merry said, but she must have forgotten, and it's a shame, when I think of what happened later. I didn't give her the pamphlet back, and she didn't ask me about it again.

She had bought us each a chocolate Feast ice cream from the village shop, and we sat and ate them, being silly and light-hearted, doing stupid voices. Merry was much more relaxed when she wasn't with the others and could be her own person, and I remember this afternoon she was just really funny. We finished our ice creams and staggered up the chalk path, still giggling at her impression of Aunty Ros arriving at a Letham's school reunion. I could hear ringing in my ears, and then, underneath it, the sound of splashing. We turned into the pool.

There, sitting at the edge, caramel legs splashing lazily into the green water, was Kitty, her hands up over her head, retying her scarf over her hair. Her body was arched, her eyes were closed, face turned to the sun. In the water stood Joss and I saw him looking at her, at her breasts, then down to her legs. He saw us a split second after we saw him, and splashed his sister with water.

"Hi!" He leaped out, grabbing one of the ragged patterned towels and wrapping it around him. "How was the walk?"

"Great," said Merry, undoing her sundress. I stiffened in horror, then I saw her swimsuit was underneath, and I chastised myself for being such a little prude. "We got Mummy's sugar, and we picked up the pork loin. I'll dash it inside, actually." She kicked the dress away, and then, picking up the heavy string bag, swung it over her shoulder. "Janey, are you going to swim?"

"Oh," I said. "Yes."

"I'll fetch your swimsuit then."

"OK. Thanks."

I stood awkwardly clutching one arm. Joss on my own was fine, but the two of them together made the dynamic different. Kitty stayed where she was, her head lolling from side to side, the patches where Joss had splashed her bikini dark red. She was humming something, half singing under her breath. She giggled to herself, and I looked at her, curiously. Joss came and stood next to me.

"We've got the place to ourselves, this afternoon. Mummy and Dad are at lunch."

"Oh. Where?"

"Over at the Lord Lieutenant's, somewhere toward Taunton. Big fancy lunch, PF loves that kind of thing." He gave a funny laugh.

Kitty reached up behind him and took a swig from a bottle.

"Give it here," said Joss, and he came toward her and stroked her shoulder, and then drank from it himself. "Janey?" he said, proffering it to me. I still didn't like the taste of white wine. It reminded me of the disaster of the school ball. Of being out of control and unable to stop throwing up. Hating it. Feeling utterly ridiculous that yet again I'd read the rules wrong.

"Yeah, go on," I said, trying to sound nonchalant. I took a gulp of it, wincing at the too-sweet, rancid taste.

"Have a good glug. Don't want Merry seeing it," said Kitty. She nodded at me, head still rocking from side to side. Her lips were parted, bottom lip caught between her white teeth. She drank from the bottle again, a dribble of liquid running down into her ear, and she giggled and wiped it away and managed to make that seem cool. Joss was watching her again with this strange, glazed look, and then he blinked, and turned to look at me, handing me the bottle, and I drank again from it. The story of the Reverend Diver, and Pammy's urgent, queer little voice were still insistent in my ear, like they were both alive, real, calling to me. I could feel the hit of white wine, ice-cold, deadening and heavy on my empty stomach.

"Let's put music on," said Joss, clearing his throat into the silence, and tinny acid music started playing. Synthesized sound, repetitive, a lone woman's voice soaring over the top, the repetition below it lulling one into movement... I remember feeling the beat drumming itself through me.

Unlikely as it seems, I was a good dancer and I knew I was. Daddy had been a great dancer, but so had Mummy—they both loved jazz. Daddy in particular. In the early years of their dating, Daddy had taken my mother to Ronnie Scott's to see Humphrey Lyttelton and Vic Price. Dancing reminds me of Daddy, and the few times I'd seen them both happy together.

So I started swaying from side to side, moving one shoulder up and down, feeling the warmth of the late-afternoon sun on my face too. I patted my headscarf, another beautiful floral sixties pattern edged with gingham, which Sylvia had made for me. I felt a light arm on my shoulder, and Joss was next to me, and we were moving together.

I loved the music, pulsing, beating through me. Then someone had pushed Joss away, his arms from around my waist loosened, and Kitty was dancing with me. I could feel her thighs pressing against me, her arms round my waist, her breasts pressed against me. She moved—she was erratic, and I saw from her eyes she was properly drunk again, and I looked at the bottle next to us on the floor and saw it was almost empty. Joss came between us as she pulled me closer to her. I hadn't been anywhere near her since she shook my hand: to be this close to someone so beautiful, so thrillingly sophisticated was almost as intoxicating as the wine. I breathed her in, unable to believe it, and then she put her hands up, and undid the scarf around my head, pushing the material away. She ran her fingertips over my patchy scalp, slowly, curiously. Her skin was cool. I felt as though I was coming alive again.

"It's growing back," she said softly, almost to herself.

We carried on dancing together, swaying slowly, as Joss put his arms around both of us.

"Yes, girls," he said, slowly. "So…"

I wanted him to go away. Where was Merry? We three carried on dancing, swigging from the bottle, and it was wild, wildly strange. By now the alcohol was pumping through my bloodstream, and I felt on the edge of something, almost completely uninhibited. Kitty's finger was now hooked through the strap of my sundress, her other hand still on my waist, she was laughing, her white teeth glinting in the sun. Joss dived into the water—and she leaned over, that melting voice like honey in my ear:

"My father only got you here to be the other Beloved Girl with me."

She was a siren, a demon fairy, sent to lure me into something, I was sure of it…I stared at her, blankly, my mouth open, wishing I could speak.

"They've planned the whole thing. Just be careful, OK?"

"I don't know what you mean."

"Oh—Janey, you're so innocent, for fuck's sake. You've been brought down here not because they care but because you match me. They're furious about your hair. We never have anyone to stay. Especially not old friends of Mummy's. Don't you see? You're only here for the Collecting. Don't start thinking you're a family friend, or that you'll ever come back here. They don't care about you. They're drawing you in and when it's over you'll be out in the cold again. OK?"

I thought of me and Joss, down here by the pool, up in my room, snatching time alone in dark corners. How much I ached for him, and wanted him to do more, but wanted to never see him again at the same time. How washed out I felt, in a louche, exciting way. How I considered all the time doing extraordinary things. Running away. Sending Mummy something awful through the mail to Spain. Jumping in front of a train. To shake myself out of the lassitude of this lazy gilded life that felt so attractive, and so dangerous.

"Your mum wanted me to come."

"She doesn't do anything my father doesn't want her to. Come on. Just—protect yourself, that's all. You're so—alone."

She pushed herself against me again, one more time, her generous, gorgeous body enveloping mine—A voice behind us, breathless and high, came.

"Urgh! What's going on! Oh my God!"

"Oh shut up, Merry," said Kitty, pushing away from me a little, but continuing to dance. I couldn't speak, I was out of breath, my face red. "We're dancing. And drinking. And no, you're not having any, so don't bloody well ask."

With one backward glance at me she pushed away, and went back to sit by the pool. The music was still loud now, but too loud, banging at the front of my head. My stomach churned. The heat of the day, the length of the walk; I felt sick, and sat down beside her. She moved away.

"You're so weird?" said Merry.

"Stop sounding like you're in *Neighbours*."

"I'm not. Shut up, you *are* weird?" I realized she was looking at me, then she said, pettishly:

"Anyway, a sort of letter just came for you, Janey. It's registered mail. From your mum."

She handed a thick, small envelope to me. The strange, sudden, dream-like bubble that had been reality for a few minutes burst.

Dear Jane,

Thank you for your letter. I am pleased to hear you are enjoying yourself. Your father was rather under Sylvia's spell. They are an interesting family that's for sure.

You asked about the connection. Sylvia met your father as a young girl in London. He was friends with her mother. As for the rest of it, I think it is best you ask Sylvia to tell you more.

You also asked me to think seriously about what you said in your letter. I have done so. Can I ask the same of you now which is that the time has come for you to think carefully about your future. I have spoken to Miss Minas on the telephone, which, as you know, I do not like doing. I have told her to stop filling your head full of these ideas of

Oxford Colleges and other nonsense. I wish you could try to understand why I say these things, Jane love.

Even if they wanted you, it seems the height of foolishness to go to university to study ideas, and theories, and not learn how to make a living. In this day and age it is a waste of three years of your time when you could be getting a job. If you can learn to touch type, do shorthand and take dictation, you will be able to work until you are sixty and then get a good pension: people will always need secretaries. Perhaps in the future there's the chance to do something else but once you're a secretary you've always the means of earning a living.

I've been over in London for a couple of nights to sort everything out. Your father died owing a lot of money to various people. The glove importing business, the party shop, the mobile telephone business, all had outstanding debts. The house must be sold to pay people back. Jane I am sorry dear but there is nothing left for you. I have had to arrange to have the locks changed, on Martin's advice, to be quite sure no creditors who might have keys try to gain access while the place is empty.

As you know Martin worked part-time at the Citizens Advice Bureau. He has been extremely helpful. Thanks to Martin, I am confident I can keep a little money from the house, not much. Martin doesn't have much either, what with his children to look after back in the UK. I don't like having to write all this, believe me. But Daddy had no business sense: Martin says anyone setting up a mobile phone business in the age of British Telecom needs their heads examined. Martin has shares in British Airways, Dixons and Woolworths.

Miss Minas has been told she must not communicate with you again. Since you don't have a key anymore and the house will be on the market it might be best if you come to Spain for a while. The letter confirming your place has arrived here. If you could telephone to secure it I should be grateful. It is Ealing Secretarial College, 01-992-1638.

If you could send me a postcard letting me know when you will be arriving or telephone if the Hunters don't mind, I can send you a check for the flight. I've enclosed your passport, a check so you can buy some pesos to pay for the taxi, and your birth certificate in case you need ID to buy pesos and book the flight. Perhaps it is best you have these documents now in any case. I look forward to hearing from you about the above, Jane dear. Take care,

Mum x

Voices were at my back; I looked up, my head now swimming unbearably, shielding my eyes from the setting sun, sliding behind the chapel, a ball of apricot fire. I looked down at the documents that had slid out of the stiff envelope.

JANE CATHERINE LESTRANGE in small typed letters. The birth certificate, the fact of my existence. It was weird, seeing it set out like that.

The voices were closer; I shoved the documents into my pocket. I could feel my fingers crushing the letter, the determined press of the imprint of my mother's words.

"I say," said Merry. "Are you all right? You're awfully pale."

"Just—" I looked around me. At the cold, dark stone now in shade, at Joss, lounging by the pool, its still waters a dark emerald where only ten minutes ago they had been light turquoise. All at once came the sound of a car, coming up the drive. Kitty was walking away, back toward the house. She was holding two near-empty bottles of wine and, as she did, one slipped, shattering on the flagstones.

She just stood there, looking around at it, not making any effort to clear it up. After a moment, her father appeared from the driveway, her mother in the back door, Rory panting beside her.

"Clear that up, Catherine," her father said, shortly.

"No," Kitty said. "It's broken now." She stepped over it, and carried on walking. Her father started shouting, her mother calling after her.

"Darling—Kitty, your father is very angry when you—"

Rory growled, sadly.

As she walked, I saw there was blood. She pushed past her mother, turning once. I saw her face, as she looked out over the garden. She was so tired. She was eighteen, and so tired, and I understood.

Chapter Eighteen

The incident by the pool, reading both the pamphlet and my mother's letter, and the broken bottle changed me. It marked a shift in my time at Vanes. I wanted to be a good girl—I was, after all, my mother's daughter, as well as my father's. I wanted to be neat, and polite, and unobtrusive. To take my tray back up to the counter after tea in a café, to return my library books on time, to queue sensibly for the bus.

But I also wasn't that girl. I knew, when my mother left and our home became a strange limbo land, and then later, when Daddy died, that I wasn't like everyone else. I didn't belong anywhere, really, and in that respect too I was my father's child.

My mother was right: Daddy was terrible with money. He had dreams, but no ability to translate them into results. At least you tried, Janey, he used to tell me, when I couldn't do my math homework or found playing the right notes on my school recorder almost impossible. It's better to have tried. The more you try the easier it gets. And that is why the note he left me was so heartbreaking. He, who believed more than anyone else that all would be well, couldn't try anymore.

Our exam results were due in a week or so, but after the afternoon by the pool and the subsequent argument Kitty and Joss had with their father about the broken bottle, there was a change in atmosphere. As if they had been pretending, and now they weren't. And that I was now one of them, that I was complicit in what was going on.

Things that now seem so strange—Charles and Sylvia's nightly, loud, agonized love-making, how public it was, the relationship between Kitty and the rest of her family, Merry's faux adolescent behavior—I questioned them less, but, deep down, they disturbed me more. I kept thinking about Diver, striding across the moor toward the chapel. I did not think he was a holy man. I thought he was a cult leader. I knew Pammy had seen through him, too, even though she was the youngest of her siblings. I wondered what Charles and Rosalind thought of what she had written, they who clung to Diver's ceremonials like the ivy that spread like veins along the back wall of the house. I didn't say this to anyone though. I still wanted to belong.

The other thing that happened was Joss and me. Who knows how long it would have taken, had I been the old me, back in Greenford. But moving into the second half of August, in the humid, stifling atmosphere of Vanes, it was easy.

Joss knocked on my door one night a few days after the broken bottle—I was starting to lose track of time. It felt like I'd been living there for years, sleeping in that tiny room on the edge of the woods overlooking the sea. When I opened it, he was twirling the wheels of a cassette between his bony fingers. "Oh, h-hi, Janey. Can I come in?"

His eyes were wide, but his voice was gentle. I knew he was nervous. Joss was many things, many bad things, but he was not a player. "Sure," I said. I ignored the fact I was in my nightie. Or, at least, I didn't ignore this fact, I just didn't care. I think that characterizes my feelings at that particular point in the holiday. I didn't care about much then. I just wanted to see what was going to happen.

The window was open, and an owl called from the woods below. There was no wind. I thought of the bees, teeming in their millions, in the darkness of the combs in the chapel.

I thought to myself: *there's a boy in my room, I've let him in*, and then the thought came again. *Who cares? Just see what happens, for once.*

Joss came in and sat on the slim bed.

"Sorry about this evening," he said. "Mummy said I had to apologize about dinner."

There had been another argument, about Cambridge, or rather, a non-argument, because the Hunters never really put it all out on the table. It was all coded. But Charles had been horrible to Kitty. He really seemed to enjoy it, to want to bait her. And she had been horrible to Merry, and doors had been slammed, and Sylvia had for once shouted, clamping her hands over her ears. "I can't stand this. I can't stand it."

"That's fine. We're all a bit nervous, results and everything."

"I know. But Kitty can be such a bitch sometimes." He bit his lip. "And my father—he gets really angry with her. He notices everything she does. Not me. It's never me."

I didn't think this was true. I thought his father was spectacularly uninterested in all his children, or rather interested only in finding fault, in exposing them as if they were conmen, coming to his table every night expecting to be fed and unaware they were about to be unmasked. I thought of Daddy, the attention he gave to everything I did or told him, and I felt sorry for them. Perhaps it was the first time I saw I had something they did not. I took a short, deep breath and blinked. "Parents. Yours aren't too bad. Not compared to mine, anyway." I meant it lightly, but it wasn't funny and, I realized, wasn't true. I felt shabby.

"They are. You don't know," he said, moodily. "You've been here a few weeks and you think you know everything."

"Hey," I said, mildly. "No I don't." I thought of the pamphlet by Pammy Hunter. It was still in my bedside table. I hadn't given it back to Merry. I'd reread it several times. I don't know why. "I'm just trying to be interested, that's all."

"Sorry." He turned to look at me. "You've—your hair's grown."

"I shaved it again, and that seems to have helped."

He ran his fingers over it, just as Kitty had done. I felt a shiver run over my scalp, as if wind was lapping it. I paused, processing the feeling, and realized something was wrong. Joss kept stroking my head. Eventually, I said: "Please don't."

I felt almost sick—at the knowledge that I liked the way he made me feel, but that was because it felt nice and not because I liked him. I suddenly and inexplicably found him curiously repellent, and now that the thought was there it would not go away. He was a fake, a phony, insubstantial, like clouds. He was not Kitty, vital and alluring and real, poor Joss. He just was not what I had built him up to be.

There was a short, potent silence, and I could have asked him to leave. But I didn't.

Instead I took the tape, and plugged it into my own Walkman. We listened, one earbud each. Bob Marley, the Undertones, Dire Straits, some snatches of Wagner—he took pride in being eclectic. This, all in silence, as he stroked me, his hands rubbing my back, over my thighs, my breasts. Eventually my neck grew stiff from leaning toward his, and I moved away. "Thanks," I said. "I really like it."

"Mm," he said, and this time he slid his hand between my thighs, pushing them slightly apart.

The thing that characterizes this whole operation is my indifference to it. I suppose in a way it made it bearable. I don't think he took advantage of me, or I him. What stands out is how *impersonal* it was.

Unexpectedly, and to his credit, he gave me an orgasm. A short, rather surprising one, but nonetheless I came. We were on the bed, his fingers frantically rubbing me, like a magician, or a bunny, his eyes alight, and I parted my legs a little, my head rolling back. I closed my eyes, and thought of his sister, and their parents, and Paul, and I felt it happen.

"Can I?" said Joss, eagerly, and I nodded.

"Oh. Course," I said, and we moved toward the pillows, and I lay back. He produced a condom, and I watched his penis, bobbing in front of me.

I'd read *Forever*, and every other week Claire and I pored over "Body & Soul," the advice page in *Mizz* magazine where Tricia Kreitman briskly told hapless teenage girls their periods were perfectly normal, that they hadn't had sex if they'd only done that, that they probably were pregnant, and that a cousin shouldn't do that to you at Christmas. Besides, my girls' school was instructive on this subject both in lessons and out of them, and once again I was grateful to Miss Minas. So I helped him put the condom on. I squeezed him when it was all on, and his eyes bulged, and he swallowed.

"Careful. Sorry. God. I'm sorry."

His erection wilted a little. I realized then that while I was an informed teenager, more aware of my rights and the fact that sex, the first time, was bound to be a disappointment than I was about many other things, Joss seemed mortified. He tucked his hair behind his ears, as if determining himself to do it, and leaned down toward me, kissing me hard and hitting my nose. The leather thong he wore round his neck swung into my eye.

"Ow," I said.

"Oh God," he said, and he bit his lip. "That's my shark's tooth." He fumbled to untie the thong from around his neck. "I—I got it off a guy in Camden Market. Brings me luck. It's like, a hundred years old. Sorry."

"Don't be sorry," I said, in a breathy voice, like I found being hit in the face with an old tooth, and him, irresistible. He was attractive, I still thought so, even if I saw too that I didn't like him much anymore. After all, he was a boy, with a nice body, and I liked the feeling of him kissing me, of our skin together, the newness, the secrecy, the excitement of it. I found that I liked it all—if I forgot it was Joss. Poor Joss.

"I like it," I whispered. "It's OK."

I pulled his head down toward my breasts, and felt his rubber-covered organ edge up my thigh, jabbing me. I pointed it in the right direction, and gradually, after a while, we got there. I loved this new, insouciant me, who layered new experiences on top of old, unbearable ones. And I knew what to do—besides *Mizz*, and the more advanced *More*, there was a terrifying book about sexual technique Claire's mother had under her bed, which Claire and I had once or twice managed to sneak out and stare at in horror.

And I enjoyed it, actually. I enjoyed the sensation of him pushing into me, and of being in control of it all. And I liked feeling grown-up. That I was on the edge of new discovery. And he enjoyed it. I thought of Paul again—his soft brown hair, shiny, his big tortoiseshell glasses, his kind smile.

When Joss came, he gave a low, shuddering roar. It was almost like an impression of an army major assembling his troops. It was so sudden, I heard myself give a little shout of laughter, which I quickly turned into a moan of approval. And then it was over.

"Hey," he said, stroking my head with one clammy hand. I wanted him to go. It was too hot, in that stifling, airless room under the old eaves. "You're pretty, you know that, don't you? Even without hair."

"Th-thank you."

"And all that's good in dark and light, meet in her attic, and her eyes."

"Th-thanks."

"It's Byron," he explained. "He wrote it. 'To His Coy Mistress.'"

I didn't point out his mistake. What was the point? There was some movement from outside and I felt the slight suggestion of a cooler breeze waft in through the window, and the stirring of the sea. I sat up. "You don't have to stay," I said.

He looked a little surprised. "It's OK," he said, shortly. This wasn't the right thing to say, obviously. He lay against my chest, and his head squashed into my breasts, and it was uncomfortable. And I wanted to put my nightdress back on, and just get into bed and sleep.

We were silent for about five minutes. I only started to feel bad then to be honest, the feeling I had used him. And slowly the realization that I had made a mistake, somehow, played a bad hand.

"I'll let you get some sleep." He gave me an awkward, hideous kiss where we both pursed our lips. "Thank you."

"Thank you," I said. "That was my first time."

"Mummy said it would be," he said, pulling on his shorts then shrugging himself back into one of his floral shirts. "I mean it," he said. "Really, thank you."

"Sylvia?" I said, stupidly.

"You don't think that's weird, do you? It sounds odd. But we were talking about it."

Perhaps it was normal for boys to discuss taking the virginity of an old family friend's daughter first with their mother. It didn't seem particularly normal to me. But the more time I spent with them the more I couldn't see whether or not *I* was the one with the problem.

I wanted to appease him now, not show that I was offended, so I said: "No, course not," and waved my hand, almost airily.

Then he was gone, and I was left alone in the dark room, staring out of the window at the dark night, a feeling of nausea growing inside me.

The following day I found myself alone with Sylvia, clearing the table outside after lunch. I think she probably engineered it, but I looked up and everyone else had vanished.

"How are you today?" Sylvia said. She was loading the old willow pattern plates onto the wicker tray, and she paused, brushing crumbs from her hands. The bell-sleeves of her floral lawn cotton shirt swung as she moved, to and fro.

I knew the real reason she was asking, and that she knew what had happened. In fact I felt sore, inside, and my thighs ached. But I couldn't face telling her I thought she should mind her own business. So instead I chose to misunderstand her.

"I'm fine. A bit nervous. I didn't sleep well last night. It's silly, when the exam results can't be changed. I know I've failed, so I don't know why I'm even nervous."

"You don't know that."

"Sylvia, I wrote *Tuesday* as one of the answers in my English exam. Just *Tuesday*."

"Of course. Rory, get *away*. There's no leftovers for you. God, this heat." She looked down at Rory, hanging around hopefully at her feet, and pushed him with one leg. I kneeled down, ruffling his soft ears, feeling his wet tongue on my knee.

Then I picked up the water jug, and a stack of glasses, and put them on the tray.

"Janey, do you still want to go to university?"

"More than anything."

"Yes, yes." She said it impatiently, like she knew the answer. "And have you really tried to talk to your mother about it?"

"Of course."

"Your father wanted you to go." Her face was watchful, secretive.

I thought she was having a go at me for not trying in the exams. I said: "I couldn't get my brain to work. I didn't care. It's so stupid of me. There's no money, anyway. I have to get a job. My mother says she can't support me."

"She's selling the house, isn't she?" I can remember her watching me, her small, set face unreadable.

"Yep. Daddy had all the debts. And she and Martin need the money. He's got kids too."

I was constantly hearing about Jeanette and Adam. Jeanette

was training to be a dentist and Adam wanted to be an artist, a job which apparently necessitated him being bailed out by his father several times a year. According to my mother, they were virtually perfect in every respect.

"You're entitled to a share of the house, Janey," Sylvia said. She glanced around. "You know that, don't you? Your father—oh, but perhaps you don't want to discuss it. But you are."

"It's fine," I said, and held up my hand. A bee buzzed, really loudly, right at my ear, and I jumped, and she laughed.

"They are annoying, aren't they? Come, bring those in." She pushed Rory again, harder this time. "Oh damn you, Rory boy. No." She was cross suddenly, her voice vicious. "Stop begging. Always bloody begging." The force of her leg surprised him. "Shoo! Go on! Go and find Charles."

With a yelp, he trotted slowly down the steps and across the lawn. "Is the gate out to the chapel closed? Yes? Oh, Janey, please don't stack the glasses like that next time. They're crystal, and they'll crack."

"I'm—I'm so sorry."

"Don't worry. It took me a long time to understand all this." She smiled, brushing her black bob out of her face with one arm, rubbing the lavender between her fingers.

We went inside, to the cool of the kitchen. I carried the plates over to the sink. Some of them were cracked, with chips at the edges, I noticed now. Sylvia pulled gloves on, and started running the tap.

"They vanish when it's time to tidy up, you know? But that means they don't know what I get up to half the time, do they?" She squirted rather too much washing-up liquid in, with a large looping movement. "Now, let me get started, shall I, and then I'll go and check on Rory. Poor old boy, he's suddenly rather old, but I should have more patience. It's my greatest failing."

"I think you're very patient," I said, softly.

"It's not patience when you're not there anyway," she said. "If you've taken yourself somewhere else."

I watched as a shelf of bubbles rose up over the bowl, sliding down the side. "Daddy always said patience was all very well as long as you don't have to be patient for too long."

She turned to me with a smile. "In that, as in all things, your father was right."

"How—can I ask you something?" I began, trying to keep the quaver out of my voice. But it was time. Every other occasion when I'd been on the verge of asking, something had happened, or Sylvia had vanished on some pretext. I had to ask her. "How did you know him?"

She looked down, closed her eyes, then opened them, and stared up at me.

"Your father saved my life, darling," she said. "Didn't you know?"

"Where from?"

"I was almost killed in a—an accident. He was there, he leaped in. Sometimes I wonder, though…" She broke off. "I wonder what would have happened if things had been different that day. And, Janey, I don't know the answer."

"I—" I rubbed one leg with my shoe, awkward, like a stork. "I'm sorry. He never talked about it. About lots of things."

Sylvia fiddled with the buttons on her shirt, then put her small hand to the hollow below her throat. "No. No one really did, afterward."

The foam in the bowl hissed, and hummed, as it began to sink down into the water. She was still.

"I knew your father as a child. He and Mummy were very close. My poor mother." She stopped and I nodded, encouragingly. "I'd have been all alone in the world were it not for Simon. He looked after me. He encouraged me to go to art college—oh, to do all the things Mummy would have wanted me to do. He was my legal guardian for a while, that's why I use his surname, as a memento, a thank you to him, and that's why I wanted Kitty to have his name as her middle name. So there'd be a connection." Her eyes were alight—she was smiling, her lovely face lit up, as was so often the way when people talked about my father. "He honestly—you know he had a way about him, and I noticed it when you came to stay before, because he did it with you—he brought out the best in me. He listened to me. Even if I wasn't saying anything. Isn't that right?"

I nodded, and tears started in my eyes, but it was OK. It was so good to talk about him with someone who understood. "That's what I miss most about him."

"Oh yes, darling." She rubbed her temples. "Oh yes. And I was quite small when I met him, only twelve, and he made me feel like an important person. Like I mattered. My father didn't ever do that, and Mummy had so many problems she couldn't. Simon always did. After Mummy died, you know, he sorted me out. It wasn't just art college." She swallowed. "Oh God, Janey. He even bought me my shoes. Imagine that, my shoes. All the wrong size, and all of that, but he was trying to help, to do it right." Sylvia looked quite different, like someone else entirely. Her eyes were dark crescents, glinting with memory.

"Oh, me too," I said. "You know, when Mum left and he had to take everything on—" I stopped. "I'm sorry, it's not the same."

"It's very similar, Janey. How strange, I never thought of it before. He had a practice run looking after me."

"I didn't realize." We looked at each other, smiling.

"Come here," she said, and she took me into her arms, pulling me toward her. She smelled of lavender. She was very thin. "Oh Janey, I'm so sorry." Her ridged nails pressed into my shoulders, and I could feel her warmth, flowing into my tired body. We were still, and then she stepped back. I said:

"When Mum left. He had to do all of that. Periods, and everything. And he did it really well," I said, realizing this was true, and that I hadn't ever felt how strange it was. "He hired a student to be there when I got back from school to cook me dinner, and he was always back by six. I'd have done my homework, and then we'd just chat. I'd help him clear away and then we'd go for a walk, or discuss the news, or watch TV. He never made it seem hard, or stressful. He'd just got on with it."

It hit me again in the throat, that I would never see him again. That I still could not understand why, how, what had happened to him to make him feel he had to kill himself. To leave me.

I let my head hang, my chin resting on my chest. I couldn't speak, or even look at her. The full tide of grief, the waves that receded and then crashed over me at the strangest times, hit me, and this time it was so powerful it was an almost physical reaction. I could not reach for breath. The bee buzzed around me again; I brushed it angrily away, too forcefully.

"Oh Janey," Sylvia whispered, very very quietly, and I knew she knew what I was thinking.

Her face was so close to mine. "My darling, beloved girl. You *were* so beloved to him, you understand that, don't you?" I was swaying, worried I might faint. She caught my hands. "You know— it wasn't you. It was that he couldn't live anymore. I understand. Do you—you do understand? Please say you do."

"No," I shook my head. "Not really."

I could hear the others, outside, someone shouting at someone else. It recalled me to myself, to where we were.

"Listen." She waved a washing-up brush at me. "You damn well listen, Janey. Simon Lestrange saved me. He saved countless people's lives out in Italy, did you know that? And my God, he wasn't like some people." And she actually spat on the floor. A wobbly gray-white blob, like a jellyfish, landed between us. "He saw such terrible things, in the war. He couldn't get over them. But he left a sort of legacy, of doing good, of spreading love. And he loved you so very much."

"You must have missed him, if he brought you up and then you married someone, weren't you quite young?" I said, awkwardly trying to veer away from the subject.

"Oh. Well, sort of." She turned away. "He introduced me to Charles, actually."

My face ached; I was so surprised I must have showed it as she nodded.

"Yes, he knew him in the war. Yes. So—well, I married Charles, and moved away. I didn't see your father for years." The basin was full, water splashing loudly, and her voice was sinking with every word, I realized, slowly, subtly decreasing in volume so no one but us could hear. "He tried his best to make sure, but—" She stopped.

Now was the moment. "Sylvia."

"Yes?"

I plunged in. "He left me a note, when he died. It was about you."

She turned the tap off, and put her wet hand on mine. The kitchen was silent, and all I could hear outside was Rory whimpering, more loudly now. Someone was still shouting.

"Ah," she said, with a soft hiss. "Do you have it?"

I nodded.

"What did it say, my dear?"

She took both my hands in hers, clutching them tight. I cast my eyes downward, darting them from side to side. "It said: *Rescue Sylvia.*"

"Yes," she said, softly. "Yes, my dear. But how? Yes." She stuck her little chin out, like a determined child. "Oh, Janey. It's too late for me. Darling Simon." She made a clicking sound, like a key turning in a lock. "He didn't believe it was possible. That was the problem."

The whimpering from outside was louder, more a kind of screaming. As thudding footsteps approached the house, I realized. Something had happened.

"Why?"

"Help! Oh Jesus, help!"

She and I were locked together, her hand on my wrist, her velvet eyes boring into mine.

"Mummy! Rory! They've—oh Jesus, they've got him!"

"They've—what?" And Sylvia broke away from me, water splashing everywhere, and ran to the door.

The midday sun was blinding. Sylvia was running, across the lawn, followed by Merry. Someone was screaming—I saw in the gateway by the entrance to the chapel that it was Kitty, and as I emerged, outside the boundary of the house, I saw why.

Rory was leaping up and down, with more energy than I had ever seen, and for a split second it didn't make sense, and then I saw them.

He had obviously wandered out of the house and into the ruins. Later, we noticed the ancient candlestick, left by me and Merry on the chapel floor, propping open the door. Poor blind Rory must have stumbled into it, knocked it over, and this had disturbed them—maybe they were trying to break away again. They were stinging him, over and over again, covering his patchy, balding body, the sound of their raging hum, rising and falling, but all the time unbelievably loud, and with it his whimpering, agonized, harsh screams. It was the worst sound I have ever heard.

"No!" Merry screamed, darting forward, but Kitty held her back, throwing her arms around her.

"Don't be stupid, they'll get you," she said, calmly, her face white, golden hair falling over her shoulders. "Stay there."

"You too," Sylvia called. "Kitty, you mustn't go near them. *Rory—*" She covered her face in her hands and ran toward him and the swarm, kicking out blindly with her feet just as she had done to Rory only a few short minutes ago. It made no difference. Suddenly Rory stopped jumping, the rasping keening scream ceased and he sank to the ground, and was still.

Merry was sobbing. Sylvia retreated, brushing them away, her eyes peeking over her fingers which were clamped to her mouth, knuckles white, as if the effort of stopping sound coming from her mouth was almost too much for her.

At first I couldn't quite process what I'd seen, that it had happened. And when I looked again, they had swept off, moving surprisingly slowly, a black specter drifting toward the edge of the woods.

"Aunty Ros said it'd happen, if we left it too long to collect, and Mrs. Red," said Kitty. She put her arm round her sister. "It's OK, Merry. Darling, it's OK. He was old. It's done now. It's OK."

I knew she didn't believe it.

"He—wasn't—wasn't that old," Merry sobbed. Kitty kissed her hair, tenderly, looking up at the sky with huge fearful eyes.

Sylvia was quite still. I heard Joss and Charles, thundering toward us. The wind, out toward the sea, was picking up. It ruffled Rory's dear, matted, patchy fur. I saw him move, just a twitch of the nose, and realized that was the moment he actually died.

"What the hell—oh Jesus," said Charles, and then he stopped. "Dear Jesus." He flinched, turning his head away.

They stood there, the five of them, and no one went toward Rory, as if they were afraid to touch him.

"Did they all go?"

"No." Kitty answered him. "It wasn't all of them. I'd say it was about a third."

"Good." He held his arm up, shielding his eyes from the sight of it. "We'll have to bury him," Charles said, after a moment's pause. "The pheromones are dangerous. The stings are all over him. It might attract them back, or a rival swarm, or the hornets and wasps. Get him in the ground while he's still warm."

"Dad, how can you?" Merry sobbed. Kitty squeezed her tightly.

"If we leave him here overnight something else will come along and tear him to bits," said her father. "I'll go and get the shovel. Damn them. What on earth is it with them, this year?"

"I'll get his basket blanket," said Kitty. "We can wrap him up in it." Sylvia, as if roused from a stupor, nodded.

"Do, my darling girl. Do. Please be careful, Kitty. They may come back this way."

Thudding footsteps sounded around the side of the house; Kitty groaned. "For God's sake," she hissed. "Not now. *Not bloody now.*"

It was Rosalind, of course, I knew that before I saw her. The glazed expression, the furious set of her mouth both at such variance with each other. She was marching even more crazily than usual, toward us this time, arms swinging wildly about.

"I'll give you one, O,
One come for the comb, O!"

"I can't listen to this," Joss said, quietly. "I'll go and get the shovel. Jesus, Mummy, this is—it's too much. It's all too much."

Rosalind had stopped, and was staring at Sylvia. She bared her mouth in a wide smile; I saw then most of her teeth were brown, rotten or missing. "Did they get something?"

"They killed Rory," Sylvia said, shortly.

*"Two, two, the beloved girls, clothed all in green, O—*What a shame. I'm sorry. Still, he was very old. *One is one and all alone and evermore shall be so!"*

I saw Sylvia turn away, loathing on her face.

"Do you remember when they killed Sybilla? Charles, do you remember?"

"Course I do."

"Who?" I said.

There was a silence, as Ros looked up, and around, utterly blank.

Sylvia said: "Charles's little sister. Pammy, she was called. She was the Outsider one year and it all went wrong. Ros tried to save her, didn't you?"

Ros nodded, her eyes bulging. I put my hands in my pockets, looking at them all. I felt scared, for the first time, of them all, of the house, of how...*wrong* I'd got it. I looked at Sylvia, my salvation, but she was looking at her husband, chewing the inside of her mouth, her fingers working at a head of lavender, the buds falling to the ground.

"Charles—Charles, darling? We can go now."

"Good *God*," said Charles, his voice strained and thin. "No, Sylvia. Not now. What the hell is wrong with you?"

"Oh." Sylvia shrank back. "Of course." She muttered something to herself, I saw her staring at the ground. "You're right."

Kitty had appeared with Rory's blanket. She handed it to her mother, who stood clutching it tight, like it was a child.

"Thank you, my darling."

I couldn't stay there, looking at Rory's heavy, still form while Joss and Charles clinically discussed the best way to bury him. I followed Kitty back into the garden, grateful to be away from there. I was shaking.

She was walking fast; the fluttering of her long red-and-gold skirt sounded like water slapping on rocks. I caught up with her.

"I'm sorry about your dog," I said.

"You should have listened to me, Janey," she said, quietly, as we reached the terrace steps. "Get away now. Just leave. Can't you see?"

"Oh, go away," I said, infuriated, because she was right, but I wanted to be here, a part of me told myself. I had earned it. "This isn't the time, Kitty—I know you're angry but—"

"Angry!" She turned and I could see a vein throbbing at her temple, her flushed cheeks, the fury in her eyes. "I'm not angry."

"I didn't know about Pammy—about your father's little sister. I didn't know she died like that."

"She didn't want to take part. She told them she wouldn't be one of the Beloved Girls. Said the whole thing was nonsense. Said she was leaving the first moment she was old enough to go. That she knew Diver was a crook. Did they tell you that? My father did once, when he was drunk, and knocked on my door, at midnight, Janey. Before my mother hauled him away. I kept him talking, Janey, that's when he told me. They made Pammy be the Outsider instead, and when the bees started attacking they locked themselves in, they left her outside, and they heard her being stung to death. Did you know that? No? That was fifty years ago, and nothing's changed." Her golden hair shook around her face; her nostrils were flared, a vein pulsing in her throat. "I think about her all the time. No one remembers her. She'll just be forgotten. I saw the booklet, in your room. Don't ever lose it, will you?" I shook my head, then I nodded, not sure how best to demonstrate I would not let her down. "I told you before. They've only invited you down here to make you come with me. You know why I hate the bees so much? I'm allergic to them, and they don't care. They care that we can walk in procession together, because we look similar. Haven't you noticed?"

There were identical twins at my school. The first was very beautiful, but something had not blossomed in the same way with the second twin, and she was just—in the cast of her face, the shape of her nose, the look in her eyes—quite plain. Yet they were almost exactly the same. Some curious alchemy. Kitty and I were not twins, and she was beautiful and I was not, but our faces were the same shape, something about our eyes and our noses. I'd noticed it before.

I didn't answer. Instead I said: "That's awful, Kitty. What happens if you're stung?"

She shrugged. "I ended up in hospital the first time."

"That's not right—" I began, and looked up to see her smiling.

"Of course it isn't. But it doesn't fit. So it can't be true. PF needs me to be part of the whole show. He's hopelessly in debt. He hasn't sold any antiques for ages and he hates Mummy earning the money. He hates Mummy!" She was laughing, hysterically. "Giles's father is super nouveau. He wants to buy into what we've got. Keeps offering for the house, or bits of furniture PF's trying to sell but the price is always a joke. He knows PF is desperate. So PF pimped me out to Giles to put them off. They like the idea they can buy a slice of the Hunters, the old traditions. But it'll only keep them at bay for so long."

"But…Giles is your boyfriend."

"He's not. I hate him. He's—" And she shivered, and was pale. "I hate him. I hate them all. But I can't do anything about it, unless I escape. I'm in this beautiful home with this beautiful life and I'm trapped. You are too now. I'm so sorry, Janey."

"I thought you wanted me out."

Her voice softened. "I wanted you to get out because I love you. I always did, remember? When you came to stay and I thought you were the best thing ever. Did you think of that? I wanted you to be safe, and I thought if I was horrible enough you might go back home, and you'd be safe there."

I felt dizzy, as if darkness was clouding in on my peripheral vision. "But your mum wouldn't—"

"Mummy's lost it. Your dad killing himself, I think something collapsed, some pole in her mind holding everything up."

She pulled me to her. Her hair whipped around her face, strands of it wrapping themselves across her features, like spun-gold cobwebs. She kissed me, grabbing my shoulders, the pads of her fingers digging against my bones as her tongue dug into me, and our lips pressed together. She raised her hands to my patchy, itchy scalp, moving over it with tenderness as her tongue moved in my mouth, probing, tasting. She was like salt water. I have never, ever forgotten that kiss, or the way she touched me—wholly with comfort, with love. With Joss, it was like possession.

"She always wanted us to meet. We've got the same names, the same secrets. Catherine Lestrange Hunter. Jane Catherine Lestrange. She wanted to bind me to him. So that you and I were connected, even if she wasn't. Do you remember what she gave you, when you came to stay?"

"Of course I do." I hesitated, because I was never sure if the others knew she had given him to me. "Her teddy bear. Wellington."

"Wellington Bear. You still have him, don't you?"

"Yes." He was in my room, my most treasured possession.

"Do you know how she got Wellington Bear? Did your dad ever tell you what happened?"

I shook my head. "He never really talked about her. Apart from once or twice."

"I know some of it. But there's more I don't understand. How she ended up here. And I've got to work it out. I'm close." She looked away, muttering under her breath, and then reached down to the ground. "I gave you a bee the last time you were here, do you remember?" And delicately, she picked up a dead bee, and put it in my open hand.

"Here. Hold it. She won't sting. Trust me, I know."

Her slim fingers gripped my forearms, her hair flew around her head, the sun cast no shadow at all. I could barely see, it was so bright. I closed my eyes, clutching the dead, soft insect, feeling it scratch my palm. She whispered:

"I'll tell you all of it, once you say you're with me, not with Joss. You have to choose. Do you stand with me, or with him? Decide, Janey, open your eyes, then decide."

I opened my eyes instantly. I stared at her, and let the bee fall to the ground. We were utterly still. I knew that from then on everything had changed.

"You," I said. "Of course."

Part Three

1959

Chapter Nineteen

One late-spring morning, as snowy-pink petals rained down upon the pavements of Chelsea, a man walked down a quiet side street of red-bricked town houses just off the King's Road. He was singing, partly to maintain an air of normalcy, but mainly to buck himself up, to stop himself from losing the thread of life, because he did not feel like singing. He did not feel like living. This happened often, and the way he had found to combat it was to do something that required continuation: a tiny action to stop the greater desire—one bullet in the head with his old army revolver—from overwhelming him. He knew how to do it. He was fairly sure that, at some point and one way or another, he would do it.

He was Captain Simon Lestrange, and he had been dismissed from his job as a glove salesman at Peter Jones in Sloane Square that morning, for being intoxicated while at work. It was true that he had partaken of drink the night before with an old army acquaintance and had not shaved as assiduously as he should have, but he was not still drunk—it was bad blood between him and the Gentlemen's Outfitters, Mr. Timms, a pokey, mean-spirited old humbug, in Simon's opinion.

Simon's drinking companion had been known by his fellow soldiers, out in Naples at the end of the war, as the "Galloping Major." He had been so christened by one of the many privates who disliked him and his autocratic air, because of his rather ludicrous "what-what" style, and because he bored on at length about himself. He was young, very thin and reedy, and fancied himself a terrific ladies' man, famed for chatting up every woman he met out there—old or young, usually young.

The Galloping Major had not been heard of for some time after the war, and regimental drinks without him had been enjoyable affairs, inasmuch as you could enjoy reminiscing about your time out there. But he had reappeared a few months ago, one of the growing band of antiques dealers who frequented Portobello Market and the King's Road, haunting the old ladies mummified in their crumbling stucco Belgravia mansions, whisking away their fine Sèvres vases and English Delftware pots. "I told her I'd give her a quid for the thing and that was doing her a favor and she believed me, poor dear!" With the passage of time—fourteen years since the end of the war now—the Galloping Major seemed convinced he and Simon had been friends. He'd get hold of Simon by telephone, and ask if he wanted to "meet for a pint." He rarely paid, but he was someone to drink with, and he'd been in Naples, so theoretically they both understood what the other had seen.

"Old officers must stick together, eh, old boy?"

He had lost his slender frame but had the same conspicuously outmoded attitude to everything. He claimed to find Chelsea risible. "Full of mods and beatniks and ponces, what what?"

Simon kept hearing that "what what?" today. Their old army comrade Hobbs, the pub landlord, had retreated to the back parlor when they'd appeared. He remembered the Galloping Major of old. "Didn't like the fellow in Italy, don't like him now," he'd told Simon, bluntly. "Sorry, Captain Lestrange."

He did not know where he was going—he could not go home to his lodgings, because Mrs. Weston did not like boarders returning during working hours while she was cleaning and—he was certain—entertaining callers in her grubby terraced two-bed in Hornsey. And, anyway, Simon preferred Chelsea.

Thinking of the Galloping Major again made him recollect there was a nice pub somewhere near here, the Phene Arms, where he and some other old regimental friends had met once or twice. He'd head that way and drown his sorrows with some of the month's wages he had in his pocket, and then work out what to do. He thought he might actually end it all tonight: he had this morning specifically located his trusty army service revolver, purloined during the chaos of their exit from Naples. But it would leave a mess for Mrs. Weston. He couldn't do that to her. She was a nice woman even if she did steal from him. Somewhere else, then.

Seeing the Galloping Major had been a mistake. It brought the war back, and the Galloping Major never wanted to talk about those days, preferring instead to sit sideways on at the table, the better to chat up young girls, cadge cigarettes and complain. He was younger than Simon, only twenty-two when he'd been posted to Italy. Simon tried, charitably, to attribute some of his behavior back then to his youth.

They had been in Naples at the liberation in 1943 and had stayed for a year, helping to rebuild a flattened city: hundreds of thousands dead or injured, an occupying force driven out, a country having to shift allegiance and reimagine itself in an unrecognizable world. In the midst of all of it, Simon had witnessed the explosion of Vesuvius. That was what people still asked about. They'd heard enough about what had happened in Italy in the war not to want to ask more. "You saw Vesuvius go up, didn't you? What a show that must have been, eh?"

He had seen people killed by the sliding hot black lava that spread down the hillsides faster than oil, young boys racing each other against the lava, getting trapped, burning to death in front of him. That had been bad enough, but Simon wanted to tell them other things. Things no one ever mentioned, that were never discussed, not by his old comrades, things he couldn't get over. He'd tried to bring it up with the Galloping Major the night before, with no luck. The lines of women, skirts raised aloft, sitting inside the hall beside the bombed-out harbor, their children gathered outside as the women waited for the soldiers, who would come inside them, then hand over their rations. The animals, cats, dogs, dead and dying, everywhere on the streets, people making bonfires to cook them. The mothers, half naked in rubble, breastfeeding squalling children, siblings climbing around in the dirt dressed in tablecloths, curtains, rags torn from anywhere and tied around them. Baroque palaces, torn in two, churches with no steeples, houses smashed to rubble, old people, curled up on the streets, waiting to die. They were ignored—no one had time for the old, not when the young were dying of starvation. The blind, emaciated children holding hands in a row, bursting into the army cafés, crying, screaming, begging for help, hands held out for food.

Oh, he had seen such terrible things. And there was the smell—of rotten, dead and dying humans and animals. There were days when the horror of it draped itself over him, and there was no one to tell him that, yes, it was wrong, that he had been brave, that he had tried his best, that this was the worst of the world and now it was over, that this was very rare, that he had been very unlucky to witness it.

The more you pushed it away, the more it came back when you did not want. He knew men who'd been there and who, afterward, had killed themselves but he and the others never mentioned them. It wasn't done. And then there were some chaps like the Galloping Major, for whom the horror barely seemed to register, for whom it was abroad, could come back to England, return to the old family home in the country and simply file it away.

There was a little boy, who he couldn't stop thinking about today, who had cried, clinging to his leg, begging him for food. His body was covered in lice bites, his feet wrapped in rags. He wore a dress, someone's dress, as a tunic, torn at the knees.

"It's the Eyeties," his commanding officer, Brigadier Jupes, had said. "Hysterical. On the make. He's got a mama somewhere pushing him out onto you. Forget about it."

But he couldn't forget, how could he? When it was particularly bad he felt he couldn't breathe deeply enough. It would make him dizzy, give him a swooping feeling in his stomach, which was usually empty anyway.

Simon suddenly had to stop, leaning against a railing, looking up at the sky, flecked as it was by the branches of a cherry blossom tree.

London was beautiful, now, more beautiful than he had known it for years, and spring showed it at its best. The air was sweeter, too, away from the traffic, the coal smoke and smog of the river. *Come on now*, he told himself. *Come on and pick yourself up. One foot, keep on walking, then another foot, and all shall be well, and all shall be well.*

It was particularly bad today. Simon told himself firmly that he mustn't meet up with the Galloping Major again. He breathed in, closing his eyes. *Three, three, the rivals...* That song. Why did he keep singing that dratted song? The damned man, he whistled it all the time.

It was a miracle, actually, how it happened, but it did. He heard a voice, nearby—he really did, he knew it right away, it wasn't like other voices he heard. Someone was singing, another song, a lullaby, and it was sweeter, clearer than the other voice. He carried on walking, one foot in front of the other, toward the noise.

At the end of the road was the Royal Hospital, flanked by two mansion blocks, and just before them, on his left, was a little cottage, a building transplanted from an English country village into the heart of town. It was creamy white, with small leaded windows. There was a delightful garden in front, strewn with late daffodils, bright purple and blue anemones, budding jasmine clambering up a wall, and in this little garden, quite incongruous, sat a girl, on the lawn, raking her thin fingers over the stomach of an enormous marmalade-and-gold cat. She was singing as she stroked him—"A Nightingale Sang in Berkeley Square"—then she looked up at him and smiled.

"I'm sorry," she said. "Was I singing very loudly?"

For the rest of his life Simon would remember this moment of discovery—the oasis of it, the cottage, set back from the road, and this girl—not quite a young woman, he saw that now—with her laughing face, her dark eyes, slim hands, the way she caressed the cat, who was like a small tiger really, clambering all over her, making noises for her attention. She was fixed in his mind now, and whenever he was unable to concentrate on anything else, sometimes it helped to call her to mind. Sometimes she could banish the thoughts.

She was dressed simply, in an embroidered coral flared skirt, a cream peasant blouse. A blue and turquoise patterned scarf was tied round her hair. She looked up at him, and gave him a big, generous smile, and held out her hand.

"My mother used to sing it to me," she said. "And I was trying to remember it again. How do you do? I'm Sylvia Raverat."

Simon Lestrange was not in the habit of sitting on the wall of strange front gardens chatting to young girls, but he found himself doing just that, as the cat—whose name was Morris—crawled over her lap and on the grass. At one point he reached up one casual elongated paw and leisurely scratched Sylvia's face, but Sylvia only said: "No, darling. Not nice," and carried on talking, as a red welt appeared on her cheek.

There was a cloth spread on the lawn, along with the remains of a tea party, at which several guests remained: two teddy bears—both huge, with large silk bows around their necks—a giraffe, in green, and a glassy-eyed doll in a broderie anglaise frock. All of these were upended and lying on the lawn. A miniature tea service, exquisite pink and cream, was scattered across the garden, crumbs and tea everywhere. Beside the cloth, a sketchbook and pencils, laid across the pad. He always remembered that detail. How neat they were, perfectly sharpened.

Sylvia did not seem to notice the mess. She was not self-conscious. There was a strangely adult quality about her, and Simon could not be sure of her age. She might be nine, or fifteen. She clasped Morris to her with pleasure, but otherwise left him to roam disconsolately about as they chatted. Where was Captain Lestrange from? Did he know this part of town? What kind of gloves? Where had he been stationed? Had he been into Soho, to one of the espresso bars? The busses into town, were they good? Did he use them?

"Haven't you been on a bus?" he said, astonished.

She laughed. "Not for the longest time. My mother used to take me. But I don't live with her anymore."

Simon felt stupid. "I...see. That's sad."

"There are far sadder things." But she didn't meet his eye. She clasped Morris again and kissed his thick marmalade fur, then raked her fingers through his ginger stomach. A neatly tailored woman passed them on the street, glancing into the pretty little garden. She ran her eyes over both of them.

"Hello, Mrs. Pinney," said Sylvia, eagerly.

"Hello, Sylvia," the woman said, gripping the pushchair she was holding even faster than before.

Simon saw the look in Sylvia's eyes as she turned to scoop tiny teacups onto the tray.

"Look, I'd best be going," he said, heaving himself up from the wall.

Her hand flew to the reddening scratch on her cheek. "Oh, stay, won't you? Just for a bit? There's a spider in the kitchen, and I'm terrified of it. I don't want to go back into the house." She grinned at him, and he saw the wide gap in her teeth, the shine of blue glinting in her black hair.

He was so often alone. He did not hesitate. "I'd love to," he said, and as Sylvia clapped her hands in pleasure he swung one leg over the low wall, carefully avoiding the flowerbeds, and stepped onto the lawn.

She handed him some tea from one of the tiny leftover cups. Simon rubbed his eyes, wondering if he had somehow stepped through the looking-glass.

"Thank you!" he said. He felt nervous, uneasy, all of a sudden— he had climbed over another man's fence into his garden and was sitting there as if he owned the place. But it was too late now.

He reached out a hand to stroke Morris—but the cat batted one paw at him, sinking its arched claws into the pads of his palm, like hooks, and gave a strange, yowling meow.

"Morris! Don't be awful." Sylvia sat down in front of Simon, unhooking each claw. "Sorry. He's my best friend. I love cats. I'd love a dog but that's not really done in London. One day. Don't you have any?" She took the tiny cup from him.

"No."

"Do you have any children?"

"I'm not married. No nieces or nephews, either." He smiled, as she poured a tiny amount of tea into the cup and handed it back to him. "Thank you. What about you?"

"I don't have children," she said, laughing. "I'm twelve."

"I knew that—not that, I mean I knew you didn't. I mean do you have brothers and sisters? Or cousins?"

"No, it's just me and my father. And Mummy has a sister. But she's on Daddy's side." She shrugged, and reticence forbade Simon from asking more.

"What do you do all day?"

"I go to school, silly. Over the river. But today I was off. I wasn't feeling very well."

She lowered her face and he saw she was blushing.

"I'm sorry to hear that. Are you all right now?"

"It's fine." Her face was bright red. "Just girls' things really."

He was mystified. "Girls' things?" Then he was silent, they were both silent, utterly mortified.

Morris distracted them by rolling over on the grass and stretching himself out. "Why did you call him Morris?" he said.

"I love William Morris. Well," she corrected herself. "I *did*. I'm mad about De Morgan now."

"Who?"

"A designer." She smiled. "He built a house just down there actually, on the river. Mummy's father knew him."

"Have you always lived here then?"

"Mummy's family always has. On Wellington Square. It's changing now. It used to be very quiet. Like a village with lots of artists and so forth. But it's different." She wrinkled her nose. "Daddy hates it. Mummy rather likes it. Me too."

"How?"

"Oh, Bazaar, and the Fantasie Café and the boarding houses, and all that. There's some fun to be had." She looked up at him with a heart-stopping smile. "I want to be a designer when I'm older, you know. I'm going to go to art college, and learn how to make prints. And do what I want. All the time."

Simon folded his arms. "Oh, really?"

She met his smile. "Really. Have you always lived here, too?"

"Since the war. I grew up in Sussex. And Egypt. And I was in Italy during the war."

"How wonderful, to have lived in so many places."

He found her enthusiasm infectious. "It was. It is. The attitudes. The ideas. No one's . . . stuck."

"Where are you now?"

"Now I'm in Hornsey."

"Horned-sea. I don't know that bit."

He smiled. "I'd imagine if you've always lived in Chelsea you wouldn't end up in Hornsey, though it's a perfectly nice place to live. But I'm not staying there."

"Aren't you? Where will you go?"

He took a deep breath. "I'm not sure. But I won't stay. I want to live by the sea one day. Kent, or, or—Sussex. The south coast." Images swam before his eyes—dying men, the smell of rotten bodies, rubbish, rubbish everywhere. He felt he shouldn't be here anymore. "Do you know it there?"

"We used to go on holiday to Bexhill."

"Ah, then. Somewhere near there would do me. A little cottage with a pebble beach. A boat, so I can catch fish. And I'd have a shop."

A smile split her solemn face. "How exciting. With a bell over the door. Selling what?"

It was like he was a child again, sitting on these small chairs, talking about what you wanted to do when you grew up. "Well... Gloves are my business. But I'd expand. Gloves, umbrellas, Burberrys, boots, you know the sort of thing. An emporium. I'd find a nice little high street in a seaside town. Retail is the thing, that's what one keeps hearing. Something to keep me going for a time."

He stopped, remembering she was twelve, but Sylvia was resting her chin on her knees, hands clasped around her legs. "It sounds lovely. Freedom. All those lovely years to do what you want, just stretching ahead of you."

But Simon now dreaded the concept of time as an endless horizon, rolling out ahead of him. "Oh, I don't know about that."

"I do. *The days are long, but the years are short.* My mother says that."

"Yes." Simon found himself staring at her, at her young face, unlined, at the blank expression in her eyes. "Yes, it's true, I suppose."

There was a silence, and something passed between them. "I hate the sea," she said, lightly. "I hated those holidays. Water, no buildings, just horizon. And dead-eyed fish on the beaches, bodies and shipwrecks just out of sight. I want to live in London. All my life. I never want to leave."

He realized she had asked him all about himself, and he had asked nothing more about her. He was terrible at gleaning information; too British. He opened his mouth, but a telephone rang from inside the house, and instantly her expression changed.

"I'm afraid you have to go," Sylvia said, flapping at him with her hands. She tugged frantically at the silk scarf around her head. Morris, sensing the change of mood, shot up onto the high brick wall at the side of the house, and then disappeared. "Daddy said he'd call at four p.m. And he always knows if someone's here. I'm sorry." She was moving toward the open French window. "He doesn't like me to leave him waiting. Goodbye. Please come back? Please?"

She was gone in an instant, shutting the door behind her. Simon climbed over the low front wall back onto the pavement, wondering if it had all been a dream.

It was another two weeks before he saw her again. He'd thought of her every day since, but he always thought it odd when people used to say that as a marker of devotion. How many thoughts did one have in a day? Thousands, sometimes millions: far too many, anyway. It was natural he'd think of her, and that monstrously vast cat, the tea set and neat pencils, in that secret garden in the heart of Chelsea. The mysterious father ringing up. He wondered about her, about her mother. She needed someone to look out for her—could he help her? No, of course not. Couldn't face it. Any of it! Intimacy, affection, bonds, love. Better to keep on walking.

There was one day in early May when he had been turned down for a position at a glove shop on Jermyn Street, and another in Knightsbridge, Beauchamp Place. It was not the rejection he minded, it was the way they did it. "No, sir, I am afraid the position is no longer vacant," the manager in the second place had explained, flipping the "closed" sign to "open" with one practiced flick of his own white-gloved finger.

"But the notice is still up in the window."

"I have not yet had a chance to take it down. Good day to you."

"I'll watch then, while you do," Simon had said, madly.

The man had flared his nostrils, glaring at Simon. "I must ask you to leave, or I shall call the police."

"Call the fuzz then," said Simon. "I'll wait. Just do the decent thing and tell me the truth. I'm not—Oh, hang it all. Good day," and he'd crammed his hat onto his head, sunk his fists into his capacious, grubby Burberry, and slunk down the street, toward the pub.

But the Phene Arms—where he had taken to visiting since that day, as it made use of the hours to walk there and back—was dark, the door barred. "Bereavement. Closed until further notice," the sign in the window said.

Simon stood still, not quite able to take this news in. The Phene was warm and welcoming, and there was always someone drunker there than he—an old geezer, or an artist, slumped at the bar, snoring loudly, and no one seemed to care. Little disappointments were unbearable to him at the moment. They suffused everything, seeming to be confirmation of the worst thoughts he had.

He walked on up the road, away from the river, and in a few minutes was on the King's Road.

His shoes were still damp from the rain and rubbed tightly; he was glad to sit down at the bar of the Chelsea Potter, take off his coat. He ordered a whisky and looked around; the place had just opened for the evening and was still quiet. Spring sunlight shone weakly in through the large windows. An old woman, head wrapped tightly in a scarf, peered in through the glass, her milky-blue eyes pointing in different directions, her wet mouth unresponsively slack; Simon jumped, and reared back, and she shuffled from side to side, but did not move. He drank the whisky as though he were thirsty, watching her. She swayed slightly.

"She's blind," a voice beside him said. "She'll be off in a minute. Don't worry about her."

He turned to see a woman sitting at the bar next to him. She raised her glass to him. She was elegant, in a way he couldn't quite decode. Her clothes were plain: a little black velvet jacket and a gray wool skirt, but they were well-cut, perfectly so; Simon knew these things, just as he knew the skill it took to cut a piece of kid leather with shears. Around her neck was a jauntily tied black-and-white scarf. "She has a silver-topped walking stick," she told him. "And a niece waiting at home for her in Belgrave Square. Rich as Croesus. She just likes a stroll every afternoon."

She had thick black hair laced with white, in a crop; she tossed it defiantly, and smiled at him. A cameo brooch hung listlessly on the jacket, and little diamonds in her ears. She was not, he thought, more than forty. She offered him a cigarette from an engraved tin, flicking it open with the same certainty the proprietor of Loudon and Sons had turned the sign over, rejecting him.

"Oh," said Simon, accepting it gratefully. She lit it with a flourish, then one for herself. There was something reckless about the way she moved. "Thank you very much. She startled me, that's all."

"Have another drink," she said, eyeing him up. "Keep me company."

"Well," said Simon. "Perhaps I will."

He had never been one for picking up strange women, though he'd done it before, just not enjoyed it. It wasn't for him. But there was something about this woman, her directness for one, that was entirely refreshing. "Another whisky?" he said. "I'm Simon. Simon Lestrange."

"Gin and vermouth," she said, sliding the glass toward him. "I'm Hester, by the way."

"Hello, Hester Bytheway," he said, stupidly, and she laughed, and he realized and he laughed too, for the first time in weeks, the whisky flooding him with bonhomie. Who cared about losing one's job, about the desperateness of life, about the things he saw at night when he closed his eyes, when there was this moment here, a woman laughing with him, a warm pub—he waved to the landlord, morosely polishing glasses by the bar hatch, for a refill.

"Do you live around here?" he asked.

"Yes. I live *and* work here. Wellington Square." She jerked her head northwards. "You?"

"Oh. Hornsey. North London."

Her generous mouth pouted; her heavy brows contracting into a frown. "I've never heard of Hornsey." She pronounced it Horned Sea, just like Sylvia had done. "Sounds marvelous. Forgive my ignorance. Bloomsbury's about as far north as I go. Although I did visit a friend in Northumberland, before the war. Where is it?"

"Hornsey's north of Bloomsbury. Not as far as Northumberland, but getting there."

She shrugged. "Noted. And what do you do there, Mr. Lestrange?"

He told her about the gloves, and Peter Jones. He told her

about looking for a job, and how he liked walking around London. And drawing, and everything else. She had large, bony fingers, and she slid them up and down the shiny pole of the bar while he was talking; it was hypnotic. She was, he knew, not sober. He wondered how often she was in there.

"What about you," he said, eventually. "Am I allowed to ask what you do?"

"Oh, this and that. I didn't used to work before I was married. Now I have lodgers; the house is too big for just me. I cook and clean, and yell at them about gas. One of them changed the locks, I had to get the police in. So, there's a room going, if you need it. Seven and six a month." She fluffed her hair.

"Who are they, the lodgers?"

"Oh, they're not a bad bunch. Mr. Thaddeus, he's a bookkeeper, boils a lot of cabbage, and Dr. Lovibond is a young historian, takes himself very seriously, rather in love with me. Liz, Mrs. Krapolski, she's a widow. She was married to a Polish engineer but she's English in fact. She's a reader for a publishing house. It sounds like a rather nice job; I keep thinking I should do something like that. This...It's not much of a living, to be honest. But I have to work now, you see." She stubbed out her cigarette, finished her drink with that direct movement of hers, and signaled for another. "I have to keep the house."

All this varying information buzzed around Simon's brain. He said, tentatively: "Your husband—"

Her face contracted, her mouth became pinched. "Oh, God. Please let's not talk about him. Or that little bitch he's with. Please."

"I'm sorry." Simon retreated immediately, and rubbed one eye, trying to maintain his composure. He considered himself adept at knowing how much to ask. It was unusual to get it this wrong.

"Don't worry. Who has time for another sob story?" She gave him a smile that broke his heart; her large, mobile mouth stretching into a half-grimace. "My husband took our daughter, but left me with the house, and I'm stuck paying to keep it up and trying to clear out the bad tenants and get good ones, which is why I ask strange men in pubs for drinks, and all the while just down the road...he has Sylvia."

"Sylvia—" Simon swallowed. A man sat down on the other side

of her, and Hester turned almost angrily away from him, closer toward Simon.

"My daughter. She's twelve. I'm not allowed to see her. I'm a danger to her, you see."

"A—danger?" Simon's utter horror of sticking his nose in, the greatest offense, was fully awakened. He shifted on his stool.

"Apparently, my dear. That's Digby for you. He's a monster. Devil in a bowler hat."

Simon was embarrassed. "Oh. I—I am sorry." He tried to get the conversation onto a more established footing. "How long have you been married?"

"Thirteen years. I was eighteen, believe it or not."

"I don't believe it, no," he said, hoping gallantry would save him. He desperately wanted to be able to say the right thing. "You must have been young when you became a mother."

"I was nineteen. Mummy was eighteen when she had me. Daddy believes one should start early. Not in Digby's case. He was ancient when he married me. The first night…oh my God." She drained her glass, and placed it firmly, loudly, on the bar, and nodded for a refill. "Paunches and veins and dried skin everywhere. Disgusting. But—but, I was born to it." And she shrugged. "I was a deb. Debutante presented to the queen, you know. It's a breeders' market. Digby broke me in." She blinked, eyes fluttering shut for slightly too long. "But I wasn't the right ride for him, so he got tired of me, and now he's thrown me out to the knacker's yard. He's got his eye on a bishop's daughter, would you believe it. One day you'll hear I've been boiled down for glue." She took a sip of the new glass of gin and vermouth, looking at him over the cut glass, her thick black lashes trembling, and then she smiled. "Christ, that's an awfully long metaphor, isn't it? I don't even like bloody horses. That was another thing wrong with me. Darling Alice did." Her large comical mouth turned down, and she was lost in thought.

"Who's Alice?"

"Alice was my other sister. I have an older sister, too, but we never got on—she's on Digby's side. Anyway, Alice and Mummy died during the war. They were on their way home, just around the corner from here. After that, I didn't really care much what happened to me. So, when Digby came sniffing round, Daddy said yes and I agreed, even though I knew what he was like, why his first wife left him, how old he was…but, God, I made a mistake. He's the Devil. Like I say. But no one believes me. Or wants to believe me." She arched her back, stretching, looking carelessly around. "Don't you find, that's the trouble with pointing out any wrong? People don't want to believe the person who's pointing it out. They want to believe everything's fine. So they'd rather think it's the person, me in this case, making it up—" Hester stopped again, her gaze resting on the bottles behind the bar, then rattled the packet of cigarettes, but it was empty. She grimaced. "I don't have her. She's my daughter, and I don't have her, and she needs me…She had me every night, to brush her hair and read her stories. *Ballet Shoes* was her favorite, have you read it, Mr.—oh, I can't remember your name, dammit all. Have you?" Simon shook his head. "Pauline, Petrova, Posy. She always wanted to be Petrova. I washed her clothes, I folded them just so—who's doing that for her? Her clothes are always crumpled, she wears any old thing, she's had her hair cut off so he doesn't have to bother with plaits and things. She should be with *me*. She started having her periods, the curse, you know, and she was utterly terrified—she needs her mother then, goddammit…" Slowly, she let her gaze slide, so her eyes were almost closed, and then, suddenly, she pinched herself on the forearm. "God, Hester. No self-pity. That's enough of me."

She patted the empty pack of cigarettes again, and he saw her eye fall on an open packet that the stranger on her other side had opened. He had taken one out, laid it on the bar. His attention was momentarily distracted by the barman, and Hester coolly took the cigarette, rolled it so snappily toward her and slid it into her pocket that Simon blinked, unsure whether he'd just witnessed it or not.

It wasn't so much the stealing of one cigarette, it was the smoothly covert way she did it. That, more than anything, was what stuck with him, then and later.

She turned and saw him. "Don't," she said, quietly. Her pupils were dilated; her expression was wild, and blank at the same time.

He had seen it once before, with a mother, queuing for bread, in Naples. She had waited all night outside the bakery, and when the shipment had come in, others had pushed—of course—he was there to ensure ordering distribution, what a joke! People were trampled; he saw old people fall, one old woman balling herself up, as the hordes streamed over her, not caring that they stamped on her. A baby girl was lost in the throng, slipping from her mother's grasp, crushed, like fruit on the floor. Simon saw this—it was almost impossible to believe it, what desperation makes of humanity, what it does. Watching Hester, Simon saw what she was like. And he was not surprised when she said, in that sideways, frank way:

"You've had a bad time of it. I can tell."

"How do you know?"

"I always know. Call it a curse. Ah, I'm right. You don't want to live much either, do you?"

There was no other noise in the pub. He felt short of breath, light-headed.

"I—" He honestly didn't know what to say. "Yes. Yes, Hester Bytheway. That's it."

"It's Raverat. But Bytheway's better." She nodded, with a small smile.

"I'll call you Hester Bytheway, then."

She nodded. They smiled at each other, as though a pact had been made. He had the most curious sensation of wanting to reach out, to hold her very tight. Her legs were swinging on the stool, as she pushed the beer mat around with her fingers, not looking at him. "Well, there we are," she said. "Let's cheer ourselves up...Listen, Simon, I'm so sorry—" She looked up at him, but her gaze slid to the window behind, and she froze. "No. *NO!*"

And then, suddenly, she rolled off the bar stool. He thought she'd fallen, but she hadn't, she was half staggering, half running to the windows, and she banged on them, at a passer-by. "You said you'd telephone with the next date, Digby." Her voice cracked, and the slim figure in the warped glass jumped back with shock. "Give her back to me? Or bring her round, just for a day? Hey? Are you listening? *Digby, listen!* My love! My little love! *Hey!!!*"

Simon heard the smashing of the glass almost before it had cracked, heard Hester's scream of despair. And, as the landlord, roused from his melancholic stupor, came around the bar with a roar of outrage, Simon saw Sylvia's young, heart-shaped face in the window, the fear in her eyes, and her expression as she saw him, then tried to place him, and then did. A man, in a hat pulled over his head, grabbed her arm, yanking her forward. He turned, shooting a glance at Hester. Simon saw his face. A square jaw that tapered to a pointed chin, gray narrow eyes, a wide nose. As he saw Hester he smiled, slowly. It was horrible.

Hester had sunk to the floor and was moaning, apologizing, bargaining; Sylvia hurried on, her father's hand under her elbow, glancing back at her mother. The look in her eyes was heart-rending: longing, mixed with shame.

"Simon," Hester was saying, weeping loudly, and she turned her white face toward him, and he saw the terror on her face. "I'm sorry. I'm so sorry. He's got her. He threw me out. I can't see her. I can't get a divorce. I—I can't do anything. I *can't do anything*." She swallowed. The landlord was looking at her, shaking his head, disapproval plain to see. She took a deep breath, trying to calm herself. "It's hell. It's utter hell. I'm sorry. Sorry."

He kneeled down beside her, feeling something fall, swoop deep inside him. "Don't worry. Don't worry, Hester Bytheway. I'll help you home. I'll—I'll help you."

Chapter Twenty

Simon moved into the spare lodgings in Hester's house in Wellington Square a couple of weeks later. As the taxi turned off the King's Road into the long, quiet square she was waiting for him. He could see her, a small lone figure as the cab drew in: legs apart, hands by her sides, like a toy soldier waiting to be placed somewhere.

"That you?" said the cabbie, jerking his head at Hester, who, when she saw him, tore the rag she was wearing over her hair off and waved it frantically though he was only a couple of feet away.

"Yes," said Simon, shortly. Nerves had overtaken him; this whole thing, this obsession with Chelsea, that it could save him, was ridiculous. He had given notice on his perfectly nice rooms in Hornsey and thrown over the interview in Finchley with an old friend of his father's. What would his dear old mum say if she knew? She, who had grown up with a dirt floor and asked for absolutely nothing more than a warm bed and a full belly.

But Hester flung open the door of the black cab, so forcefully that most of his worldly possessions tumbled out: an elephant's foot waste-paper basket, inherited from his father and crammed with books, an old Gladstone bag full of valuables like his father's Egyptian District Officer silver salver, his mother's teapot—Royal Doulton, formerly her pride and joy—carefully wrapped in a sweater, more books and a battered pair of shoes. They slid onto the Royal Borough of Kensington and Chelsea's worn flagstones.

"You're here, you're really here," she said, jumping up and down, her smile so broad he could see she had several teeth missing at the back of her mouth. But she was so like her daughter, her swift, impulsive kindness and intensity, that he had to smile.

"I am here," he said.

"Well. Don't hang around! Come on!"

Simon paid the cab and watched it drive away. He instinctively understood that he felt at home here, in this little village of shabby stucco houses, cafés and garden squares filled with impoverished young people, making things, doing, being, *living*. He credited his new appetite for life to the Chelsea atmosphere, and Hester's need for him, and his for her. Last week, they had stayed up all night, walking slowly from Bloomsbury back to Chelsea, not doing anything else, mostly strolling in silence. They were—lost souls, he supposed, and that was fine.

"Come up, come up," said Hester, grabbing the rusting handle of the giant trunk that held his clothes and scraping it toward the steps. "I say, help me, would you! Or am I already your servant, is that how it'll be!"

"Never, Lady Bytheway," he told her. Somehow, they dragged the trunk and the rest of his meager belongings up the stairs. It was a warm spring day, and he was perspiring by the time they reached the second floor.

"Here we go!" Hester flung open the door forcefully. It banged, making him jump. "S-sorry," she said. He wondered again, at her dilated pupils, her too-loud voice.

It would formerly have been the master bedroom—a vast, drafty room in pale lemon, with a dull chandelier hanging from its cracked and partial cornice. The floorboards were original, he guessed, untreated oak, and that summer every time he walked on them barefoot hundreds of tiny splinters embedded themselves in his soles. The windows were huge Georgian affairs, with hinged shutters—you fastened them with a rusting metal bar which frequently jammed. The fireplace was vast: deep, and tall, the size of a small Scout hut. Simon could hear the cheep of baby birds, nesting in the chimney. On the huge pink and gray marble mantelpiece was a spray of the first delicate roses, lemon yellow, the faintest blush of salmon at their edges. They were exquisite.

Simon was touched. "They're—you shouldn't have."

"I very nearly didn't," she said, carelessly.

"No, really," said Simon. "Flowers are so expensive—"

"Oh, it doesn't matter, does it? They're from Harrods—I love Harrods—I used to go with Sylvia, to the toy department—I go there to cheer myself up. I wanted to get you something

241

but—anyway, someone gave them to me." She wouldn't meet his gaze. "Listen, will it do? Bathroom next door, your kitchen's just there"—she pushed open some folding wooden doors to reveal a small alcove with a dresser, a counter with two gas rings and a kettle. "It's your own. You're the only one who's got that. Ten pounds a month, didn't we say?"

Simon was gazing around him. "Yes," he said. He turned away from the roses, and drank in the sunny room, the empty shelves on either side of the fireplace, the pots of geraniums on the window sill, the coal merchant shoveling glittering black lumps of coal into an ancient hole in front of the house opposite. "It's wonderful," he said, his eyes shining. "It's London, isn't it? It really is."

"Yes!" Hester clapped her hands. "Dear Simon. It's going to be marvelous. You're a brick for helping me out. I'm sure you'll have a job in no time. I'll get Sylvia back off Digby, and she and I will go to Harrods again, it'll all be so jolly."

At first it seemed Hester was right. He got a job on Sloane Street, working at Durrant's, a small but exclusive outfitters selling only the finest gentlemen's gloves, umbrellas, waterproof boots, and wallets. Mr. Durrant had long since died and the shop was owned by an elderly Italian, Mr. Agnetti, well known in the business. He was most exacting in his standards, but kind. Simon found it did him good, having to be meticulous again, well turned out. Mr. Agnetti was formal, his manner dry. He had a system for everything, and customers who had been with him for years. Ordinarily his fussy precision might have irritated Simon, who dreamed big, and could see how the shop should be appealing to new customers, selling gloves and scarves in bright colors, the kind favored by Princess Margaret. But, for now, he was very grateful for the job.

It was a quiet place to work, and that suited him too, just Mr. Agnetti, Simon and a girl known only as Miss Inglis who answered the phones, placed the orders and kept the books. She was quiet, precise, with small doughy hands, and small eyes, and lived with her mother in Clerkenwell, and this was the only information she gave about herself, though often Simon would turn into the back office to find her watching him, intently. He didn't mind; he knew girls liked him. He had always known it, just as some people know they are good at math. It didn't help him.

Simon began sleeping well again; there was something about the immediate quiet of Wellington Square, against the backdrop of noise from the city just beyond. He still had nightmares—the little boy in the dress, the soldiers plunging into starving women. But there was a routine now, and it helped.

He'd leave early for work, wandering through Chelsea up to Sloane Street, and most of the time he didn't cross paths with Hester in the mornings—she wasn't an early riser—and in the evenings he'd stop off somewhere for a pint on the way back, and perhaps a pie or a light supper somewhere in Chelsea. He walked as much as he could. It tired him out and helped quell the dreams. Some of his free time was spent helping Hester with the seemingly unending list of tasks required to keep 11 Wellington Square from collapsing into the dust, like one of the bombed-out houses opposite that was now a gap, like a child's missing tooth.

Sometimes he took little Miss Inglis from the shop to the cinema—she was fond of jazz, like him. He even went to tea at her close, dark flat just off Leather Lane with her mother, who only spoke Italian, and spent most of her time embroidering altar cloths for the Italian church on Clerkenwell Road.

"My mother likes you," Miss Inglis had confided in him, as they left the Gaumont on the King's Road after *The Thirty-Nine Steps*, looking about them and smiling at the fact that it was still light. "She thinks your Italian accent is good. And she said you were well turned out."

"That's the gloves, I'm sure," he'd said, lightly.

"No." She considered this carefully, as she tightened the knot on her raincoat. "It wasn't the gloves."

"I meant—oh, never mind."

"Were you making a joke?" She had raised her small blank face to him.

"Only about gloves. A very poor one."

"Yes. I see." She blushed. She'd told him once she knew she was dull. He found himself liking her more for it. "Well, goodbye, Simon."

"Would you care for a cup of tea?" he said, gesturing to the coffee bar on the corner of the road, thronged with people, fun in the air. He felt it. But Miss Inglis merely nodded, and they walked together in silence.

He couldn't help thinking of Hester, in his bed that morning, rolling around as she attempted to twist the bedsheet into a toga without using her hands, her mop of thick dark hair bouncing, her breasts flopping from side to side, her smile as wide as her face, and he realized it wasn't the same, not at all. As he held the door open for Miss Inglis he longed to be back in Wellington Square, the easy familiarity of his new home. Sometimes he'd walk back along the river, watching the light on the water as the sun set out to the west on those lovely late-spring evenings, and the sense of something changing seemed to him to be everywhere.

Sometimes he'd be at home reading or listening to the gramophone and there'd be a knock at the door and it would be Hester, holding a bottle of gin and two glasses, and they'd drink together, sitting at his small mahogany drum table that his father had inherited from a maiden aunt. Once Hester stubbed a cigarette out on the wood by mistake and he had been surprised at how furious it made him. "Darling, I'm sorry," she said, carelessly. "I'll give you one of mine." Sometimes she'd dance: she had worn a groove into the carpet of her bed-sitting room jiving to the records she played constantly. She loved rock'n'roll; he preferred jazz. Sometimes they didn't say much. Sometimes she made him howl with laughter—she was like that, she knew just what to say to set him off.

Calamitous events seemed to befall Hester all the time. Her mink coat got caught in a Piccadilly Line train door, and she had to take it off and lose it or else risk death by running down the platform. Her wedding bouquet had had an upturned pin in it, and upon her arrival at St. George's, Hanover Square, she had leaned down to smell the arum lilies, when she saw the sharp point of the pin, one quarter of an inch from her eyeball: she could have been blinded. When Sylvia was a tiny baby, she had fallen down the stairs when their old lodger, a marble salesman from Czechoslovakia, had dropped one of his marbles in a hurry, and she had curled up, covering Sylvia as she fell, instinctively, and it was a wonder she hadn't broken her neck...

Simon was never sure about some of these stories—there was a photograph of her on her wedding day on her dressing table, and her bouquet was sweet peas, not arum lilies—but he'd seen enough of Hester's life after a month with her to know drama did seem to follow her around, which was unfortunate because she didn't really seem to welcome it. He didn't want it either.

They didn't sleep together for a week or two, but it soon became almost perfunctory, and she seemed to expect it. The first time it was she who, after several glasses of gin, unbuttoned her shirt and hopped onto the bed. "Oh come on," she'd said, and he'd followed her, and they were naked, evening sun streaming into the little room. Afterward, she'd patted him on the chest and said: "Well. Thank you, darling. As you were," sat up, and pulled on her skirt. Sometimes she'd ask him to do things he didn't like, if she had drunk a bit too much. Sometimes he would take her against the window, pressed up to the glass, at dusk. She was sometimes drunk. Sometimes she'd come to him in the middle of the night, eyes red, and he shouldn't have, but he was lonely too. She never wanted to stay. He never went to her.

She wouldn't talk about Sylvia. "I have to keep quiet. I have to be good. I'll get her back one day, she'll come back here. And I'll go to Harrods, and buy her a huge damned teddy bear. Big enough for her now she's almost grown-up. And I'll keep her safe. Till then let's not, Simon dearest. It makes me ragged inside, thinking about her."

Chelsea was a village, the Arts Club at the western center, bordered by the river to the south and Fulham Road to the north. Her daughter was in that village, and sometimes, he knew, she saw her, from afar, walking to school, or sitting in the garden. He had stopped strolling past the little cottage, he didn't know why. But he knew Hester did, he knew she spent her days prowling the streets, hoping for a glimpse of her girl. Still, unlike the rest of London, indeed England, in Chelsea no one seemed to care where you were from or what you did. Girls in slouchy sweaters, boys with longer hair, no twitching curtains in dank boarding houses, less grime and filth and more hope than in the rest of the city. Life had taken on some sort of shape, to his surprise. He couldn't see beyond the next few months; Simon knew Hester lied, but Simon was—yes, he was—sometimes almost happy.

Chapter Twenty-One

Simon was never entirely sure of the arrangement between the Raverats, whether Digby Raverat was actually suing his wife for divorce, nor of Sylvia's role in it. Her solicitor, an ancient man who had always handled her family's affairs, was clearly not up to the job, and considered the whole matter of divorce, and the Honorable Hester's behavior, distasteful. Simon had the feeling Digby was a cat, playing with Hester, the mouse, trying to hurt her, disorientate her.

Sometimes Hester would take a telephone call in the echoing chilly hallway. Her pleading would float up to him—always the tone, never the actual words. Afterward she would thunder back upstairs, weeping silently, bitterly, and refuse to come out of her room, and Simon would slink back to his quarters, not knowing how to help, and hoping she didn't think it was just that he wanted her. Other times, usually at the weekend, she would dash out suddenly, in a flared green skirt printed with pink apples, a sign she was cheerful, pulling a scarf over her head, gold hoops dangling from her ears, flashing in the sunshine. She would be back in the evening, and would race up to tell him about it.

"I saw my girl today. We went on the Serpentine, and we took two busses. We rode on the top deck—she adores them, and she was so sweet with the conductor, called him 'sir.'"

"I took my girl to tea at Fortnum's today. We used to have tea parties when she was here. She still holds the cup just so with a little finger—oh, Simon, it was awfully sweet."

Sylvia never stayed over—though her room, next to Hester's, was kept ready for her. It still had a baby's cradle in it. There were brightly colored cloth children's books, tooled in gold, and Kate Greenaway prints on the damp walls. And there was a patchwork quilt, neatly folded over a wooden rocking chair, and sheep's wool stuffed into the gaps in the floorboards and in the window frame.

Still, though, the draft from the window was strong enough that sometimes Simon would pass by and see the chair gently rocking on its own, as if fulfilling its purpose in that empty, sad little room.

Occasionally he was still taking Miss Inglis out and about. Sometimes they'd go for a drink at the Hart, just off Sloane Square, where they'd sit in expectant silence, she nursing her cream sherry, he his whisky and soda. He liked the companionship, the quiet. She didn't require anything from him. Didn't want him to give himself up, to take, take, take. "I never know what you're thinking," he'd said once, in a rare effort to try and flirt with her.

"No," she'd said. And given him a small smile.

He'd walk down to the Six Bells pub, where there was jazz on Monday nights, or up toward Victoria, to drink in one of the quieter pubs in the streets leading toward the river. He had given his address to one or two old friends—occasionally he got a post-card or a letter forwarded on from them, including one from the Galloping Major (*In town hunting for treasure*, he'd written. *Care for a drink next time I'm up?*), but he never answered.

Simon was glad his mother was dead—both of his parents, in fact. She had been so proud of her son, in his dress uniform, had been so mortified when he returned from the war, gray-faced and silent. How far he had sunk from their dreams for him: living in a one-room bedsit in Chelsea with a married woman with whom he enjoyed carnal relations, spending his evenings walking, or in jazz clubs or espresso bars, mixing with all sorts. He had taken up painting again—he thought perhaps he might give it a serious go, if there was interest in it. He had shown one to Miss Inglis, who thought it was good, though she thought everything he did was good. He'd shown the same little painting—of barges by Albert Bridge—to Hester. "What a reductive load of crap," she'd said, briskly. "You can paint, Simon, but I wouldn't give this to my worst enemy. I wouldn't even give it to Digby. There you go."

"I'd like to meet Sylvia again properly," he said one evening, as he was watching Hester climb back into her skirt. She straightened up and paused, haunches still facing him, then slowly turned round.

"Why?"

"Because…well, she's your daughter. And I haven't seen her to talk to since the day I invited myself in for tea."

She tied her white shirt up into a knot, fluffed out her hair. "Darling, that's very kind, but there's no need."

He shrugged. "Of course. I merely—I did think…if she comes to live here…I barely know her, and if …I thought we—" Sweat started to run down his brow. "It's of no importance, after all."

Hester came and sat down on the bed. She patted the dull, snagged surface of the eiderdown near his leg, as if unable to bring herself to comfort him. "Don't be like that, Simon. It's vastly complicated, that's all."

"I don't understand it, really, I suppose," said Simon. He could hear himself, like a bleating goat.

"I don't either. Look—" She leaned forward, so one creamy, blue-veined breast fell heavily against the shirt, almost out of the material. He looked away, wanting to concentrate. "I have to be whiter than white. Digby knows I have lodgers, but if he knew I was—you and I—well, that'd be curtains. I'm not sure he even knows you're here at all."

"What's the difference between me and the others?"

"I don't want to fuck Mrs. Krapolski or Mr. Thaddeus," she said. "What about Lovibond?"

"Maybe Lovibond." This was their joke about the young, earnest, awkward history lecturer who had rooms on the top floor and clearly had a crush on Hester. He was recently down from Cambridge and was always popping round. "Mrs. Raverat, I have a leftover scone. Mrs. Raverat, I wondered if I could polish the chandelier? Mrs. Raverat, would you care to borrow my transistor radio?"

At that very moment there came a creaking sound from upstairs; young George Lovibond getting ready for bed. They were silent, Simon trying not to laugh. But Hester said: "Please promise me you'll be careful. He'd know. Raverat…he just knows everything." She gave a little shiver, and sat up again, tucking herself in, as if afraid he was watching. "I can't explain it."

"You always say that."

"Yes…" She bowed her head, closing her eyes briefly. "All right then. Before we were married, there was one time—one time, at the Dorch—I laughed at one of his friend's jokes about him, and afterward in the corridor he grabbed my arm, so hard. I couldn't move it for days. He'd twisted it half off." She looked up at him, and he saw the violet shadows under her eyes. "He didn't do it again, not until after we were married. It's when he's drunk. He loses control. I think it's the war. He was Digby Raverat, jolly good chap, first to pour the gin, didn't matter if someone else had paid for it. Oh, then the war came and he couldn't fight, and he applied for a few posts, doing hush hush stuff, but he never got anything…he was living off my money and all our friends were dying or being terrifically secretive and there was he, this joke…he's a joke, darling. A bad one.

"He drinks too much. I do too, of course, he got me drinking, I barely touched it before I married him." Her long lashes rested on her white cheeks. "Course not. I was a kid. But both of us drank together, only he gets nasty. Really nasty, Simon. The slightest thing…He's sorry afterward. He says he is. But it happens. And I have to be good. I have to get Sylvia away from him. Then I can start to make plans, darling."

"How can you bear to let her live with him?"

"He would have killed me if I'd stayed, Simon." She put her hand on his arm, gently, as if shielding him from her awful truth. "I had to leave. I was left this place when Daddy died. I had to leave." A shadow crossed her face, like clouds scudding in front of the moon. "Or, rather, I asked him to leave…and he did. He walked out one day when I'd gone to Fulham to buy some more cheap woolen carpeting for the bedroom floors. Packed everything up, and took her with him. So perhaps it was all a huge mistake but…What can I do?" She laughed, almost pityingly. "The law isn't on my side. Nothing is. He has them all lined up. Liz, the doctor, Pandora, they'll all say the same thing. That I went loopy after I had Sylvia and I drink. If I make a fuss I won't ever see her again." She said again: "You don't know what he's like."

They were silent. The wistful sound of a Polish folk song

floated down from Mrs. Krapolski's gramophone above them. "Who's Pandora?"

"My best friend. We did the debutante's Season together. She's married now, living in Ireland. She's Sylvia's godmother. She saw her on a bad day...I wasn't sleeping well, Nanny had left..." A shadow of memory passed over her face. "A bad day. Digby was so cross with me that evening—" She gave a deep shuddering breath, as if struggling to hold on to her composure.

"Aren't you afraid he'll—hurt Sylvia?"

Hester ran her hands through her hair. "It's not the same—she's learned to keep quiet." She swallowed; he knew she was struggling to maintain her composure, and he wished he hadn't asked her about it. "He barely sees her in any case. He's out all day. It's five minutes in the evening and his housekeeper brings him a drink and he gives Sylvia a kiss and tells her to say her prayers. I had her all day." She closed her eyes; it was unbearable, Simon felt it too. "I taught her to read, to throw bread for ducks. I brushed her hair every night, I folded down her socks, I mopped her up when she tripped, or when she started school. I know her. She looks like a fragile scrap of a thing, yet she's tough as steel here." She thumped her chest, her mouth downturned in misery. "She needs me, Simon. She's growing up and she needs me. So I have to do this. Live like this, to get her back. You see?" Her lovely face crumpled, but she didn't let herself cry. With a small sob she said: "It's bloody hard, I tell you."

"She's a lovely girl," Simon said. Their fingers tightened. "You should be damned proud of yourself, Hester."

"Look, will you promise me something? That you'll look out for her?" She inhaled, her shoulders rising again, and scratched her head furiously, as she did when she was nervous. "If something...happens to me? Will you?"

He took her hand. He said, solemnly: "I promise I will."

"Daddy's dead, her aunt's dead, my mother's disowned me...I'm the last of my family. She has no one, no one to take her side. Promise?"

He reached over and took a sip from the glass, his hand clasped around hers. "Yes. I promise. For the rest of my life. I'll look out for her."

"If I can simply wait out a few more months, he'll get bored. It's if I annoy him, or challenge him—he can't stand it, he can't stand being made a fool of, or thinking his friends are laughing at him. He's already furious he married the daughter of a baronet and she got fat and didn't go with him in bed the way he wanted and didn't have as much money as he thought. He wants me out of the way. That's the thing. Out of the way and then he'll marry…oh, the bishop's daughter, or any of those new debs. Fresh meat, more money, and he can carry on as if it all never happened."

"You don't—you mustn't say things like that," Simon said, feeling nauseous.

"No, darling. I mustn't. But you've promised now." And she mimed a throat being slit, and something about the way she did it, her face white in the darkening light, the knowledge of her nakedness under the shirt and skirt, was as matter-of-fact and brutal as anything he'd seen in Naples. It haunted Simon, for the rest of his life.

Chapter Twenty-Two

Miss Inglis got into the habit of teasing Simon about Hester. She read the society columns in *The Times*, and got the *Picture Post*. In June, she was most exercised about Princess Margaret's hat choice for Royal Ascot. She knew all about Hester.

"The Honorable Hester Bingham," she told Simon. "They said she was the most stylish deb of her season. Me and Mama read all about her. That was the first season after the war, you know, and she wore a Hardy Amies dress when she was presented to the King and Queen."

"Mmm," said Simon, pushing a beer mat around. They were in the Star Tavern, just off Belgrave Square, he having persuaded her to see an Arnold Wesker play about working-class life in rural Norfolk at the Royal Court. It had not been a great success. Miss Inglis had worn a silk shantung dress and her best jacket, navy blue velvet. "I might as well have not bothered," she said. "Everyone there was so dirty. It wasn't what I thought the theater would be like, not at all."

"I thought it was very interesting," he said. "The struggles of ordinary people and all that."

"Ordinary people are dreary." She wiggled back in her seat, making herself more comfortable, and pulled the seam of her dress around. "I don't want to watch ordinary people on television. Or see them up on stage, or read about them. I want to escape."

"Don't we all," he said, touched, and he clinked his glass of beer against her sherry. She met his eyes and they smiled, awkwardly.

Afterward, walking through the dusky Chelsea streets, he felt her small frame closer to him than she had been before. There was something oddly touching about her primness, after the weeks of Hester's sensual, abandoned approach to life. They headed down the King's Road toward her bus stop. "Why don't I walk you home," she offered, gamely.

"It should be the other way around, shouldn't it?"

"It should, but I'm on the King's Road now. It's very exciting. I don't ever get this far in my lunch hour. Besides, I want to see the famous Wellington Square, don't I?"

"I suppose so," he said, but his heart sank, and he felt the whisky he had drunk out of the hipflask earlier, hastily, in the Gents sloshing together with the beer in his stomach. He didn't want Miss Inglis meeting Hester. He didn't know why, just that it was a bad idea.

But he smiled politely, and listened as she chattered away, more voluble than usual—sometimes it was hard to keep up a conversation with her. Perhaps it was the sherry.

"Did you see *The Horse's Mouth*? Princess Margaret went to the premiere, a couple of months ago now it was, and she wore a beautiful dress. Huge bow. Mother was going to go, but her knees weren't good, although she used to walk into Covent Garden every day." She stopped, facing him. "I've told you that, haven't I? She worked on the fruit stall with her father." As if confessing something.

"Yes, I did see it." Simon kept on walking. He could feel the last of the whisky, sliding around the hipflask in his breast pocket. He wondered if he could just swig it, here and now.

"She's so beautiful, don't you think? Poor lady... She was so brave, what she did—I say. Is this it?"

"I turn off here. Are you sure you don't want me to wait for the bus with you?"

"No, ta. I said I'd walk you to your door, didn't I?"

She took his arm, looking up into his face, and he smiled gallantly as if he could think of nothing nicer. They turned off the King's Road and toward the square, the white buildings glowing in the dusk. Honeysuckle draped itself over the wall leading to Hester's house. "Which house is yours?"

"That one," said Simon, stopping. "The one with the lighted windows, and the people in the doorway."

He could hear voices, slightly too loud. Hester was talking, and at the same time someone was singing. It was that song. That dratted song again.

"Four for the honey makers,
Three, three, the rivals,
Two, two, the beloved girls,
Clothed all in green, O,
One is one and all alone and evermore shall be so."

"Is that her?" Miss Inglis whispered. She drew closer to him, pulling his arm, and he smelled her scent. Yardley. It reminded him of the shop, of the endless working day, of tedium and despair. The little house by the sea, the market town, the boat—all these things he had proudly promised Sylvia he'd have one day were further away than ever.

"Yes," he said, looking at Hester's black outline, illuminated in the glare from the hall lights. "That's her."

"Who's that man?"

"Not sure." But Simon stopped, at the sound of the stranger's speaking voice.

"Awfully kind of you," he was saying. Hester looked up. She was vacant, her eyes bleary.

"Well, there you are, there you are. We're all pals, aren't we? All pals." She gestured at Simon, flapping her hand at him, like a broken wing of a bird. "Simon. He says he's a friend of yours. I'm *so* sorry," she said, some of her great charm washing over him. "I seem to have for-forgotten your name."

Early evening was, he knew, the worst time for her, when she was used to washing up tea things, running baths, laying out nightdresses, reading stories—and her daughter was twelve, and could do all these things for herself, needing her mother less and less with every day that passed.

The figure turned around, lifted his battered tweed cap. "Simon, old man. Good to see you. You mysterious beast. I've been trying to get hold of you for weeks, what what? Went to see your old landlady and she directed me here." He came toward them and then

ding

The street lamp went on behind them, bathing the square in electric light, capturing the four of them for the quickest sliver of a second, frozen at that place and time. Always, to the end of his life, Simon could recall the scene. Hester's black silk shirt. The Galloping Major's hat. Miss Inglis's arm, thrust through his.

"I'm so sorry," said Hester, holding out her hand. "You must be Miss Inglis."

"Oh, call me Eileen," said Miss Inglis, nonplussed. "Lovely to meet you, Mrs. Raverat."

"Hester."

"H-Hester." Eileen wiggled forward, staring frankly at Hester, and Simon inwardly shuddered. He looked up to find the Galloping Major watching him, cigarette in his mouth. Simon knew then he hated this man on Hester's doorstep.

He remembered suddenly how he'd shot a thief they'd met on the road up to Vesuvius. The sound of crumbling stone, of walls cracking under the heat of lava, came from behind them. The smell of sulfur hung so heavy in the air sometimes it was hard to breathe. It made you cough and choke. The man had leaped out from behind a plume of smoke, it seemed, and as Simon stood there, aghast, the Galloping Major had coolly pointed his pistol at him and fired. He'd done it most efficiently, then put the gun away, moving the dead, emaciated man out of the road with his boot—quite gently, but with a boot all the same. Then he'd smiled, stepping over the brains—"One less dago, Lestrange," he'd said, though Simon was his superior.

Desperately, Simon tried to block out the song, playing in the back of his mind again, and the sight of Hester's ravaged face, her slack mouth. She had been worse and worse lately. He knew he must stay calm, to help her. He felt now that there was a precipice, he stood close to it.

"Well, old man," said Simon, intensely awkward. "It's awfully good to see you. I'm sorry if you were expecting a drink. But I was just showing Miss Inglis where I live. I have to walk her—"

"Eileen, please," said Eileen, proffering her hand to him now. "Nice to meet you."

"Hunter," said the Galloping Major, and, yes, that was how he introduced himself, that stiff clicking together of the heels, like the Nazis. "Charles Hunter."

Hunter. He'd almost forgotten his name. Charles Hunter.

"You from round these parts?" Eileen said, as they shook hands. He could see Eileen sizing Hunter up and suddenly he knew she would find him wanting. It was good to know.

"Me? Oh, no. I'm from the other side of the country. Different world altogether. But I'm down here often, doing business. Antiques, don't you know. Seeking out treasure." He gave Miss Inglis a leering smile—the younger the better, Simon remembered. Miss Inglis was in her twenties. Too old for the Galloping Major.

"Do come in for a drink," said Hester, to fill the silence. "Both of you. Please."

"Thank you," said the Galloping Major. He stared up at the tall house, and Simon knew he was appraising it, wondering what treasure he could winkle out of poor, ruined Hester.

"No, I'll be off," said Miss Inglis. She shook Simon's hand. "Mum worries if I'm too late. Goodbye, Simon. No, you don't need to walk me. The bus stop's just there. Thanks for an interesting evening. I'll see you tomorrow." She stared up at Hester, almost hungrily. "G'bye," she said, awkwardly, ignoring Charles Hunter altogether, and she trotted back down the narrow street to the King's Road.

"In we go," said Hester. Over the Galloping Major's head Simon frowned at her—she glared back at him, clearly feeling he was to blame for it all. Both of them stepped back to allow Charles Hunter in first. The door closed behind them, and the square was quiet again, the buzz from the electric lamp the only sound.

Chapter Twenty-Three

Every other Wednesday afternoon Mr. Agnetti left Durrant's early, to go into Soho and meet up with old friends, those he had been interned with in a prison camp on the Isle of Wight during the war. It seemed remarkable to Simon, but he harbored no ill-will toward the British for this treatment. "They had to be sure of us," he'd say, buttoning up his coat with swift precision. "Isn't that so, Miss Inglis? We were lucky to be left alone. We were proud to serve in the camps."

Miss Inglis, who had been two when war broke out, and whose Scottish father had died parachuting into Greece, would nod politely.

The shop was heavy with silence after Mr. Agnetti had gone. Simon would sometimes look up from a ledger book or his card file to find Miss Inglis staring at him, her cheeks very slightly flushed. Then she would swallow, and look away.

Today, Simon was busy at the typewriter, laboring over what he hoped was a letter of constructive criticism to a supplier in Warminster about the stitching of some cotton gloves. He had persuaded Mr. Agnetti to switch from his long-established supplier in Derbyshire to these people, and it was all rather awkward. Mr. Agnetti, normally so mild-mannered, was annoyed and had pointedly asked several times that Simon write the letter and mail it today.

It should have been a simple matter but Simon could not seem to order his thoughts. He was sleeping badly, the last week or so. It was too hot. His new life wasn't new anymore, the golden sheen worn off, the dull metal underneath plain to see. He didn't know what to do, how to help. The previous day, damned Charles Hunter had been round at Hester's, valuing furniture.

The Galloping Major had even got his foot in the door with Hester's husband. He'd been round to price up a bible box at Digby Raverat's house, at Hester's insistence.

"It's mine, and he stole it," Hester kept shouting. "He's no right to it, it's been in my family for eons. It's very valuable. *Very* valuable. Elizabethan." She'd lowered her voice: she was more and more convinced Digby's spies were everywhere, bricked into the walls, hiding behind railings. "Charles saw Sylvia. He saw her, introduced himself, gave her my love."

The Major had been invited back to the Chelsea cottage. Digby Raverat said he was a sensible fellow. Had had him look at a portrait of Hester's grandmother he said was by Sir Edward Horner and worth a bit of money. He'd brought a book for Sylvia—*Daddy-Long-Legs*.

The whole thing made Simon angry, and it was ridiculous, when to him the Galloping Major was such a thin, insubstantial person. It was very strong work indeed to accuse an old army comrade of dishonesty, but Simon knew that, like the other chaps you found all of a sudden up and down the King's Road, tweed jackets and mustaches and country gent accents to the fore, Hunter was no antiques expert.

"Oh, I know he's a bit of a cad," Hester had said, impatiently, a few days before. "But at least he's got a *plan*, Simon, darling. He can *help* me."

Angrily, Simon fiddled with the typewriter ribbon, his fingers clumsy. He had to get this letter right, not only to show Mr. Agnetti he was right, but to make himself feel like less of an utter damned fool…

Mr. Agnetti had only been gone for five minutes when the door of the shop banged open, and a fresh July breeze swept into the stuffy interior. It was so sudden that Miss Inglis, halfway up a ladder in the back room fetching some new stock, gave a small squeak. Simon, who had been laboriously deleting "unaceptable," looked up.

"Sylvia," he said, with surprise. "Why—hello, my dear. How are you?"

He had not seen her for several weeks. Digby Raverat had been more difficult than usual about letting Sylvia visit her mother. There had been an incident. Hester refused to talk about it, but she had had Sylvia for the day and taken her to Fantasie, a coffee bar on the King's Road that was all the rage, then to Bazaar, where she'd bought Sylvia a sweater.

Sylvia swore she hadn't said a word about it but Raverat did and he was furious. Sylvia was only supposed to visit her mother, not leave the house. This was breaking the rules, and Digby made sure his solicitor reminded Hester what happened if she didn't stick to the terms of the proposed divorce agreement he had put in front of her. Namely, that she would lose all access to her daughter.

"Just a damned sweater. Nothing sexy. She's twelve, she's starting to be interested in clothes" was all she'd say, that evening, nursing a large gin and vermouth and what appeared to be the beginnings of a black eye. "He wants to pretend he's living in Belgravia. It's not like that here, it never has been, it's a place for people to create, not to ossify . . . Oh, Simon—" And she'd winced, touching the cheekbone. "Christ, that hurts."

He'd given her his steak from the fridge, reluctantly, it had to be said, and he hated himself for this meanness. But Simon was growing tired of it. Of her, of him, of it all, the wretchedness of it, the unhappiness, sheer bloody misery of knowing Hester woke up every day in hell, that sweet, sad Sylvia did too, that they were both being broken by this man.

The previous week, he'd glimpsed Sylvia's small, pale face at the window as he walked to the Phene with the Galloping Major. He was incapable of shaking the man off. Simon wasn't really sure where he lived, and attempts to inveigle other old army friends to come and drink with them were always unsuccessful.

They'd strolled past the cottage, where the fresh spring flowers in the garden had given way to yellowing grass and dead roses.

Sylvia had leaned up against the window, almost as if she was waiting for passers-by. Her face had lit up, and she'd waved cheerily at him. He'd winked and waved back, doing his silly walk where he pretended to be going downstairs, and she'd laughed—he could hear her laughing.

"Ah, Sylvia," the Galloping Major had said, turning to look at her. "Pretty thing. Some good pieces in that house, if only her oafish mother could pull herself together. We'd make a killing."

Simon crossed the road, patting his companion's elbow as he did to chivvy him away, and quickly changed the subject.

Sylvia stood in front of him now, panting, her pale cheeks flushed, the strap of her coral sundress slipping over her thin shoulder.

"Sylvia. What's the matter?"

She leaned over the counter, struggling for breath. "I'm sorry, Simon. I didn't know who else to ask."

"What's happened?" He pushed the typewriter away. "Is it your mother?"

She nodded. "She's in Harrods. I left her…You have to come and talk her round. I'm—" She gave a great sob, as if gulping in air to help her breathe. "I'm s-so sorry. But she'll ruin everything if you don't. She's lost it. She's taken something—drunk something— but I can't get her to leave, and she's making a scene. I just went round to see her because she telephoned…and she dragged me out to Harrods…said we'd buy something, have some fun…"

Simon's heart hardened against Hester, only for a second. He thought of Durrant's, left without anyone out on the shop front, and what Mr. Agnetti would say if he knew. "I can't leave the shop, old girl. I—"

"Yes, of course." Sylvia covered her small face with her hands. "B-but someone will call my father. You have to come and get her home. You—you must, Simon."

Simon hesitated.

"Go," a voice behind them said, with repressed excitement. "I'll be perfectly fine here, honestly." Miss Inglis appeared in the doorway from the stockroom.

"Are you sure?"

She put one small, cold hand on top of Simon's. "Yes. Go, Simon."

He looked down at it. "Thank you—Eileen."

"I won't tell him, don't worry. We'll sort it out later."

Sylvia was tugging at his arm. "Oh, Simon, please come. Let's run."

She was in the toy department when they arrived, having run up the stairs, past the chilly sedateness of the Food Hall and the giant china fruits, the men in white serving ladies in furs, then the perfume counter, where heavy fragrance hung in the air. They ran through the outfitting department, far grander than Durrant's, a whole floor of discreet, dull grays and navys and browns, up the winding stairs, the traffic on the street below rumbling through the open windows.

Hester was walking around in a circle, taking tiny pigeon steps, and flapping her arms up and down like wings. No one else seemed to be taking a blind bit of notice; that was the extra-ordinary part of the whole thing.

She looked up and saw them, and gave a big smile, her neat white teeth shining. "Mummy's here!" she said, proudly. "Darling girl. You're back."

She ambled toward them, and stopped at a stepped series of golden scalloped shelves held up by golden pillars. Each shelf had a bed of cotton wool upon which rested dolls of increasing size and opulent dress.

"Doll heaven," she said, fingering the silvery wings of a stiff porcelain-headed angel, the velvet epaulets of a stern-looking drummer boy. "Beautiful."

"Hester," Simon said quietly. "What's going on?"

She shrugged, her arms floppily exaggerating the gesture. "We thought we'd come out and buy my little girl a present, didn't we?"

He looked at her, and saw she really was out of it; stoned, or drunk, he wasn't sure. This was a new development, the dope she was taking.

Simon didn't know what to do. It was all wrong, all of it. Everyone was in the wrong place. Sylvia shouldn't be dashing from shop to shop, panting, her unbrushed hair hanging in streaks over her hunched shoulders as she stood watching her mother in a toyshop full of things for little children. She should be at home in the cozy kitchen at the back of the house in Wellington Square with the old range and the large radio on the dresser, drawing. She loved drawing. And Hester shouldn't be here, fingering these gaudy lifeless dolls. She should be there too, boiling her daughter an egg, looking over her shoulder at her work. Sipping from a cup of tea, scarf tied around her hair, overalls on having just painted another room ready for a new lodger.

There was a life for them—it was tangible, just within reach, and he could see it. It was cozy, and calm, full of possibility. He didn't care whether he was part of it or not—that didn't matter.

He took Hester's arm, gently. "Hester, my dear. You shouldn't have brought Sylvia here." She stared at him, with blank eyes. "We need to take her home. I'll do it, now. You go back to Wellington Square."

Hester swooped her arms up and down again, clucking, and then laughed.

"Hester." He shook her arm. "Digby. Remember? He'll be home from work at six."

"My—oh. Yes." She screwed up her face, with a superhuman effort it seemed. She put her hands to her cheeks, then looked around, and picked up one of the teddy bears, a soft marmalade-colored animal with a large burgundy bow, and squashed it under her arm. "My girl Sylvia." She went over to her daughter, stroked her dark head. "I'm so sorry. It's all wrong, isn't it? But it'll be right one day. You'll see. One day."

Sylvia put her head on her mother's arm, cautiously, uncomfortably. Hester patted her awkwardly. He saw how she blinked, swallowing, trying to recover herself. She handed the bear to her daughter. "Here. Mummy's bought you this."

"Oh," said Sylvia. She held the bear rather awkwardly and looked at her mother. "You bought it? It's for me?"

"Yes! Of course. He's my present to you. He's called...let me see. Wellington Bear." She smiled, her beautiful dark eyes shining, and mother and daughter looked at each other. "Almost Wellington Square. He's a reminder of me. Of your old room, and home. You'll be back there soon. I promise." She swallowed the last words. "You need a teddy bear when you're growing up. Sometimes more than when you're a child, you know."

"Do you?"

Hester started stroking her daughter's hair. Her face was completely white, as if she knew it was over, that she had made the final mistake, and the minutes were now ticking away.

Sylvia nestled her head against her mother's chest, eyes darting around the shop.

"You do." Hester kissed the bear's head, then her daughter's head. Her long black eyelashes fluttered against Sylvia's hair, the firm, expressive fingers clutching her wrist.

Simon's head was pounding, a cramping pain at the front of his forehead that stretched over his right eye and over his face. He could hardly see.

Hester took Sylvia's hand. "Come on, darling. You must hurry back now. I'll see you soon."

"Promise, Mummy? You'll speak to Daddy?"

"I promise. I know I haven't kept my promises before but now...Yes, darling."

"Come on, Sylvia," said Simon. "We'd better get going. Bye, Hester. I'll see you back at the house. I'll fix you a drink and we'll have—have a nice supper. Yes?"

"Yes," she said. "Off you go. Hurry!" And so Simon pulled Sylvia away, hurrying toward the elevator.

But as they waited, Sylvia looked up at Simon with a nervous smile, leaning into him.

"She's drunk," she whispered to him. "And I don't think she's paid for that bear—has she?"

"I've paid for it," said Hester, loudly, reappearing behind them, and they both jumped. She smiled at one of the doormen. "What, did you think I was just marching out of here with a stolen bear?"

The doorman touched a gloved hand to his black top hat and nodded at her. "Mrs. Raverat. Very nice to see you again, ma'am. And Miss Raverat, of course."

Simon ushered them all through the door and down the stairs instead, unsure what to do next.

"It's a villain's name, isn't it?" Hester was babbling. "Raverat. I've always hated it. Sylvia, when you do something with your life, don't call yourself Raverat, will you, darling? Let's think of a much better name for you."

"Will you be all right?" Simon said, as they emerged into the humid July evening. Fumes—coal tar and petroleum—hung stickily heavy in the air. He felt he shouldn't be abandoning her like this.

"I've taken up enough of your time already." She tossed her cropped hair, a flash of the old Hester, and put her hand on his arm. "Dear Simon—hey! Let me go! Let go, I say!"

She was yanked away from him, from behind, and he couldn't see by whom, not at first. "I say!" Hester screamed, trying to wrest herself out of his grip. "Look here, get off me!"

"You're stealing again, you dirty thief."

Digby Raverat's soft, dry voice could scarcely be heard over the traffic. Where had he come from? He was behind Hester now, one hand clamped around her upper arm like a vise; Simon could see the white knuckles, the pink fingertips pressing into her sleeve. "Slut."

The worst person Simon had known so far was an American corporal who'd sodomized little boys in back rooms of shabby restaurants in Naples, and then demanded money from their parents afterward, to keep quiet about what he'd done to them. But he looked like a villain—thick, slicked-back hair, hairy hands, a scar on his neck only partially obscured by his uniform collar. He thought of him now for the first time in a long while; the family whom he'd had to visit, as one boy had died afterward because of what the corporal had inflicted on him. Simon wasn't surprised when he heard afterward that the corporal had been quietly stabbed on the Via Foria, after Ascension Day, his body tied to a cart and dragged around the city—some said he wasn't fully dead, as one eye in that jowly, handsome face was blinking, the other too swollen shut to open.

Later, Simon would try to remember what Digby Raverat looked like: some marker, to store him away under the heading "Villain." But the truth is he was a very nondescript man. The curious square jaw and pointed chin, that was all he could recall. Light-gray hair. He was small, and beautifully dressed as ever, in his pressed dark-gray suit and spotless trilby.

"I'm taking Sylvia home," he said. "You—" He suddenly pushed Hester viciously in the chest, like a child in the playground, and she staggered backward. "You can stay here, my dear. On the street."

"No," said Hester, righting herself, leaning against Simon. "G-get away from me. Here's the bus," she said, and she held out her hand to her daughter. "Sylvia, shall we get on?" Perhaps she was determined, in her stoned or drugged or drunk state, to preserve some normality in these last moments.

"You are a thief," said Digby Raverat, and he was smiling, quite pleasantly. The streets were still bustling; Knightsbridge matrons, in swinging coats and court shoes, coming out of Harrods, bidding farewell to the doorman. He wrenched Hester's fingers so that she winced in pain. Raverat took the teddy bear from her, holding it by one ear. It dangled in the breeze. Sylvia gave a small sad cry, as her mother tried to snatch it back, but he batted her away again as if she were a fly. "You stole this bear, and you're drunk. I've reported it to the police."

"I say," said Simon. "You've no proof."

He laughed. "Who's this? Oh, I am sure I can guess. The new lodger, yes? I was there upstairs. I was watching you. You're quite the little lapdog, aren't you? I saw her take it, old boy." Hester was scrabbling at his arm, as his grip on her tightened. He turned to her. "Get a good look at Sylvia, now. You're never seeing her again. Your mother was right. You're a slut."

Simon said loudly: "I say. Don't talk to her like that. She's a good mother."

Someone jostled Simon, and he pushed them out of the way, angrily. He could feel the situation sliding out of his control. Sylvia was pressed against the shop windows, utterly still. Simon knew she had seen this kind of scene before, and worse.

Digby Raverat took a pocket watch out of his waistcoat. "Five oh one p.m. Hester, be reasonable. You drink, and steal, you take other men as lovers—you really must understand"—he was smiling gently—"my position. So, shake hands with your daughter. Say goodbye nicely."

He took Sylvia's arm roughly and Sylvia pulled back, against the window. But he dragged her away, so that her black school shoes scraped along the pavement.

"I don't want to go with you," she said, in a small, clear voice, as another bus swept past them, close to the edge of the pavement.

"I'm afraid you must. Don't make a scene."

"Don't touch her," said Hester. "Let go of her arm." Digby Raverat tightened his grip on Sylvia, and Hester's voice rose, clearly, magnificently, above the roar. "I said, let go. You can't tell me what to do. You can't always control me. You try, you've tried every day," but then she started struggling to get the words out, overwhelmed with sobbing, heaving breaths. "You're—I don't understand why you're like this—why are you like this? I don't want you, I don't want your money. I just want to live with my daughter, and that's what she wants too. Do you understand? She needs me."

"Nonsense!" said Raverat, with an arch look of surprise. "They'll ask you in court, Hester—how many times have you returned her late? How many times have you been drunk when you're with her? What about the time you dropped her when she was three? Or when you left her behind in that restaurant? These things, these things, my dear. You're not a fit mother." His voice hardened, and he tightened his grip again on his daughter's arm, so that she gave a small howl. "It's over, Hester. Understand that."

Hester shook her head. "N-no," she said, her gaze empty. "I won't. N-no. Damn you."

"Hester," said Simon, suddenly really alarmed. "Not here. We'll discuss it later. Come home with me and—"

If he hadn't said anything, would she have moved? But she did. Afterward, he could recall it in perfect slow motion, every split second—

The omnibuses, lumbering along the road, the setting sun, blinding one's vision when one turned toward it. The crowds on the pavement, weaving slowly between their small group.

Raverat was still gripping his daughter's arm. Hester stepped forward, and took Sylvia's other, free, hand. "There," she said, with a small smile. "Darling, he shan't hurt you again. No one shall."

She looked up at Simon, that frank, lovely face of hers with the glimmer of a smile playing over it. "You're lovely," she said. "I'm so sorry."

Holding her daughter's hand she closed her eyes, and Simon understood then what was going to happen, but he was too far away—he stepped forward.

He heard the screech, and the scream, and saw, for one split second, the last moments, as Hester pushed Digby into the path of the bus, and as she was yanked along with him. Simon reached out one hand and grabbed Sylvia's shoulder, enough to make her turn, hold back, for the briefest split second—enough, just enough.

The bus hit Hester, knocking down her husband, crunching

them under the tires—he heard the sound of bones smashing, a body puncturing. Simon's vision went dim, and when he opened his eyes again something had been thrown up into the air—Sylvia, flying in an arc, hitting the front of the bus, then thrown to the side, out of sight.

Silence, then screams, then shouts, then cars hooting, people calling. He rubbed his head, blinking, trying to see. He was on the pavement, eyes level with the road.

Underneath the bus in front of him there were two separate piles of clothes, a smell of petroleum and burning and something disgusting, drains, feces, and someone was screaming, her mouth was open, and he was scrambling to his feet, swaying, and he couldn't hear anything, anything at all. Finally there was silence. As though he had stopped being able to hear. He stepped on something soft and looked down. The teddy bear was on the pavement, legs neatly splayed apart, watching the scene with beady amber eyes.

Part Four

1989

Chapter Twenty-Four

"Pass it around, Janey. Oh God, you've bumsucked it."

"I haven't."

"Yes, you have. Jesus. Haven't you had a spliff before?"

Janey raised herself up on her elbows. She was laughing, and her face was red. "No, of course I haven't, you bloody idiot." We smiled at each other, getting used to each other, this new, intensely enjoyable connection. "I'm square, remember?"

I do remember. I remember everything.

This is why she was cool, that Janey Lestrange, my dearest friend, my new life, my other half. She didn't care. She didn't realize then that she didn't care, but she didn't. She was shy and awkward and clever—Jesus, she was clever. That first evening when she arrived and Joss was banging on about some stupid poem of his and she stood there looking at him, one quizzical eyebrow raised, her thin, dry hands clutched together the only sign of how nervous she was, and her curious patchy dark head.

Even though it was almost dark, Joss was wearing sunglasses. He raised them, fumbling slightly, and said in a drawling monotone:

"Slowly, Miss D and two Us. It's not a straw. You're inhaling. Not sucking."

We had purloined a bottle of cooking sherry from the kitchen. Our mother was in her study. Since Rory's death she'd stopped going upstairs with my father after supper. She would tidy up, for ages, in the kitchen, then go and work. My father was pottering around on the terrace. The pater familias, shut out from the marital bedroom. He could go up, of course, but he didn't want to be alone. That's the thing about him, I realize. He couldn't stand being alone. All my mother wanted was to be left alone.

In the dark corridor before we went out to eat that night, Mummy had clasped my hands tightly and pulled me into her study. Her wide, sparkling eyes were huge.

"Kitty, darling. The place at King's. Are you absolutely sure you won't go?" Her low, beautiful voice thrummed through me—every syllable weighted with restrained, exquisite pain. "We should tell them, one way or the other."

I knew who she meant when she said "them." She meant Professor Lovibond, the owlish professor of history who had interviewed me. "I knew your mother," he'd said nervously, as I shifted on my seat, angry that he should bring it up. "She wrote to me a month ago, mentioned I'd be interviewing you."

"She what?" I'd said, forgetting to add verbs. I remember the view behind him, the mud-green Cam, waterlogged fields, spiked edges of ancient buildings poking into view through the leaded windows. I did not feel at home here. I knew I never would.

"Lovely girl. I remember her mother too. A bad business," he'd said and then when I'd looked bewildered, had added hastily: "Anyway, nothing to do with today."

Discovering my mother felt she had to interfere in the application process did not add to the quality of the interview. I had folded my arms, trying to hide how upset I was, and my answers became monosyllabic. The light from his desk lamp glinted on his round glasses so I couldn't see his eyes, but I could still make out his gaze that started at my too-short denim skirt and then slid up my body, the gaze I had noticed men now tended to give me. *Nice legs. Bet she's a handful.*

I'd been relieved when I hadn't got the place. I didn't want to go. Not on those terms, and increasingly, not on any terms. I wanted to see the world. Really see it.

But Letham's had taken action. They hadn't got anyone into Oxbridge the previous year, and they really wanted to have their cake and eat it—they needed to maintain their impeccable social image ("We are exclusively for daughters of the gentry") with the promise of an excellent education ("Let's face it, most of them will marry and never work again, but they need to go to university. Shove 'em out into a nice place full of Oxbridge rejects, but add one or two to the Honors board in the Great Hall and what happens afterward isn't our problem, is it?").

My history teacher, Dr. Forbes, was an old pal of Professor Lovibond, they'd been up at Cambridge together. Mummy wrote another letter (I found out afterward) and Forbes had had a word. I often wondered how it had gone. "I say, old boy, I'd love it if you reconsidered *re* Hunter...Catherine Hunter, that's it. Yes...yes, I know. Fierce competition. *Fierce.* But awfully clever girl. And it looks good on dispatches, et cetera."

I was brighter than most people I knew; I understood this, more fundamentally than I understood I was beautiful. That was something other people said after staring at me, it wasn't something I consciously worked at. I didn't ever *try* to be beautiful. Dr. Forbes, for all he was a sexist old dog and, after what happened with Mimi Rosenthal, patently not a suitable person to be teaching in a girls' boarding school, had a brain like a finely tuned machine, and exhorted us to acquire the same, to treat it well, keep it oiled, up to date, carefully tended. I enjoyed this. Most of the other girls took no interest.

But I'd wanted to go because I had been properly accepted by them. Not because they'd rejected me first time round, and because two men sorted a place out for me with some help from my mother. I kept saying: "Someone who really wants to go can use the place. It's not fair." I could have flunked my exams, but I'm not like that. I still wanted to be the best, of course, and I was.

But now I looked at my mother, and I said: "I've been thinking about it. Perhaps it'd be good if I went."

"Oh! Darling Kitty." Her hands, tightening around mine, the scent of lavender rising up as she hugged me, the buds she kept in her pockets crushing against me. She was frailer than me, quite tiny, I noticed, for the first time. "You won't regret it. Really."

I hugged her back, then released her. Holding her, I said: "But if I go, there's a letter I want you to send them. You have to promise you'll write what I say."

"Anything."

"I want to defer for a year."

"What?"

"You said anything, Mummy."

"OK. But what will you do?" Automatically the little hands reached into the capacious pockets of her skirt, rubbing the lavender heads together; the scent rushing to fill the air between us. She inhaled. "Daddy won't want you hanging round—he's not keen on you going in the first place."

"Mummy—you promised. And there's something else, too." I swallowed. "It's really important."

"Go on."

"I want to have your name. I'll go if I can be Catherine Lestrange."

"What?" Mummy said again. She took a step back, into a pile of sketches, which cascaded to the ground. "Why? What on earth for?"

"I just said. Didn't I? I want to change some things in my life. You changed your surname when Simon became your legal guardian, didn't you?"

She nodded, lips pressed tightly together. "Yes. But that was to stop anyone getting hold of the house, and my possessions—he had to move up north for a job, and it meant—" She shook her head. "Yes. I changed it. Did it officially and everything. I didn't want my old name anymore."

"There, you see? You're on my birth certificate as Sylvia Lestrange. I checked. That's all I need. But I don't want…" I pointed behind me, I circled my finger inward, a whirlwind. "…*this*. I don't want any part of this anymore."

My mother took a deep, ragged breath. "But are you saying you'll go?"

"Give me time. I'm still not sure."

She looked down the corridor at a sound from outside. Quietly she said: "You have a couple of days. That's all. Most people would kill for the chances you've had." Her jaw was clenched, the tension of years. She released my hands and reached up, stroking my hair; I flinched. "Yes, Charles! I've got the salad dressing!"

I'd stared at her, wondering if she was allying herself with me or not. I couldn't read any of them anymore. "I know that, Mummy. Will you write the letter?"

My father appeared in the doorway. He glanced around the

study, taking in the papers, the gouache, the stacks of material. I saw the disdain on his face, melting into something like contempt.

"Hurry up then. Good God, it's not that hard, is it?" His eyes slid over me, and the black fog of hatred I had for him suffused my chest.

"Come on, fatso," he said, and reaching toward me, still with that odd look in his eyes, he pinched my waist. I yelped and squirmed away. He chose to take it as a joke. "Here we all are then. Let's eat," he said, stepping out of the dark hallway into the evening sunshine. "What what?"

I rubbed my ribcage, tears smarting in my eyes. Mummy followed him out, then paused in the doorway. "Listen," she said, her mouth barely moving. Her face was hard. "OK, I'll write the letter. You can take my name. We'll not say anything for the moment. But you—you think carefully about what you're doing, Kitty. My name is hard come by."

I have thought, I wanted to tell her. *I've thought it all through.*

I'd got three As, in history, English and Latin. Joss had failed two of his exams, but gained a D in history. My father found this hilarious, and kept slapping him on the back. "Bloody historian we have here! Perhaps you should have been the one to apply to Oxbridge, Joss! Have a change of heart! A regular boffin! Do you need glasses! What what!" Joss had nodded, as if he found it amusing. PF didn't say anything to me.

We'd had champagne at dinner, but neither Joss nor I deserved it. Janey's headteacher had collected the results from her school and rung her here. Later, I had heard her in the tiny cloakroom on the telephone to her mother, burrowed far into the coats.

"Would you at least let me talk to Miss Minas just to see if—Yes, I know. I know. Yes, Mum."

Afterward, Joss had stood silently beside her, as she rested her head on his chest. It made me feel furious. All through supper she said nothing, though we included her in our toasts. "Come on, Janey," my father said at one point, irritated: she wasn't important enough to have feelings that derailed his evening. "Toast our historian here, even if you can't be happy for him."

"Cheers, Joss. Well done. Kitty, well done. You deserve it." Dully Janey had raised her eyes and clinked her glass against Joss's.

Taking the dishes in after the main course I patted her arm.

"Hey, Janey. Won't you tell me what you got? I won't laugh."

She shook herself slightly, putting the plates down on the kitchen table. "You're right. It's just embarrassing. When I set myself up as some kind of clever clogs. I got the same as Joss. A D. And two Us."

"Oh," I said. I felt a sinking disappointment on her behalf.

"And I was predicted two As and a B. It's not that," she said. She pressed her lips tightly together and I knew she was trying not to cry; I knew her determined little face so well by now. "It's Daddy. Wondering what he would have said if he was still here. He was so proud of me. He wanted me to have everything he didn't. He wanted me to go to university. I'm letting him down. And it's all I wanted. But it's more than that. I just—a day like today is hard without him."

"But you screwed up the exams because you'd just lost your dad," I said, squeezing her shoulder.

"It's the feeling of having lost something else. Not just him." She picked up a chocolate mousse, and went back outside.

I wanted to tell her I had always felt a sense of loss, as a small child. That Aunt Rosalind told me once I never cried out as a baby, when someone took my toy, or I was hungry. Joss did, all the time. And yet I was frequently to be found in my crib with tears rolling down my cheeks. I don't remember this. But my earliest memories are about feeling something was missing. I never felt safe at Vanes, or that it was a refuge. I have never liked it here but it's more than that, as if some past memory from someone else has bled through to me. I can't help it, but I feel like a stranger here. Since I was old enough to walk I'd stare at the picture of the Reverend Diver downstairs, unable to look away, as my eyes met his curious, flat, hooded gaze that seemed to follow you up and down the hall. I was too young to realize this feeling of separation from your home wasn't usual. But his face haunted me. I was the outsider, not Janey. She wanted to belong here. I didn't.

So we went to the pool after supper to celebrate. I climbed up the stone steps out of the water, watching wetness slide off me, feeling the heat instantly on my shoulders, my back. I saw Joss watching me, watched him twitch his groin with one absentminded gesture as I patted myself. I saw Merry, knees up under her chin, head bopper headband bopping sadly atop her head, sitting on one of the chairs beside the pool, scanning us all, unable to understand it, the dynamics—poor Merry.

I remember it all so clearly. "Running up That Hill" came on in the background, on the tape machine. I remember pulling the sundress over my head—a faded number Mummy had made with her own material, dusky pink and coral blooms, and the huge pockets she loved, slipping my battered canvas shoes on, shaking my hair out, catching sight of myself in the quietening waters of the pool.

"I'm going for a drive," I said, rolling my swimsuit and towel under my arm. "D'you fancy coming with me?"

Merry looked up hopefully, but I was staring at Janey.

"Sure," said Joss. I ignored him. Janey's eyes met mine.

"Oh," she said. "Right." She nodded and got up.

"Where are you going?" Joss demanded.

"Giles's gig at the Good Leper. Some people are meeting to celebrate the results."

"Giles?" Joss's mouth wobbled, his eyes half closed. "I rang him yesterday; he never said anything about it."

Janey had pulled her T-shirt dress on—also pink and coral, but stripes, and pockets. I remember glancing at her in it, next to me. Behind us. Merry was singing along with Kate Bush.

It's a small thing, but I sang along with her, looking at my dress, Janey's dress, and that and the conversation with Mummy, all of it danced together in my mind, and I think the new idea came to me then, fully formed.

I saw then how we could do it. I saw then how it would work.

So I said: "Giles isn't your boyfriend."

"Is he yours? Kitty. What is it with you two?"

I shrugged. "I don't know really."

Giles likes you, my father had said, around a year ago, when he had brushed against me in the hallway, pushing his flabby frontage against my breasts with a slight grunt. *He's calling you tonight. Be nice to him, won't you?*

"Well, I have a right to know what's actually going on. Are you going out with him?" Joss's eyes closed again, and his lips fluttered. I thought he was trying not to cry, but then he sneezed, three times, and gave a yelp. "Jesus!" He brushed a bee out of the way, into a puddle of water, where it flailed wildly. I stepped backward, out of habit.

"Did it sting you?" Janey said, leaning over him, with a faint display of concern.

"No—no, it's fine." Joss flicked the bee into the pool, morosely, as if accepting defeat. "It's Kitty we have to be careful about around bees. It's dead, Kits, don't worry." He flicked it back at me, and it landed at my feet. "Look—do you have to go?"

"Tell Mummy I'm showing Janey the sights. I don't know when we'll be back."

"But Kitty!" Merry stood up. "Dad wanted to run over the Collecting stuff."

"I know what happens by now, for Christ's sake." I tugged Janey's arm, impatiently. "Sorry, darling. Come on. Let's go."

I had worked out early on why Janey had really been invited to stay—they needed another eighteen-year-old girl, to stand with me, one of the Beloved Girls. In normal years, it wouldn't have mattered, but somehow, something to do with Joss reaching his maturity, this was the Ceremony that mattered. My father's obsession was absolute: this year would be the high point of his life, being able to display to the Leigh-Smiths and the grand families of the county, and also the locals, the Reds and the Culneys, who remembered the old stories, that he, Charles Hunter, still held sway here. That he mattered.

Mired in my own teenage myopia, I didn't realize until after Rory was killed quite how desperate Janey was. She had night terrors, and bit her nails and skin until they were raw, with spongy, pink or yellowing patches around the cuticle. She had lost her father, who was her world. So raw with grief for him was she, and deadened with misery, that she was willing to consider anything. Janey had suffered so much, and I think the trauma meant she had lost the ability to consider, to solve, to adapt. She blundered around, those first few weeks while I was watching her, wondering when she'd come to me. She chatted up my mother. She listened obediently to my father, she palled up with Merry—she even fucked Joss—how obvious. As though with each member of the family she was trying something different. She went through all of them, and I was just there, waiting.

"Are we really going to the pub?" she said, as we went across the lawn, water still dripping down our bodies, between our legs, onto the grass. I looked up to see my father watching us from the terrace, a half-smoked Café Crème hanging from his bottom lip. He was diminished since Rory's death, suddenly older, this long, lingering summer sucking him dry. I knew that too.

"Of course we are," I told her.

I reversed carefully down the drive. As ever, Joss had backed the car into a tight wedge by the oak tree and never bothered to turn it around.

"You didn't do that, did you?" She pointed to the mangled side mirror.

"Do you mind? Joss caught it on a gate on the way back from the pub."

I could see she knew what night I was talking about. She'd been here only a week and Joss and I had gone to the Good Leper because the band was playing. He'd drunk too much and insisted on driving home; the boys had told him he had to be careful, with me in the back. It was out of the question I'd drive, of course. It was one of many nights at the Good Leper where I'd wished to be somewhere else.

You'll ask, well, why did you go? It's hard to say. I knew I was treated badly. But I knew I had to go otherwise it would cause more trouble. The trouble with being a victim is you often don't realize you are one. Part of me still told myself I was lucky. That my life without them was so bad it was worth it. That I didn't care.

That evening, the last time I'd sung with the band, seemed a long time ago. "It's like you've only been here a couple of days, but actually that evening was another lifetime."

She nodded, simply. "The days are long but the years are short, that's what Daddy used to say." Her hands were patiently folded in her lap. She was very restful, I'd noticed. Her movements were gentle. She never raised her voice. "I just want to be straight about this, properly clear. Why have you decided to like me, now? Is it because of Joss?"

I turned onto the main road from the drive, and as I did caught a flash of a face, peeping around a curtain in Ros's gatehouse sitting room. "What about Joss?"

"Well, me and him."

"Ha. No."

"What is it then?"

I didn't like the line of questioning. "Sit tight, will you? I always liked you. Don't you remember? I had to wait till you worked some stuff out. Till you started to see through it. Forget about stupid A-levels. Let's celebrate that instead."

The Good Leper sat at the heart of Larcombe, at the mouth of the stream that flowed down from the woods. There was a little iron bridge from the harbor leading to an artificial island from which jutted a small pier. As a child, I longed to live in one of the sweet cottages on the island, blue, red, green front doors each and gardens filled with listing hollyhocks. It was eight o'clock, and the remaining day trippers on the rocky beach were packing up for the day.

It was less than two weeks since my father's birthday, when we had sat out here on a fresh summer's day eating fish and chips, when there had at least been a smattering of rain. That summer, the heat was constant, and it seemed bound up with something else in the air. It had been the hottest May for almost three hundred years. And as the heat grew an atmosphere seemed to creep into everything, too. Isolated though we were, I was part of this generation of young people who'd grown up with Thatcher. She was my formative political memory; she was in total control. When I'd slip out to meet Sam Red in Larcombe or Minehead he'd talk about youth training schemes, how there was no work for any young people, how there was no money in the countryside, only in the city, especially London. Something was changing that summer. I knew it, I felt it. Young people were going to mass raves, getting high, taking E and acid: they just wanted to dance, not worry about anything else. I'd been to a rave near the school, and not been caught, and it was amazing. I'd danced for three hours without stopping, in a field in the middle of nowhere. Everyone around me loved everyone else. There were no barriers, no impediments to change. And change was happening, it was in my father's copy of *The Times* every day. It was happening in Europe, people swimming across rivers to leave East Germany, people protesting in Hungary and Czechoslovakia. I'd read about it, in the newspaper, heard it on the radio in the kitchen while Mummy cooked. No one else at home was interested. But I noticed. I noticed how stuck we were, and how different it was to the rest of the world. There was change in the air, and even here you could sense it.

"I hate August." I leaned down to lock the Mini. "That feeling of summer coming to an end."

"It's your birthday in a week, isn't it? Aren't you looking forward to it?"

"That's partly why I hate it. We haven't got long, have we?" Then I stopped, and caught her arm: I felt very protective of her, suddenly. "Before we go in, just listen, OK? Don't let any of them get to you. They say stuff, but it's just banter. To wind people up."

"OK," said Janey.

I had my Converse on, and my hair was almost dried, so I ruffled it, making it as big as possible. Wendy James would have approved.

Janey looked at me. "I'd love to be you," she said, unexpectedly, and I saw her look down at her T-shirt dress, her loafers.

"You really wouldn't. At least—" And I stopped. "Never mind, let's go."

Arm in arm, we went into the pub together.

Chapter Twenty-Five

I'd known Giles Leigh-Smith since we were children. His father was County Sheriff and they lived up toward Bossington in a huge, ugly, Edwardian mansion, dirty yellow, and extremely drafty. They were always having parties with a marquee and hired waiters and lots of rented champagne flutes—they were that kind of people.

Initially we'd rather ignored them; we were "old" county, and they were a bit nouveau. Mrs. Red called them "jumped-up." But this changed as the eighties progressed and money was the thing rather than class; my father cultivated Mr. Leigh-Smith, who had money to burn if it meant social acceptance. Mr. Leigh-Smith wanted a house to match the gold-tooled books he'd paid a bookshop in Mayfair to supply; so he bought enough antiques off my father to keep the Hunter family afloat far longer than he realized.

The final piece of the puzzle was that Giles went to Farrars with Joss and was a big success: it was the kind of school that rewarded brutish, muscular young men. I'd asked him once if he enjoyed watching cricket, and he looked totally blank.

"Not unless I'm playing. Waste of time."

He was taken on a yacht two summers ago with Nico, whose father was a Greek shipping magnate, and it was a great surprise to everyone when Giles returned from the Med completely transformed. Gone was the upturned collar of the rugby shirt which had seemed once to form a layer of his skin. In its place paisley shirts from Hyper Hyper and Sols in Kensington Market. Gone the bottles of Stoly and Bolly he filched from his parents' liquor cabinet which he used to help him date-rape girls—I'd been one of them, losing my virginity to him on a pile of coats at a house party, in a haze of champagne and pain. Now he drank gin and tonics, White Russians—anything sophisticated, eccentric, unusual.

Others—notably my brother—followed suit, and within a term at Farrars half the year were sporting black leather necklaces and skull rings, swapping Cure and Smiths and Bowie albums. The remaining boys, the truly committed rugby types and the hopeless geeks, the fringes, looked on with momentary bemusement, and then looked away again.

Farrars was our life, you see. There were just as many girls in the neighborhood (of our kind of people, naturally), but it was what the *boys* were doing that mattered. The school had stood for five hundred years, and never mind if two masters were in prison for what they'd done to several prep school boys, and never mind if my father still had nightmares not from his time in the war, but from his years at Farrars, where the headmaster selected a boy every week to cane for no reason. There was a grand arch at the entrance, in Portland stone, so once you'd passed through it you knew you were on Farrars land.

Joss never really talked about school, though the Christmas of his first year he barricaded himself in the bedroom and refused to come out. My father had to break the door down. He beat him for that. Joss and I had been close, playing together on the grounds of Vanes, looking after the bees together, building dens, swimming races day after day, but after he went to school we never really were, and to my eternal shame I never asked Joss if he was happy. Really we had nothing binding us together anymore until Giles came back from this boat trip and became Mr. Camden Market, and showed Joss the way to be. Joss loved classical music, and color, and noise. He hated team sports, and the company of other men. I think probably he was very miserable until, on the whim of another boy, he was allowed to change his entire personality.

As children, we hunted in the woods, and I loved the bees and making up stories to myself in the garden. I got on with Merry well enough. I adored my father, until I was about twelve, and started to see through him, to find his gaze on me unsettling; around this time he started to criticize me. The two were linked, but separate: at first I didn't understand why he'd be so cruel, telling me I was stupid, or fat, or lazy, or a slut.

"She's turning into a beautiful young woman," the Reverend

Piper had said one Christmas at our drinks party. I was thirteen. I suppose he thought that was an OK thing to say.

"Don't flirt with the vicar, you little slut," my father hissed later that evening, and he'd actually slapped my face, then pushed me into my bedroom, shutting the door. It was the summer I started wearing a bra, and also the summer Mummy started taking our father upstairs immediately after supper, leaving him virtually comatose afterward.

Then I was stung and had to go to hospital, to have an adrenaline shot. No one seemed to know what to do with me, but the doctor who treated me airily said if they'd stung me once, it was less likely I'd have the same reaction again. We came home and no one mentioned it again, though I was terrified now, of what was at the end of the garden, of how they didn't take it seriously, of how not one of us seemed to like the life we were living in the house.

Perhaps this would have gone on indefinitely, perhaps I'd have got away. But the truth is it wasn't until Janey came for the second time that I saw how very odd we were, and by the time I'd noticed it the box was open, and couldn't be shut again. Though I'm not sure I'd have shut it even if I could.

We weaved our way through the crowded tables to the group next to the end of the bar, beside the sticky-looking jukebox, a lifeboat collection tin and an assortment of ancient-looking packets of peanuts. Ranged against the bar was a collection of young people and I saw them through Janey's eyes, though I knew them well. Polly Baring—BJ Baring as she was known, at both Letham's and Farrars—pursed her famous lips into a pouting smile. Nico, just out of hospital for downing a bottle of Smirnoff on his eighteenth birthday at the start of the holidays, was next to her, sitting weakly in a chair, black velvet frock coat, roll-up cigarette dangling from fingers, twist of curled forelock hanging over his eyes. I had been "given" to him by Giles as a birthday present. I didn't meet his eye.

Polly, my nominal best friend, turned back to Guy, her tiny

frame eclipsed by him. The rest watched me approach: Lucy, Hugo, Freddy, Bonar—these were the people with whom I spent my childhood, my schooldays and now my holidays.

"Well, here we are," I told Janey. She said nothing. I saw her rake her bitten fingernails over her balding head.

"Giles?" someone called, as I walked through the bar. "She's here, mate."

Giles came toward us: tall, broad, flashy. Janey took a step back.

"Kitty!" he said, in a voice of booming bonhomie. "Guys! Look, Kitty is here, and she's brought someone."

I kissed his cheek, but he didn't respond.

"This is Janey," I said. "You remember, she's staying with us."

"Right." He nodded, sort of, toward her, but didn't look at her. "Hey, congrats, Kitty," he said. "I hear you got your A-levels, babe."

"Oh. Yeah." I picked a strand of still-damp hair out of my face, running it through my fingers, flicking it behind my back. Lucy Calthorpe, watching, mechanically did the same.

The background chatter in the pub stayed loud, but I knew most eyes were on us, or, if not, that they knew this was happening.

"You must be really pleased. I flunked mine. But who cares?" Giles came up and put one large arm around me, squeezing me. He ignored Janey. As he got closer I smelled cigarettes, stale beer, pot and something funky. He was holding a pool cue. "Are you ready to make some music?" He twisted a lock of my hair around one finger.

"Sure am," I said, trying to jolly myself out of it. His finger turned, rolling the hair tighter. "But maybe in a bit, Janey and I might get a drink, chat first."

"Oh." He was still ignoring her. "I missed you at rehearsal the other day. Thought you'd dumped us."

"You're pulling my hair." I put my hand up to his.

"I'm just saying—you got so drunk the time before we had to drop you back at home, then you miss the next one..."

The time I'd been late, and he'd forced me to drink half a bottle of vodka, then smoke some weed, then rehearse, but I was flopping around all over the place, so he'd driven me home, stopping to make me have sex in the back of the car, in a layby. He'd screeched along the driveway, doing a handbrake turn, and opening the door, pushed me out onto the gravel. Aunty Ros had seen me, tumbling out onto the ground, skirt around my waist. But I was so drunk I couldn't tell her what had happened.

"It hurts, Giles. Stop it."

"Oh. Does it?" But he didn't stop twisting, and then he took more hair into his hand, wrapping it over and under his fist. I moved my head, to accommodate the pain, move closer to his fingers.

In my ear, as I drew closer, he whispered: "Don't fucking stand me up again. OK?"

My neck was bent, one leg and hip lifted higher as his finger rose up, the tight gold spool of my hair around it. "Yeah—yeah," I said, my eyes watering, trying not to let them. You couldn't flap or cry with Giles, he'd sense the weakness. "Look, sorry. We had the stuff with Rory, and the bees, and that girl I told you about staying—"

"I'm the girl. Hi." I had almost forgotten Janey, standing behind me. "Could you stop doing that to her hair, please? She doesn't like it."

Giles gave a bark of laughter, but didn't let go.

"Hi. Really pleased to meet you," he said, in that honeyed, English charming way that he did so well. "Luce!" he called over his shoulder. "Kitty's here!"

"Yay!" came a voice. "Seen her already. Hi, Kits. Love you."

These boys thought of themselves as radically disparate to each other, in the matter of length of forelock, preference for rugger or cricket, beer or port. (Nico was wildly different, because he was half-Greek, a fact remarked on by them all the time.) They were all white, all *definitely* straight, they all liked sport, and loved England, and would vote Conservative.

"Giles," I said. My nostrils stung, my eyes stung; every now and then he'd tighten and it would be painful in a whole new way. *Never mind*, I found myself thinking. *If he pulls harder the hair will just come out. It can't keep getting worse.* "Hey—I love curls, but shall we go and—"

"Hi! Giles," Janey's voice was carrying. "Catherine is asking you to stop. Didn't you hear her?"

I don't think he even registered she'd spoken. "Don't. Do. That. Again," he whispered in my ear, cutting across me. "If I say we re-hearse we rehearse. If I say let's go to the pub you get here early. You let me down. Don't. Why do you do this to me? OK?" He yanked the head again, and then suddenly gave a high-pitched, strangulated squawk. "Ouch! Ow! *Ow! What the fuck?*"

His finger was so tightly wound around my hair he couldn't free himself, and it took a moment, as he screeched even more loudly, a sound like a cross between a sheep's bleating protest and a bird being strangled. "What the—"

He twisted around, to see wax from one of the candles in the wall brazier was dripping into his hoodie, onto his neck.

Janey stood at a distance. Her arms were folded, her coat jacket over her arms.

"She asked you to stop," she said.

Giles glared at her, his face red, rubbing his neck. "Hey. Was that you, billiard ball?"

"Come on," said Janey, walking to the bar, through a throng of curious, staring teenagers. "I'll buy you a drink, Kitty."

She crossed over, ignoring Giles, but he watched her. His face had that set expression of studied lightness I knew so well. Janey leaned on the bar and nodded to Pete, the landlord. "Evening. Vodka, lime and soda for me please. And you? Yep. Two, please."

"Course, madam," said Pete, casting a dubious look at the Pollys, the Lucys, the Guys and Sebs and Nicos. "Single or double?"

She smiled at him. "Oh, double I should think, don't you, Kitty?"

I couldn't meet her gaze. But I knew she had seen the layers peeling off me. Like dead skin, withering in front of her eyes. She knew now I had no power. That outside the gates of Vanes, I was a wounded animal, a joke. Lucy Calthorpe, staring at Janey, gig-gled as Seb whispered in her ear. I saw her eyes, roving over Janey's patchy head, her curious uneven dress, her clompy loafers.

"Where are you at school then, Jane?" Lucy asked her.

Janey said brightly: "St. Cecilia's. It's in Greenford."

"St.... Cecilia's? Lovely. Is it girls only?"

"Yup. It *is* lovely," said Janey. "It's just *lovely. So* lovely."

"Right," said Lucy, uncertainly. Polly, standing next to her, smiled.

"What happened to your hair?" she said, swigging down her vodka tonic.

"My father killed himself, and all my hair fell out," said Janey. "Here you go, Kitty. Cheers." She clinked her glass against mine, as the others stared.

I looked at Giles. He was smoking, moodily, muttering something to Guy, a tall, raffish, vague boy everyone fancied. Guy's mother had modeled for Chanel. Now she was in a clinic with some undiagnosed condition. Guy hadn't seen her for two years. It made him very needy. He was the drummer. I liked him the most of them all. He smiled at me, and nodded.

"Hi there, Kitty. When do we go on, Giles?"

"Not sure. Pete's being a bastard about it. He says it'll put the tourists off. But I say screw that, Petey baby!" Giles turned round and lifted himself up onto the bar.

"Listen, Mr. Giles. I can't turn paying customers away and you're too loud. Better to stick to the jukebox instead, on a hot summer's evening like this."

"The *jukebox*?" Giles said incredulously. "You booked us, though, Pete. I mean—" He turned, suddenly, pointing his finger at Janey. "You. Why are you laughing?"

Janey put down her glass. "Me? Because it's funny."

He stood closer. "How so, Patch?"

"Aahh," said Janey. "Another good one. It's funny because even the person who booked you doesn't want you to play on the grounds you're too loud, which is a nice way of saying you're shit."

Guy laughed and then stopped, abruptly. "You don't know anything," Giles said.

Janey said: "I know lots, actually. And definitely more than you."

She didn't care, that was what was so fine about it all. Janey Lestrange did not care. I had grown up knowing I had my place in the world—I was:

a) Decorative

b) Charming

c) Good at setting the table

d) Leggy. "She's a very leggy girl." Did anyone say that about Joss, whose legs also grew alarmingly long, the same summer? What do you think?

"Show us, then," Giles said, with a small smile. He clapped his hands, starting a slow hand clap. "Show. Us. Then. OK, Pete. We'll stand down. We've got some celebrating to do, anyway. Another night!" He shrugged, like he'd taken the decisions. "Let's have some jukebox time, instead. So. What music do you like, Patch?"

I remember her expression. No anger, just calm. Summing up the facts, considering how best to rebut them. She reached into her pocket and removed her blue Sony Walkman. Nico, or Alex, or one of the band members, sniggered.

"A mix tape," said Cleone, a jolly, husky-voiced girl, Polly's cousin. She had left school the previous year and gone to university in Edinburgh. "Bloody love a mix tape."

"Great!" Janey pressed "play" on the CD cassette player resting on the bar.

"Coming up, the UK official Top Ten," the tape announced, in a tinny voice. "And at number ten, it's 'Eternal Flame,' by those Bangles!" And the keyboard, with its little cascade, led into the song. I half-closed my eyes. I couldn't bear to watch. She'd seemed infallible to me, but that was within the boundaries of Vanes.

Janey swayed in time to the music. Next to her, Cleone hummed loudly, slightly drunkenly. "Good song," Janey said. "Really good. We used to dance to it in the kitchen, and sing into wooden spoons, my dad and me. But this is my favorite." She fast-forwarded it, and "Days," by Kirsty MacColl, started playing.

I'd always thought it was just a sweet, jangling song—it was on the radio all the time that summer, and Janey was always playing it in her room, especially when she was entertaining Joss. But listening to it now as though for the first time, I realized how weird it was. Not a dreamy, summer song at all.

"My dad loved the Kinks," Janey said. "I love Kirsty MacColl. Ray Davies, of The Kinks, wrote it. So it was a song we both liked."

She started humming along, and for a moment everyone stopped and listened, to that bright voice echoing through the dingy, smoke-filled air of the pub.

"That's good, isn't it?" There was a silence. "Who's going to laugh at it? It's funny, isn't it, liking a song like that?"

There was something in her quiet, amused voice. Like she knew them all, and knew they were losers.

She'd stopped the tape, and was fast-forwarding it, and the trundling wheels rattled as they turned. Even Pete had stopped polishing glasses and was leaning over, listening. She pressed "play."

"More. The Queen herself, the one and only, the greatest, the woman who shows us the way…" I realized then she'd drunk a bit more than me at supper. "Madonna!"

"Like a prayer…Ahahahahahhh," she warbled. She had a terrible voice. But she held us all in the palm of her hand, that was what I hadn't realized before, with the spark in her eyes, with her quiet energy, not by shouting loudly. "Just like a prayer! Possibly the greatest album of all time, *Like a Prayer.* You're not singing, Giles!"

"You're ruining everyone's evening," Giles said, smiling. "That's why. Some chaps have come from miles away, OK? It's a special evening for a lot of us and you're not bloody getting it. Now listen, Patch—"

But Janey had pressed fast-forward again, and then stop, and Phil Collins was singing. "Yes," she said. "I've got the soundtrack to *Buster.* Yes, I bought it with my own money when I was sixteen. Got a problem with that? No?"

(I did have a problem with it, but I didn't feel then was the time to point it out.)

Janey downed the rest of her drink, as the door swung open, banging loudly. She turned and nodded. I looked over to see Joss, framed in the doorway, summer evening sun casting a halo around him. His shoulders were drooping, and he was panting—he must have run down the hill.

"I yelled at you to stop so you could give me a lift," he shouted. "I wanted to come too, Kits."

I shook my head at him, hopelessly.

Janey pressed play one more time, and Transvision Vamp came on. *"Oh baby, I don't care…"*

She started dancing, and I saw then that she really could dance—and I remembered that time at the pool, when we'd danced together, when I'd realized again that connection between us. Her lithe, androgynous body moved smoothly, her hands above her head, fists touching. She swayed, smiling, eyes closed, mouthing to the chorus.

Two or three other girls started dancing—Cleone, Polly, even Amarinth. Lucy stayed stock still, looking up at Giles for his reaction. The boys were also silent, as if not quite sure what to do.

I saw Joss, suddenly, in the doorway—terrified, and angry, and I felt sorrow. We'd left school. We didn't have to face any of those people again. I was out of there, I had left already, but Joss knew he would always be here. In the pub, in the village square, at the church on Christmas Eve, at the school for his son's first day at Farrars. He was incapable of change. He glanced at Janey.

"You said she was fit, Joss," Giles said. "Mate. Come on."

"Come," I said, and I finished my drink, and took Janey's arm. She stopped dancing, obediently, and I knew we were as one.

"Are we going now?"

"Yes," I said. The edges of my vision were blurry. I blinked and gripped her arm more tightly. We turned for the door, and I inhaled the scent of the party—cheap perfume, sweat, cigarette smoke, beer, fried stuff, bleach.

"You're not going, are you?" said Giles, in surprise, as if he couldn't conceive why I wouldn't want to stay.

You never seemed nervous, Janey said to me afterward. *You seemed in control, all the time. You'd smile that smile. And you looked like you were sure about everything.*

"I don't want to be here. I don't want to sleep with you anymore. In fact"—I blinked, trying to make the whirring visions go away—"I don't want to see you again."

I said it softly, but I had my keys in my hand, in case he tried to hurt me.

"I'm not sure I've finished with you yet." He gave a slow smile. "So...Yeah. Let's wait and see."

"No, let's not." I shook myself, and clenched my jaw. "You have finished with me and I have with you."

His face pressed close to mine. There was no expression in his dark eyes, which was worse, I wasn't sure why. One eyelid twitched. "Like I say. I decide."

"Janey, let's go," I said, and I stepped away from him.

"Look, Kitty," Joss began. "Not that it's a big deal, but Nico's filled me in, and it's a bit—well, it's really uncool the way you've ruined everyone's evening so—"

"OK, thanks. Bye, Joss," I said, patting his arm.

Outside, the air was fresh, and sweet; the crisp scent of autumn. I felt a horror slide over me, the idea of something ending and something new around the corner, something terrifying. It flooded me, when it came, this idea, and was often all I could think about.

We got into the car and I drove away, fast.

"That was—" Janey began, as we climbed the hill. "That was intense. Are those people seriously your friends?"

I swerved into a layby fringed with heavy beech trees, and turned the engine off, then closed my eyes, willing the blurry moving images away. "Yes," I said, through quick, low breaths.

"Are you OK, Kitty?"

"Course I am. I've had this before." I put my hand on her arm. "God, Janey, you're cool." I started to laugh. "And you're crazy."

She gave a snort. "Am I? I don't care. More and more, I'm realizing I don't care. A bit like the song."

"What don't you care about?"

Janey leaned back in the seat, rubbing her scalp, eyes narrowed.

"Oh. Well, I suppose—any of it? Class, patriarchy, feudalism, conforming. My mother is obsessed with all that, with who mattered, who was at the Greenford Ladies Society luncheon that week, who had a new hat, who went to a garden party at Buckingham Palace. The irony is she's the one who had an affair and broke up a marriage." She laughed. "You look blank." We were both silent, and I heard an owl hooting somewhere in the distance. "It's later than I thought." I looked carefully at her, at her thin, sculpted lips, her high cheekbones, her wide eyes. She put her hand on my cheek, traced my lips with her finger. Then she kissed me.

I'd kissed her before, but this was different. She had come to me.

"I suddenly wanted to," she said, leaning back. "Sorry. Phew. I'm— I never behave like this. Most daring thing I've done is not tell a boy I liked him."

"I wanted to as well," I said. "Do I taste the same as Joss?"

She blushed at that. "I deserve that."

"Sure."

"Do you mind?"

"What? You kissing me or you sleeping with my brother?"

"Both."

"No, neither of them," I said. We stared at each other, flushed, eyes wide open. Hers were deep, deep blue, I'd never noticed before quite how pure their color was, like the darkest sweet peas in the sheltered spot of the garden. "Listen, Janey." My hand tightened its grip on hers. "You have to help me. You want to escape, don't you?"

She hesitated. "I—I don't know."

I tried not to show my irritation, or my desperation. "You—you can see this place for what it is, can't you?"

"It's not as simple as that," she said, looking me over. "You're sick of it. It's new to me. It's kind of magical, Kitty, and it's not being at home and—I—I like it here."

"No, you like Joss's willy," I said frankly. I moved closer to her. My heart was beating in my throat, and behind my eyeballs my head was pounding. "Listen. You know he's not for you. You know he wants to stay here forever. That's not what you want, Janey! The Collecting is next week, and the day after you're supposed to go home. We haven't got long."

"Until what?"

"I'll be eighteen. For the first time in my whole life, I'll be able to do what I want." My voice shook. The edges of my vision were in focus again but I still felt slightly faint. "I want to get away from here. I don't ever want to come back. I can help you, and you can help me. If you want to, that is. If you don't—it's over."

Janey's face was dark in the shadow of the car. "Depends what you want me to do."

I pulled the key from the ignition. "Listen, let's walk back across the fields. I can't drive anymore. I'll leave the car here, Joss can come and pick it up tomorrow."

"The fields?" Janey looked horrified. "How?"

We clambered out, leaving the car pressed into the verge, and climbed over the gate, into a field heavy with nodding, sandy wheat. Two over, harvesting had already started, and the land was gritty with yellow-gray stubble. The milky-white moon was enormous, hanging low in a silver-blue sky.

"What's that?" Janey pointed up to the moor, behind us. Outlined on the distant horizon was a collection of stones, sharp square edges against the moonlight.

"Those are the Vane Stones. They've been there for probably a thousand years. They're one of the highest points around. They catch the sun and reflect it back. They say you can tell what the weather's going to be like by looking at them." She looked totally blank. "Like a weather vane, you see. The house is named after them. You can see them from the front of the house, Joss's side that looks over the moor."

"They're glittering."

"They do that, when there's a full moon. It's beautiful up there. You can see three counties. And the stones are huge. Mummy and I camped out there, once." I'd forgotten how she and I used to do things like that. "It was brilliant, it's totally wild. You drive off the beaten track, along a winding, twisting road, through the heather. Further and further away from the coast up onto the moor. You can't see another soul. We found a huge bank of bracken and slept on it." I was smiling, remembering Mummy's excitement at gathering water from the stream, at us making a fire. "It was so much fun, except when Rory ate the sausages we'd brought for our breakfast." I thought about his soft head, the bulky feel of him against my ankles, and a sob rose in my throat. "I'll take you. We can go up one day. It's beautiful, Janey."

"I'd like that. The Vane Stones." She stared up at them again, at the purple-green ridge of the moor. We walked on.

There was no sound apart from the owls below us, and the rustling of our feet trampling through swaying, heavy wheat, prinked here and there with poppies. Now, I think we'd be shot.

Occasionally a fieldmouse would dart across our path, making Janey start.

The stillness, the heavy heat, the alcohol, the pain in my head where Giles had pulled my hair, all were like a clamp and I walked faster to slough it off, dispel the panicky blackness of the mood that I could feel descending on me.

We were in sight of Vanes; I could see the arched windows, glinting, as though they were watching our approach and winking at us. The moon hung exactly above the house. It seemed to be a living thing, tugging at the stones, coating the parched lawn in flecked silver, washing the ancient flagstones with light, pulling us in toward it. The weather vane creaked, very slowly, turning around, though there was, I realized, no wind. It was stifling hot. The whole place was like a model of a perfect English house, from afar. And we in it were rotten. When had we become rotten? I do not know, but I feel desperately sorry for those two girls, on the edge of the fields, about to step back within the boundary of the house.

Chapter Twenty-Six

I put down a wicker basket of items I'd collected from inside. "Here," I said, taking out a bottle of wine and some mugs. "Have a drink." I pulled out the nighties I'd taken from the laundry basket. "And get ready for bed, in case we have to creep back inside. Or if we want to sleep outside." The truth was I wanted to change, I didn't want to wear the sundress, which smelled of cigarettes and beer and the fetid atmosphere of the pub. Something had shifted inside me, and it was because of her, and the strength having her there gave me to act.

I took off all my clothes, and dived into the pool. My parents slept at the other end of the house, and Merry might wake, but she'd know if she heard us down here that it wasn't her business. Poor Merry, it never was.

The feeling of cool, green water on my naked body was beautiful. It was sharply cold, and fresh. I emerged, shaking my head and smiling. The pool was so deep one rarely touched the bottom, unless one dived all the way down. To be entirely covered with it, to look down and see the moon on the surface, my breasts, my legs treading water, was to feel clean again.

"Did you ever like Giles?" said Janey after a long silence.

"No. Not really."

She took a gulp of her wine out the mug. "Why did you go out with him then?"

I shrugged, which is hard to do while you're treading water, so I slid under again, and swam the length of the pool.

"I don't know. His father does business with mine."

"Wow. I didn't think you—"

"What?"

"Well, you're Kitty, aren't you? You could have anyone you want."

"I'm at school with girls. And I'm Joss's sister. Some guys feel funny, asking me out. And as for meeting anyone not from Joss's school—who else is there? He sort of ... picked me. Started ringing up and asking me out. After a while I sort of couldn't say no. PF kept on at me, kept saying it'd be helpful. Giles bought me all these presents. He'd bring the vodka when we went out. Everyone wanted to be with him. For a time I suppose it was ... like belonging. I didn't ever think I was like that." I shrugged. "Turns out I am."

"Don't you go anywhere else? Friends of friends' houses? Minehead? Parties?"

"It's all the same gang. Always. And they don't hang out in Minehead."

"I like Minehead," said Janey, thoughtfully. "I like the curve of the bay. And the wooden huts."

I thought of Sam Red, the grandson of old Tom, whom I'd met up with a couple of times in Minehead arcade, and also behind the arcade, rather like something out of *Grease*. We'd kiss, and do stuff to each other. It was kind of fun. I'd only gone to meet him to alleviate the boredom of the previous summer, when the other girls—Polly, Lucy, Amarinth, Eliza, were into three things: talking about the same group of six or so boys, skincare, and the merits of shopping for ball gowns at Laura Ashley versus Fred's off the King's Road.

Joss fitted in with Giles's gang, because he adapted. I couldn't work out how to. I wondered about Sam Red now. He was nice. He was a great kisser, and there was something about the combination of his mop of unruly thick hair, AC/DC T-shirt, jeans and sneakers that I found extremely attractive. He *was* attractive. But I couldn't have told anyone I knew that I hung out with Sam, even if I omitted to mention what we got up to. They'd have found it weird. And I'd have got more grief from Giles.

I didn't understand why Giles wanted to be with me. I think he liked having me, knowing I was the prettiest girl, and yet knowing I was his to denigrate and demean in every way possible.

I climbed out of the pool, and dried myself. I put the nightdress on. Janey did the same, not watching each other. I poured myself some wine.

"Anyway," Janey said. "Doesn't sound like much fun to me, only being allowed to hang out with the same group of people the whole time."

"It's hardly like *you're* drowning in friends," I said, irritated that she understood so well. "That Claire girl you're always going on about, and Ems, is it? And...who else?"

"It's different. I chose to be like that."

"Oh really? What about that boy, Paul?"

"I know," she said. "I'll probably never see him again, unless I go home. And I'm not going home."

"You might do."

"You don't understand." Janey dangled her feet in the pool, her toes pointed. "Claire's left, and she won't be back. The others have gone away too. And usually it was just me and Daddy. I didn't need lots of other people. I did stuff with him. He was my best friend."

She bowed her head, looking at her reflection in the still water. "I know. I'm sorry, Janey." My heart ached for her. "I wish I'd known him better."

Janey poured herself another cup of wine. She raised it to me, then drank. In the silence, I pressed my wrinkled, cold fingers against my goosebumpy arm, then glanced up. She was watching me.

"I found him," she said, after a few minutes. "He was in the garage. I can't forgive him, that's the thing. That's what's making me so angry. He knew I'd find him. I don't understand how...If you love someone..." She shook her head, body bowed over so far she was almost bent double, kicking the water. "Suppose you had someone you loved more than anyone or anything. Why would you leave them? And why would you let them find you, make it even worse than it could be?"

I didn't know what to say. I slid one hand out toward her, and touched her arm.

"I see him, you know. Whenever I close my eyes. His tongue was swollen, gray and purple—it stuck out. He looked so—so stupid. Undignified. That's the worst bit. I hate myself for it. For even thinking that. But h-he d-did. I don't understand why."

"Did he leave a note?"

"Yes." She looked up and directly at me. "Yes, he did. Do you know what it said? It said: *Rescue Sylvia.*"

"Oh." I sat back.

"How did he meet Sylvia?" Janey asked. "Daddy said she was his ward, but that's all."

I wrinkled my nose. "I don't...really know. All I know is he was a lodger with my grandmother, in Wellington Square. After she'd left my grandfather who had custody of Mummy. And your dad promised to look after Sylvia if anything happened." I rubbed my still-throbbing scalp. "So he looked after her. Mummy says he was always on at her to work hard."

Janey gave her small, twisted little smile. "He did the same with me."

"After her mum died Simon—your dad, I mean—he stayed on in the house and took care of the lodgers and he made sure Mummy went to school. She changed her name to make it easier for them. She said something today about it. About how it helped protect her. But then your dad lost his job, and had to move away for work. I think that's when it went wrong. Your dad wasn't there."

The music, the glistening ripples of moonlit water, the pull of the moon, the steady drip from my wet hair down my body and onto the ground—all were hypnotic.

"I've been thinking lots about our house. How it's just sitting there, empty. I had a birthday party once," Janey said. "We didn't have lots of money. My mum got really worried there wasn't enough food. So she goes to the corner shop, buys armfuls of Golden Wonders and Monster Munch and when she comes back, Daddy is running up the walls and jumping off. And he's blowing a kazoo in time as he runs up. And there's this group of kids around him, totally transfixed. He said one of them started crying, so he had to take action." I realized she was smiling, and crying. "We all ate the chips and he turns the oven on, and he shrinks the chip packets in the oven and each kid got one to take home. He said it was a special token. And my mum was so furious, it wasn't how she wanted the party to be at all. And everyone said it was the best party they'd ever been to, and she just couldn't see it. The next week, and the week after, at school, children kept coming up to him, clinging on to his hand, begging him to do it again. And he'd say: *Do what?* and they'd say: *Oh, any of it!*"

We both laughed. I tried to make it sound natural, but I was at sea, trying to read cues I couldn't quite decipher. Joss and I had one birthday party when I was seven, some suitable children in the neighborhood and a few locals too. All grouped round the swimming pool, and most of them too afraid to go in, because the water was such a strange, vivid green. Mummy made lavender bags, and quiche, and told us we could run around the garden. But the children were scared of the buzzing from the beehives, and there was nothing else to play with, and they weren't allowed inside—my father's stipulation. Someone fell in, and had to be rescued, and it was all rather grim. Two months afterward, I was invited to Sam Red's party, in Larcombe Village Hall. Sandwiches, jelly, twenty children running around screaming with joy and a magician called Mr. Majelika who made a rabbit actually appear out of a hat. Was it the first time I realized being one of the Hunters wasn't actually all it was cracked up to be?

To have someone here with me, someone who understood, whose mind worked the way mine worked, after all these years, was glorious. But it made me see how unusual our situation was.

"Sorry," Janey said, wiping her nose neatly with a tissue. "I got sidetracked...I don't really understand what happened. With Daddy and Sylvia in London."

"I don't really know either. Just that your dad got a job in Northampton. Somewhere like that. Did you know where?" Janey shook her head. I took a deep breath. "Janey, when he came back she'd taken up with...with my father. They were married when she was eighteen."

Janey's expression said it all. I didn't ever tell people this. I'd been poking through the study and found the marriage certificate, hanging out of a paper file on a shelf. That my father had married my mother when he was forty, and she was eighteen. I don't think Joss knew. He could work it out, sure, if he wanted to, but somehow there was a big difference between her being twenty-two years younger than him now and then.

"He took her down here for the weekend when she was seventeen. Showed her how wonderful it was."

Janey's mouth was curled downward. "So, like...your age."

"Yep."

Even saying it made me feel queasy. I tried to think of Mummy being driven down toward the house for the first time. How alone she must have felt. Sensitive, brilliant Sylvia Lestrange, so alone she felt she had to marry a man I was sure she didn't love, walk into a world about which she knew nothing. Had she had a friend, to speak out for her? Where was Simon, when it happened?

"I once heard my father talking about how nice it was, being married to someone younger. Hugo's dad, Sir Andrew. He told him it was *easy to break her in*. The girls he knew from growing up, a lot of them were land girls or WRNs or WAAFs. They didn't really care for being bossed around. They were Ros's friends. They went off and did their own thing. He's never liked that."

"Oh, God," said Janey. I could see it in her eyes: disgust, pity, horror, re-evaluation. "But how—do you mind me asking, how do you feel about your dad?"

"I don't know." But I did know. I forced myself to meet her gaze. "OK. I don't like him. He's only interested in what he's interested in. And it's not children. It's not me or Merry. And Joss he is interested in, but only if he conforms. I feel sorry for Joss most of all in a way. And Merry, poor lamb. What happens to her I don't know. The irony is she's most like Daddy of all of us." I moved closer. I wanted to make sure I got it right. "He's never cared about Mummy's life. He made her leave art college. She was so talented."

"She still is."

"Yes, but she lives a sort of half-life. She has sex with him every day, and I know she doesn't want to. I don't know why." I paused, and then pushed the heel of my palms into my eyes. "At least I don't want to know why."

"What does that mean?"

I shook my head. I wasn't ready to tell her what I thought. *She sleeps with my father to keep him busy. To keep him sated.* "She's barely there most of the time. She wants me to leave, that's why she wants me to go to Cambridge. To get out."

"Has he ever—" Janey's eyes locked on mine. "Kitty—has he ever done anything to you?"

I shook my head. "It's—looks. And touches. He pushes against me, 'by accident.' He stares at me. I've seen him watching me get changed. He's come into my room, once or twice. He stands there, asking me about Giles. Mummy's appeared, and taken him off."

"Your father," she said, hoarsely.

Bile was in my throat; shame, horror, embarrassment. "It's as if he's waiting. Waiting for something. But he's never quite got up the nerve." I rubbed my head.

I thought she might try and change the subject, or let me know how disgusted she was by me, by what I'd allowed to happen. But she just said: "I'm so sorry. That's awful, Kitty."

I took a deep breath. "Let's not talk about it again, please." She nodded. "*This* is what I wanted to talk to you about. I'm leaving. I'll go—anywhere. Traveling across Europe, then down into Africa. I'm going to take the car. I'll leave right after the Collecting, next week. There's loads of other people there, they'll never notice."

Bless her forever, she didn't look horrified. She said calmly: "Won't you go to Cambridge?"

I shrugged. "I don't know. I've deferred the place for a year. I just know I have to get out of here, and if I tell them, they won't let me. So I thought I'd just do an evening flit. And, Janey—here's the thing. Will you come with me?"

She kneeled up, hugging herself. There was a spark in her eyes I hadn't seen before. "Yes."

"Yes? Seriously?"

We stared at each other.

"We have to plan it without telling anyone," I said. "We leave a letter. We say we've gone traveling, that we'll be in touch. Are you sure, Janey?"

Janey nodded. "I'm sure. What's there for me? I've screwed up my exams, the house is being sold. Mum's making me go to secretarial college. I don't even know where I'd live." She laughed, like it was funny. "I've got absolutely nothing else to go back for." She bit her thumb. "Well, almost nothing."

"Good." I saw the hurt in her eyes at my pleasure, but I wanted to keep going, in case she changed her mind. "We need money. I've got a Post Office account. I just need to—get the account book off Mummy...now..."

"That's OK," Janey said, softly. "My mum's sent me some money."

"There, see? And I've got money too. Aunty Ros gave me and Joss a check, when we finished our A-levels."

"Yes...That's great." She nodded her head, in time.

Back to life...Back to reality.

I shook her knee. "Janey. Think of the places we can see…"

She nodded, and half raised her soft, prickly head. "Can we go to Rome?"

"We can go to Rome. Definitely."

"I want to see the statue of Marcus Aurelius. Dad was always going on about him. He drank champagne under him after the war. And I want to jump into a fountain. Don't care where."

"We'll do all that," I said. I'd never have doubted otherwise, but I knew traveling with Janey would be great. "I want to go to Toulouse. Fermat was from Toulouse." She gave me a funny look. "What? He's a genius. And Toulouse is pink. The stone. They call it the pink city. *La ville rose.* In the evenings, the stones glow rose-gold."

"OK," she said, laughing. "We'll go to the pink city."

I was laughing now too, lying on my front, hip bones rubbing against the cold stone. "I'm so sick of hills, Janey. Toulouse is only a hundred miles from Spain. And then from Spain you can get a boat to Africa." My heart was thumping so hard at saying these things out loud.

"Yes, Kitty!" Janey clapped her hands. "Morocco. I want to go to Marrakech, too." Her eyes were alight.

"And Fez. The souk. They have bars of sandalwood perfume, the whole city smells of it. And ancient silk hangings laid out on the ground. And spices in wooden bowls, and blue dye—" She laughed at me. "What's so funny?"

"It's not. I can see you wafting around the souk in your long blond hair, buying up kaftans. Looking like a Getty. Very Kitty Hunter."

"What do you mean?"

"Oh, the look—" She wafted a hand at me, my flowing floral dress, my hair, my Converse. "You know what I mean. It's quite seventies. You look, yeah, you look like one of those rock group-ies. You've got that sort of vibe going on."

"Don't be silly." I stood up. "I'm not like that."

Janey folded her arms. "You're so funny. You don't realize, you're one thing, but you look completely like another thing. When I last saw you, five years ago or whenever, you were just the one thing. A clever funny girl who was loads of fun. But now…" She sketched an outline of a woman, helplessly, with her hands. "You're another thing."

"I'm not. I'm the same."

"But you don't *look* like that. That's how people see you. Mostly it's the hair. You can't help but look beautiful, Kitty. It's just a fact. Hey, it's a good thing!"

I was silent, then I said: "It's not."

"Come on." Her eyes were kind, but she was still smiling. "It is."

I reached in and took the scissors out of the basket, and started chopping off my long, thin hair, tugging at each chunk as it fell away glinting, like candy floss spun from a whirling metal barrel. "Help me," I said, nodding. "Help me!"

She looked horrified. "Kitty—what the hell are you doing?"

"Please," I said, with a forced smile. "Help me."

"Oh Kitty." She came forward, and took the scissors, and then Joss's battery razor, which he had no cause to use and wouldn't ever miss. After a few minutes my hair was everywhere around us. A heap on the floor. I picked up a clump, then some more.

"Look," I said, leaning over into the water, nudging her to do the same so that we stared at the moonlit water. "Don't you notice anything?"

"Oh," said Janey. "Oh. I see."

Our reflections stared back at us, with golden strands of looped hair scudding the surface: Janey's face, thinner, the eyes a little darker, but other than that, we were strangely similar.

"It's…It's odd, isn't it?" Janey poked at the water with her finger, so that the surface was disturbed, white-gold blocks of light rippling in between our fingers.

Baby, can I hold you tonight?

In the distance over by the low black bulk of the chapel, as ever, the low, constant vibration of the bees, working away, even at night-time.

Nine days to go.

I felt, rather than heard, the crunching of feet on the gravel. As I looked up, my hands still clasping Janey's, I saw the gate to the pool swing open with a bang and Joss limped in toward us.

"I could hear the music halfway down the drive. You'll wake someone up." He was out of breath, as if he'd been running. I could smell the stale beer and cigarettes on him, as he drew closer.

"Who? They're all sound asleep."

I turned, facing him, the scissors in my hand. He froze. "Jesus, Kits. What have you done to your hair? Is that my razor?"

"I got back tonight and fancied a change."

"Oh my God. What will—they all say?"

"I don't know, Joss. What will they say?" But I was terrified, now I'd done it. I daren't look in the mirror. Joss sat down on one of the wooden loungers nearest to us. He ran his hand over his head. "Blimey. We look similar again," he said, with a smile. "Well, a bit similar."

Janey and I moved apart. He took Janey's hand, apparently carelessly, but I knew it wasn't.

"Anyway, they're not all asleep. Aunty Ros isn't. She's awake. I could hear her singing."

I said to Janey: "Getting ready for the Collecting. What else does she have to do?"

"I still have no idea what *I'm* supposed to do." She shot me a look.

"Oh, don't worry," said Joss, airily waving a hand. I closed my eyes, and imagined us. In a square, somewhere in Spain, or France, an utterly foreign place. Together. Warm, spicy smells, cigarette smoke, the clink of glasses. We'd pore over our Lonely Planet guide, or just sit in silence. Free to be who we wanted, to decide where we went next.

When I opened my eyes Joss was clumsily stroking Janey's face. She caught his fingers and held them to her skin, smiling at him. I felt a bolt of rage shoot through me, as my brother turned in, toward her.

"I missed you, Janeypoo," he said, softly. " 'Twas lonely at the pub wivout you."

Janey said: "Giles…he's a prat, Joss. I don't know why you're friends with him."

"Giles is a good pal to me. He's supposed to be your boyfriend, Kitty." He looked up at me. "You know no one will want to go near you when they see what you've done to your hair."

"How's my hair different to hers?" I said, pointing at Janey. I felt furious with her for not saying more after that, just sitting there watching, letting Joss touch her.

"It's not her fault. She lost it because… *because of her dad*," said Joss. He pressed his fingers onto Janey's breastbone, and kissed the top of her head. I gathered up my clothes and punched off the tape player. All was silent.

"Think about what we said, Janey," I said quietly. "I'll leave you two alone now."

In the silence without the music from the cassette player the Collecting Carol started circling around in my head, as it did all the time now, whenever there was silence.

Three, three, the rivals,
Two, two, the beloved girls,
Clothed all in green, O,
One is one and all alone and evermore shall be so.

"Thanks, Kits," said Joss, so patronizingly. He stroked Janey's neck, pulling her closer for a kiss. I strode back toward the dark house.

Janey caught up with me as I reached the terrace, the curling, prickly lichen digging into the soles of my feet.

"Kitty."

I turned around.

"I said I was with you before," she hissed, and the fury in her voice took me by surprise. "I said it, didn't I? And you doubt me just because I'm fooling around with your brother. Why shouldn't I? Don't we need to keep him onside? Don't we need to act like everything's normal?"

"If we're going to leave it all behind…Yes…" I said, slowly, my hand on the door.

"I will risk everything," Janey said, her eyes burning. I saw how angry I had made her, and it was thrilling. "I'll do this, I'll run away so they can *never* find us. I've said I will. Don't you trust me?"

"I—I do," I said. "I promise I do."

"This only works if we're both in it together."

She held out her hand. We shook, and I said:

"I'll make plans. I'll book a ferry. Work out what to do with the car. Where we'll go…"

"Good. Good. So…don't doubt me." Her fingers pinched my wrist. "Don't ever do it again. We're leaving. Together. You and me."

"OK," I said. I smiled at her, shaking my hair, before I remembered it wasn't there. It was in a pile, by the pool, abandoned.

Chapter Twenty-Seven

As Janey said, someone—probably I—had forgotten to explain to her the full tradition of the Collecting, and so it was a surprise to wake up a week later to my Aunt Ros standing at the end of her bed.

"Where's your green dress? Hm? Is it ready?" is what she'd apparently said.

Joss had only just gone back to his room. Janey called me in, and I arrived to find Aunty Ros going through the dark and scratched chest of drawers in the corner of the room, removing Janey's clothes and shaking them out.

"Your mother should have sent you down with something suitable," she said, as though Janey were a new housemaid arriving to wait on the Queen. "Don't you understand?"

"Sorry," said Janey, sitting up in bed. She wrapped the worn quilt more tightly around her—she was naked. I stood in the doorway, watching them.

"The Beloved Girls wear lovely long green dresses. Oof, there you are, Catherine, looking like goodness knows what. Honestly," said Aunty Ros, her currant-bun eyes disappearing into her wrinkles as she screwed up her face in reproach. "What Miss Lord would say were she to see a Letham's girl turn out like you—" She slammed a drawer, furiously. "Nothing in here. Nothing at all. Don't you have *anything* that'll do?"

"Nope," said Janey. She ruffled her hair, which was, I saw in the morning light, growing back, and fairer than before. "I'm sorry. I didn't think when I was invited here that I'd be asked to take part in a pagan ritual."

"Don't be sarcastic with me, little girl," said Aunty Ros, waggling her finger. "I know all about you. I know you've got your claws into the twins. Both of 'em." She shook her head. I realized she was getting herself worked up—she was more and more unpredictable lately. I patted her shoulder.

"Aunty Ros, there's the Dickins and Jones dress I wore when I was Georgina Lowther's bridesmaid. That'll fit Janey. And it's quite like my dress."

"You'll look like boys," said Ros, in despair. "Both of you. It's the Beloved Girls. *Girls*—you should look the part."

"Princess Di has short hair," said Janey.

"Her Royal Highness Diana the Princess of Wales has appropriate hair." Aunty Ros clicked her heels together. "She doesn't have hair hacked off with a blunt pair of scissors like a—a—gypsy." She shook her finger at Janey again. Her voice rose. "St. Bartholomew's Day, or rather this year the twins' eighteenth birthday, is the most important day of the year here. You can sneer at it all you want. But it means something, to Kitty's father and me. I always took part in the Collecting—every year after I was eighteen, I was a Beloved Girl. Before that I'd walk with the procession. Daddy carried me if I was too tired. One year, he let me remove the comb myself. Got stung twice, I didn't cry though!" She stared out of the window, at the delicate morning sky, pale blue and lemon yellow. I could feel autumn, pressing against the glass, longing to be let in. St. Bartholomew's Day always made me feel like that.

But we weren't doing the ceremony on the usual day. Saint Bartholomew's Day had come and gone, and we were doing the ceremony on our birthday, in two days' time. And every day we delayed, the bees grew angrier. My father had stopped checking on them, after Rory died. He said it was best to leave them to it, not to open the hives too often, to guard against robber bees and wasps. The previous day after breakfast I had heard Mrs. Red ask him if he was going to replace the queen.

"She's a bad one, Mr. Charles." She'd rubbed her hands viciously on the tea towel, then leaned back against the sink, arms folded. "Get a new one. A new queen will put them in a better mood."

But Dad shook his head. "She's fine. They're all fine." He'd been leaning against the kitchen table, an amused look on his face. He'd stepped forward, patting Mrs. Red's arm. "Dear Mrs. R, have a little faith. I think I know what I'm doing, after all these years, what what?"

Mrs. Red was old enough to remember Pammy, my father's sister, dying. I'd asked her about it once. "Little thing she was, small for her age, and they made her stay outside when they were in. Terrified she was. Kept saying she didn't want to stay. Well, they took too much, and disturbed them, and they turned, flew straight out the door, got her. Her poor little heart." She'd shaken her head, wiping her eyes. "Such a clever girl. Kind. It was dreadful, Kitty, dear. Absolutely dreadful."

I had seen the look she gave my father as she moved past him, to put the dishes back on the dresser. Then she glanced up, and caught me peering through the door, and her face twisted from alarm to something different. Jubilation. I didn't understand it, not then.

"We'll practice this evening, so we're all clear," said Aunty Ros now. "It's the biggest one yet, it's important to get it right. Everyone needs to know their part."

"Do we have twelve hunters?"

"Oh yes," she said. She opened the window, letting in morning air. "The Red family, the Culneys, Pete Crawter from the Good Leper, and so on. They're honored to do it."

Janey gave a repressed chuckle, and Ros looked at her suspiciously. "Is it funny?"

"Oh, I don't know." Janey reached out for her nightie, then pulled it over her head, stretching out her arms and yawning. "It's—you're all so obsessed with it. I find it a bit funny, that's all. All to celebrate Joss's birthday. Not even Kitty's birthday."

Ros took her time folding up a sweater and placing it carefully back on the chest of drawers. "It's tradition, Jane."

"I know it's tradition, but—" Janey hopped out of bed and stretched again. "I don't mean to sound rude. But the world is changing. You know, a thousand people had a rave not far from here the other week. All those men and women who drowned on the *Marchioness* last week. They were young, they had their whole lives to live. Some of them would have changed things. For the better. It just seems so—I don't know, strange, to be obsessed with this ceremony, when it—it's got nothing to do with real life."

"Have you lived in the countryside before?" Jane shrugged a *no.* "Of course not. Listen." Ros hitched up her skirt, rolling her head round her neck in an alarming fashion. "What's your favorite clothes shop? And what's your favorite thing to eat? Quickly. Tell me."

"Um…" Janey held one arm, the other dangling, head on one side. "Dash? Topshop? And my favorite thing is…well, it's toast, actually. With lots of butter. And apples."

"There. So not far from here, there's the Lowthers' fields of wheat, hundreds of acres of the stuff, they sell it to Sainsbury's mainly, that makes flour for the bread you eat. And the sheep who make the wool for that sweater, they're grazed all over these parts. And we make the honey. Hugo's family, they make vegetable oil. You drive half an hour east and all of Somerset is one big apple orchard. My family used to own coal mines not far from here, so your family could keep warm. You don't think about where it comes from. You see it and think how strange we are. But there's a connection, a connection to the seasons, to the land." She opened the drawer, hypnotically slowly, and slid the clothes back in. We watched her. "Listen, Janey Lestrange. I don't listen to the news. I don't need to know what's going on today. I know what matters." She jabbed the top of the chest of drawers with one stumpy finger. "We lose that connection and we are in trouble. If bees don't fly around collecting pollen on their legs and brushing it off onto other plants, the plants don't get pollinated. If they don't get pollinated, we don't have apples for you to eat. We don't have most fruit and vegetables, we're dead in twenty years."

Janey looked at her, obviously not believing a word of this. "OK."

Aunty Ros said, grinding her jaw: "I ask you simply to understand that this is a little corner of the world that follows the rhythm of the year, that respects it, and the ceremony with the bees is one way of acknowledging that. And that's why it means so much to people."

"Yes, Ros," said Janey. She nodded. "Sorry if I sounded rude."

"Fine. Why don't you come down with me and we'll find that dress of Kitty's. It's hanging in Sylvia's wardrobe. You can see if it fits." She handed Janey some knickers. "Leave your nightie on, you'll change afterward." Janey nodded meekly. "The hunters, the honey makers and the three rivals will be here at six."

"Who are the rivals?" I asked.

"Some friends of Joss."

"Oh," I said. "Giles?"

"Yes. Joss asked for him specially. Your father's pleased. I imagine you are, too!" Ros smiled, her face creasing into unfamiliar lines. "Kitty, dear, that reminds me. I've found a nice hairband you might want to wear, to cover up the haircut." Ros gave a chuckle, determined now to indulge us, as if it were all a big game. "I don't ask for you to be in crinolines, but it's nice to be young ladies now and again, Kitty, and the ceremony is so special—"

"Thank you," I said.

She bent down and patted the bear on Janey's bed. "Come on, Janey, dear. This is a pretty little room. It was mine when I was a girl."

They passed out of the room, leaving me alone in there. I stood for a moment looking around, wondering what a young Rosalind Hunter would have got up to in here. I was pretty sure I knew. On the shelves were rows of old Angela Brazil books. The built-in cupboard under the eaves was filled with boxes of letters and photographs. One summer I'd gone through them all, hoping for some scurrilous boarding school anecdotes, but it was all crushes on head girls and endless stories about the beneficence of Matron or the headmistress. I remembered the tale of a girl who had broken her leg falling from her pony—you were allowed to keep ponies at Letham's then, but the stables had been demolished after the Second World War. Young Ros had written a five-page letter home about how the headmistress, Miss Shaw, had given the girl her own handkerchief as she lay on the ground waiting for a doctor to arrive and set her leg. "She told Arabella she could *keep the handkerchief*. I long for a broken leg!"

Joss and I used to quote this to each other, when Aunty Ros was particularly manic about Letham's or anything else. *I long for a broken leg.*

There were a few mentions of Charles ("he's a fine fellow; Father says he thinks a great deal too much of himself though") and Pammy ("everyone says she is a dear little thing, thoroughly excited about becoming a Letham's girl!"), but nothing about her death, though Ros would have gone back to school two weeks after it happened. She'd been wiped out of history. I realized, looking at the box, I'd never even seen a photo of Pammy. She was my aunt, and I had no idea what she looked like. What had she wanted to do, to be? No one knew. When her siblings were dead, no one alive would remember her. She wasn't even a ghost. Apart from the leaflet about the bees she was gone, forgotten.

I started going through Janey's things. The striped T-shirt dress that suited her cool androgyny, the strange baggy T-shirts with messages on them, the second-hand skirts and dresses, the hideous brown sandals. There were her underpants, on the floor, and bra. I picked up the bra—her breasts were smaller than mine. I held my fist inside the cup. I flicked through the books on the bedside table, and the letters.

I still miss you,

her friend Claire had written.

I'm sorry it sounds so weird there. Are you sure you can't come back and go to secretarial college here? Do you want me to ring your mother? If she knew you were willing to agree I'm sure she'd help you. What can I do? I want to see you before I go to Birmingham, Janey!

The Radio 1 roadshow was in Somerset this week, somewhere like Western something, with a pier? I wondered if that was near you, did you see it? It was Mark Goodier, I do not understand why you think he's fit. I got all the questions right on Bits n Pieces, but it's not the same without you there, Janey. I miss you.

I saw Do the Right Thing last week and Paul Rolles was there with another girl, thought you'd want to know. They were all over each other (it was grim).

Loads of girls from school have been going to raves, there's a place out past Ruislip, apparently it's great, maybe we can go when you're back…

I hope you are OK. I think about you a lot. I hope you don't miss your dad too much, Janey. Let me know if you want me to talk to your mum.

Love from Claire

(Your Best Friend in case you'd forgotten)

PS Got some Tooty Frooties waiting 4 when U R back. And my dad bought me the double album of Sign "O" The Times.

I hated this letter, I hated it so much my first instinct was to scrunch it up and throw it away, then I realized Janey would find out and I'd look mad. I was mad, but she couldn't know that. I bit my finger, wondering what to do. I hated Claire, with her view of the world, her trying to drag Janey back into normality with her. Janey didn't want to be normal, she wanted to stay here, here with me.

Then I read the letter from her mother. Her mother was pretty awful. My mother, for all the horror I felt quivering around her at times, loved me, I knew that, I knew it fundamentally. I wasn't sure Janey's mother did.

You cannot go to university to study ideas, and theories, and not learn how to make a living. Even if they wanted you in this day and age it is a waste of your time, of money, of everything. You're not one of them.

You're not one of them.

I could hear Janey downstairs, talking to Aunty Ros. I could see it all then, as clear as day. I ran downstairs, avoiding the creaking stairs. The house was silent in the early-morning stillness. I crept into Mummy's study, and pulled out the electric typewriter. I had watched Mummy write a letter with it five days ago, the letter that was now hopefully resting on the desk of the Dean of Admissions at King's College. It was that which had given me the idea.

I'll go, I told her. *If you do this for me.* I started to type, ignoring the voice in my head which said: *You're betraying her.* I wasn't. I was doing what was best for her.

Dear Mum
   I am staying on at Vanes and then going traveling with Kitty. I've had a great summer. I love it here. I don't want to go to secretarial college.
   You've made it clear you've no interest in me or my future. Now I'm eighteen, I don't have to

---

do what you say. Hope you understand that. I
don't expect you to provide a home for me any
more. You can handle the sale of the house,
Mum. I will be in touch about my share of the
money. Despite what Martin says, I've got a
friend here whose father is a solicitor and he
will advise me on how we divide up the proceeds
when it's sold. Or you can just give me half,
which is the minimum I'm due given you were
divorced from Daddy.

You can write to me, I'll send a postcard
with details of what my address will be.

Take care, Mum, it's for the best, isn't it?
Hope this brings you some relief. Tell Claire
if you see her that I fancied a change and to
keep the Tooty Frooties for next time.

Janey x

I printed it out on our headed paper, and signed it with Janey's
small, tight signature, which I'd taken to practicing, over and over
again.

It was very quiet in the house. Mummy was outside, deadhead-
ing flowers, my father was dozing in the study as he always did
after breakfast.

"What are you doing?" I spun round, to see Joss in the doorway.

"Oh," I said. "Just something for my Cambridge place. I have to
send it off today." I smiled at him. "I hear Giles is one of the rivals."

"Yes, and Guy and Nico. Good chaps." Joss swallowed, and
pulled at the black leather thong around his neck, from which
hung the shark's tooth he told everyone he'd bought in Camden
Market but which in fact was bought in Minehead at an establish-
ment confusingly named Mavis Crystals and Joss Sticks. "Listen,
Kitty—he's... Um—it's all right, between you two, isn't it?"

"Course it is, Joss."

"Oh, good." Joss looked enormously relieved. He fingered the
shark's tooth. "Because, you know—uh, if he wasn't treating my
little sister right, I'd have something to say about it."

"Of course," I said, marveling at this. "No. It's ... fine."

"OK."

"And Joss?"

"Yeah?" he said, fingering some of Mummy's old textiles.

"I'm your big sister, by the way." I blew him a kiss. "See you later."

I ran to the mailbox, at the end of the drive, and mailed the letter. On the way back, I passed Aunty Ros, humming as she hung out her washing in the tiny little gatehouse garden.

"Dare to strive, strive to dare!" she called loudly. "Are you ready for tonight, Kitty?"

"Sure," I said. I pulled my sleeves, easing them over my thumbs, and went back along the drive. Inside my head, it felt alternately light, fizzing, bright and heavy, as though my brain was pulsing, aching with trying to work, to process, to complete.

Chapter Twenty-Eight

The rehearsal went well. Janey and I were demurely obedient, hands clasped in front of us. The twelve hunters were a little too overexcited and had to be told by my father to calm down. It was their job to walk at the front of the procession, two apiece, starting the singing. They had to be local because they had to know the words of the song. It's an old, strange variation and the rhythm needs to be right. One year I remember a gang of them including Tom Red's father, Jim, drank too much beforehand, and got hopelessly out of sync, then crashed into each other at the door of the chapel. Joss and I were about nine and thought it was very funny. But Aunty Ros and my father were not amused.

The twelve hunters were: Matty Culney, Jed Culney, a gaggle of Reds, including my old friend Tom, Pete from the Good Leper, the Yarner boys, and two sons of the Thomas family who came on holiday at the same time every year and liked to pretend they were locals while they were here. They took the whole thing immensely seriously, though not, of course, as seriously as my father. "You're Hunters for one evening only," he kept saying to the locals, trying to nudge those close to him. "Don't get any ideas into your head, will you? My wife would kill me!" And everyone would laugh, the Thomases sycophantically. Mummy just stood there, dangling the key in one finger, watching him, with her vague, vague smile.

"*So* charming," I heard Mr. Thomas saying to his wife as their sons walked out, ringing the handbells.

The five walkers were Joss, my father, Merry, Ros and Mrs. Red, all carrying the smoke and bellows. Mummy was the Outsider. The honey makers were four women from the village, Mrs. Culney, Pete Crawter's wife, and so on.

One of the rivals was missing—Giles had said he'd make it later. Anyone else, and they'd have been thrown off the team, but my father said nothing. The two remaining rivals, Guy and Nico, walked behind us, holding their spoons.

"Why are we here, man? This is fucking stupid," Nico hissed, and was nudged by Guy.

The Outsider always picks a helper—Mummy, at my father's prompting, selected Ros and she, greatly pleased, very much enjoyed the ceremony of opening the door to the chapel, as my family gathered around her to pretend to push the smoke into the tombs and into the roof. We used the smoke to calm the bees down, before we opened up the ancient hives.

Even though this was a practice run and the tombs and the ceiling would not be opened until the ceremony, I hung back. I was not terrified of bees—I had grown up with them. I knew their moods, what kind they were. I knew too that they didn't sting you unless they absolutely had to. But I didn't like being in the midst of them. That was why I loved being by or in the pool. There were rarely bees there.

We didn't ever talk about the time I'd been stung. I don't think my father could quite believe it, that he had a child who was allergic to bee stings. It was like his cousin's daughter Clarissa, who, we'd been informed in their much-mocked Christmas round robin, had an allergy to dairy. "Dairy allergy indeed," my father had said, laughing hysterically. "These girls, honestly. Like Kitty and the bees. Load of nonsense!"

"It's serious," Mummy had said, in exasperation. "If she's stung again, her heart could pack up. The venom sends her into some kind of shock."

"What, and it doesn't with us?" said my father. "Come on, Sylvia. No one likes being stung. It's one of those things. Your daughter just likes to make a fuss."

Mummy had pushed open the door with her bottom, carrying two platters out to the dining room. I'd seen her face, as I hovered in the hallway. "Jesus Christ, Charles. Do try to understand."

I think he took it as evidence of my betrayal. That I was a Bad Daughter, in some way. Merry, jumping eagerly behind us all, wouldn't develop something as ludicrous as that.

Some people at the back—the lads, the twelve hunters—were humming the Collecting Carol, as the setting sun flooded into the open door of the chapel and the old leper window. A sharp wind came in, and Janey, wearing the silly bridesmaid's dress into which Ros had forced her, shivered. In my mind, I was thinking how useful this rehearsal was. How I could see it all now, the food laid out in the drawing room and kitchen and on the terrace, the champagne with which they were all liberally plied beforehand, the tasting of the honey.

I knew too that this year the honey was madder than ever, though no one ever admitted it. Something to do with the rhododendron bushes that ran along the north wall of the garden, and the reason why my father never sold the honey. We mostly ate the spring honey. But you never ate rhododendron honey in large quantities. Once a year, in summer, was enough, and it was the reason they were all there, giggling, nudging each other. Everyone knew.

In Minehead Library a few summers ago, whiling away the hours of a wet August at home I had read in a dry, long-forgotten book turned the wrong way on the Natural World shelf about a similar honey in Anatolia, in a part of Turkey. I remember the sound of rain on the large glass windows, shutting the book quickly, afraid someone might spot me. It made perfect sense. *"In large quantities can have an hallucinogenic effect."* I wondered if a member of my family was the person who had read the relevant passages and neatly underlined them in pencil. I came to consider if it hadn't, over the years, got into their blood somehow, permanently changing them, driving them mad. Whether that is why no one had been able to save Pammy.

As the rehearsal finished and the participants dispersed, I was thinking about what we'd need to pack, how we'd get the bags in the car without anyone noticing, whether the letter requesting the name change had arrived at Cambridge.

My daughter is delighted to accept the deferred place as discussed on the telephone, Mummy had written. *Please note that the name on the exam certificates (which I am delighted to enclose here) is not correct. She now chooses to use my name. Therefore Catherine*

Lestrange will be taking up the place in the Michaelmas Term of the following year i.e. 1990. Please could you confirm by mail or via the telephone that this change has been made and is acceptable.

Yours sincerely,

Sylvia Lestrange

"Two days to go, my dear!" my father said, slapping me on the back when the rehearsal ended. "Just two more days."

"Where's Joss gone?" I said to Janey.

"He's gone down to pick up the car. Your father wanted him to." The car was still where we'd abandoned it last week, on the edge of the field after the night at the pub.

My parents walked back to the house together, and I watched them go: she so small, slight, the tension in the distance between them to me a palpable thing, and we were alone by the pool. It was early evening, electric-blue light, the Seven in the western sky, low as ever they went, and there was an edge to the warmth. Summer was almost over.

I swam, and Janey joined me. We did not speak—lately, we found we didn't need to. In places, I noticed, her hair was now longer than mine. I wondered if she might want to have longer hair. I'd chosen to have short hair. She hadn't.

"Do you—like Joss?" I said, when we were sitting at the edge of the pool with our feet dangling in the cool water.

"I like him, yes."

"You know what I mean."

"Of course. I'll say it again. I like him. Possibly more than you do."

I laughed. "I don't dislike him. He's my brother. It's just—" I took a can of beer out of the ancient cool box by the table. "I don't know." I wanted more from her.

"Try me."

"It's incredibly strange to me, the idea that he and I were in the womb together. That we were face to face, touching each other, together. And we have nothing in common. Apart from you."

Janey shook her head. "I think you have more in common than you think."

I drank another can of beer and we sat in silence, for a long time. Like I say, there were no words. Gradually, the energy of the house dipped. A light went out here, and then there.

"Kitty," Janey said. "What will you do? After we've traveled? Will you come back? Will you go to Cambridge?"

I stuck my finger into the beer can. The sharp opening cut into my skin. "I don't want to let them down." But I didn't want to. I didn't want to have to make decisions about the future. I didn't *see* the future. That was the difference between us. "What about you?"

Janey eased herself into the pool. "I'll get a job. I might try and retake the exams. Get into university. I don't know." She blinked. "Not sure how I'll afford it."

I thought of the letter I'd written and hadn't told her, to her mother. I thought of all the plans I'd put in place. *You're lying to her. It's not lying. It's...organizing things.* I was keeping secrets from her, and it was best that way. For the moment. I told myself that was the truth. My fingers were wrinkled, freezing cold, but I didn't want to go inside. If only. In the distance was the faintest of roars, like water rushing, or an engine.

"This time next week," Janey was saying, "we'll be—What?"

I'd stood up. The sound I had heard was a car engine. Footsteps on the gravel. "Stay still," I said. "Don't move."

Janey froze. There were voices. Low, very quiet. Outside the boundary, somewhere in the trees, our friend the owl called. I could hear the footsteps, on the terrace, then silence.

"They've gone," said Janey, very quietly. "It's nothing."

"No," I said, terror making it hard for me to speak. I knew the pattern of the sounds. There was no sound when you walked on grass. I knew they were coming.

"There you are!"

A voice in the doorway, holding the wooden door open. I looked over, to see my brother, half slumping against the stone frame, his floral waistcoat unbuttoned, hair disheveled. He had a red wine smile around his mouth.

"I brought some friends back," he said, very quickly. I could tell Janey didn't understand him. He couldn't look at me.

"You didn't drive like that."

"Someone left the car in the lane. Silly." He waggled his finger.

"Hey, Janey. Hey." Then he turned. "Giles! Guy! Nico! I found the girls!"

He really was in a state; I'd seen my brother drunk, but never that drunk. I couldn't imagine how he'd driven the car up the road. What had they given him, in such a short space of time? He staggered across the flagstones to the side of the pool, and was sick into it.

"God, Hunter, you're disgusting." Giles was behind him, the other members of the band flanking him.

"What are you doing here?" I said. I felt prickly with panic. My swimsuit seemed to be shrinking, with me inside it.

Giles had his hands on his hips. He looked down. I remember his face, seen from that angle. Flattened, wide, the black hair sticking out, the black stubble gray on his chin. He had jeans on, with a thin belt. He wore loafers without socks.

"I came to see you. Don't you want to see me?"

"No," I said, looking up. "I don't want to see you. You should have been here earlier, and you shouldn't have got Joss this drunk. Look at him. What did you give him?"

"Hi, Kitty," said Guy, as Janey hastily swam to the other side of the pool, away from Joss's dispersing puddle of vomit, and jumped out, shivering. She looked like a half-drowned animal, her hair in patchy spikes. "Thanks for having us. We won't stay long."

"Oh," said Giles. "I don't know about that." He took a bottle of wine out of a plastic bag. "I think we might stay for a bit, don't you, Kits?"

Nico was giggling, rubbing his gums; Joss was still bending over the pool, hands on knees, trails of spittle swaying from his mouth. He was groaning, low. "Joss," Janey said. "Joss—oh God. That's disgusting...Joss."

"I don't feel well," Joss said, his face white, and he stared at me, our eyes locking, the two of us, once as close as it's possible to be, that tiny connection still there.

"Joss..." Janey wrapped herself in a towel. "Come here...oh God, don't be sick again. What the hell did you do to him?" she demanded. "Joss! Come back!"

Joss ran toward the door, stumbling as he went, and she turned back toward me, and shrugged. "Back in a minute."

I could hear her, calling his name, softly, across the lawn. I watched through the open gate, and then was grabbed from behind as Giles hauled me up, underneath one armpit.

"We're going into the pool house," he said to the others.

"Are you OK?" said Guy. "Catherine?"

A man with a conscience. Or the beginnings of one. I often wonder what happened to him.

I looked back but Janey was gone. I should have called out for her. She would have come, of that I'm certain. But I didn't. Girls should, but they don't. Girls should make more noise but they're told not to. To box themselves in. Be loved and be quiet.

"I missed you tonight, Kitty," Giles said, in a soft voice, but so the others could hear. He stroked my hair; those fingers on it again. I wanted to scream. He opened the pool house door, courteously, and I went inside. The smell of warm wood, of soft mildewed fabric curtains, of towels; it had always been one of my favorite scents, the aroma of home, what I dreamed of when I came back from school during the holidays. I loved this warm, safe, old room. I turned around, about to ask him to leave, and he shut the door. Then he kneed me in the stomach, catching me off-guard, so I buckled, and fell to the floor. "There," he said. "I don't think you've been very nice to me lately, Kits. I thought you might want to be nice to me now."

He raped me, though at the time I didn't think it was rape. I didn't want him to stroke my hair, then my neck. I didn't want him near me at all. I said no, but he said I wasn't being friendly, that I had humiliated him. I didn't want him to take the strap of my swimsuit down, but he said I was too full of myself, that I had badmouthed him, shown him up, made him look stupid, that I owed it to him to be nice now. I didn't want him to push me onto the ground where my little sister's old red bathing suit from last year lay under the bench, kicked away and furry with dust. I looked at it as he covered my mouth, and pushed up inside me as I screamed in silence.

"There," he said, "this is nice, isn't it? If you just try, a bit. Last time you made no effort. Polly puts some effort into it."

I didn't want his weight on me, his smell, of rancid sweet decaying alcohol and the pressure of him on my hips and breasts, his jigging, frantic fatness, the pain of it inside me, how raw it was. Red, hot, sore—people say those words to describe sex and I think how strange. He went harder and harder, clutching my breasts as though they were handles. That hurt so much too. But the penis inside me was the worst. It rubbed, every time a little more, until I started to panic, and believe it wouldn't ever be able to get out. I couldn't breathe. I kept trying to breathe. Giles wasn't looking at me anymore, his head was down. Like it was an endurance race. So I just stared at the edge of Merry's swimsuit—I remembered the day we'd bought it, in Debenhams in Bristol, for some reason, where Mummy had taken us shopping. I tried to remember where we went for lunch and when the edge of the pain returned I pretended it wasn't me. That this was happening to another person.

I was not me anymore.

I took myself to another place. Ignored him pulling my fingers back, him yanking my hair, grabbing my breasts and squeezing them, the sound of it.

He spat on my stomach when it was all over. I looked up at him, and didn't say anything. I learned then, really then, the power of staying silent. I was wrong, of course, but to me it felt like power. He jammed two fingers inside me afterward, and said I was disgusting, and as I stood up, looking down, trying not to think about how to breathe, I heard him laughing, as he wiped his fingers on Merry's towel.

"Bye, Kits," he said. "See you at the ceremony. Have a wash, will you? You stink."

The others had gone—vanished into the night. I stayed inside and then emerged into darkness. The Seven were still there, even lower in the sky than before. I wanted to swim but the pool was dirty now, everything was. When I was certain he had gone—I didn't know how he'd get home, and I didn't care—I crept up to my room. I stuffed torn-out pages of my old school books under the door, creating a wedge, and then climbed into bed. I went straight to sleep. Which was the strangest part of it all.

Chapter Twenty-Nine

The following morning, I crept downstairs. Sun was stealing into the kitchen, along the passageway and out to the garden. I opened the back door and stood, inhaling the fresh air for a moment. There was a very slight breeze, but it was still too hot, already, though it was barely seven.

My mouth was dry. I was so sore inside and my muscles were aching: my stomach, my hips. My hands hurt where he had gripped my wrists. My scalp stung, where he'd pulled the tufts of my shorn hair. My eyes were sore, though I hadn't cried.

No one else was up yet, it seemed. I picked up the car keys, and left the house.

The sea was too cold for the early day trippers who squealed and stumbled away from the uneven shingled shoreline. Not cold enough for me. I swam for ages. The salt stung my eyes, sluiced my torn body with pain. The water across the bay looked calm, liquid gray velvet shot through with teal, but sometimes the strength of the tide pulled me violently in, toward the rising bank of gray stones on the beach. I didn't mind, being battered about like this. I was a strong swimmer. I wanted to feel nothing, to feel numb.

I came out of the water, wincing as I walked on the hard stones toward my beach shoes and towel. I sat on the beach, aching all over, the stones digging into me. I liked it.

I didn't know that I was a victim, that he had done a bad thing to me. I felt it, inside, outside, but I wouldn't have believed it if someone had told me. All my life I'd been told to put up with something or other: that I didn't have a choice about where I went to school, what friends I made, what boys I dated, what clothes I wore, even where I went after school. What would it feel like to be in charge of one's life? What would it be like? What would I choose to do, if I could?

I could never go into that pool house again, I knew that. I could feel seawater, seeping through me into the thin old towel I had taken from the bathroom.

I'd pushed so many people away. I had been living this lie of Kitty who is a goddess and in charge for so long that really I would have to start again, unpick it all, become another person. I didn't think I could. I wished the decision could be taken out of my hands.

After a while, I realized I was shivering. I pulled a sweater over my head, looking at the bruises forming on my legs, and the scratches from the night Janey and I walked across the cornfield.

I looked up at the cairn on the top of Exmoor, the Vane Stones, black in the shade. The Reverend Diver was up there, I remembered. A suicide, therefore not permitted to be buried on church land. I thought about my young Aunt Pammy, dying outside the chapel, aged only twelve, her family drunk on honey and unable to help her, and the pamphlet her only legacy because we never, ever mentioned her otherwise. Later, in the afternoon, the Stones would turn fiery gold. I put my shoes on, stood up carefully and walked slowly to the car.

As I came along the drive, I turned the radio off. All was silent and I knew the house was still sleeping. I eased myself out of the car, walking slowly, like an old woman. Something moved above me. I looked up.

Janey's face peered out from the window of her bedroom. When I got inside, she had obviously run down the stairs and was waiting for me.

"Hi," she said, awkwardly. "Are you—OK?"

"No," I said, with a smile. "Thanks." I bent over slightly, unable to stop a strong, aching pulse jabbing inside me. The saltwater stung badly now that the cold had worn off. Janey stared, her eyes huge.

"What happened?"

"Giles. Giles happened."

Realization crept across her face.

"Oh. Oh, Kitty. Did he h-hurt you?"

You didn't say rape, then. Rape was crazed strangers waiting for you in dark alleyways, it wasn't neighboring boys from nice schools with rich fathers.

"Yes," I said, scrunching up my lips and nose, as if asked to comment on the weather. "Yes, he did a bit."

"I—oh shit." She was knitting her fingers together. "I went with Joss. To his room. He was in such a state. I wanted to go back, but Joss said you two were always like that, always fighting. Oh no—" She saw, and I saw, we had been played.

She reached a hand out tentatively toward me, but I moved away. "Shit," she said again. "I knew I should have stayed, Kitty—I'm so sorry."

"You could have asked. You should have."

"Yes," she whispered. "Yes, I should have."

"You could have come in. You'd have seen." I rolled the bathing suit up in the towel, squeezing the moisture out, as much as I could. I couldn't look at her.

"I—what if you didn't want me to come in? You—you'd have been furious. I wasn't sure…" She started fingering her scalp again, anxiously. "Joss said—"

"It's the thirtieth of August," I said. "You've been here for what, five weeks? If you haven't worked out that when Joss says something and I say something you should always listen to me over him then we're not friends. I believed you before, when you said you were with me, not him. We're not—whatever this is."

She was pale, her bottom lip caught in her teeth.

"Anything, Kitty. I'll do anything. I know. I messed it up. They—" She shook her head. "No, it's my fault."

"Look," I said, relenting at her expression. "Next time don't stand by."

"I won't," she said. She cleared her throat. I saw her blinking and nodding. "OK," she said. "You too, though."

"What does that mean?"

"I mean, you—oh, I don't know."

I heard the creaking of the staircase, someone coming down-stairs. "Come here." I dragged her inside, into the utility room, and unrolled the towel again. "You're my friend. You're the only one I trust. What the hell does that mean?"

"I mean…" She looked up, and her eyes were glinting with tears. "This—it's getting out of control. You—me—Joss—what's happened. Running away. This ceremony—I shouldn't have come here."

"Go home then," I said, hugging myself. "Go back to your empty house."

"You know I can't," she said. "Neither of us can now, Kitty."

I turned the washing machine on and moved closer toward it. Blood was drumming in my ears: I could not lose her, not now, not when I was starting to see what I had to do, what really had to happen.

"But we're not children anymore. Polly Baring, look at her. She'll meet some posh guy like her and marry him and settle down and never know what's going on outside her door. We can't choose that. We don't want to choose that. We've seen something else."

"I'm sorry," said Janey, quietly, and I felt her smooth, cool little hand slide over my other wrist. "I'm so sorry I didn't help you." She rubbed her face.

"It's OK," I said. But it wasn't. I wanted her to be as strong as I'd imagined she was, and she wasn't. How could she have been?

"Whatever you want to do, Kitty. Tell me. Whatever."

"I've written to your mum," I said, suddenly. "I forged your signature."

She froze. "What did you say?"

I put my hand on hers. All the time, I was warming up from the ice-cold of the sea. My heart was racing.

"I've cut the ties, if you want. I did it well, promise. Promise. I said she didn't need the hassle and that you were eighteen and could decide on your own future. And I sort of hinted that you were entitled to the money from the house, and that you had a solicitor ready to check it all over, and that you were willing to give her half."

"It's not about money—"

"It's not, but honestly," I said, more brutally than I'd intended, "I don't think she cares that much about you, does she? I honestly think she'd take that money if you didn't point it out to her."

Janey nodded, her face pale. "No, sure...Sure."

"Perhaps I shouldn't have done it." I rubbed my eyes. "I'm sorry."

"Perhaps you shouldn't. But we're even," she said. "It's OK. Jesus." She shook her head. "It's OK, Kitty."

"I don't care...baby...I don't care," I sang, quietly, and we smiled at each other.

I sank down onto the floor, raking my fingers through my cropped hair, sticky with sea salt. Janey sat down next to me. We were silent for a moment as the washing machine rumbled loudly, feeling the cool stone floor on our skin. Every moment that went by meant last night was in the past, and the ceremony, the moment of our release, was drawing closer.

Chapter Thirty

Mummy was in her study when I knocked, softly, the following day. One knew when she was working there because the radio crackled incessantly in the background. Mummy never seemed to notice: my father, Joss and I found it unbearable.

"Come in."

Checking no one was watching, I went in and shut the door carefully behind me.

She was at her desk, her mother's old kitchen table, scrubbed and re-varnished, and pushed up against the wall where a fireplace had been bricked up. There were shelves on either side, crammed with battered King Penguins, other books on design and a few curios: ostrich eggs, a set of Russian dolls, a matchbox with a dead beetle, dead, curling leaves. A large white anglepoise lamp loomed up as if staring at you. Pots of pencils, tubes of paint, and other equipment were shoved to one side of the desk. It was organized chaos.

This had been my grandfather's study, and when Mummy came to the house in the sixties, she had boarded up the fireplace, painted the room white and put up the shelves. It wasn't like the rest of Vanes, dark wood paneling, intimate, claustrophobic. It was spare, and cool. North-facing light. She had had framed some of her own textiles and hung them on the wall, like gold disks: "The Hive," the one everyone had in the seventies, and the "Lost Garden," the coiling roses. "Lion," which she had designed for Joss for our seventh birthday, and which was now on duvet covers, placemats, even mugs. It was "The Hive" that was the first one though, and it was everywhere, on curtains, cushions, oilcloths on kitchen tables…She'd signed a deal with the department store, which paid her a flat fee. She got no commission on any of those sales.

On weekends back from school I used to do my homework in

this room, curled up on the window seat. Mummy would tell me about her childhood in fifties London, freezing smog, her grand-mother's floor-length mink coat, seeing Winston Churchill being pushed along in a wheelchair in St. James's Park, and the happy, ramshackle life in her mother's icy-cold house in Chelsea: the eccentric lodgers, how some of them became friends, about life after the war, leaping around bomb sites, the Festival of Britain, being taken to Harrods by her mother once a year to choose her birthday present.

She didn't ever tell me how and why she was taken away by her father, or what she had seen happen between her parents, or how it affected her. She didn't really talk directly about her mother, al-ways stories that danced around her. "Look at those peonies, Kitty. My ma loved huge, blowsy flowers like that. Adored them. Every spring she had to buy a bunch." "Ah, *Genevieve*'s on. It was my ma's favorite film, you know."

After Eileen Lestrange rang her, back in March, to tell her that Simon had died, I'd found her in there, sketching, and when I asked her who it was she was drawing, she told me it was her mother. "I can see her, so clearly. But there aren't any photos of her. *I* don't have any, anyway. And when I'm gone, who will remember her? Everyone else is gone, really. And she should have been remembered."

It was the same with Pammy. And I thought it was the saddest thing I'd heard.

"Hi, Mummy," I said, looking round, inhaling the soft scent of pencil shavings, of chemicals. There was something odd about the room since the last time I'd been in there, to type out the let-ter, but I couldn't work out what it was.

"Hello, darling. How can I help?" She was chewing a pencil, her thick dark hair tucked behind one ear.

"Um...well, I wanted to talk to you."

"Sounds serious."

I cleared my throat, momentarily blocking out the sound of the static crackling from the radio. I wished it could all go away, suddenly. That this was a normal day, a normal summer, that I hadn't woken up. "Well…" I sat down carefully on the chair next to her. She was drawing cats, curled and coiled into various positions. "Is this going to go on some material?"

"Textile, yes. Think it could be lovely on a cushion." Her head was down, still looking at the shapes. Her pencil moved quickly, blocking out the stripes on a curled tail, thickening the sketchy lines of a pair of ears. "Simpler…must be simple…What's up?"

"I wondered if you'd heard from King's. About the name change."

"What? Oh, yes." Mummy shuffled papers and pencils around, peering through her hair, which kept falling in her face. "Here it is. In fact, it's from the Senior Tutor. He wrote to say Professor Lovibond has left the college, hence the delay as my letter went unopened for several days. I wish I'd known, I'd have written to him. Dear boy. They're most apologetic about it." She put the letter down and looked at me. "You're all set, darling. They've amended the name, and they've deferred the place for a year. Old Mr. Forbes from Letham's telephoned to let me know, too. Said what with your birthday being the last day of August, and all that—a year's delay might be wise—apparently they had no problem with it. You need to bring your birth certificate when you go up but that's fine, we'll remember that, won't we?"

"Why's Lovibond gone?"

"Some illness. Very sad." She stared out of the window. "To have seen him again would have been so nice."

"Yes…" I was silent for a moment, lost in thought. "Mummy…would you mind, a lot, if I didn't go?"

"Mind?" I saw her eyes widen. She froze for a tiny second, then gave a small laugh. "After all that? If you don't go, what are you going to do instead? Honestly, Kitty."

I shrugged, avoiding her eye. I looked around the room again, and realized what was different. Rory. Normally he was curled up under the desk, head resting on her feet, pretending to be asleep.

She stroked my hair. "Kitty, love, what's happened? Joss said something odd last night. You've been so strange this summer. Is it A-levels? Or Janey coming to stay? Eighteenth birthdays can be a bit awful, can't they? Suddenly everyone says you're a grown-up and I don't think one is ready for them, somehow. I wasn't."

"What did you do for your eighteenth birthday?"

"Me?" She chewed the pencil. "Well—let me see. Oh yes, of course. It was Good Friday, I remember that." And she stopped short, and said, her voice quiet: "We don't need to go into it. Please, Kitty: will you take the place? I can find something for you to do for a year. I don't know. Maybe my aunt. I have an aunt somewhere, no idea where…She took my father's side." The pencil tapping grew faster. "But will you go? Promise?"

"Why?" I realized how stupid the question sounded.

"You're asking me why I want my daughter to go to Cambridge. Come on, darling, you're brighter than that."

"What did you do on your eighteenth birthday?" I said again.

Mummy looked at me. Her pale, pointed jawline was set. The dark eyes flickered with something, then dulled. "Promise me you'll go."

I met her gaze, and then shrugged. "Promise."

"Wonderful. Kitty—oh, this is good news. I know it's the right decision." She exhaled, and I realized I too had been holding my breath. "Now, let me see." She gave a big, beatific smile. "Yes. He made me go to church with him. He'd come up specially."

"Who?"

"Well, your father of course. This is my eighteenth birthday, you did ask."

"Oh—yes. Go on."

She laughed. "Who else was there? Anyway, the night before, we went to Simpson's, and I wore my new Biba dress, and he said it was a waste of money. So rude! Then he took me to the cinema." She gently tapped the tip of her pencil on the worn table surface. *Tick-tick.* "I was desperate to see *Mary Poppins*. But we saw *A Shot in the Dark*—Peter Sellers, you know. Very funny. He laughed the whole way through and then we went back…Went back to the square."

Tick-tick. "Where?"

"My house, you know. Well, Mummy's house. I had lodgers. It was an absolute pain at times, cooking and cleaning for them, but it was rather fun. At least, when Simon was still there, it was lots of fun." Her eyes were bright. "We did have some larks. Two art students I knew, a lady seamstress and a doctor. And George Lovibond—but he left some time about a year after Mummy's death, I think. I'd have sold it, I think, your father was always saying I should. Simon—Lestrange, you know—he wouldn't let me. He said it was my security—" Her eyes swam with sudden tears. "But he'd lost his job. He had to take another position, miles away. He'd come back on weekends to check up on me. I used to get so cross with him…" She shook herself. "What a fool I was."

"You weren't, Mummy. Go on."

"Dinner…cinema…new dress. So, yes, on the Good Friday, he took me to church. To atone for my sins, you know."

"Simon did?"

"No! He did."

"Who?"

"Oh! I'm sorry. Daddy. Your father did."

I was cold suddenly, and shivered.

"To atone for your sins?"

"Well, yes. But by then it was all settled between us, anyway." She covered her face with a piece of foolscap. "It had to be, he kept saying. It was rather scandalous. I was quite young. Oh, it's rather embarrassing, telling your daughter about all this. Sex, you know."

"Oh." I was silent for a moment. I could feel my blood, pumping, thudding in my ears, beating faster and faster. "Sorry—I knew you were married quite young. That wasn't the—" I swallowed. "That wasn't the first time then? Mummy, how old were you?"

"The first time? I was fourteen, the first time. But we were so careful." The pencil, still beating on the sticky desk. She looked down at it. "He'd come up every few weeks after that, especially when Simon left. And he said it was wrong, that he'd get into trouble. But I—I needed someone. You know."

"Yes," I said. I felt sick.

"Daddy made me see how impractical it all was. The danger of living on my own. I was so scared when he wasn't there. It felt right, Kitty." She looked up, defiantly. "It sounds wrong but it wasn't."

I nodded. I wished she wouldn't call him "Daddy." I'd never called him that. Not ever.

"The night before I was eighteen, we did it again. And we said we'd pretend it was the first time." She smiled, gently. "He said it

wouldn't be proper otherwise, you know. He was a little older."
Mummy's gaze slid out to the lawn, the horizon beyond.

"He was…" I screwed up my eyes, in part to hide my expression. "Mummy, the first time though…you were fourteen. He was thirty-…he was thirty-six."

"It was all quite proper, as I say. We didn't tell anyone. He was so kind about it. Even when I wasn't sure. And he took care of things—you know, odds and ends of Mummy's furniture, he'd have them valued, give me the money. She had some jolly nice pieces, you know. He knew what he was doing."

I tried to speak, but bile was swimming in my mouth, and I had to swallow.

"Anyway, that night Simon suddenly turned up. It was a surprise, for my eighteenth. He'd bought me some gloves. And, well, Daddy was there. Simon—oh, he was very old-fashioned. It was the sixties, after all. But Simon was very angry." She rubbed her face. "He made a bit of a scene, talked about going to the police—well, I was eighteen, so that was rubbish. But he said some terrible things to Charles—to your father. Charles was right to order him out of the house. Daddy, I mean." She smiled gently.

"Is that why you and Simon weren't in touch, all those years?"

"Well, I suppose so. But I had to choose. I wrote to him, after we were married, to say how happy I was. I wrote to him when Charles sold the house for me, to ask him to collect his things. He never came. I did so want to see him. To th-thank him." And her voice thickened, and she made a choking sound. "Thank him for looking after me. Darling, you're too young to understand."

"I'm older than you were, Mummy."

"Yes, but it was different. I'd seen a lot."

"How?" I stopped, and started. My mouth was dry. "Mummy—you were fourteen when he—he started sleeping with you?"

"But I'd known him since I was twelve, darling. It wasn't the same as it is now. And he was a friend of Simon's. And as he was always saying, I trusted Simon and Mummy trusted Simon, so it meant he could be trusted too. And he was such a help, sorting out the furniture, and making me see I ought to sell the house. And—you know, he always promised he'd marry me. He even took me down here, to show me what I'd be letting myself in for."

Her fingers tightened on the pencil.

"You're never quite sure, are you? But coming to Vanes made me understand he wasn't—I didn't like it you see, I was quite young still, and it hurt, the first few times, and there was the business of—well, mess, and being quite quiet, so he didn't bother me too often. Your father is a gentleman. Old school."

"Yes," I managed to say.

"I don't like your expression, Kits. We agreed we'd make my eighteenth birthday special. That's why I remember it so clearly. And the next day, in church, Chelsea Old Church. He told me it was clean now, I was clean. And that we'd be married, really that we would. Oh. Realizing I wouldn't have to live in lodgings anymore, that he could sell Mummy's house for me, that I'd be married to someone who'd take care of all of that." She was drawing on the paper now, the pencil circling round, and round. "And I did lose touch with Simon, for years, until I bumped into him at the Tate Gallery, about ten years ago. I was up in London for the week, meeting some fabric buyers. I'd just popped in, to look at *Ophelia* in Room Nine. I'm sorry you don't know London better, it's my home, really. I love the Tate, and Mummy and I used to love *Ophelia*. And he was in the same room. Oh, it was so wonderful to see him. To be in touch with him, to tell him I had a daughter, I'd given her his surname...Because Mummy had made him promise he'd look out for me and when—when—when"—and her face crumpled into a hideous, silent, howl of grief—"when I realized what being married entailed, and that your father wasn't keen on me designing anymore, and living quite away from what you know, and so young, I could have...done with a friend." She nodded, lips tightly pressed together. "And Simon, well, he was my friend, and Mummy's. He was a true friend."

Our eyes met, and there was something there, an expression of utter calm, as always. I had never seen her angry, or upset, merely irritated sometimes. What had she done to herself, to stay that way?

My mind still couldn't quite grasp the full extent of it. I thought of my father now, hanging around Wellington Square, whistling. Waiting for this girl to let him in. Wanting her to.

"Darling," said Mummy, in a low voice. "I think we have to change the subject now. Do you understand?"

"I don't think we should."

"We have to, darling. Please."

Behind the dull expression in the eyes, a muscle twitched. "I don't think about it. I can't think about it. Otherwise it seems real."

She looked down at the twisted, tangled ropes of creeping tendrils she had drawn, encircling the scribbles on the sugar paper. *Rescue Sylvia.* I stared at her. I didn't know what to say.

"He shan't hurt you again," she said quietly. *"No one shall."*

"Who said that?"

"It doesn't matter," she said. "Not now. I've told you. Do you understand? Will you keep your word and go to Cambridge? Get a degree, get a job, be a huge success, earn a living, be away from here? Do you understand?" She was close to me. She cupped my chin in her hand. "I said, Kits, do you understand?"

And I did understand. "Yes. Thanks, Mummy."

"Now, let's enjoy the ceremony, and all be together, and spend the rest of our time with Janey before she has to leave, and it'll all be lovely."

"I don't want to be a Beloved Girl, Mummy. I don't want to take part in it."

"Listen. The doctor says if you're stung and it affects you that you're unlikely to have the same reaction again."

"I don't think he was right," I said. Just the thought of it now, the ritual of going into the chapel, made my throat close up. "And I don't want to put the headdress on. I don't want people watching me. It's not going to be my house, apart from anything else. I don't want Joss's friends there."

Her eyes narrowed. "I thought they were your friends too."

"Not anymore."

Her pencil drew small, looping circles, closer and closer together. "What's happened?"

"Something happened." The pain in my throat from keeping control of myself was an ache spreading out across my whole body, joining up with the other aches, the pain in my vagina, the bruises on my thighs, my breasts, my head.

"Ah," said Mummy gently. "I see. What—what was it?"

"Giles," I said, very softly, and it hurt to speak now, my muscles almost entirely closed up. "I don't want Giles there."

"Last night after the rehearsal, was it? Joss said he had some people back." I nodded again. "OK, darling. Did you two have a fight?"

"N-not exactly."

She leaned toward me. "Oh my love. Did—did he hurt you?"

I shrugged, and bit my lip. "A bit." Out of the window, I could see birds on the wires from the telegraph pole, sitting, waiting to fly south. I chewed the skin on the side of my nail, praying she would make it right, that she would explain it.

"Right. Oh, dear God. Right."

She stood up, and paced to the window. She was saying something, under her breath. Over and over. She looked down, and I knew she was searching for Rory. "Did you get away?"

"What?"

"I mean, did he come after you? Did you try to run away from him?"

"N-no. I mean—no."

"There, you see. It can't be that bad." She stroked my shoulder. "These things happen, Kitty. All the time. It's life. It's part of growing up. I—I learned that, and when I did, I was much happier. Honestly."

His breath, hot and rancid, hammy, acidic, breathing wet spray in my ear as he rammed up inside me, again, again, again, and the sharp, sandpaper agony of it, far inside, and at the edge, and on my hips. His face... his smile. I cast my mind back over it all.

"He—he hurt me, Mummy."

She was very still, blinking a couple of times. "Darling, where was it?"

"In—in the pool house."

"Really? Had you been drinking?"

I nodded, miserably. I put my hand on her wrist. I suppose I wanted her to touch me. I wanted someone to wrap me up, gently, to shield me, enclose me from it all.

"I think perhaps you shouldn't have drunk so much, Kitty. It's been happening rather a lot lately. I—I don't mean to blame you or Giles. He shouldn't have gone too far, clearly, and I'll tell Joss to tell him. But you shouldn't have gone with him, darling."

"He—he made me."

She gave a little laugh. "Really? Did you scream? I don't think so. No. I was reading till late, I heard Joss and—ah, Janey, come in, I think I'd have heard someone being dragged off to be raped."

Then she did put her hand over mine.

"It's very unpleasant, but it happened. Put on a brave face, darling." Her finger strafed my cheek, my chin, and I shivered. "It's like the Collecting. Heaven knows there are plenty of things I didn't want to do when I was your age. What is it Daddy says at the beginning of the Ceremony? *Half for us and half for them, else the Devil take us all.* We all have to put up with things we don't like. It's part of growing up."

Suddenly the old line came to me, one that Sam Red had said last summer, as we walked along the seafront at Minehead idly watching the sunset: normal teenagers, him with a beer and a cigarette, me eating cotton candy. "It's better to be preserved in vinegar than rot in honey, Kitty."

I looked out of the window. "What's that?"

"They're lighting the incense."

"A day early?"

"They need calming down. The earlier the better."

I realized the humming I was hearing wasn't the radio, not this time. It was coming from the hives. She drew a line harshly through the sketch of the cats and looked up.

"Just carry on, Kitty. That's my advice to you. Remember, I'll be there tomorrow. I'll make sure you're all right."

"Will you?" I wanted to laugh, I felt almost hysterical. But she said:

"Don't worry. Haven't I sorted out Cambridge for you?" She cleared her throat and swallowed. "Trust me."

I can't, I wanted to say, but didn't. "I'll see you later, Mummy."

She had already turned back to her desk, humming to herself now as I left. I thought, but couldn't be sure, that I felt her eyes on my back, watching me leave.

Later that morning, before lunch, I went up to Merry's room, at the top of the house, the other end from Janey's. It was stifling hot already, not a wisp of a breeze, the sky a heavy yellow, lower than before.

She was lying on the floor, flicking through a book, which she slid under the bed as I opened the door.

"Hello, darling. What's that book?"

"Nothing."

I crouched down and flicked it out before she could stop me. *"Neighbours Annual 1988."*

Her face was instantly flaming red. "Stop it."

"I didn't say anything."

"You will though. I can like what I like. Janey says so."

"She's right." I sat down next to her. "Who's best in *Neighbours*, then?"

"Well, Scott, obviously." She looked at me, furiously, but I said nothing. "I liked Clive, too, but he's gone, and Lucy Robinson, but my favorite is Scott. And, of course, Charlene."

"Is that Kylie?"

"Yes, of course." She rolled her eyes, too embarrassed to look at me. "She's amazing. She can mend a car, and she can marry Scott. And she can sing."

"Well, that does sound amazing," I said. "I thought she'd left though."

Merry sat up. She said, in an important voice: "She has, in Australia. But our transmission of programs is about a year behind. She hasn't left in the UK yet."

"Oh," I said. I bit the side of my thumb cuticle. The nail had torn, that night, and I kept tearing the skin further and further down the thumb. "A delay."

"Yep." Merry was arranging her box of *Neighbours* memorabilia, the annuals, the album sleeves, all together. There was a copy of *Smash Hits!* with Jason Donovan on the front. The cover was folded over. I smoothed it down, and handed it to her. She put the box away, pushing it under the bed, her hands brushing my legs, but she didn't ask me to move or, still, meet my eye. She folded her arms and sat back down. There was a short silence.

"I'm sorry I've been a cow lately," I said, slowly. "I've had a strange summer."

"That's OK."

"You like Janey, don't you?"

Merry nodded. "I really do."

"Me too."

"I know. I knew you'd get on, if you could only just…just put yourself away."

I laughed. "What a funny expression." I saw her blush again, and I felt a lurch of guilt. "Sorry, I didn't mean it's silly funny. It's just so spot on." She stood up, and started arranging her ballet books, slamming them against the shelf. "I'm sorry, Merry."

She gave a small shrug. "'S'fine. Don't worry. Look, I've got to cycle to Gemma's. I'll see you later, OK?"

"Why? Oh. Of course."

"You wouldn't forget the Collecting, would you!" She laughed, a bit too loudly. "Even you. PF says he wouldn't be surprised if you didn't turn up, if you were off somewhere, but I know you wouldn't miss it."

"I wouldn't miss it," I said carefully, and I got up, slowly, too. "Look, Merry, darling. Whatever happens, I'm sorry I wasn't a better big sister. I'm sorry I wasn't nicer to you. You're great. Just remember that."

She was staring at me as though I was completely mad. "What on earth are you on about?"

"I mean soon—I'll be gone, and I won't see you as much, and I want you to remember, I—" I breathed out. "We take too much from the bees every year. We leave them with less and less. You know that. We shouldn't. Don't let them." I leaned against the bookcase. She looked at me with alarm.

"Are you OK?"

"I'm fine! I'm just tired." I pushed myself away. "And feeling sentimental, that's all. Just that I'm glad you're my sister. And I love you. Goodbye."

I left the hot little room, pausing outside, and went back to my room, down below. I could hear Mummy getting lunch ready, Joss strumming his guitar and humming along, some poems. I could hear Ros, striding across the lawn, circling around and about, and, in the distance, beyond the grounds, I could hear the bees, louder than ever.

Chapter Thirty-One

The air was heavy and dull on the evening of our eighteenth birthday, when we all finally assembled at 6 p.m.: Joss in his new dark blazer, Merry in a neon-pink and yellow ruffled skirt and white netting top, a ponytail asymmetrically perched atop her head and then, at the end, Janey and I, in our green dresses, walking slowly down the curving stairs.

In the austere paneled dining room, food was laid out on long tables and dressers: wine in silver ice buckets, jugs of Pimm's in the fridge, globe crystal champagne glasses upside down on the long dining table. There were vast platters of smoked salmon, prawn cocktails in little crisp pastry shells, mini-quiches. There was Shloer, otherwise only ever served at Christmas. Mrs. Dawson down in Larcombe had brought it up this morning. Of course, most important of all were the little fingers of toast, and bread, for those who wanted to taste the honey, and most people did. Later, we would come into the dining room, there would be drinks, and loud, relieved chatter, spilling out onto the terrace and across the lawn, as the village came together for the end of summer. Everyone was always tense with pride and then, afterward, mawkish with sentiment. When I was younger I alternately loved it and was repelled by it, like the Last Night of the Proms: I always cried at *Pomp and Circumstance* but loathed the naked jingoism of "Rule, Britannia."

Mummy and Daddy were "upstairs" again, for the first time in a while. We could hear them. I listened, idly; normally I blocked it out but tonight for some reason I wanted to take note. It was so rushed, so intense, so urgent. You could hear Daddy, muttering something, but it was Mummy, as always, animal-like. The yelps grew louder and louder, a huge, distressing scream, and then silence.

I picked a piece of dead skin from my finger. Janey caught my eye. We smiled, mirthlessly.

It was dark in the hallway. There was a murky light to the evening, and once or twice I heard thunder, gathering way out to sea. On the edge of the terrace and across the lawn was a diagonal line of hazel switches leading toward the gate, each crowned with a smoking beeswax candle from last year's bounty. There was no wind.

"There should be quite a crowd this year," said Joss, fiddling with his collar.

I gave him a small, private smile. *This is weird.* I twisted the little diamond studs I'd got for my sixteenth birthday, then ran my hand over the back of my neck; sweat was pooling at the nape. My bare skin was warm, but I was shivering slightly. The dress Mummy had given me was one she'd made in the sixties—printed Indian green cotton, falling to the ground, trimmed with cream lace. My uneven hair was prickling in places, catching in the lace collar. I felt, in short, like a lamb trussed up for slaughter, but before that on display for a good stare by as many as cared to. The advantage of the long dress was it hid the bruises on my legs and arms.

I touched the back of my neck again. "Don't," said a quiet voice behind me. "You look glorious. Like a goddess. Really."

And Janey's arm slid around my waist. I snatched at her fingers, held them tight. The strength I felt at that moment, knowing she was there with me, caught me by surprise.

Then we could hear them, hear them singing the Collecting Carol, the same song sung for hundreds of years.

> *"I'll sing you one, O,*
> *Green come for the comb, O!*
> *What is your one, O?*
> *One is one and all alone and evermore shall be so.*
>
> *I'll sing you two, O,*
> *Green come for the comb, O!"*

It always started softly, as they came up through the woods from the village, climbing to the top of the grassland, walking along the breast of the hill, ringing the handbells to call out the lepers who might be in the woods, following the ancient boundary wall that led to Vanes. There, they processed along the driveway, under the arch onto the terrace, where they greeted us, and we joined them.

"Nine for the nine bright shiners..."

"I'm scared," said Janey, into my ear. "Kitty—are you ready?"

"There's absolutely nothing to be scared about, OK?" I said. "The bags are in the car. Everything's ready."

The Hunters had been practicing. There was a swagger to their singing.

"We're doing this, aren't we?" she said, quietly.

"Yes," I said, into her ear. "We are."

"Eight, eight here we come say eight for the Spring Collectors..."

My parents had joined us by now, my father's hair neatly combed and gleaming, Mummy in a lovely silk dress of midnight blue, smelling of her delicious Givenchy perfume. Her hair was plaited, and twisted around her head, her face aglow. She and my father stood apart, on the doorstep, heads slightly bowed, the lord and lady of the manor.

"Seven for the seven stars in the sky,
Six for the six-sides of the comb."

Our hands touched. The procession was approaching. As ever, I could feel the hairs on my neck rising slowly, the ghastly anticipation, the stifling terror of the flames, the sound of the bells, jangling too loud. Lack of sleep made me stare unblinking, wired.

I could see the lines of villagers and friends, coming closer. Tradition was they didn't look at us on the doorstep. We joined at the end, holding our beeswax candles, and our smoke.

"Five for the five proud walkers,
Four for the honey makers..."

The half-sung, half-spoken lilting way they talked was hypnotic. I looked out and I could see faces I'd known all my life: Mrs. Red, Pete the landlord, Gracie and Sam, who I'd been at infants with, and the Reverend Thompson, frowning heavily—he was something of a happy-clappy trendy vicar, not at all keen on obscure pagan ancient English customs, but he dared not miss the occasion. Then there were the second-home owners, the holiday-makers who came every year, and the many retirees from all around here who loved the custom, because it made them all feel something.

There were more than ever this year, over fifty, I'd have guessed, and as they passed, I felt their presence, that final time.

Then the roar came for the last three verses:

"Three, three, the rivals,
Two, two, the beloved girls,
Clothed all in green, O…"

At the rear was Giles Leigh-Smith, dressed almost identically to Joss: navy blazer, blue shirt and chinos, brown leather deck shoes. His parents followed him. I watched him walk past, as always thinking how strange it was that on special occasions like this, women get to dress in bright colors and different styles and men are in uniform, identical versions of each other.

I saw Mummy was breathing quickly, her face pale, a tightness about the mouth. Joss and I followed them, then Janey and Merry. Usually, Rory tottered along behind. I thought I heard something, a pattering, a quick movement of feet, but when I turned, there was nothing, and Merry frowned at me.

The singing grew louder the closer we got, then to morph into something else, a jangling, too-loud reality. The whole procession didn't file into the chapel—there wasn't room. Instead they formed a ring around the abandoned old building, chanting, singing, and even from a distance the humming from inside was so loud it got into your head, your chest, your heart. The bees knew we were coming. In the distance, thunder rolled down toward the hills.

Daddy's line was the same, every year. He stepped forward to the door of the chapel, turning the key, then sliding back the long, black bolt. To us he said:

"Half for us and half for them,
Else the Devil take us all."

Then, as he opened the chapel door:

"Half for you, and half for me,
It was ever so and thus shall be."

Again, I thought I heard something, the shuffling of feet, an animal cry. I turned, again, and caught Janey's eye. She mouthed to me. *I'm here.*

Joss and I were surrounded, and propelled toward the chapel. My skin was crawling with fear, at the closeness, the heat, the noise. I hesitated, but Joss pushed me inside. "Come on, Kits."

My father followed us in, and Merry. "Come on, Janey," she said, smiling, and Janey was dragged in, too. I looked round for Mummy but couldn't see her. Then I remembered. She was the Outsider. She had to stay without us, all alone.

Inside the small space, the beeswax candles had been lit, but it was still dark and close, the air cloying with honeyed wax, even with the hole in the ceiling. Daddy squeezed the bee smoker, and the scent of dead leaves and fuel filled the place. My eyes stung. We could barely hear the singing outside, the noise inside was so loud. A new moon shone overhead; I had not noticed it, so slender was it, so precise, cutting through the pale lavender blue above.

"One is one..."

It was just us now, us and them.

The humming was so loud, you felt certain they must know something was happening. Did they remember, some hereditary memory handed down from queen bee to worker to queen bee? Did they know the song, what the footsteps across the lawn at the end of summer meant?

I was shaking. I could barely keep a lid on my terror. Ros stepped to the front as Daddy pumped the bee smoker behind her. I jumped as Janey put her hand on my back again, and I felt her trembling, and then I knew how scared she was and somehow that gave me some strength.

"Loud today, aren't they?" I heard old Mrs. Red saying from the doorway. "He needs to smoke 'em a bit more."

I knew Daddy would have heard this.

Suddenly Mummy appeared, next to her. Normally, she was silent throughout, taking as little part in the ceremony as she could. She advanced a little way into the chapel, then spread her hands apart and said, in a low, compelling voice:

"We've come to take our share tonight, on our children Jocelyn and Catherine's eighteenth birthday. We thank you for it. We thank you for them and for the life you have given us."

Who was she talking to? I always wondered. My father made a shooing motion to Mummy. I knew what he meant. *The Outsider has to stay outside.*

But Mummy hadn't finished. "We thank you for Janey, for bringing her to us this summer, and all she has given us, every one of us. We thank you for her father, Simon, and all he did in his life. May he rest in peace. We thank you."

My father paused, staring at her in astonishment. He hissed something at her but she ignored him. So he began hacking away at the mud around one of the tombs, with a chisel. Sometimes he got it wrong and had to open up a few before we found where the bees had made their honeycomb that year.

Outside, the others carried on singing the Carol, softly now. Over and over again the same verses came, and I wanted to scream. I glanced at the open door as my father tried one sealed-up tomb after another, the sound swelling and ebbing as he did.

"There's no honey," my father hissed.

"There's always the ones in the roof," said Aunty Ros. "Keep trying, Charles. Keep trying. More smoke."

My father kicked the can toward Joss. "Do it," he said, shortly.

Joss picked up the smoker, staring at it in panic. "Of course," he said, tucking his hair behind his ears.

"Here," said Aunty Ros, bustling forward. She grabbed it from him. "I'll smoke them. As you were, Charles. As you were."

Gradually, the seal of mud that had been applied back in January on the fourth tomb down cracked away. "At last," my father said, and reached a hand in.

He was never stung; they knew him. He was calm, and confident, king of his world, certain about what to do. His withdrew, and we could see he was clutching a torn-off section of golden-yellow-brown comb.

"Got it," someone yelled outside. "He's got it!"

He sliced it in two, as honey started dripping onto the ground, and the bees made more noise. The Three Rivals banged their silver spoons against their glasses; the Hunters cheered. I shrank against the wall of the chapel. I felt the back of Janey's hand, the knuckles brushing mine.

"Half for them and half for us!" my father called, his voice trembling. "Joss, come forward. Joss, my son—take the comb, taste it first—" He turned to me. "Kitty. Here, taste some."

And then it happened. Someone outside shouted. "What the hell's that?"

"They're in the roof," someone else called. "Look at them."

I froze. "What?" said Daddy, sharply. He looked up, we all did, apart from Mummy, still hovering on the threshold.

In addition to the combs kept in the tombs lining the walls of the chapel, there were the rows of comb nestled in what remained of the roof. The bees had been there for ten years or so now. And they were leaving.

Where the chapel was open to the sky was a black cloud, like a cloak, floating across the whole of the roof to the edge of a broken buttress. As we watched, it rose up into the air.

"I said so," Mrs. Red called. "Good Lord, he was right. They're really leaving."

I ignored her, snatching the ivy headdress from my head. "It's fine," said Mummy, in a soft, sing-song voice as she carefully put half of the first piece of comb, dripping, oozing, amber gold, into the bucket. "There's more here. They're still here." And even after all of it, even knowing what a single sting could do to me, as I saw the honey, a drop of golden light, sliding from the comb, my mouth watered, as it did every year.

My father's eyes were bulging. "It's not fine, Sylvia. Do shut up. Why—why are they swarming now, for God's sake?"

Mummy was still awfully calm. Her eyes downcast, her movements slow, gently she prised the comb from Charles, put the other half of it back in the tomb. "They're not swarming. They're leaving. Stop the Collecting, stop it now. They're angry with you. Half for us and half for them. You've always taken more than half, Charles. You take too much. You always do."

Someone started to scream. "No! No, don't!"

"Move away! Get away!"

"Tell them to be quiet," said my father, sharply now. "Don't aggravate the others."

"Come on," said Aunty Ros furiously prising open another tomb, thin fingers white at the knuckles with the pressure. "Carry on. Tell them for God's sake to shut up. Sing. Sing something. Dammit, sing them something."

But we were silent, inside, as outside, then came another scream. "I've been stung!" The noise was indescribable, a vibrating, roaring rush, it wasn't a hum. It grew louder every minute.

All summer we had known there were too many bees and that

they hadn't built enough comb. All summer they'd been making too much noise, and for years we knew these were bad-tempered bees, aggressive. They didn't like the people, the light from the candles and, of course, the heat.

And then from the opened comb inside the chapel brown-black forms were emerging from the dark hole. Overhead, I saw a faint flash in the sky: lightning, coming in from the Bristol Channel.

Suddenly I knew I had to get out. I felt the danger and knew with certainty that my father didn't see it. I grabbed Janey. "Come on," I said as, outside, there was more screaming. I looked at Mummy. Her dark eyes were blank.

"You take too much, Charles," she said. "You always did." She put her hands on Merry's shoulders, and propelled her toward the door, pushing her gently away, and then she did the same to Joss, but he moved away.

"Let me go, Mummy. I'm fine. Absolutely fine."

All the time, the bees were emerging from the opened comb. More and more, like oil, sliding over the dull stone, across the wall, some flicking off and into the air, hovering, and all the time outside, the noise grew. I could hear them shouting. "Get out, guys!"

"Come on. Come," I said. "They're angry. I don't think it's safe, honestly." I looked up at the ceiling, my hand holding hers. "Come on, Dad—"

My father was wrestling with the final tomb, hacking away at the mud seal. You could hear the roar of the bees inside, and, above, the ones in the roof.

"Stay *there*!" He kicked his leg out toward me. "Kitty—why *must* you make everything so damned difficult!"

His kick caught me in the stomach. It winded me, and knocked him back against Aunty Ros, who was cutting the comb in two. "Steady, Charles," she barked. The two of them froze, for a second, turning to face me—*they* could be twins, I realized, they were virtually identical, with their large, ruddy, moon-shaped faces, deep-set eyes, thin mouths. Ros dropped the comb she was holding, and it sent the bees crawling all over it flying everywhere, just as my father wrenched open the mud seal of the final tomb. Some were stuck in their own honey, some flew out of the combs, with a huge thrumming explosion of sound. Most landed on the floor, and then there was a noise even greater than before, and then chaos seemed to descend, as they rose up from everywhere, swarming around us all, in an angry roar.

Mummy pushed Merry and Janey out of the door. "Go!" she shouted. "Is that you, Joss?"

"No, it's me, Giles," came a voice, through the droning thunder, the flying black dots that zoomed everywhere.

"You're dressed the same," my mother said. "Like a pattern, like a pattern." She laughed, wildly. "Take them up to the house. Get them out of here. Now. Then come back."

"Yes, yes of course, Mrs. Hunter—"

I saw Janey and Merry disappear. "Right, you two," Mummy said, and she grabbed our arms. I could barely make out Joss—in his navy jacket and chinos he was, as Mummy said, identical to Nico and Guy, amidst the gloom and the chaos, and he was *my* twin. We gripped hands, staring at each other.

It was seconds, of course, but it seemed to last for hours, huge, stretched-out gulps of time. I could hear Aunty Ros, screaming, plucking at her hair, her dress, pulling bees off her body, her mouth wide open, her face bright red. "Sylvia, you stupid woman," she barked. "Get back *in*, goddammit! Kitty and Joss have to stay! To watch it all! To taste the honey. You're ruining it! You're ruining it all!"

"Kitty can't stay, not now," my mother shouted. "Can't you see what's happening? Good God! Wake up, the pair of you!"

"Jesus, Sylvia," said my father, almost casually, and he yanked her away from the door.

And I saw Mummy reach for him. She was much smaller than he and it was done in a split second. She could not overpower him, and the insects everywhere. With one hand, she shoved me and Joss outside again, despite Joss's protests. She took my father's forefinger in her other hand and bent it back, as far as she could. He howled, bending over.

"Go," she said to us, and I saw her jaw, set as she turned to him. "I'm the Outsider," she said, quietly. "And I say who goes and who stays."

As my father yelled, batting away at the comb, I heard my aunt calling to him. "Is it nearly done, Charles?"

"Just a little more. A little more..." His voice shuddered.

Outside, Joss and I stood, breathing deeply, as my mother emerged into the daylight.

The first swarm was hovering by the terrace, as people scattered, screaming. The table and chairs were knocked to the ground, plants trampled.

Sam Red appeared next to my mother. "Need me to do something, Mrs. Hunter? Have you called the police, or whatever? Gran thinks you should—Are they still in there?"

"Yes," said Sylvia. "I'm afraid they don't want to come out."

Sam put his hands on his hips. "They're not settling anywhere. You should leave, Kitty, get inside or something. Listen, someone needs to get them out. What, do they think they're immortal?" He made to move forward, but Giles elbowed him aside.

"Leave it to me," he said. "I'll go in, get them. OK?"

"Fine," said my mother. "I'm going to call 999. Thanks, Sam. Thank you ever so much, Giles. Get them out, and I'll lock the door." She pinched my cheek. "All shall be well, my darling." She smiled, very quickly, and raced back up to the house.

Giles was staring in at the chaos within the chapel, not moving. My father was screaming again. "I—" he said. "I—"

"No," Joss said, clearing his throat. "I should go in. He's my father."

They were all around me, so loud, flying so close to my ear, my face, that I could feel the vibration of their bodies. A pain started in my leg, instant, like a forcefield, shielding my body, shielding me.

"Great," said Sam Red, nodding. "They might listen to you. Hurry."

Giles looked at me, and smiled. The pain was worse. I backed away from him.

"Someone, shut the damn door!"

I closed my eyes, feeling Giles's hands on my head, his thumbs jabbing into my mouth, the feeling of his hips agonizingly grinding against mine and I ran toward the drive, as a huge, black wave of pain twisted my chest, as if someone was tearing out my heart, squeezing it, clamping it. I couldn't see. The others didn't. They were running toward the chapel door to close it and someone—I think it was Merry—was shouting.

Then I felt a cool hand on my shoulder.

"You're ill. You've been stung." I looked up, and Janey was standing next to me, wreath awry, her face pale and stained with tears. I nodded.

"Oh Janey."

Her hand pressed against my forehead. The noise, the chaos receded. I found I could hardly breathe, and yet the touch of her skin was cold, soft, infinitely comforting. "Are you OK?"

"I am," I said. I looked at the chapel, saw Mummy was back down there, locking the door shut. I saw her pat the old door, grimly, as she walked away with the key.

"All done," she called. "Move away, everyone. Inside. Move!"

I thought of Giles's twisted smile, his curious light-blue eyes, the certainty that he knew he could do it to me again. I swallowed, letting my mind play over ten, twenty different scenarios. I could see everything, the pain making everything ultra-real, like a light shining into all my thoughts—suddenly, everything was clear.

I paused, for a moment, breathing hard. "Right. Let's go."

"*Now?* Kitty, we can't go, not now."

"Why not? We were always going to slip away. Isn't now a better time than any? In fact—don't we *have* to go now? I do, anyway. It's not safe." I thought of Giles's calm, mocking face. Of my aunt and father, melding together as one. Of Mummy, stumbling as my father pushed her away, the touch of her fingers on my cheek. "I've left my father a note. On the hall table. Below the Reverend. I don't want to stay." I blinked. "I—I can't stay any longer."

"Are you OK?"

I grabbed her hand. "Please. Let's go, Janey. Let's just drive, shall we? Like we promised?"

Everywhere, all around, people were yelling. I covered my ears. Beeswax candles, branches and crystal champagne glasses lay cracked and broken on the lawn, in a trail leading to the chapel. Above us, the sky was darkening, and I saw two black clouds of bees. The first was still swooping in circles above the house as the remaining guests retreated inside, the sound of crumpling glass and screaming, absolute primal terror everywhere.

I looked up and saw the second swarm was floating away

toward the woods, back to where they'd originally come from, all those centuries ago. And then I saw Mummy, ushering everyone away from the chapel, moving people out of the way.

"Where's—where's Joss?"

"He's out. Mummy said so. Isn't that him?" A dark figure, hand running through hair, was racing toward the house. "Look, Janey, you can't go back and say goodbye, not now. OK?"

"Course not," she said. "It's just…"

We'd reached the car. I could smell the brake fluid from other cars hanging in the air. And more thunder. Behind us, up on the moor, there was still some blue sky, edged with lemon.

Janey stared at me, brushing a couple of bees out of the way. "Kitty, are you sure you want to do this?"

"I think so." Another wave of hot, blinding pain convulsed me. My fingers were numb, my limbs heavy. "Open the door, and help me in, then you drive for a bit."

Our bags had been packed for days. My rucksack had the documents, both passports, the cash we had carefully assembled. We'd even laid in some travel sweets, the sugary pastel-colored squares caked in icing sugar, bought at the post office and now resting in the glovebox. As Janey carefully bumped us down the driveway, I looked in the side mirror, but no one was watching. As we turned out into the road, I heard the sound of an ambulance, then saw it, coming toward us. But it zoomed straight past, another emergency, somewhere else, and then we were on the main road. How strange, I remember thinking. There are other emergencies.

We drove in silence for a while, winding higher and higher up along narrow lanes. Occasionally I would point toward a turning, and Janey would take it, calmly. The sky was darker than ever, but still it didn't rain. Out to sea, you could see the storm. Once, lightning cracked overhead. The windows were open, to let what fresh air there was in.

"I—I feel a bit better," I said, after a minute or two.

"Are you sure, Kitty?" Janey waggled the gear stick, biting her lip and looking in the rear-view mirror. "Was it just that one sting? Do you think it's not too bad?"

"It's my leg, so it's further from my heart." I stared out at the gray sea, the occasional drop of rain on the windshield mixing with bird shit and the dust of summer.

"Why didn't you ever just tell them you couldn't do the Collecting? That it's too dangerous for you?"

"I—I've tried. I don't know." I shifted in the seat. "I felt it was evidence, deep down, that my father is right. I've always felt that."

"Of what?"

"That I'm against the family in some way. That I'm betraying us." She shook her head, vehemently.

"But that's not your fault, Kitty! None of it is."

"Oh, I know. Mummy's been saying for years we should get Buckfast bees, and my father always ignores her. They're placid and easy. These guys aren't. They're European dark bees, I think." I rubbed my head. "But my father doesn't care, nor does Ros. Remember, my aunt died in there. They saw it happen. Their father wouldn't get rid of them. They believe all the stories, honestly, that they and the bees are their survival, that they need each other. So the bees have to come first." Her mouth fell open—she had forgotten. "Aunty Ros was cross when it happened. She clearly thought I was making a fuss because I didn't want to do it. I think that was the first time I realized—"

"What?"

I shrugged. "How screwed up it is."

Janey nodded. "Oh yes. Yes, Kitty." She turned, and the car swerved.

"Hey. Steady on."

"Wow, I'm so sorry." Janey grabbed my hand. She took a deep, ragged breath.

"I—can we do this? This is pretty wild."

"We can't go back," I said, and I nodded. "You know I can't go back. I'd rather die than stay there."

I turned on the radio. It was Kirsty MacColl, "Days." I smiled. I didn't need to look at Janey. It was perfect.

I hummed the first four notes, softly, tapping the dashboard, smelling the wet air, and she joined in, and for that moment, climbing up away from the house, we were free, and everything was worth it. All of it.

I began to feel the most unlikely thing; I felt hope. We had done it. We had got away.

"What about your family?" said Janey. "I mean, what will you tell them?"

"Don't worry. I left a note, remember," I said. "They'll shrug their shoulders and tell everyone I ran away and that you've gone with me. *Typical Kitty*. I can see it. My father won't come after me. He knows I could get him sent to prison for what he did to Mummy. And the fake Queen Anne giltwood mirror he sold Lady Lowther two years ago for two thousand pounds that he bought at a flea market. He'll stay silent. They all will."

"Will you miss them?"

One is one and all alone, and evermore shall be so...

"Miss them..." I paused. For a second, I wondered about Mummy. Ordering me out, marshaling the others away from the chapel, taking charge. "Don't know," I said.

I turned the music up as loud as I could and sang, and all the time pain was making my vision fold up and in on itself, so the world seemed to be melting at the edges, like celluloid burning up. My arms ached, my ears, my nose...the tingling of my lips hurt more every second, as did the rasp in my throat which was like something alive, scraping away, something active. I pressed my hands to my face, to cool myself down and found my fingers were puffy—they did not look like mine, part of my own body.

A tractor came toward us, slightly too close, and Janey stared ahead, concentrating for a few valuable seconds. It gave me time to think, to clear my head. Something my English teacher used to quote came back to me, even as my heart was cramping, clenching with venomous pain. *"The long divorce of steel falls on me,"* I murmured. Dr. Lovibond had said it at my interview, staring intently at me.

"You know the quotation."

"Of course."

"Does your mother ever talk about her? Your grandmother?"

"No—not really."

"The long divorce of steel. It came for her," he'd said, blinking intently at me. "For both of them."

I looked down suddenly, feeling an itch on my sleeve. There

were two bees, one on my arm, one in the tiered lace ruffle of my dress.

Suddenly I was tired. I watched one, its abdomen bumping gently on the dress as it crawled across the layered material toward my skin, toward its own death.

And then I had a flash of realization; I saw that this was what was meant to happen.

Sometimes you get lucky: this was one of those times. Strange to talk about luck, when everything is ending. But it had been luck that had brought her there that summer: Janey had come to free me, we were two halves, as one. Through her, I could disappear, and I could live on, and up till that precise moment I'd been stumbling along making plans for our escape, with no real idea of what came next.

Then, with the wind moving away from us, howling down the wooded combe and out to sea again, I felt it and I looked down, lucky enough to watch as the creature raised its abdomen, as the barbed sting slid into my body. Like a needle, coated in fire, pushing into me.

If it was the end for the Hunters it was the end for me. Not Janey. She must be the one to get out of this, to pull free.

"Turn up here, toward the Vane Stones," I said.

"Here? OK."

There was no one around, up on top of the moor. The sun was setting on the last day of August. Below us, the bay, the windswept trees of the ancient woods, and the yellowing grass, dry with the end of summer. Across the Bristol Channel the lights of Wales were starting to flicker. Clouds scudded across the sky, their shadows licking the land, and I could see rain falling out to sea, in silver-flecked showers. And there was sunshine, in patches, shining like gold treasure in the water. It was ever-changing, this view, always something new.

I stared straight ahead.

"So we're booked on the ferry leaving Plymouth later tonight," I said. "We'll be in Roscoff at breakfast."

Janey nodded. "I've got my bag. Your rucksack has all the documents...passport, money, sandwiches. I think we're OK."

I took a deep breath as piercing pain seized my heart, my lungs, seemed to grip at the back of my head. I wanted to savor the last precious seconds of us, together.

"I know I let you down before," Janey said. "I'm sorry. But now we're doing it. We're having the adventure." She smiled, a proper smile, her thin, soulful face lighting up. She was beautiful. "Don't you agree?" And she turned to me and saw my expression. "Kitty? Are you OK?" I turned from her, just slightly, and put my hand up to my face as if shielding my eyes from the sun. "What's up?"

"I've been thinking." I cleared my throat. "Change of plan. I think it's time we parted ways. Do you want to keep the mix tape?"

"Why?" she said, laughing. "Are you off?"

"Ha." I opened the car door. "Yes, basically."

"Don't joke, Kitty."

I reached down, digging around in the detritus of the car, and took my backpack, and threw it toward her. "Here. Take it. Look, I don't know how to say this, but I've changed my mind. I don't want to go traveling. Not with you. I just needed to get away."

Janey laughed. "Don't we all." But there was a puckered frown between her eyes. "This isn't funny, Kitty. Are you—are you OK? Can you see? Is there any more pain?"

"Oh Lord. Please," I said, taking a stick of Wrigley's and breaking it up on my tongue. "Please, Janey—don't be clingy, will you?"

She stared at me.

"Clingy? What are you talking about?"

I slung her bag over my shoulder and gave her a curious, almost pitying glance. "I'm heading off myself. On my own. And look, I've arranged it so you can take the place at Cambridge. The matriculation list says Catherine Lestrange, I got Mummy to write and ask them to change the surname. The place has been deferred for a year. You just need to show them your birth certificate. It says Jane Catherine Lestrange, doesn't it?"

"Yes, but—"

"Tell them Professor Lovibond got the date of birth wrong on the form." Quite casually, I chewed the gum in my mouth. "He's left now anyway. You're Jane Catherine Lestrange, I'm Catherine Lestrange Hunter. Get it? They're not going to suspect anything, it's too unusual a name. And, anyway, why would they? You just say you're using your mother's name now. We told them." I inhaled, wondering if my subconscious had known all along that this was what I should do for her, if this was why I'd laid my plans. "It's all worked out pretty well—it's best if we're not together after this really. Now we can both go off and do our own thing." I nodded at her. "Yeah?"

Janey put her hands on her hips. She gave a short half-laugh, half-cry. "Kitty, why are you being like this?"

I had to bite my lip at the sight of her sad, sweet face. *I'm doing this for you. I'm doing it all for you.* "You can take my place. Go to university. That's why I'm doing this."

"I don't want to go off and *do my own thing.* The whole point of this was we went together. I don't want to go to Cambridge. Apart from anything else even if I—I wanted to go, how on earth will I get anyone to believe it's me and not you?"

"Why not? I'm Kitty Hunter. I'm not Catherine Lestrange. Never have been. They won't be looking for Catherine Lestrange. She's a combination of the two of us. You get to be a—a new person. It's simple, and it's really rather genius. It's a third person. She's both of us. If someone asks you if you know a Kitty Hunter you just shake your head. *Sorry, that's not me.*"

"But I don't want to go, not like that!" She laughed, helplessly. She was standing on the other side of the car, arms folded around herself.

I sighed. As if I was trying not to show how irritated I was. "Isn't that all you've ever wanted? Don't you deserve it? Wouldn't you have got those grades, if you hadn't been mad with grief? Is it your fault? No." She opened her mouth, and I moved in for the kill. "What about your dad, Janey? Wouldn't he want you to go? What'll you do instead? Go back to Greenford? To an empty house? To the secretarial course? Listen. I feel bad about it, but not *that* bad. We both used each other, didn't we?"

She was sobbing. "No. No, we didn't, Kitty. I thought I'd found you—I thought—"

I shrugged. "Look, we had fun, didn't we, this summer? But we're pretty different. I'm—well, this is what I do. I'm trouble. Ask anyone."

She shook her head, her mouth turned down with the rictus of crying, half laughing. "You're not, you're not that person. Stop pretending."

"I'm pretending now, am I?" I opened my eyes wide. "Listen, Janey. It's been a laugh and you were a good person to have around, I'm not saying you weren't, but you have to admit we don't have much in common. And I'm not sure I can go across Europe with some girl from the suburbs who wants to talk about her dad the whole time and doesn't really know what she wants to do with her life."

"So where will you go?"

"Maybe head west. Cornwall. Hang there for a bit. Try my luck in London, get a job…"

"Are you still angry because I didn't save you, that night with Giles?" Janey's small mouth was turned downward, and she kept closing her eyes heavily, as though she could barely stand to look at me, to take it in.

I shrugged, and curled my fingers, digging them into my palm. "I'm sorry. I know it's a change from what we agreed. But that's how it goes."

"We're in this together, Kitty. Don't."

I cleared my throat delicately. "Look, I never once pointed this out but at school I wouldn't even have acknowledged you. Do you realize how lucky you were? How my father says Mummy's lame ducks will eat us out of house and home one day? And you're the biggest lame duck of all, Janey."

"Stop it, Kitty. Don't do that." She moved toward me. "I know what you're trying to do. And I don't believe you. I saw the real you. I know you."

A few spots of rain landed on her green dress. The wind ruffled the folds of fabric on my sleeves. I cut across her.

"Listen, don't miss that ferry. If you go back to the house, they'll want to know where I am and it'd be a shame if you got arrested for my disappearance, or something, or God forbid they call your mum. You'll have to go to Spain. Live with her and Brian, or whatever his name is."

"Kitty, look." Janey cleared her throat, and smiled. "I know you've had a really bad time. It's me, remember? But let's do this together, not apart." She came around the car, toward me. "You can't just—be nobody. You can't—not exist anymore. I know

Giles hurt you, and your father…and everything…We can find a way through this though. Us two. Come here—"

I'm doing this for you. It hurts because I'm doing it for you. In response, I dug out an envelope from my backpack and hurled it with all my might, right into the middle of the purple heather and rusting bracken. "Here's your papers. The ferry ticket. Your stuff. Bye then." I cleared my throat, battling to keep it steady. "H-have a good life, Janey."

She swiveled away from me with a desperate cry, eyes following an arc to see where the paper envelope landed. She looked back toward me, in agony. "Stay. Just stay there, Kitty!" and then she turned and ran toward the thick scrubby moorland.

The second she'd gone I dropped behind the car, clutching her ridiculously unwieldy bag to my chest. I fell out of her sightline, crawling down onto the lane a few feet below us. By the time she looked back, only ten seconds later or so, I'd vanished. At the lip of the lane was the path that led to the Vane Stones.

I could hear her calling my name. "Kitty! Kitty!" Like the cry of seabirds, circling overhead. "Kitty!"

The large envelope I'd thrown was one of Merry's *Smash Hits!* magazines that she got on subscription. She'd shoved it in the car the other day when we'd gone to get milk and forgotten about it.

Arching beech trees and a tiny drystone wall edged the boundary at the top of the moor. There was no one around.

"Kitty! Come back! Don't leave me!"

Tears ran down my face, and my heart ached, physically hurt. I slammed my hand to my mouth, so that the sob that escaped me was muffled.

I had to let her go. I had to. I smiled as I saw how easy it would be for her, how perfectly I had arranged it, how well my plans had fallen into place, and I hadn't even designed it like this: I had agreed I'd take up my place at Cambridge if I was allowed to be someone else. That someone else was her. She was me. I had completed the circle. I had made it good. I had not been able to rescue my mother any more than Janey's father had, but I would rescue his daughter instead.

The five large boulders of the Vane Stones were surrounded

by windswept thorn trees, twisted by the years into curious shapes. I sank down behind the largest stone, as her voice carried on toward me.

I thought of them as Diver's stones. They'd found the young governess from the house here, her neck broken, her clothing in disarray. I'd always known he'd lured her up here and then killed her. I knew that was why he'd killed himself. That was why he'd been buried here, I was certain. I knew Pammy had known that too. She'd known how rotten it was. I knew that they had in some way caused her death, exposed her to danger. I knew these things, because the blood of my ancestors ran in my veins and the honey from the same hives coursed through me. I couldn't shake it off, and I'd tried for so long.

"Kitty! Come back! I'll do anything! *Kitty!* We can't miss the ferry!"

I hadn't woken up that morning expecting to betray Janey. I knew she wouldn't betray me, either. I knew she'd look in my bag and find all the papers she needed. My passport and hers, tied together in a ribbon. The letter, from King's College, Cambridge, confirming Catherine Lestrange's place. All our money, combined. And, prosaically, apples, and sandwiches. And even some Tooty Frooties.

I knew after a while she'd drive away. She had no other option. I didn't want to be found. We understood each other. I thought and hoped she'd truly believe I didn't like her, that I'd been playing her all summer, that I'd planned this out. It'd make it easier. I knew that she'd never fully give up on me, though. A buzzing thought came to me that suddenly I didn't want her to, that I could cry out, that she could come and save me, but I squashed that part down, like my father squashed bees under his thumb.

She stayed longer than I'd thought. She got as far as the Vane Stones, but I knew the little cavern, in the hollow of the hill behind the largest stone, and I hid in there while she stumbled around. I could hear her sobs, her muttering to herself and I bit my lip so hard I tasted the metal of my own blood. Janey, my kind, clever, sparky Janey. *I have to let you go.*

I curled myself up, as tightly as I could, so I couldn't hear her broken voice calling for me.

It stopped raining, and over the bay yellow light broke through the gray clouds. It was an hour later I think that the battered blue car that had picked her up only five short weeks previously was bumping down the track across the moor. I backed out of the tiny space in the rock ten minutes before, propping myself against the stone, clutching her bag. I looked down, away from the sight of the car.

There was the remaining bee, still on the ruffles of the dress.

I caught it, held my hands together, an open ball, and shook up and down, then I opened my hands, cupping them to my chest. I heard its furious buzz, and felt it sting me again. Surely I'd done enough now? I leaned back against a rock, feeling the rain on my face. The buzzing that had been so loud all my life had suddenly gone. I waited to feel the terror—but it didn't come.

"Of course."

I took out Wellington Bear, hugged the soft, matted fur, and smelled his soft head. He smelled of my mother, and of Janey. It was silly to want this final attachment, I know. But now, holding him tight, I was ready. The whole summer, from her arrival to these last moments, flickered in front of my eyes, like images on a screen. All of it. I remembered it all, the good and the bad. And I realized, as the heat of pain mixed with the scent of heather, and as the buzzing of the bees and the new, sudden warmth of the evening sun washed over me, that I had been ready forever so long. It flashed before me, like flickering images on a screen, the whole summer, and I remembered it all. I was ready. I waited.

31st August 1989
To: Charles Hunter,
Vanes, Somerset

After the Collecting, we are running away. We are telling you so you make sure they don't come looking for us. And if they do, we'll tell them about you. We know your little secrets. We know what you did. We know all your deceptions.

We don't want to live like this anymore. Janey doesn't want to go to secretarial college, she wants to study and do something with her life. Kitty doesn't want to go to university and then marry someone and be a posh housewife, she wants to travel and get away from here. Far away FROM YOU.

But no one listens to us when we say these things. We've been told what to do and where to go all our lives.

We're not listening anymore.

Where we're going, you won't find us.

Wherever you look, we'll be invisible.

We're never coming back.

SIGNED:

The Beloved Girls

Catherine Hunter & Jane Lestrange

Part Five

2018

Chapter Thirty-Two

Catherine rang the doorbell of the large white stucco house and stepped back, trying to ignore her shaking legs. She was tired and still felt dirty, though in fact she had showered that morning for the first time since Friday. More than anything else though, she was incredibly thirsty. Whenever she had imagined cutting loose, taking herself out of the lie that was her own life, she hadn't considered thirst would be her main preoccupation.

The road was busy with traffic, but few pedestrians. Still, she felt uneasy. She had come up out of Warwick Avenue Tube station, head down, scarf covering her backpack so it couldn't be seen on CCTV. When she'd bought the backpack, two years ago, she'd made sure it was as nondescript as possible. But, still, it didn't hurt to be careful.

Standing there, she did her checks, the ones she had done every day for the past twenty-nine years, and only halfway through did she remember once again that these checks were redundant. It was over.

"You've got a form of OCD, I reckon," Jake had said once, leaning in the doorway of her office, waiting to go to lunch, as Catherine did her checks out loud:

"One-two-three-four-five. OK, I'm ready."

"What do you keep in that bag, anyway?"

"Oh, the basics. A fake passport, ten thousand pounds in cash and a lightweight wig, in case I have to suddenly cut loose and revert to my old identity," she'd said, and he'd laughed.

Sometimes she asked herself if enough time had elapsed. If she could just admit to being a different person, not only in name. For she was not Janey anymore, she was not that brave, worn-down, but hopeful girl who had got on a boat and woken up in a different country and had to start completely from scratch. But the answer was never what she wanted. To be that brave, to admit what she had done was to admit she had left Kitty behind to die. That she had stolen a place that wasn't hers at one of the best universities in the world. That she had lied at every step of the way, to everyone who knew her, and to those who loved her. Of course she could never go back.

Catherine rang the bell again. It was bank holiday Monday and this was the third day in a row she'd come here. There had been no answer before either and she was too afraid to wait, or ring the other apartments to ask the other occupants of the building if they knew anything.

Most of the other houses on the road were mega-mansions. Behind her was the canal, with the waterbus that took you through the dark, slimy tunnels to the zoo. They had taken the waterbus for Tom's ninth birthday, and he had fallen in the canal, and Davide had had to dive in to fish him out, and then they weren't allowed to stay on the barge. Thinking of this, and Davide's rage, and he and Tom both dripping wet and covered with stinking green algae, cabs refusing to take them home, ending up in a McDonald's on the Edgware Road, she wondered how they had ever managed to laugh about it. But they had. They'd all ordered Big Macs and Tom had been allowed an extra portion of fries. "I'll let you have them all, Tom," his big sister had announced magnanimously, eyes wild with jealousy.

It was 4 p.m., and Catherine and Davide should have been on the Eurostar back. What were they all doing now; right now?

This was the third day without them. She shook her head, knowing she mustn't think about them too much. It was best that way. Leaving, escaping the horror that her life had become made sense until she started to think about Davide and the children. She had sent a postcard from the station so they wouldn't worry.

I've done the right thing. They probably are better off in fact. I can't be with them anymore. I've been seeing ghosts. I smashed up the study, I sent the letters. I don't remember doing it but they're in my handwriting so I must have. I can't make it better. I'm so sorry. I love you all.

She wasn't sure where she'd sleep tonight. She was thinking about this, and whether she could bear another night on a bench, when the door was suddenly flung open. Catherine jumped, clutching her bag to her chest.

"Hello?" said the woman in the doorway, politely. "Which one were you looking for?"

"Oh. Flat C."

Catherine looked her up and down, drinking in the sight of her—the once frizzy dark hair, tamed into a glossy black mane like a cloak over the slim shoulders. The pale face, the perfect, slightly too-dark arched eyebrows, the slim fingers clutching the door. She was understated and glossy, in espadrilles, expensive jeans, a paisley silk-printed smocked top. She tucked a lock of dark hair behind one ear, and gave Catherine a cool smile, showing slightly too-white teeth.

"That's me. How can I help you?"

"I—I came before but you weren't in—" Catherine began, but now that she was here she didn't know what to say, not to this cool, beautiful stranger. How to start.

"I was away for the weekend. What is it, please?"

"I—I wanted to ask you if you'd heard." Catherine cleared her throat. "Heard the news about—"

Relief swept across the woman's face. "Oh! I'm so sorry. I'm not interested in religion, thank you so much." She made to close the door, but Catherine put her hand on it, and stopped it. The woman's eyes flew wide open. "Excuse me! You can't—"

"Merry," Catherine said, quietly. "Merry, it's me." The door stayed where it was. Catherine peered around the frame. "Merry? Did you hear me?"

The head poked out again, eyes bulging, pupils fully dilated. "*You,*" she said, slowly, swallowing. "No. It can't be. It's—you. No."

"It is. It's Catherine."

"You're not Catherine," Merry said. Her eyes darted up and down the road. "Listen, I don't know what—what this is. I saw in the paper that you'd gone missing. Catherine." She gave a quick, hissing snort. "I know who the hell you are and you're not Catherine. You're Jane Lestrange. The question is where you've been, and another question is how on earth you did what you did and what the hell happened to my sister, and how on earth you've got the nerve to show up here after all this time when—Jesus."

Merry shook her head, her face slowly flooding with red. She scratched at the corner of her open mouth, then closed her eyes. "I—No. I can't. No. Goodbye."

And she shut the door in Catherine's face.

Catherine stood silently for a moment. Then she shrugged, and knocked on the door again, softly. She looked over her shoulder, at the trickle of pedestrians making their way down the street. A little boy in yellow wellington boots, just like the ones Tom had had, followed by a nanny carrying his bags and coat. Two glamorous Russian ladies. An ancient man in red cords, who reminded her of Quentin Holyoake. Time ticked on. A dog barked. A helicopter went overhead. There was no answer.

So Catherine knocked again, as hard as she could, ringing the bell at the same time. Then she bent down and pushed open the letter box.

"I'll stay here and shout until you let me in," she bellowed. "I'm not going anywhere. I have to talk to you."

The door opened again. Merry peered out. "Get inside."

Inside, junk mail littered the communal hallway. The windows on the stairs were filthy, coated with years of London dirt. Merry hurriedly led her up a wide, curving staircase, carpeted in worn-out shagpile. Catherine followed her meekly. It was nice to be inside. She'd been mostly outside for two days.

"Come in," Merry said, gesturing. "Quickly, please." Catherine saw her glance up and down, taking in the grubby trousers, the thin navy sweater and scarf, the messy hair. "Take your—coat off," said Merry, wrinkling her nose. "I have to do something. Back in a second."

Left alone, Catherine advanced slowly into the room. Years of advocacy, examining evidence and sussing out clients, and years of playdates with her own children meant she was expert at summing up families, and houses. The ones she liked best were the ones where your assumptions were challenged: the house in chaos with empty Fruit Shoot bottles, dirty diapers and baby wipes scattered on the floor but a pile of library books on the window sill. The aging hipsters with bare floorboards and minimalist Scandi designed furniture who unexpectedly offered you a slice of Colin the Caterpillar cake with your cup of herbal tea.

As she glanced around Merry's home she felt she was destined to be disappointed. In contrast to the communal areas, the interior of the flat was a vast, chilly, hollowed-out space. There would be no surprise inflatable llamas hidden behind the Eames chair here. Where once there must have been paneled connecting doors linking to another room, now there was nothing, just white blank floors and walls and, in one corner, a curling iron staircase, down which pale silver light glowed from the floor above. Other than faint traffic noise it was very quiet.

The only personal touch was on the mantelpiece, where there were four or five gilt-edged invitations, addressed to "Darling Melissa" and "Ms. Melissa Hunter": gallery openings, receptions, fundraisers. At each end of the mantelpiece was a photo of Merry. One was of her laughing in a group of people that included a famous philanthropic Hollywood star. He was smiling at Merry, whose flawless skin shone, her eyes glittering. The other photo was black and white, and showed Merry at Vanes, aged about three, Catherine guessed. Her arms folded, her rotund tummy extended, a comical frown across her brow, almost hidden by her heavy dark bangs. Next to her, on the lawn, sat Rory, as a puppy.

Merry reappeared, silently, as Catherine was debating whether to help herself to a glass of water or whether that wouldn't be on.

"Love the place," said Catherine, gesturing at the empty, echoing space.

"Sit down," Merry said, pointing to a sofa so pale it seemed to blend into, and become indistinguishable from, the spotless floorboards. She reached for Catherine's bag. "Can I hang this up?"

But Catherine snatched it away so fast she flinched. "No. Thank you. Sorry. It's got all my... It's got important things in it."

Merry stared at her. "Uh. OK." Her phone lit up with a message. She looked down at it, then up at Catherine, and flashed her a smile. "What can I get you? A cup of tea?"

"Oh, a glass of water, please, Merry," said Catherine. The phone lit up again. They both looked at it.

"Sorry. I have a gallery opening tomorrow, hence why I'm working on a bank holiday and everything's rather chaotic."

"It looks it," said Catherine.

Merry got up without replying and padded over to the kitchen, a white passageway that Catherine could see led through to another reception room, with a vast pale oak table at its center.

"I didn't mean to joke. This place is beautiful," Catherine said. She shook her head, wondering. "It's—it's not what I'd have expected of you. That's all I meant. The Merry I knew at four-teen, anyway."

"Yes, well. It's quite different from Vanes, isn't it? I took time picking every single item out. I wanted to be quite sure nothing reminded me of home." She handed Catherine a glass of water. Catherine drank it in gulps, and put it down noisily on the glass table in front of her. It made a clattering, cracking sound. Merry winced.

"So how have you—" Catherine began, but Merry put up a hand.

"No, no. No. I'm asking the questions, thanks. You were in the newspaper, did you see it? I did. They said you're my sister, which is kind of strange, wouldn't you agree?" Merry rubbed at a droplet of water that had fallen onto the table.

"No," said Catherine. "No, I didn't." She wiped her mouth and sat back on the sofa. Merry watched her. "What did it say?"

"They say you'd been acting strangely. That your study was broken into while you were away. *The Times* had it that someone was following you. Something to do with that guy, you know, the one you defended."

"Grant," said Catherine, slowly. "Grant Doyle." She put her hands to her face. "Did it say how he was?"

"He's still in hospital. That's all they've mentioned."

Catherine's fingers twisted in and out on themselves. She whispered, in a low voice, "Poor Grant. What have I done? That poor boy."

"Poor boy nothing," said Merry. "He murdered someone. I wouldn't worry about him."

"I was his barrister. His defender, and I threatened him," Catherine said in a rush as if she was confessing. "He's barely eighteen."

"People were talking about it, at the gallery this morning. *At work*. They were wondering if you'd run off because you knew something about him or he had something on you. And I had to sit there and smile, pretend I'd never heard of you. *Catherine Christophe, that missing woman?*" She put on a high-pitched, silly voice. "*Sure, I've heard of her. She stole my sister's identity, she might even have killed her.*"

"I didn't steal anything."

But Merry, swifter than Catherine this time, leaned forward and snatched the rucksack away from Catherine. With quick, nimble fingers, so like her mother's, she opened it, rummaging around.

"Give it back to me."

"Absolutely not." Merry pulled out a shiny nylon fanny pack. "What elegant accessories you have these days, Janey." Swiftly, she took out Catherine's passport.

"I see your birthday is the thirty-first of August. If you're not impersonating her, then how come you've stolen her passport?"

Catherine reached for the passport, pressing it tightly between her fingers "I didn't. I told you. I didn't steal anything. Merry, I came to explain. To say I'm sorry—"

Merry was laughing, the hollows under her eyes pronounced. "Listen. I've done what Mummy wanted. As always. I've kept out of this for almost thirty years. How did you get her name, and your photo? How come it's *your* photo?"

"I said my passport had been run over. It was." She'd been proud of that idea. She'd balanced the hard, black and gold cardboard on a stone outside the hostel in Toulouse, then backed the rental car over it, up and down, so that it ripped down the middle, and was crushed, the photo saturated in mud from the gutter, the whole thing unrecognizable. "I went to the British consulate in Toulouse and cried. I said it had fallen out and I'd found it like this on the street. I had Kitty's name on the ferry tickets, as proof of travel, and my birth certificate with me. It was no problem, not back then." She corrected herself. "Kitty's birth certificate."

Catherine observed wryly that, despite the disdain and horror on her face as she relayed her story, Merry could not help but look a little impressed at this. "You still stole her identity though."

"It wasn't stealing." Catherine swallowed. "She gave me all her documents. She told me I had to take them. You weren't there—I didn't have any other options. You have to understand that. What she—what happened." It was very strange saying any of this, after so long. Her mouth was completely dry.

"Forgive me," Merry said, crisply. "Forgive me if I don't, quite."

Catherine pulled the rucksack back onto her lap and tucked the documents inside. She was silent for a moment.

"A couple of things started up this year. And I—I found I couldn't cope anymore. I think that's what's happened to me. The house came on the market, and I found out right after the trial had finished. I had to bring my mother back to the UK and put her in a home. She doesn't know who I am. My daughter was turning eighteen. And then—"

I've seen her. She's come back, Merry. She's still here. She follows me around. And she's not who... she's not who I thought she'd be. It's all wrong.

But she couldn't say it.

"All of those things. All together, clicking into place, like a sort of machine in my mind, it—it—brought her back again. And it wasn't the story I'd imagined for her."

"What story?" Merry said, and her tone softened. "Kitty, do you mean?"

"What happened to her. I think about it all the time." She hugged the rucksack to her, tightly. "Whenever I couldn't sleep or when I was feeding the children and trying not to go mad with tiredness, or when I'm walking to work or there's a long, very boring closing argument I...I'd think about what she's doing. What she'd have become. I think she'd have been a designer, like Sylvia, don't you?" Her eyes shone. "Orla Kiely, or Cath Kidston, or someone like Donna Wilson. Colorful, edgy, British style. She'd sell Sylvia's prints, too. And she'd live in a house in Hampstead—I'd picked it all out. And she'd wear cashmere joggers, and be awfully stylish. She'd never marry anyone but be really glamorous, and popular, and out at all the best parties—she's Kitty Hunter, remember?" She glanced around at Merry's cool, echoing home, at the invitations.

"Catherine—"

"And I had her winning awards. And opening shops. In 2019

she's going to open three more concessions. One in Bicester Retail Park." She smiled. She didn't care anymore. "And 2020's going to be her biggest year. I had her opening stores all round the world in 2020. Hong Kong, New York, Sydney." She smiled. "I know it sounds crazy. But it helped me…remember her. Because there's no one else to talk to about it. I go to another place, instead of the horror of it, when I start thinking about that summer, about what happened to her, if she's still…I left her." She shook her head. "I'm to blame."

Merry was silent for a long time. "Oh Janey," she said, eventually. "Jesus. I don't know what to say." Her pale face, with its dewy, perfect skin, was drawn.

Catherine squeezed her eyes tight shut. "All the things happening this year—Mum, Carys, the trial, the anniversary. I couldn't control my thoughts anymore. I—I smashed up the study."

"You broke into…your own study?"

"I didn't know what else to do. It was the night before we went away. At Easter. I was working late, and the others were all out. I had to release—something." She shook her head. "Oh God. What have I done? What did I do?"

She had set aside the evening to tie up Grant Doyle's paperwork: the billing, some queries from the solicitor, but she found she couldn't. Instead she had sat scribbling things down, as she sometimes did, things Kitty might say, memories they had. She'd done it for years. She thought it helped keep her alive.

And that night she had googled the Hunters, for the first time ever. She had never let herself look them up. She was always afraid of what she might find out, how it would affect her ability to be this new person. But, that night, she couldn't stop herself. It was too much, finally, and she'd clicked on a story.

HOUSE OF TRAGEDY UP FOR SALE
Ancient chapel where Charles Hunter and his sister were killed during bizarre "Collecting" ceremony and eldest son severely injured to be included in sale; campaign to have it listed underway

Like the time she'd been in a café with Jake and a bee had flown in, or the time a woman called Polly, on a tour of one particularly competitive London day school, had looked at her a little too closely and said: "You know, I'm sure I've met you before. You weren't at Letham's, were you? No? Are you from Exmoor?" or when she'd just started training to be a barrister, and didn't reply when a senior criminal barrister called for her help during a trial: "Catherine!" he'd shouted at her afterward. "What's wrong with you! Don't you answer to your own name, goddammit?" Like those other times, when Catherine was threatened, she had no means of coping. She had never learned how to. She shoved it away, deep down, where it couldn't disturb her, time and again.

This time some final tie binding this tightly woven, other her together was loosened. She had felt it slipping away, had, quite calmly, stood up. She had pulled everything off the shelves, inadvertently breaking the window, smashing mugs and pulling open box files, scattering papers everywhere. She was glad, as ever, that Mr. Lebeniah was deaf, that they were on the end of the terrace, that the people in the houses that backed onto hers were either away again or absent while their basement extension was completed.

As it was happening it was liberating. She told herself this would make her feel better, that it would sate something inside her, and she kept thinking of the girl she'd defended for strangling her abusive stepfather who used to cut herself, to release something, to control something she could not control. All the time very quietly, sobbing so hard, wishing there was someone, anyone, who understood. But there never was. When she had left Kitty behind, she had accepted she would always be an outsider.

She had locked the door on the study, and gone downstairs, tidied up the kitchen, so that when Carys and then Tom got back, they found her pottering around as normal, and when Davide arrived home, late and a little the worse for some excellent Puligny-Montrachet after a dinner with clients, he found Catherine in bed, attempting to concentrate on *Wolf Hall*.

"All set for tomorrow?" Davide had said, sliding into bed and snuggling against her.

"Oh, so much. I can't wait to get away."

He smelled of cigars, and wine, and aftershave, and he

undressed her, and she climbed onto him, and afterward slept very well, because that door was now locked and no one would go in.

Except she left the key on the hall table, and when they got back ten days later Carys did go in, to get an envelope. Would any of this have happened, this unraveling? If she hadn't left the key on the table for Carys to unlock the study? If Eileen hadn't come back, if Vanes wasn't being sold, if Grant hadn't got precisely, completely under her skin. Catherine stared, unseeing, at the floor. What if Quentin hadn't had his stroke? What if she hadn't broken her toe? She just didn't know.

Most of all, she didn't understand Kitty's return. The idea that she was real was as frightening as the idea she was imaginary. The letters that kept arriving—had she written them? Catherine thought she had. Sitting there on the sofa, she was certain she had. Hadn't she? But she couldn't remember now.

She'd tried a mindfulness course a few years ago, and it had been a laughable failure. "You?" Davide had said, when she got home that evening and she'd told him. "You only think ahead, *chérie*. I do not think being mindful is part of your—your make-up."

He had no idea. How every thought was monitored, every impulse measured, how she looked over her shoulder, up at the sky, around the family table every day, every night, looking to see when the wind would change, when she would have to take herself off, slice herself out of the family, so that they could get on without her.

The buzzing was so loud in Merry's empty flat now that Catherine shook her head. "Anyway, that's—that's what—it is." She picked up the empty glass and put it down again. The room was chilly. "How have you been all this time, Merry? You mentioned a gallery opening—what exactly is it you do?"

Merry gulped. "Sorry?"

Catherine said politely: "What do you do? I don't know anything about you, Merry. And I'm so sorry."

"Jesus." Merry laughed, her mouth wide open. She had two black fillings. "You really want to do this now? Fine. I had to leave Letham's, after it happened, because Mummy said there was no more money for school fees. I studied art history at Edinburgh, and then I moved to London. I own a gallery in Fitzrovia, and I represent young British artists. I'm off to Miami in December, we're launching someone new tomorrow evening, and I'm hoping to take him there. I have several clients I'm really excited about. I'm single, though I was engaged briefly fifteen years ago…" she paused. "I couldn't—anyway. But, no, life is good." She glanced round the flat, smiling, nodding. "So I'm fine. I'm really fine."

"That's nice," said Catherine. She had to get rid of the sounds in her ears, people calling out for her. "How often do you go to Miami?"

Merry gave a shaky laugh. "You turn up after thirty years and what you want to know is whether I'm a frequent visitor to Miami. What next? Am I excited about the Royal Wedding? Do I prefer hummus or guacamole?" Catherine shrugged. "What about your kids, for God's sake? Won't they be worried sick about you? Your poor husband. You just left him at the station?"

Catherine looked up at her. "I sent them a postcard. To say I had to go away for a few days. That I wouldn't—do anything silly."

"The police don't seem to think that. It's bank holiday Monday, Catherine. They won't have got it, not if you mailed it Friday evening. It's 2018, there are other ways."

"I have a—a pay-as-you-go phone." Catherine paused.

"Pay as you go? Aren't you, like, a barrister?" Merry's voice was full of scorn, like a teenager again.

"I threw my old phone into the canal. This one lives in there." She nodded at the fanny pack. "I worked out, when I went up to Cambridge, the only way I could face it, could cope was if I had—a plan to disappear if I needed to. I've amended it over the years but it's basically the same. I take this everywhere, you see."

"But you've got it all wrong. There are people out there looking for you. People who love you. And you don't care. If that was me—" She stopped.

Catherine shook her head. "Please don't. I had to leave. There were signs."

"What kind of signs?"

Catherine stood up, and paced over to the window. "Oh," she said, with a blank smile. "I can't say that. You wouldn't believe me."

"Try me," said Merry, quietly.

Catherine looked round. She was hungry, and tired. She wondered if she was really here. Whether she was hallucinating. She hadn't really slept for three days, and hadn't eaten since the previous night, when she had queued up outside the Pret a Manger on the King's Road for the handout of surplus food at closing time and had been given a goat's cheese and pepper wrap and a muesli bar. Neither items she'd have chosen in her old life, and she'd smiled grimly at the idea of asking for something else. "Sorry to be a pain, but have you got the crayfish baguette? And a Very Berry smoothie?" She had the money, but was paranoid about CCTV in the shop.

Besides, the handout was very civilized. It was her and several normally dressed people. One mother, with two kids. One had a battered *Paw Patrol* backpack, like the little boy down the road for whom Carys babysat, and huge dark eyes. His sister carried a very stiff pink rabbit that she stroked while sucking her thumb. They were both expressionless. Bored. Years of her criminal-law work had taught her being poor is boring, among many other things. You wait a lot. For busses. For appointments. For people who tell you what to do. An old lady, with dank white long hair hanging around her face rustled several plastic bags in her pockets. Catherine had found herself wondering: will that be me, in twenty years' time? Two young men, in their twenties, Turkish or Eastern European, she'd guessed. They'd grinned at Catherine as they took their food, waving their wraps. "Good, good food. Fuck Tories, huh? Fuck them!"

Why had she come looking for Merry? Why had she bothered this fragile, sad woman? Catherine cleared her throat.

"It doesn't matter. I came because I wanted to apologize."

Merry folded her arms. "How did you find me?"

"I looked you up," said Catherine. She watched someone walk past and wondered how long it would take if she were to walk back home. She supposed she couldn't really go home again.

"You stalked me."

"It's basic data mining, Merry. I got your building regulation application form off the internet. For this, I presume." She waved her hand at the hollowed-out flat. "Melissa Hester Hunter. Your mother gave you all unusual middle names, which helped."

Merry opened her mouth to say something. Instead she laughed. It rang around the empty flat. She stood up and came toward Catherine, her footsteps clattering on the shiny floorboards, so they were facing each other. "You show up, out of the blue. After thirty years. You smell awful, by the way. You look half deranged, you're barely blinking, do you realize that?" Catherine put her hands up to her face, to shield herself from Merry's voice, the noise. It was very loud in there, the bouncing sound drilling into her tired mind. "I loved you, Janey. It wasn't just Kitty who did. I loved you, so did Joss, and Mummy. We all fell for you and you disappeared. You left one note, threatening to blackmail our father. That's it."

"It was her," Catherine whispered, hands still up around her face. "Kitty. I went because of her. And then she vanished. In front of my eyes. It's the truth, Merry. Honestly. I loved her, as much as you did."

"Fine. Even if you went because she forced you to—"

"She didn't force me. But it was her idea. She planned it all. And then she...she let me go."

"But where did *she* go?"

Catherine shook her head. "I don't know. She'd been stung. She was in pain. I know she was. But she said it was nothing."

Merry stopped. "I saw her just after it happened...she told me she'd been stung." She bit her lip, and suddenly she was a child again, a scared, lonely child, and Catherine saw the damage they had done.

"I promise I don't know what happened to her. I think she crawled out of sight and hid herself and I think she probably died." Catherine took a deep breath, and exhaled. "I wondered if you guys had ever heard. If your mother knew."

"Why would we know?"

"I thought she might have got in touch with you if she could. I thought she'd at least contact Sylvia. She never heard from her?" She saw Merry stiffen. "How is Sylvia, Merry? I went to her exhibition the year before last. It was wonderful. Is she—OK? I thought about going down to see her—what do you think?"

She glanced out onto the pavement, as Merry stepped away from the window, tapping on her phone again. Someone was looking up at the two of them. A tall, heavy-set man, hands in his pockets, shaved head. Catherine stared, suddenly alert again. "Do you know that person?"

"No," said Merry, shortly, looking down. "It's one of the security guards. Place is crawling with them round here. It's the Russian billionaires." She cleared her throat. "Sylvia. Sylvia is...well, she's fine. I don't think it'd do you much good to go and see her. I mean she's mad, really, but she's been that way for so long we're used to it. Voted for Corbyn. Voted for Brexit. She was arrested in March with some group of environmental terrorists, essentially. She glued herself to some railings." She flicked her hair away. "One isn't quite sure what triggers it, but she definitely changed after my father died. Or reverted. That's what Joss says. You know, we were pretty much frozen out by everyone after what happened."

"Everyone?"

"Well. Not the villagers. Not the Reds, the Culneys, the old families. But—our friends."

"Some friends."

Merry ignored this. "Mummy made me leave, go to the local school, and then there was the business with Kitty—the police—all of it." She closed her eyes, as if recalling it all, and then, opening them again, said in a tight little voice: "I'm so sorry, I'm being terribly rude. Would you like some tea? More water?"

"No, thanks—" Catherine sat down again. Her hands, sweating, slid off her joggers, onto the cream sofa. "What business with the police?"

"What? Oh. Well, after Kitty went missing. She'd left the note saying you were both leaving, addressed to my father. But the police made a stink about it. Wanted us to produce her. Out of nowhere. And we couldn't of course, 'cause she'd gone abroad!" Merry laughed, moving over to the kitchen. She put the kettle on and started pushing open white handleless drawers, taking out cutlery and cups and saucers.

"But she—hadn't," Catherine said, quietly.

"Well, we didn't know that, did we? We didn't find out for years. We just weren't sure. We knew it wasn't Kitty up at Cambridge—Mummy came and sat outside the college and saw you."

"Came to King's? She *saw* me? Why didn't—she—why didn't she say something?"

Merry looked at her hard. "I guess you'd have to ask her that."
She shrugged, and silence fell between them, heavy, unyielding.
"We knew Kitty couldn't still be abroad, surely. She'd have run out
of money. And it was years after by then, and someone—I don't
know who—some friend of a friend it was, rumors, said they'd
heard Hunter's daughter, the one who'd run away, had ended up
as a barrister in London. Giles's ma came over especially to tell
Mummy. Which was jolly decent of her in fact."

"Giles." Catherine rolled the name around her mouth. "Giles
Leigh-Smith."

"Yes, of course, who else?" Merry looked impatient, as though
to say what other Giles is there? "He lives in the same house. Married a lovely girl, Bella, he's a pillar of the community, he's
really—been so kind, trying to help Mummy, reaching out to
Joss—Joss was very ill, he was stung about a hundred times, you
know, his heart stopped twice. But Mummy's been awfully rude to
Giles. Wouldn't let him across the threshold. I don't understand
why. It's been embarrassing, and of course it's one of the reasons
people turned against her. They always had their suspicions about
her, and then after all of it she starts designing again in earnest
and she's so successful, her stuff's everywhere, you know. It—looks
wrong, to them. And I have to say I can't blame them, can you?"

Catherine didn't know how to answer, but Merry didn't seem
to notice. "So for Ginny Leigh-Smith to take the trouble to come
and see Mummy and tell her she'd heard Kitty must be in London, well. And Mummy said it was none of Ginny's business
where Kitty had gone and she knew she was OK. She was in-*cred-*
ibly rude to her. That really broke the last of the links with the
families near us. Poor Joss, it's made it very hard for him, to keep
up the house, the traditions, you know." Merry hugged herself.
"Not that we do any of *that* anymore.

"It was twenty years ago now. She came up to London, to wait
outside the law court to see this barrister, the one she'd heard was
Catherine Lestrange. She waited all day till about four when they
all emerged and it was you, on the pavement, huddled with some
others, someone shaking your hand, someone crying over you.
Mummy said you looked so glamorous. Together. That your hair

had grown back much darker. You weren't like the old you. So…Mummy toddled back to Somerset. She said she was right all along. She'd seen all she needed to. And she sort of shut herself off. Said that was how it was and we'd screwed up your life enough so we should leave you alone. She started working properly again right after that. So she's filthy rich, there's the irony."

"She came and saw me…both those times," Catherine said slowly. "And she just left."

"Yes. I wanted to get in touch with you again. I insisted, really. So we came up together, looked for you again a few months later but there was no sign of you."

"I was married. We lived in Paris for a year. When I came back I'd changed my name." Catherine swallowed, sifting through it all, the concertina'd pack of facts jammed up together. "What—what does Sylvia think happened to Kitty, then?"

"Kitty?" Merry shrugged. "I don't know." She shoveled loose tea into a pot. "I have no idea what goes on in Sylvia's mind. I don't think I've ever known. We all joke about it. She could have murdered her and we wouldn't know."

"We?"

"Me and Joss. And Paola, Joss's wife."

"Joss is married?"

"Why are you so surprised?"

"I'm not," said Catherine, but she realized Joss was still eighteen to her, not a man the same age as her, the same as other men her age: a bit paunchy, a bit gray, a bit stiff sometimes.

"Yes, a lovely Italian girl. She's very clever. Organizes Joss. He needs that. She got rid of Mummy, too, moved her out to the gatehouse. Mummy doesn't really get on with Joss, you know. Hasn't for ages. He asked her to leave—oh, ten years ago now. Tried to sell the gatehouse from under her, but she refused to go. Still refuses. He's had to renegotiate with the buyers, accept a much lower offer. He was furious with her."

"And—what does Joss think about Kitty, what happened to her? What does he think about me—taking her place at Cambridge?"

Merry sighed, as if it was all rather tedious, having to explain it.

"Listen, Janey. Catherine. Whatever you call yourself. You have to remember the stuff with the Collecting was a long time ago now. It's not something we think about that often. We're not close, as a family." She smiled faintly. "My father and Aunty Ros, well, they were in their sixties—Ros was almost seventy. We all have to go some time, don't we? They knew the risks with those bees, and they refused to replace them with a more docile variety. And I don't think we see it quite the way you do. It was terrible, of course, but it was almost thirty years ago now. When he came out of hospital Joss wanted to move on, not live constantly in the past, like our father. He's right."

For the first time Catherine felt something she hadn't felt for years—decades, even. She was the outsider again. It was so odd, like when she'd smelled the scent of Amarige—Claire's favorite perfume—on someone at the theater just before Christmas, and it was like being punched in the stomach, being teleported back to Claire's bedroom, listening to Soul II Soul, lying on Claire's Littlewoods duvet—she'd seen it right there, the pastel squares of apricot, blue and green, the posters of Prince and Nina Simone on the walls, the mirror with the pink-glass trim.

Her own past, who she had been before that summer of 1989, had entirely disappeared. The sitting room of her childhood home, with the bobbled, mint-colored, slightly shiny three-piece suite which had been her mother's pride and joy, the potted plants and neatly arranged copies of the *Radio Times*, the bookshelves either side of the gas fire, stacked with Daddy's and her books: Robert Graves next to *Adrian Mole*. The stairway, with the thin oval window in stained glass—a rainbow over fields. The oddest little details, things the mind held somewhere, shut far away out of sight. She was no one now. And suddenly she could see eighteen-year-old Janey again, shorn-haired, standing on the terrace as the family looked her over, the relentless August sun beating down on them all, the evening of her arrival at Vanes.

She jumped, as Merry bent down and handed her a cup of tea. Her mind was whirring. *I shouldn't have come here. Not here.*

Merry's voice broke in on her thoughts. "I did used to wonder, though. After Mummy came back from seeing you at Cambridge.

Did people really think you were Kitty? I can't imagine anyone getting the two of *you* confused." Merry poured herself some tea, delicately.

"Well, they wouldn't, would they?" said Catherine, forcing herself to focus. There was a bitter taste in her mouth. "Everyone at Cambridge knew me as Catherine Lestrange. That's very different from Kitty Hunter. You don't look for someone you didn't know was supposed to be there but isn't there, do you? No one really asked."

In the twenty-nine years since, of course *some* people had asked. The first time was an old friend of Charles and Sylvia's, she never knew from where. He'd been at King's himself, was in Cambridge for lunch, decided to look Charles's daughter up. She'd heard him asking one of the porters. "Kitty. Kitty Hunter."

She'd been hurrying back from a tutorial on the Pazzi Conspiracy, her mind full of popes and plots, hugging folders to her chest. A bright, hopeful March sun washed the quad in warmth, the cobbles digging into her thin-soled sneakers, and then she heard the voice ringing out, and she could still hear it, years later, the exact timbre, the tight, upper-class drawl.

"Kitty Hunter. I tell you, she's here at King's. Look again, if you don't mind. Or Catherine, perhaps."

"And I'm telling you, sir," the porter had firmly replied. "There's no one of that name here."

"History. Give me the list for history."

He'd scanned it with his finger, as Catherine watched, pretending to fiddle with her backpack, heart in mouth, hardly able to breathe: "Iveson…Jordan…Lestrange…Oh. Hm. How odd. I could have sworn…"

"You're not the first person, I understand," the porter said grimly. "Perhaps she told people she was going there. Or the parents did. It's happened before."

"Her parents aren't—actually, her pa's dead. Very sad. I—" He'd scratched his head. "She ran off—or perhaps she didn't go, in the end. How curious."

And he'd tottered off, bald head gleaming in the sun, and she had slid past the porter, out onto King's Parade. So Charles was dead; she had not known this before. And no one knew the rest of it. For the first time, she felt free.

Her mother was easy enough to deal with—she spent Christmas with her, and once, maybe twice, a year, when Eileen was in England, she came to Cambridge and took her out to tea. Easy enough to explain she was using her middle name, not her first name—she had gone through a phase, like all eleven-year-olds, of wanting to change her name. Eileen never asked about Sylvia, and the family at Vanes, nor what had happened to Kitty, beyond mentioning her once. "I never liked the sound of her," she'd informed Catherine. "One of those girls who causes trouble, you know? Wherever she is. If Sylvia's not worried, you shouldn't be." Besides, there was a weary familiarity now in her dealings with her mother. She knew she only had to lean on her a little too much: "Mum, can I come and stay for a bit, I'm having a bad time at university—" and Eileen would retreat, pleading a full house, Martin's children staying, an outbreak of Legionnaire's disease in their apartment block—anything really, as long as it kept Catherine at bay. Whenever she felt Eileen was showing too much interest, and might want to stay a night, she'd do this, and it was almost funny to see her mother back away. Almost.

After she and Davide moved to Paris, and then back to London, somewhere along the way she understood she didn't have to bother with her mother anymore, since her mother wasn't ever going to bother with her. She didn't give her mother her new address or phone number, and let one email go unanswered. Not greatly to her surprise, after a year or so Eileen didn't get in touch again. Her mother. And so they lost contact entirely, for twenty years, until one day Catherine realized she had to just check she was OK, and discovered her mother had advanced dementia, no visible support system, no other family, and that she was responsible for relocating her and paying for her care. Which she did, because she had to.

She had represented a woman whose mother had changed the locks after her father died and refused to let her daughter have any mementos from the family home, who held the funeral in private and then sold the house and with the proceeds moved to Florida. Catherine was used to hearing stories about families that made you realize your individual story might be unusual, but the level of family dysfunction was far from unique.

The one stumbling block was Claire. Claire, her best friend, who knew her as well as her father. She'd written to Claire on her year off, sent postcards. *Traveling for a while. Hi from Prague!* But Claire had sensed something was amiss. She had contacted her mother enough times for Eileen to eventually write to Catherine. *Please could you tell your friend Claire I've passed on her messages. Perhaps you could contact her yourself now.*

So she'd invited Claire for the weekend, and it had been awful. To have to be Janey again, to answer Claire's questions about the place at Cambridge. Claire was the weak link—she could have rung Miss Minas. "Your favorite pupil got to Cambridge in the end, Miss Minas" and then the cat would be out of the bag, as they'd check the records and find out there was no evidence for a St. Cecilia's girl having gone to King's that year. She was lucky Claire was enamored of her new life in Birmingham, already saying she never wanted to leave. All Catherine had to do was make Claire think they weren't friends anymore. So they had fun that weekend, she took her to Cindy's, to a comedy club, to the college bar, where there was a karaoke evening, anything that took up time but meant she didn't meet enough people who might want to question Claire about Catherine's background.

At the end of the weekend they'd hugged. Claire had pulled Catherine tight. "I think it's weird, changing your name, but I see it. I see it. I see you, babe. OK?"

The smell of her perfume and the smooth feel of her skin against Catherine's cheek, the way she loved her, just loved her, because she was her friend. Catherine remembered, in the few seconds of that hug, wondering if she should give it all up then, confess then. "You just keep on working hard and get that first and do your dad proud. You come to Birmingham, OK?"

Catherine had avoided going for a year. She'd gone traveling over the holidays, back to France to see Davide again, then spent Christmas in Spain with Eileen, and only managed to get to Birmingham at the end of the second year, by which time there was enough water under the bridge for it to seem naturally stilted. She'd gone to the pubs, oohed and aahed at the campus, had a curry at Claire's favorite curry house, but all the time with a degree of restraint. She acted—perhaps it was then she realized she was a good actress, and could be a good barrister.

It shocked her how easy it was, afterward, to let the friendship slip away. But she had loved Claire, like family. And the loss of her, which was never made up for at Cambridge, or in London, was a constant source of pain. But what other way could it have been?

There were other people who stared, who asked questions, but only a couple of times. Some girl, a friend of a friend from Kitty's school: "Hi, are you Kitty Hunter? Letham's?"

"No."

"The one who—oh, there was some scandal. She ran away. Some like, random thing at her family's house? My brother swears his best mate snogged her at a ball. Someone said she was here, doing history. Isn't that you?"

And she'd assume a patient, polite face. "No. That must be someone different. I'm Catherine Lestrange."

Her friends, and Catherine, began a joke about it. That she had taken the place of a girl called Kitty whom she'd murdered to get to Cambridge. Whenever it happened, at Cindy's, or in the college bar, Catherine would smile and, surreptitiously, would touch the little pouch she'd taken to carrying in her handbag, where the passports were, and Kitty's birth certificate, and the cash she'd saved, and one of the letters that arrived from Davide, twice a week every Tuesday and Friday, without fail.

You said you were not sure, that it was too hard, that it was too easy at the same time, you said these things, Catrine. But it is a small miracle, is it not? That I met you. That we had that time together. Six months! It is a small miracle that we are made the way we are, that we fit so well together. I am not afraid of the future. You know we say a coup de foudre—*yes, it was instant like that, but for me it was also certain, and strangely calm. We both know it, don't we?*

Come back to France this summer. My parents will host you. As you know, they love you. As do I. My fierce English girl with the crop and the smile like Isabella Rossellini only more beautiful. I like writing these things down, when I say them to you, you roll your eyes, but they're all true. We have only a sea dividing us, Catrine, come back. No one else matters, the past does not matter, we matter. Put yourself first, with me.

She had folded and unfolded this letter so many times that it threatened to fall apart entirely and she was terrified that it would. As if, without this physical evidence of his love for her and his reasoning, her resolve was weakened.

"You have to remember, I'd been away for a year too. I felt much older than a lot of them, and I kept myself to myself. Some of the others, especially the boys—straight out of public school, they were like kids in a sweet shop. They behaved like idiots. I just wanted to work. I was older than a lot of them. I'd been through a lot. After I left—her—I drove, I drove to Plymouth, I ditched the car. I got on the ferry like she told me to, I got to Toulouse like she wanted. I lived there for a time. It's where I met my husband." Catherine exhaled. "And it made everything different."

"Does your husband know?"

"I told him I changed my name, to honor a friend. He knows I didn't have much connection with my childhood, but I think he put it down to Daddy dying and my mother leaving. He thought I didn't want to talk about it much." Catherine shrugged. "He's a man, Merry. And we've been together longer than we have been apart, you know. We met in France, on his turf, and I suppose it stayed that way, and I liked it. At the beginning, I explained a bit, some details. I said I'd left home and wasn't close to my parents. Which was true because I wasn't close to my mother. I never have been. And Daddy was dead."

Merry put down her teacup, smiling, then pressed her cool hands to her flushed cheeks. "You seem to have been very lucky."

"With Davide," Catherine said, calmly. "Yes. Yes, I have."

Merry arched her head, backward, staring up at the mantelpiece, the photos, the invitations. She rubbed her neck.

"You've been lucky in other ways. You didn't see Joss in hospital, realizing he couldn't speak. You didn't have to watch Daddy and Aunty Ros die. That's what I saw. She went in front of me. She was holding her throat. Like she was strangling herself. And the house, and the gatehouse, and the chapel, and our life there, our friends—it was all gone, in one afternoon, after that. And you two were gone too."

Catherine nodded.

"Merry—I'm so sorry. I should have tried to make sure you were OK. I mean, obviously you are." She gestured round the flat. "You look amazing. You've obviously made a—a success of it all."

"Yes," said Merry, crisply. She glanced at her phone. Then she said: "No one calls me Merry, by the way. Not anymore. It's Melissa."

"I see." Catherine nodded. "Melissa."

A silence fell, awkward and hard-edged in the cool room. They smiled at each other mechanically. *I have nothing else to say to her*, Catherine thought.

She gathered her stuff and stood up, slinging the rucksack over her shoulder. "Look, I'd best be off. I'll—"

"Where? You can't go! We're having such a nice chat. Here, have a sandwich. You must be starving." She glanced down at the phone again and Catherine's brain suddenly started clicking, connecting, again.

"Oh, no thanks. But maybe a bit more milk? In my tea?" Catherine said, slowly.

Merry got up, pleased, and went to the fridge, and the second her back was turned and she opened the heavy, metallic fridge with a *whoosh*, Catherine leaned across to glance at the phone, glowing with new messages.

Keep her there. Police on way

Police say they are five mins away. Shall I tell mummy?

No merry don't let her go. Make her stay. Don't tell Sylvia, she mustn't know she's still around. They mustn't meet. She'll muck up plans if she heads down here. It's tomorrow. Get the police to take her off yr hands.

"Thank you so much," said Catherine, standing up. Merry spun round, in alarm. Catherine crossed the endlessly long room and took Merry in her arms, hugged her tight. She was very thin—too thin. Her shoulder blades dug into Catherine's wrists and hands. She was not, anymore at all, the childish adolescent Merry who had jumped up and down with joy, who danced through meadows, who loved Jason Donovan.

After a moment, Merry hugged her back. And Catherine whispered in her ear.

"I am so very sorry. None of this should have happened."

I am sorry for you. I was raised with so much love, she wanted to say. *I was so loved by him. It didn't matter about my mum. He loved me, he understood me, he made me confident, and strong. You Hunters, you never had that. You never had it, from either parent. Daddy couldn't stay in the end but he knew that he had done enough. I know he knew that. And...*

Perhaps that means I have been lucky. I'm standing here. And I may not look it, but I am OK. I must be OK. All shall be well.

"Do you know something?" said Merry.

...He was so close, his voice in her ear, it was almost as if she could feel his breath on her skin...

"We used to rather laugh at how much you straight away wanted to be like us. You were quite weird, Janey. Did you know that? Kitty did, especially."

Catherine half closed her eyes, the better to protect herself, to hear his voice again. "I know."

"You *know*?"

"Yes, of course," said Catherine, almost impatiently. "But I couldn't help myself. All of this, all of it is because I couldn't help myself. And it wasn't my fault." And, suddenly, somehow she felt a little lighter. "It wasn't." She was desperate to leave. "Look—"

Merry took a step back. Catherine found herself thinking how skull-like her face was, the fine, smooth white skin stretched taut over her cheekbones, her forehead, her chin. And then she said, slowly: "OK, I'll tell you something. Mummy still believes in her."

"What do you mean?"

"Mummy doesn't think she's dead. She says she sees her."

She was watching Catherine carefully, the button-like eyes fixed on her, bony fingers twiddling the small, flashing diamond on her necklace. Catherine felt a twitch start up, above her left eye. "Where does she see her?"

"I don't know. Around." Merry gave a thin smile. "Around, Catherine." She folded her arms.

Catherine didn't respond; she didn't know how to. She merely nodded, and patted her rucksack. She put her hand up to her eyes, and said abruptly: "Listen, can I quickly use your bathroom? I'd like a wash. And—you know. Don't know when I'll be in a bathroom again."

Merry looked appalled at whatever *you know* might be. "Oh. Of course. Next to the hall, down there. Take your time. Stay. Listen, if you don't want to go back to them, tonight—stay here! Stay for a glass of wine, anyway."

She followed Catherine into the hall and, when Merry was satisfied Catherine was inside the lavatory, she could be heard going back into the living room again, collecting the teacups, clattering in the kitchen.

Silently, so very silently, Catherine opened the bathroom door and then tip-toed toward the heavy front door. She didn't shut it behind her—Merry would hear it. She crept back downstairs, rucksack on her shoulders, through the dingy hall, then outside, and she ran.

Catherine knew perfectly well they couldn't arrest her, that there were no grounds, but she mustn't be caught, not now. She told herself this as she ran, hair flying behind her, her toe suddenly twingeing again. She was less than five minutes from Paddington station, and she knew what to do. She ran beside the walls, so Merry couldn't see her, and then ducked into an underpass and then, when she was certain no one was following, she kept on running. Earlier that day she had checked on a computer at Marylebone Library. There was a train, leaving at 7 p.m.

Though there was no one behind her she was sure she could hear Merry's voice, thin, high, anxious, calling her, all the way to the station. A copy of that day's *Times* was scattered around on the floor. She knew she was in it. She kicked it out of the way. She would not be caught by them. She could disappear again and again, if she wanted to. She knew how to. She had started this and now she had to finish it: she was going back to Vanes.

Chapter Thirty-Three

The rain kept stopping and starting, and she wasn't sure whether to stay put or keep on going. It was wild and windy, with a close humidity everywhere and sudden bursts of sun, which felt incredibly hot for May. Palm trees clustered together next to whitewashed holiday bungalows in quiet lanes leading toward Langford. Behind them, the looming rise of Exmoor, in front the sea. She had forgotten how strange this corner of the world was, an unsettling oasis against the wooded twisting flank behind, and the bulk of the moor above.

Catherine walked along the lane, her sneakers soggy, her head hot under the baseball cap. It was so quiet, apart from the wind, and the birdsong. No planes, or helicopters, or idling engines. No drilling, no beeping pedestrian crossings, no shrieks from children playing. She'd forgotten how much the English countryside unnerved her. Still, blossom spread above her in bright green trees arching over the lane; nodding, pale pink foxgloves and wild roses dotted the hedgerows. It was a glorious time to be here, even for a city girl like her.

Suddenly a tiny, terrified mouse shot out from the hedgerow, scuttling down the lane and disappearing further down the way. Catherine started violently, the rucksack jolting on her back, then she found herself smiling. When she was a child, her primary school had gone every year to Horsenden Hill for a jolly summer picnic, and most of the class, her included, had fled screaming from the horseflies, the midges, the wasps. She had been hysterical with fear on the famous occasion a mouse ran across the kitchen floor and her mother screamed and, as if out of a film, stood on a chair. Daddy, ever practical, had cornered it and bashed it with a shoe, then picked it up by the tail, its small gray body swinging from side to side, almost comical, as if it had never been alive, been real. "How could you, Simon?"

"Kill it or touch it?"

"Touch it! It's disgusting! Full of disease."

Daddy had thrown it into the bin, and her mother had screamed again.

"My dear, I lived with rats the size of cats when I was in Italy. It's just a mouse. It's terrified. And it's dead now anyway."

This incident had occurred just before her mother had left and she had wondered afterward if the mouse had tipped her mother over the edge. Then several years later, that summer at Vanes, her horror when, one evening, a mouse had run out of the fireplace and across the drawing room floor. Kitty had barely raised an eyebrow. Joss had looked up, startled, and then gone back to strumming his guitar.

She knew there were worse things than mice. But she hated them. So, now that she was a grown-up, she paid an exterminator every year to come and block up any holes in the skirting board, seal up cracks in the floorboards, put brush strips on the doors. Carys, who showed strong incipient signs of hardcore veganism, much to her father's distress, objected to the poison under the dresser, the glue traps under the sink, and would remove them after Davide and Catherine were in bed. Tom didn't care. Tom didn't care about anything much.

It was strange, the way distance gave you clarity of thought. She loved her second-born child but she had always worried she didn't really understand him, not in the way she knew the bones of her busy, purposeful daughter. She'd always tried to, filling his days with cello and chess and football, and he did it all with a sweet smile, never seeming that interested in any of it. And now, when she thought about him, the casing around these thoughts—her unspoken fear for him that he wouldn't find his place in the world—had vanished. *It doesn't matter that Tom's not this or that*, a voice told her as she walked, her toe aching a little. *It doesn't matter that he doesn't know what he wants to do. He's sixteen. It matters that you've left him.*

Her daughter, her rages, her anger at everything, her hobby horses—the three months after she adopted from a friend, who had long since tired of it, a stinking, dying lone guinea pig with a large sore on its back had been long months for the whole family—her passion for the environment and commitment to real change, all these things Catherine could not exactly walk in total step with but she could understand. She thought of Tom, giving money to the homeless man. Of his big, toothy smile, his handsome, still not quite finished face. Of Carys in her office, pale, tired face, sticking-up hair, how intelligently she had tried to grapple with what her mother was telling her, how little she, Catherine, deserved her as a daughter.

She hadn't seen them for four days, and it was now the pain of what she'd done, believing it to be the best, the only course for them, that was starting to unfurl itself, a grinding, inner agony that seemed to pull her toward the ground. Missing them was like a physical ache, in her chest, behind her eyes, in her shallow, fluttered breathing—lately, she couldn't ever seem to draw a deep enough breath to fill her lungs with air.

I have spent so long living this life and protecting it, she thought to herself as she gazed out to sea. And it's mine, but I really don't know it very well. And now I think it might be too late, and I don't want it to be too late. I desperately don't want it to be.

After the first time she'd met Davide, he had told her he knew *tu n'étais pas dans ton élément*: "in English, that you were a fish out of water." That was the thing he had always understood about her as fundamental to her being: that she did not belong. But he thought it was because of his first impression of her that day, not because for two months by then, and for the subsequent next twenty-odd years, she had been lying about her very existence to him.

Coming here again, she couldn't stop thinking of that departure, which she remembered in forensic detail. The drive across Exmoor to Plymouth, in sleeting rain, trying to handle Joss and Kitty's temperamental car. At Plymouth, she had ditched the car on a quiet residential street not far from the ferry where there was a corner shop at the end of the road, and then she had thought to send Sylvia a card, written in capitals.

THE CAR IS ON PARADE STREET, PLYMOUTH.
DON'T LOOK FOR US. WE'RE FINE. THANK YOU FOR RESCUING US. RESCUE YOURSELF, NOW.

The shaking terror as she showed the ferry tickets, which were like shiny checks in a book, with multiple carbon copies, as though they were Charlie's Golden Ticket and must be preserved. Leaving the country in the pouring rain, on the ferry, the stink of fried bread and cigarettes everywhere, and the newspapers still full of the same news—as if the world hadn't changed—the *Marchioness*, a drug that could stop those who were HIV positive from developing AIDS, and Princess Anne separating from her husband. She had huddled in the corner of the café, hiding behind a fog of smoke and a cup of tea, and, as the night wore on, she allowed herself to sleep. Only that morning she'd woken at Vanes, in the little bedroom she'd come to know so well, with a measure of security. Now, she was alone, and terrified, and yet she kept on going. She wouldn't go back to Vanes. Kitty was right, there was nothing left for her there. She had to keep traveling.

The next day she woke in France. There was a delay allowing the drivers back to their cars, and a straight-backed army type in a tweed jacket had rapped his passport loudly on the iron barriers, so that they rattled, and the cavernous deck had shuddered. "I'm *British*!" he'd shouted, almost screaming.

The rain started again as it kept doing, a bright, glittering shower casting rainbows across the bay. Catherine pulled her thin fleece tightly around her, feeling the ache in her shoulders from the swinging rucksack. It was late afternoon. Time to press on.

In France, where it was about ten degrees hotter, and where everything was opening up after August, she had taken a train south, traveling without knowing it toward her husband, toward the love of her life, but on some level sure she was journeying toward something.

Davide knew her feet were always cold, and that she liked a strong black coffee first thing in the morning. He knew she despised the Royal Family, and was more left-wing than most French people, which was saying something, but made straight for any copy of *Hello!* at a hotel or someone's house and could identify the most obscure of the Queen's grandchildren. He knew her shoulders were painful because she hunched over her desk. He knew she loved London, knew every street in the place, and that she adored her work, the discipline and the focus her job required.

She still loved him as much as ever, maybe more. His dark beetling brows, his expressive eyes, his perma-tanned skin, his Gallic elegance and precision, his humor, his pragmatism. He was not moody. He was reliable. He was sometimes rather too precise and reliable, and tedious over matters of what to give the children for tea, more formal than other people she knew, but then none of these things were bad, necessarily. Her children ate spinach, and were never late, thanks to their father. "Everyone should have a Davide," mothers at school would say wistfully, as Davide took Tom out for steak on his eleventh birthday or traveled to Hert-fordshire on a rainy Saturday in February to attend a glitter-slime-making conference with Carys, aged thirteen. Catherine would want to laugh, to say: I had a good template. I was raised by a good father.

As she walked along the old paths, bursting with new life, she saw again that those years of wonder with Simon had given her the ability to navigate a difficult childhood and adolescence. She had grown up with a father who took her to the library every week, who taught her to cook spaghetti, to sing jazz standards, to love his adopted city, who had imbued in her a sense of curiosity about everything, a passion for fairness and justice. Losing him had almost broken her, but she had survived, because of his love and what he had taught her, his beloved daughter.

She had got in late to Taunton the previous night and stayed at an anonymous hotel at the edge of town. That morning she'd watched a report on breakfast TV that Grant Doyle was in intensive care. They didn't know if he'd make it. The tide of sympathy was turn-ing toward him. There was talk of a petition by former pupils demanding an inquiry into bullying past and present at Jolyons school. The other members of Dan Hammersley's gang, the others who'd tortured Grant, were openly being named in newspapers.

Catherine had noted almost as if she were a spectator that there was no mention of her. She had stopped being of interest. She was just a missing woman, a bit crazy (probably menopausal), someone who'd fallen out with her husband—she was not the story anymore. Women went missing all the time, after all.

She stood still as the rain thundered heavily down, dripping onto her shoulders, thinking about Grant Doyle. How much he had reminded her of someone, not her, she knew, but Kitty. His intensity, his insecurity, his too-confident way of walking which hid his fear: everything about him. She had made him into a bogeyman, when he was just a bullied child: she had made Kitty into a goddess, when she was no more than the same. She saw this calmly, again from a distance.

Perhaps she will be there. So I have to go, she said to herself. I have to see it, see what it's become. I can decide what to do afterward. I'm not sure I can go back home again. I don't think I'm good for them. But first I have to go back up there.

She stood shivering, waiting for the skies to clear, staring up at the hill.

The path was the same. Narrow, twisting, dangerously close to the edge. Bramble blossom, hawthorn and elderflower sprang out impulsively, the rain and sudden spring heat making everything look obscenely, wildly green. The sun was out again, slipping toward the western horizon. She had to stop a few times to catch her breath—it had been four days since she'd disappeared, four days of sitting around in hotel rooms or on park benches or in trains and she could feel her muscles ossifying, her taut body slackening. Her tendons ached with the pull on her legs as she climbed; sweat oozed down her back, and Catherine felt alive, exhausted, exhilarated.

She put her hand up to her eyes, as she looked around, orientating herself, and then she walked west, up toward the outline of a ruined building, cast into golden relief by the sun.

The tall stone gateposts topped with pine cones at each end—they were still there.

The long, low house turning itself toward the sea, it was still there, the stone gleaming whiter than ever before. But now black marks dotted the walls, like hundreds of spiders, still clinging to the brickwork. She realized it was where ivy had been pulled down.

The shutters were closed tight in almost every window, and the gate was fastened shut. The curious hive-shaped gables, curving up into the roof, four of them—she hadn't noticed how strange they were that summer. Her tired brain kicked in, asking questions, seeing patterns. What came first? The windows shaped like hives? Or the bees, looking for hives? It wasn't so big, really, nor so grand. It was a lovely, large house, but not the mansion she'd held at the humming center of her imagination all those years. It was just a house.

Catherine shook herself. She felt depleted, a bit like the bars of the battery on her pay-as-you-go phone, down to one. Wherever she was she had been waking, at two, at three, then five, mouth working, eyes snapping open. The house grew larger as she approached, no signs of life, though she felt it was watching her.

She crossed over the path that threaded through the edge of the wood toward the driveway, and kept on along it, following the northern boundary of the house, until she was standing in front of the chapel. Her sneakers were soaking wet with mud and spring rain.

Catherine stared at the chapel, blinking. It was more a collection of stones now than a recognizable building, only this time there was some almost comically ineffective red and white plastic tape draped around it, fluttering like a large ribbon around a present, and a "Danger: Keep Out" sign propped up against the listing north wall, next to a Building Preservation Notice signed by the local planning authority.

Butterflies fluttered in and out of the dark, overgrown clump of faint-flowering brambles and trees that had sprung up around the ruins. One wall was partially erect, the curious diagonal iron bars on the window that splayed out in a half-fan pattern still there, though they were rusted half away to spindly points, like used sparklers. The rest was all rubble, the floor barely visible. No one was looking after the place. It was silent, the droning gone. The bees had never come back.

Picking her way carefully across the threshold, she remembered how she'd looked at the thyme and wildflowers springing up in the cracks and thought: this place isn't anything special. And then she saw it.

It was laid out on the altar, the carved stone rectangle at the back of that small stage. Half of the altar still stood, the stone roundels of skulls and bees and crosses abruptly terminating where one jagged edge showed how it had been broken in two. Such violence required, to break a monumental object like that apart.

On top of the altar was a comb. And, littered around it, like soft, dark amber petals, dozens of dead bees. She blinked—surely it was the light, her tiredness, her mind, playing tricks, tricks upon tricks. What was real? She didn't know. Wasn't even sure, in that moment, if she had made it here, if this wasn't some dream. Golden, drenched in light, oozing amber, thin hexagonal walls pricking through the honey, some palest yellow, some the color of deep, unguent toffee, and Catherine knew, knew that it was real. She knew if you stuck your finger in, it would taste like no other honey she knew, caramel notes of raw, rasping sweetness that melted on your tongue, caught at the back of your throat, lingered on your lips...

Someone had been here, and had left a slab of honeycomb on the altar. She turned, expecting to see a face at the leper squint, but there was no one.

Carefully, Catherine dipped first one finger, then two, then three, into the honeycomb. She did not stop to think who'd left it there, where it had come from or even why it was there at all in May. She simply feasted on it. It was glorious, sating, unimaginably delicious.

A movement made her look up out of the cracked building toward Vanes. She saw that in the gathering dusk, a light had been turned on in the hall of the shuttered house. Catherine wondered what it would be like to simply walk across the lawn, knock on the door, ask to be let in. How her younger self, who idolized the family and the place so much, would have loved that.

The gardens were overgrown, so different from Sylvia's day. The back door through which they had run in and out was cracked, faded from red to a weather-beaten pink. The wooden table and chairs on the terrace were dark gray. One chair had lost a leg, listing onto its side, like on that final day here when she had seen the furniture toppled, everything upended amid the chaos of the swarming bees.

She realized the house was dying now, in its last stages, sloughing off its final skin. The feeling of the summer heat reaching even the flagstones on the soles of her feet, the back door that swung inward too violently—there was a small recessed circle in the brick wall, from the door knob, centuries of people coming and going. Catherine suddenly remembered with a jolt how carefully Kitty used to open the door, so as not to disturb her mother when she was working. None of the others had bothered.

Her sneakers were so wet now she could feel water pooling between her toes. Catherine unlaced them and took them off, and the socks, and she stood on the stone in her bare feet. She wanted to feel more than she did, to experience some kind of elemental connection to the place, something transformative, symbolic. She took out of her rucksack the pamphlet written by Pammy Hunter, which she had held on to all those years. She would leave it there, leave it behind, a memorial to Pammy, and Kitty, and all of it. She reached out, to place it on the altar.

But she couldn't do it. She wanted to keep it with her. It was part of her life, her story, and not to be left. She didn't want either of the girls to be forgotten. She wanted to be able to reread this story, if she needed to.

So there was nothing there for her. Only the sweet taste of the honey, and the feel of damp stone under her feet.

"Bye, Kitty," she said, gently. "Bye, Janey. I miss you both. I'm sorry it happened. I'm so sorry."

Then she stooped down and picked up one of the dead bees. She held it in her hand, feeling the tiniest prickle of the body against her skin, just as she had that first time Kitty had given her the bee, that October weekend, all those years ago. And something made her say: "Hey! Kitty! Wherever you are." She could hear her voice bouncing against the bricks of the chapel, echoing on the wall outside. "I came back. Thank you. Thank you for the days you gave me."

She stood in silence for a while as the wind blew through the ruined building. She could hear the tape, clicking against the wind, like Morse Code, tapping out a message to the air, the sea, the sky. And for a moment it was easier not to move, to keep herself utterly still.

When she felt she could, and before she lost her nerve, Catherine took the little blue Nokia phone out of its bag and tapped in

Davide's mobile number, blinking hard to try and remember it right; she never called it because it had been programmed in her phone for as long as she'd had a cell phone.

He answered after one ring. "H-hello?"

"Davide." She had to clear her throat, then terrified in a tiny second that she wouldn't be able to speak, that he wouldn't hear her, that they'd be cut off, that she'd lose him—"Davide? Davide—" And she was crying.

"My love—my love." She heard the breath whooshing out of him. "Hey. Hey! It's Mum."

"Mum!"

She could hear screaming, a thudding noise.

His voice was a sob, whispered. "Where are you? Are you OK?"

"Yes, yes, yes. I am. I'm totally fine. I'm so sorry. For everything—" She swallowed, trying not to cry. She could hear him, crying. She had never, ever heard him cry. "I had to get away. I had to, for a bit—"

"Mum!" Carys's voice was loud, as she spoke right into the phone. "Mum, where are you?" She wasn't even angry. She just sounded terrified.

"Hi, Mum," Tom called. "Hi."

"Hi, darlings," she said. Tears slid down her cheeks. She looked around, at this place she'd thought about for so many years that held no power for her anymore.

"I'm so sorry," she said. "I couldn't cope anymore. It burst."

"What burst?"

"The—thing I had around me. I can't explain. Not yet. I had to get away. I know I shouldn't have done it. I know—I know how much you must have worried."

"Um—*yeah*," said Carys. "Um—a *bit*."

"We'll talk. When I get back."

"When will that be?" said Davide.

"What are you going to do?"

"Mum—you won't do anything—will you?"

"I promise I won't. I promise. I shouldn't ever have put you in this position." She couldn't stop crying, heaving sobs that she tried to keep as quiet as possible. "I'll tell you all about it. Tomorrow. I promise."

Tom broke in: "They found your phone in the canal, Mum. And your stuff. It was like you'd—"

"I know. I know. I am so sorry. Mothers aren't supposed to run off. They're not supposed to break down. They're supposed to—not do this." She cleared her throat, wiping her face, but the tears came again as she thought about her own mother, and Sylvia, pressing Wellington Bear on her all those years ago. "Look," she said, turning around and around in the hexagonal skeleton of the chapel. "I will talk to someone, when I'm back, someone who can help me. Things happened to me, when I was your age, darlings. And I spent so long thinking I'd caused it. And…" She glanced at the sealed-up tombs. "It really wasn't anything I did. None of it. And it's taken me a long, long time to realize that." She scratched her head. "In fact, I'm not that sure I even believe it now, saying it out loud, though it's true."

"Did you go back to your home?" Davide said, clearing his throat.

His voice—to hear his kind, low voice, here in this place.

"Sort of. My love, where are you?" she said. "Can you just tell me where you all are?"

"Sure," said Carys. "We're in the sitting room, and we've got a takeaway, and Tom has his weird pale-blue joggers on, and I'm in my unicorn onesie hoping for a miracle, and Dad's started smoking again so he's been out the back and stinks of cigarettes. And…Mr. Lebeniah brought round some flowers this evening, and Jake came by earlier for a drink. He said that guy is out of the woods."

"What guy? Grant?"

"That's it. The creep. Anyway. And someone called you. Some old school friend. She saw the picture in the paper. She said she knew you in West London, Mum, but you were called Jane? Is that right? She was called Claire. She looked you up in the phone book, who even does that? She sounded really nice…"

Catherine held the little phone away from her ear. "OK," she said. She nodded. "That's great. Yes, I was known as Jane, back then. Claire was—she was my best friend." She felt sick at what would have to be explained, and then she shrugged at how easily Carys had just unpicked it for her. She looked down at the bee in her hand. It was time to remember other things.

"I didn't go back to my home," she told Davide. "I went back to Vanes. And I'll tell you all about it when I'm back."

As she spoke, she turned toward the house, and a door opened. She could see a figure emerge, stand on the terrace, looking out. Catherine backed herself against the wall.

"I'll be back tomorrow. There's something I have to do tonight. Is that OK?"

"Of course—it's late," said Davide. She could hear him, shushing the children.

"I love you. I love you all. I'll come back. I promise. I promise."

She must have stayed there a while, because the sun had almost disappeared behind the cliffs as she emerged. Still in her bare feet, she stood on the springy, soft mossy turf, feeling the warmth of it soaking into her skin. She was here again. She had spoken to her family. There was a link between these two formerly separate worlds. She had stood on this ground and heard their voices.

Catherine walked the few steps toward the stone gate that led into the garden of Vanes, through which she had run so many times that summer. She saw, with a plucking feeling at her heart, the gateway to the old stone pool; the gate was open, she could see the green water, glinting in the setting sun.

It was an hour or so since she'd eaten the honey; she'd had nothing else since breakfast other than a banana and some water. She felt light-headed, bursting with energy, and she wondered if the rumors about the honey and its strange properties were true. The colors around her were incredibly bright. The world seemed calm, and at the same time pulsating with life. Every leaf, every blade.

She stood still for a minute, there under the archway, looking for one last time at the house, the terrace. The back door opened again, suddenly, and a man came out. He pointed at her.

"Hey, you!" he called, his voice carrying across in the wind.

She stood still, as if it wasn't obvious he was talking to her.

"Hey! What are you doing, poking around? I saw you going into the chapel. It's condemned property, OK? It's dangerous. Clear off!"

Catherine took a step back. She slid her thumbs under her rucksack and stared back at him. She could see now for certain that it was Joss; of course it was.

He was wearing a moleskin waistcoat with gold buttons that gleamed, a checked shirt, dark-green trousers. He was red-faced, and those lovely hazel-gray eyes that she had once gazed into glared furiously at her as he gathered pace. The Byronic lock of hair that used to fall into those eyes had gone; most of his hair was gone, in fact. His stomach was a little round half-sphere; the rest of his once-wiry, languorous frame had expanded, like a balloon filled with too much air.

Joss, it's me. I took Kitty's life. She gave it to me. I lived it, and it was good. So good. Ah, Joss—

But she couldn't bring herself to say hello. She couldn't bear to think that was Kitty's twin, nor did she want to trample on the last traces of nostalgia she might have had about that summer, to see the man the boy had become.

"I say! Hey!"

He was walking across the lawn, following the path they'd always taken. He was coming toward her. Catherine dropped the bee that she was still holding in her hand, forgetting about her sneakers, and backed away.

"Here! You!" he was shouting. He was getting closer, and she could see him, squinting at her in the last of the light from the sun. *"Who is that? Tell me who you are!"*

"Goodbye," Catherine called. "Goodbye!"

And she started to run, bare feet surprisingly agile on the springy turf, till his shouts faded and there was no answer, only the sound of sea and air.

Catherine went back along the footpath and turned off toward the main road. She didn't know where she would sleep tonight, only that she should get out. This was her last night. Tomorrow she would go home.

The first night she'd slept in a hotel, the second two nights out in Hyde Park, and she could barely remember them now...that was the worst period, where she knew she couldn't go back but couldn't seem to go forward at all. And she had been afraid she might try to end it. She had been so afraid. Now she was out of it she realized how terrified she had been.

At the end of the short path through the woods was the gatehouse. But it was not empty. There was a light inside and she could hear loud music, guitar, something with drums. And then she remembered what Merry had said. "She lives in the gatehouse now."

Catherine had no idea what time it was. She stood rather woozily on tiptoe, and peered above the overgrown hedge, spiky with spring growth. Staring into the sitting room window she could see a figure, hunched over an empty grate. At her feet, a discarded box from a pre-prepared meal, a plate and some cutlery, and jewel-like colored foils, twists of chocolate wrappers, scattered across the floor.

It was Sylvia; she knew, without seeing her face. The black hair, tied in a loose bun, heavy bangs shot through with gray. The sharp angles of her shoulders, the way her knuckles whitened as she clenched her hands together in her lap, beating in time to the music; all this, Catherine knew, without having to see it. How like Merry she was, and like Kitty had been, in her swift, intelligent movements, and how little she resembled her son.

Sylvia looked up, suddenly, as if she sensed something out of the window. Catherine stopped still, keeping completely quiet. "It's late," she heard Sylvia say, very calmly. "Who is it? Who's there? Is it you again, Kitty? Come to blow my house down?"

The wall was covered in strange markings, set out in evenly spaced-out hexagons: as Catherine peered closer she could see a block of brightly colored diamond patterns, next to perfectly controlled swirls of color, clambering, spiked thickets of rose studded with little decorations, woodland animals on endless repeat. The whole of the small room, she realized, was a hive in different patterns.

Catherine's head still ached. She stared again, as the hive played depth tricks on her eyes. The room seemed to be layered, the walls alive, three-dimensional.

The wind behind her gusted and a tree scraped on the roof, the window rattled and suddenly the door flew open, banging loudly, and Sylvia appeared in the doorway, staring out at Catherine, as the music swelled and a woman's voice howled.

"Oh. There you are," she said. "I wondered when you'd come."

Chapter Thirty-Four

Catherine was ushered inside the tiny gatehouse and Sylvia shut the door carefully, peering out, head swiveling back and forth down the road.

"Unwanted visitors," she said, obscurely. She slammed the door smartly, then leaned against it, arms folded behind her back, her lovely dark eyes flashing. "So you're here. At last." She looked down at Catherine's bare, muddied feet but said nothing. "May I take your coat, my darling?"

Inside, the music was so loud things rattled. A guitar, a drum beat, a wailing, distanced voice grew, swelling toward a chorus. A glass, a precariously balanced photo frame, a cup and saucer on the cluttered dresser shook—with a jolt that made her feel sick, Catherine recognized the cup and saucer, a pink willow pattern, from Vanes. "I like the music," she yelled. "What is it?"

Sylvia gave her a strange look. "The Stones, darling. 'Gimme Shelter.' How the devil are you? And sorry to be awkward, darling, but what should I call you?"

"Oh. Catherine. Th-thank you." She shivered.

"I know," said Sylvia, rubbing her hands together. "It's chilly, isn't it? I like this bit. She was called Merry, you know."

"Who?"

"The backing singer. Listen." She grabbed Catherine's hand. "Rape…Murder…" she wailed. "Did you hear that? When she duets with Mick. Her voice cracks. She was pregnant. She lost the baby later that night." She shook herself. "What a song, man. It really is far out. The Devil's in it. Clayton. Merry Clayton, she was called. I always liked that name, you see."

Catherine blinked. She didn't know what to say. "You don't seem surprised to see me."

"I'm not. 'Catherine,' did you say you call yourself?"

"Yes. Did you speak to Merry? I went to see her yesterday. Did she tell you I was here?"

"Merry? Goodness no. Haven't heard from her in over a year. She's in league with Joss, of course. They're always messaging, usually at the same time as he's telling me off for something or other." She mimed a texting action with her fingers: "*Nnn nnn nnn.* Merry's *very* grand now. Too busy to come here, which is fine with me." The beady eyes were watching Catherine.

"I thought she might have rung you, that's all."

"No. I knew you'd come back." She gestured Catherine toward the cozy little sitting room. "I'll turn the music down. Great thing, a record player. Doesn't break, you don't need to download anything. I listen to 'Gimme Shelter' all the time." Her weather-beaten face cracked into a smile. "It's a good thing I don't have any neighbors. Come in."

She disappeared into a side room and Catherine heard the sound of a needle being removed. Catherine followed her, pushing aside some curtains in Sylvia's fabric, then stopped and stared. The walls were covered, not just with hive drawings, but other drawings, children playing, rain storms, a green parrot pecking its way round some curtains, scribbled onto the wall, in ballpoint pen, or felt tip, or whatever appeared to be at hand. There were photographs, pinned onto cork boards that were stuck up on the walls. Peeling old snapshots with white borders, and newer ones. A little girl with a huge smile and a large tabby cat, sitting in a garden. Children on a lawn. Merry and Joss, arms round each other. Joss and a dark, slim woman obviously taken on their wedding day, and—and—Catherine peered more closely, and stepped back, as Sylvia reappeared from a closet at the end of the room.

"That's me," she said, in some surprise. It was from March. She was leaving the Old Bailey with Grant Doyle. Ashok Sengupta, Grant's solicitor, was standing behind her, wearing an irritable expression. It was very strange, looking at the picture, to see herself during that period, when she had felt all the time as though she couldn't breathe. When even looking at her children gave her a pain in her chest. When she did not sleep, and ghosts seemed to follow her everywhere.

Suddenly she ached for Davide, for her husband's arms around her, for the taste of his kiss, for the feel of the bumps on his skull when she held his head in her hands, for the feeling of walking down the street with him, close enough to touch, of the sound of his voice, light, amused, cynical, kind. He knew her, knew the bones of her, what kind of person she was, and what did the rest of it matter? It didn't, oh it didn't.

Her breathing quickened again. She stared at Grant Doyle, at his dead eyes. "Where did you get this?"

"It was in *The Times*. I still get a paper," said Sylvia, with some pride. "And I buy *The Times*, to test myself. Because you know a lot of rubbish gets talked in the media. One must be alert, to the truth. If one simply swallows the *Guardian* whole every day, one doesn't question anything. Although they were wrong about Brexit, weren't they? Dead wrong. *The Times* has been rather keen on your disappearance, darling, but there was nothing about it today. Just that boy. I don't like his face much, do you? A very unhappy child. Now. Would you like some rhubarb schnapps?"

"Oh—I'm not sure." Catherine looked around her.

"Come now. Just a little glass. It's homemade. Where have you got to go to?"

"I don't know," said Catherine, with a laugh.

"Where are you staying tonight?"

"I—don't know." She paused, and took a deep breath, and found that the air seemed to fill her lungs, that she was still, for a moment.

"Well," said Sylvia, watching her. "Even more reason to have a drink then. Come with me, my dear. Yes. Come." She led her back through the tiny hexagonal hall, into a kitchen. In Aunty Ros's day it had been unchanged from the eighteenth century—plain shining painted walls. A large butler's sink, old material below it, and a couple of shelves.

Now, the layout was the same but the room was transformed. The walls were drawn on all over with sketches and patterns, as in the little sitting room. The tankards were gone, in their place plastic cups and china jugs and mugs emblazoned with messages. "I'm From Minehead, what's your excuse?" "A Gift from Exmoor." "Ohhh Jeremy Corbyn." Where Ros's Letham's Ladies' College photograph had been was a mark around the wall and a snap of Corbyn himself in the space, stuck up with tape. There were

Extinction Rebellion stickers on everything and several joss sticks, one partially burned with a trembling ribbon of ash, stuck into a plastic cup. Across a photograph of the Hunter family from the 1900s—ruffles, lace, hats, pointed collars, lined up outside the chapel, carrying the smokers, the handbells and the spoons, not one smiling—someone had cut and pasted in different letters taken from newspaper print the legend:

> Why Does Karl Marx Hate Earl Grey?
> Because all proper tea is theft.

Catherine thought of Merry's flat. She started laughing, so tired now she was quite dizzy. "I love it."

"Love what?"

"Well…What you've done with this house. It's not very… Aunty Ros, is it?"

"Not really, no. But not many things were poor Ros, my dear. She was against far more things than she was for them. Ghastly, ghastly woman. Do you know, she'd be ninety-eight if she were still alive."

"Good grief." Catherine took the tiny cut-glass crystal tumbler of schnapps offered her and clinked it against Sylvia's. "Cheers." Their eyes met. She swallowed it down. "Oh. This is delicious."

"Thank you. I have a little vegetable garden around the back. I grow most of my own food and store the rest. Half for me, you know." She gestured out. "Look."

Catherine peered into the dark. In the long thin strip between the house and the road she could just make out an assortment of sticks and, as a car drove past, its headlights threw into relief the outline of a large, neatly managed vegetable garden. "That's very impressive."

"It has to be. I don't want to rely on anyone. And it keeps me busy, when I need a break from drawing. Although I always want to draw."

"You're working again, I know—" Catherine began.

Sylvia looked down at the glass. "I had to. There's so much I still want to do. So much I couldn't do when I was married. I—I used to tell myself: *One day there'll be a chance. One day.*" She glanced up quickly, her head jerking with a small, swift twitch. "The rest of the time I cooked, I had the children, I drove around doing errands, I entertained…and I gave Charles what he wanted." She drained her glass. "I thought of it like ticking a box. If I'd ticked the box it was like marking another day off in the calendar, and then I could sleep."

"Marking a day off till—"

Sylvia looked past her. Her heart-shaped face was set, her gaze fixed on a distant point. "Till I'd be on my own, able to work again. Free. And now I am free. To work all day if I want, so I do. I've just finished a new design actually, I'll show it to you, later. I sell direct when I'm dealing with somewhere like Liberty. They take what I've got, and I use a variety of names."

"Don't you want to have them all under one name?"

"Absolutely not. I don't want to be recognized, not anymore. I don't want *attention*. I just want to do the work, make sure people use it. Furnishing fabric, oilcloth, napkins. I did some lovely place-mats and tableware last year for IKEA. I like the idea that millions of people will use it. It's fun."

"I didn't know that's what you were doing. Merry told me you were working again."

"Why on earth would you? I don't want anyone to know. It pays well and it keeps me independent. And it means Merry and Joss leave me alone. In fact, I have that son of mine over a barrel." Catherine blinked. "I must have poured a couple of hundred thousand into that great hole of a house for years, paying his wife's consultancy fees, setting up his podcast studio and all this other rubbish. But I've said no more now. Why do you think he's selling? He wanted to evict me from here, my own home, but I soon put a stop to that. Do you know, I've learned to be quite tough when I want to be. This is my place, and I'm staying. Here, come." Sylvia stood up, and Catherine followed her back into the sitting room. "There. That's one of my designs." She pointed at the chair, a gray-blue fabric with a house like Vanes, with pointed gables, and spare, Scandinavian detailing around the house.

Catherine smiled, the hair on her neck starting to prickle, the feeling of it moving up to her scalp. "Sylvia. I have that in my bedroom. At home. The curtains. I picked it myself. I—it always reminded me...I—" She stopped, unable to say more, and shook her head. "You designed it."

Sylvia was nodding. "I did."

Catherine managed to say: "I love it. I look at it every day. When I was in bed, feeding my babies. It always made me feel— calm. Which is strange, I picked it because it reminded me of Vanes."

"Perhaps it's because, in some way, it reminded you of happy times. Or an idea of them. So you have two children. How wonderful. I am sure you're a terrific mother. After all, you're Simon's child, how could you not be? Look at the example he gave you."

With one small sentence Catherine felt something settle inside her, a warmth, a heaviness. Her shoulders sank, she felt as though she was breathing again, that she had come up for air.

"Yes," she said. "I've been thinking about that. It's odd to hear someone else say it. To hear *you* say it..."

They were silent, looking at each other, as the wind rustled outside in the trees. A truck rumbled slowly past the house.

"I'm sorry," Catherine said, eventually. "I'm sorry we ran off." Sylvia nodded. She didn't say anything, just sank into the worn armchair. Catherine sat down, opposite her. "I wanted to see you again. To say that I should have tried to get her to stay. To avoid what happened."

"What? The bees? Charles's death? Kitty vanishing?" Sylvia jabbed the air. "It couldn't be avoided, none of it. It was coming for years. I lost a daughter, my husband, his sister, that night. And there's nothing that could have been done about it."

"That's not true. It could have been different."

"No," Sylvia said, pursing up her mouth, tightly. The dark eyes that had once been so vague, so clouded were alive, gleaming with purpose. "I couldn't stop her going. That's my great failure. I tried, but I couldn't keep her safe. But I've stopped blaming myself. I was barely there by then, hadn't been there for years. You know what I mean." She gave her a searching look. "As for the others—I saw then that the only way she might one day come back was—to a safer house. So I locked the door."

"What?"

Catherine could see Sylvia then, the Outsider in her beautiful dress, holding the key, standing outside the chapel, buffeted by the wind, her face utterly blank.

"I locked them in. Do you see? I locked them in. I saw it was then or never. But I—I made a mistake."

Catherine leaned forward. She felt dizzy, slightly sick.

"You locked them *in*, that day? It was you?"

"Yes. Yes. But I got it wrong."

"Joss was in there, Sylvia."

Sylvia blew her bangs away from her forehead and poured more schnapps. She stared thoughtfully at the floor, cradling the glass between her fingers. "I thought he was Giles. So—well, that is something I still carry. The guilt of it. I didn't care about Giles. I wanted him to die. I wanted Kitty to see that I could protect her." Her voice grew smaller. "As for the other two, I didn't care by then. They didn't care about me. He certainly didn't."

Her eyes, staring into the middle distance, flashed fire.

"But there was so much chaos, and then I turned round, and—and—there was Giles. Standing there, laughing with one of the rivals. And I saw what I'd done. I opened the door. A minute later would have been too late for Joss: it was too late for the others." She turned toward Catherine, her childlike face solemn. "I wouldn't try to kill Joss, you know," she said, matter-of-factly. "But Charles was different—I think I woke up that day, you see. I woke up when the bees turned, when they started attacking. It was very strange. I realized I couldn't do it anymore. You rescued me really."

"No—" Catherine put the glass down. "Oh my God, Sylvia, I didn't rescue anyone. I—I left Kitty. I should have found her. I shouldn't have gone."

"Kitty was very strong-willed, little one." She reached across the flickering fire and patted Catherine's leg. "She wanted to get away. To have some control over her life. She used you. I used you, to give me the courage to do what I wanted that day."

She said it so matter-of-factly.

"Really?"

"Of course. Your father tried so hard to stop it. He saw what was coming, the disaster my marrying Charles would be. And I cut him out. I was groomed, that's what we'd say now, though it's all crap, really, I'm sure." Catherine shifted uncomfortably in her seat. "Still though…" She chewed her lip thoughtfully. "You know, your father came to see me, the month before he died. Did you know that?"

Catherine shook her head. "No. Where was I?"

"You were on a school field trip. Dorset, if memory serves. And Simon drove down here. He'd come on a mission. He wanted to make me see what Charles had done to me. How he'd found him having sex with me in the sitting room when he came back one weekend. Charles wouldn't ever go into my bedroom, he said it wasn't right. So he'd make me—on the sofa." She looked up, her expression utterly blank, and poured them both another drink. From outside came the sound of the wind, tearing restlessly through the tangled trees.

"I was an orphan, and I had money, you know, from my mother, and her possessions, and the sale of her house. Charles took it all. He took my youth, and my money, and he took me—my identity. That's the thing. He'd been hanging around so long, pestering me, and I really just wanted to be left alone. After Mummy and Daddy died and I was living in Wellington Square with your dad, he started telephoning, bringing me presents, waiting till the lodgers were all out and especially after Simon—your father moved away for the job—oh, then Charles was there all the time. I told myself it was nice, having someone to look out for me. For once. I was very angry with your father, for moving away.

"Charles…he'd take me for drinks and put his hand up my skirt or kiss me…He'd say he was only trying to be nice, and I was naughty for letting him do it."

"How old were you, Sylvia?" Catherine said, softly.

"I was fourteen. Maybe thirteen. Do you understand, now?"

Catherine could only nod. She closed her eyes, breathing in deeply.

"He told me I should be grateful, and I told myself I was…I hated it, I hated it when he did it to me. I just wanted someone to make it all go away, and he said he could…he was the problem, and he made himself the solution." She looked up, and her eyes were swimming with tears, and she blinked until they were gone, then she swallowed.

"And your father was cross about me spending time with Charles, and that was fatal. He wanted me to finish college, to be what I could be. He wanted me to live like a nun, and of course I was still furious with him—I was so angry, darling, I missed Mummy so much. So Charles got his way in the end. He got what he wanted. He always did, until the day he died. He really bloody did."

She hung her head, and there was silence, broken only by the sound of another large engine moving outside.

Daddy had come here, the month before he killed himself. He had seen for himself what Sylvia was living with, how she was trapped in this beautiful prison, cooking, cleaning, servicing Charles to stop him from moving on his own daughter. How the atmosphere was poisonous, the family dynamic all wrong, and he had taken the blame for it himself, when it wasn't his fault.

It wasn't his fault.

"And so after that, your father married Miss Inglis, I think on a whim. I think he thought he had to marry someone, and she was there, and they did get on, they liked jazz, and she adored him but she didn't hero-worship him—people tended to with your dad and it was fatal." Sylvia blew her bangs out again. "Gosh, I always forget she's your mother. Isn't it curious?"

Catherine shook her head. "Not really. She forgot she was my mother for most of my life, to be fair." She cleared her throat. "Sylvia, I didn't know. I didn't know any of it."

"I know, darling. I told Kitty, the day it all happened. She didn't take it very well. She—she had had her trouble with Giles. I handled it all wrong, you see...I live with that forever." Her voice was low, breaking at the end of words. "I let her down, Janey. So when I could, when I saw how I could take my revenge, for me, for her, I took it. But he's still free. His life is unaffected by what he did."

Catherine nodded. She said, gently: "I understand." What else could she say?

"That's enough," said Sylvia, suddenly. "Let's not talk about it."

"I went to your retrospective, you know." Catherine held her gaze. "The one at the Fashion Museum. It was wonderful. I was so—I was so proud of you."

"Why?" Sylvia said, quite sharply.

"Because I know how talented Daddy thought you were. And to see all your designs and drawings lined up, what you'd accomplished, despite everything, and that's just your work, not even the stuff you do under a different name. It's a complete body of work, Sylvia. It's amazing. I look at the catalog all the time."

Sylvia was staring out at the dark night. "I went up to see it, incognito, you know. I stayed with Merry in her peculiar flat. I was homesick for my own little hive, right here. You see, all I felt when I stood there and looked at them all lined up was...sadness. Sadness for me and what I might have been."

Catherine nodded. She didn't know what to say.

"Charles, he stripped all my *me*-ness back. All those years, being someone else. Feeling utterly alone." And Sylvia threw back the remains of the schnapps, swallowing hard.

The vehicles rumbling outside grew louder and louder, but neither of them moved. Eventually Catherine said carefully: "I am so sorry, Sylvia. I know Daddy loved you. He loved your mother and he loved you."

Sylvia put her head slightly on one side. "I know he did. I think that's what made me suddenly wake up. Seeing you, marching next to Kitty. The two of you, being set up for the same kind of...it's not failure, it's a sort of tidying away of women so they won't cause trouble." She laughed, slapping her hands to her cheeks. "Oh, I had such high hopes for Joss when he was younger, Janey—I'm sorry, Catherine. You know, he liked Bowie, and he wore velvet waistcoats, and smoked hash—I thought, this boy of mine's the rebel I wasn't allowed to be. But he just went the other way. I don't mind about respectability. I mind about *community*. This idea you're better than everyone, that you and your family have to come first. It's disgusting. It's not how we should live. It's not...British, despite what Charles and Ros thought."

"What *is* that noise?" Catherine said.

"That?" Sylvia looked out of the window, at the source of the commotion going on outside. "It'll get louder later. No, I've failed Joss, and I've failed Merry. Merry knew something was wrong about that day. I think she suspects it was me, but the police were utterly hopeless. I'd complain about them if I wasn't an interested party." She shook her head, outraged, seemingly unaware of the irony. "But mostly Merry's horrified by me. Like Joss. It's quite something, to know your own children are repulsed by you. Their mother who grows her own veg, doesn't buy any new clothes, and whom they have to keep asking for money for their weddings or building works or expensive holidays. They don't know what on earth to do with me." A wide grin split her heart-shaped face, and she took a deep breath. "It's rather funny."

"Yes," said Catherine, slowly understanding. "This is you, isn't it?"

"Darling it *is*." She cleared her throat. "I really do like this life. Have for thirty years or so. I can do my work, do my thing. I stay up till three if I want, I sleep in till noon if I want. No one to cook for, no one to organize. I don't have to sit and listen to ghastly people my own age complaining about immigrants or the social-ists or young people taking drugs. It's just me."

"Do you like it? Don't you get lonely?"

"I picked up men a couple of times, but I stopped after a while. It wasn't my scene. It's fine just being me. Great, actually. All those years when I couldn't. I wake up and wallow in it." She smiled again, blinking. "You can see why Merry and Joss are horrified, can't you? They think I should be polishing the candlesticks and the handbells and doing the flowers and helping Joss and gener-ally being the dowager Lady Hunter. Well, the bees didn't want to carry on with it and neither did I. They'd had enough. Balls to that, Janey. Bloody balls to it."

Catherine saw that Sylvia was one of those people who lived by themselves who, when you got them going, wouldn't stop talking. "I was in London last month with Extinction Rebellion," Sylvia went on, proudly. "I glued myself to some railings. The wrong rail-ings, actually. Some Russian oligarch on Great Portland Street, but he was rather nice about it. His housekeeper gave me a cookie." She gave a wide, mirthless grin, and for a split second Catherine saw the Kitty who kept appearing to her: the wide teeth, the manic eyes, and she shivered. She closed her eyes. *She locked them in*, she told herself.

"Where did you stay? In London?"

"Oh, coach there, coach back. I wouldn't bother Merry. Imagine turning up on her doorstep after two days sleeping rough and covered in glue!" She began to chuckle. "You haven't seen her, have you? You have. Oh, well, you'll know what I mean."

Catherine raised her eyebrows. "I do. Better than you can imagine." She couldn't help feeling sorry for Merry. "It was nice to see her though...I'm sorry, Sylvia, that noise isn't right. What can it be?" Catherine stood up and went to the window. The white light, flashing again. As if it was trained on her. A huge vehicle was lumbering down the driveway, the digger mechanism rocking violently as the flashing lights threw beams into the woods. She could hear shouting.

"Best ignore it," said Sylvia. "It's some nonsense of Joss's, and you're well out of it. He thinks I don't know, but I'm not stupid. Now, Catherine. Come and sit down again." She beckoned. "Why don't I get you some food, something to eat? I've got a curry in the fridge. I've had mine already."

Catherine shook her head. "I'm not hungry. Thank you, though."

"Are you sure?" Suddenly she was the old Sylvia. "How did you get down here? Where will you go now?"

Catherine put her hands out. "I'm not really sure. I—I don't know."

Sylvia didn't say anything for a moment, just stared at Catherine, chewing her lip. Then she said: "You have to go back to your children, darling. After some rest. And some food. You do know that, don't you?"

Catherine nodded.

"You will, won't you?"

"I—want to." Her throat was closing up. "I promised I would. But I keep thinking I can't."

"You can't?"

"That I shouldn't." Catherine shook her head. There was no point trying to explain a truth as fundamental as this, and she couldn't rid herself of it. *You don't understand. They really are better off without me. I'm so scared. I think it's true.*

"Is your husband nice?" Catherine smiled. "I know it's a silly-sounding question. But lots of people aren't. Is he nice?"

"He's very nice. I miss him."

"That's lovely." The older woman smiled. "Ah, I'm happy to hear that. You never belonged here, you know. You can go back, any time, darling." Sylvia's lined, beautiful face fixed her with an intense stare. "Your father was nice. He was nice to everyone. And he loved you so much. None of this is your fault, Janey."

"That's absolutely not true. Quite a lot of this is my fault. I've lied, I've run away, I've done some despicable things."

Sylvia shrugged, in her quick birdlike way. "I don't think they're so bad. But don't you think you owe it to yourself—to *him*—to be happy? To have a shot at it, anyway? You're allowed to."

It hurt to speak. "I shouldn't have left Kitty. Who knows what happened to her? She—she should have had a wonderful life."

Sylvia smiled. "How do we know she didn't?"

"Didn't what?"

"Have a wonderful life? How do you know what happened after you left?"

Catherine gaped at her. "Have you seen her?" Outside, she could hear men calling, and an engine, louder than ever now. She moved closer, shivering in the small, crowded room. Sylvia said nothing. "Sylvia? What do you mean?"

"I see her all the time. All the time." Sylvia shrugged. "And I think she's happy."

"You—see her? What do you mean? Is she—*alive*?"

Sylvia touched her hands to her cheeks. Very quietly, she said: "To me she is. Don't tell anyone."

Catherine narrowed her eyes. "Sylvia, really? What happened, then?"

Sylvia shook her head. "You don't need to worry about her. Or me. She's fine. And she's exactly the same."

Catherine said: "I don't know…"

"You're a lawyer, dear girl. Filleting the evidence, trying to get to the truth, it becomes an obsession. Sometimes there's no one truth. I'm saying that to me Kitty is still here. And that she brings me great comfort. And that if you love someone, that never goes away. I have had my darkest moments in this place." She waved her arms around. "But if you question why you were brought into this world, just consider this: we all have a purpose in life. Perhaps your purpose was to bring happiness to your father. You made him very, very happy. He gave you so much. You were so beloved and you are so like him, my darling. The tragedy was in the end he couldn't shut out what he'd seen, how he thought he'd failed. I won't talk to you about how you have an obligation as a mother or any of that. They break us that way, all of us, when they hand us the baby, and they don't ever do it to the men. But, Janey—Catherine, I'm sorry. Don't you owe it to Simon, to yourself, to be happy? And don't you owe it to Kitty, too? Look at what she gave you. She gave you what you wanted. She forced you to take that degree, she got you away from your mother, she pushed you onward, into a different life. And it's the life you were supposed to have, it seems to me. Just with a slightly different name. I think it's easier to hide away than face up to it, sometimes."

Air seemed to rush into Catherine's chest. "Yes. It's just I wouldn't know where to start."

"With some therapy, I'd imagine," said Sylvia gravely, and she smiled. "It's all there. You have to make the decision to do it. To walk down that path. That boy you were defending in that picture, what was he called?"

"Grant. Grant Doyle." She chewed at her nail. "I utterly failed him. He reminded me too much of other people. I failed as a lawyer. I think that was part of what led…" She spread her arms wide, encompassing the rucksack, the bare feet, the grubby clothing. "…to this."

"Perhaps he won't ever be able to live with what he's done. But he killed a man, you didn't. You were his lawyer, not his counselor, not his mother. You had a great deal to bear over the years, Catherine. I did too. I took my revenge. I can live with it. What you did is OK."

"It isn't OK."

"No. We will have our own ceremony, here and now," said Sylvia. She stood up, walked over to Catherine and tapped her on the shoulder. "I release you from it. You're free." Catherine nodded, looking up at her with a faint smile. "Listen," said Sylvia, gripping her hands. "This is really important. You can only do as much as you can. And sometimes it won't be enough. Sometimes it will be."

They stared at each other, fingers entwined. Then Sylvia turned, bent down. With a flourish, she pointed to the spot beside her armchair, next to the fire, and moved a flowing scarf and tall pile of books out of the way. "It hasn't worn well, so I cover it up. They didn't coat it properly. It's an old wallpaper I did, years ago. They printed up a sample roll, but they decided not to go with it in the end. Said it wasn't very cozy. What do you think of that?"

She jabbed one square finger against two slices of wallpaper, perfectly papered onto the wall. "There."

Catherine found herself looking at a densely interwoven design: roundels made up of brambles, bracken and late summer grasses, dotted with handbells, stars and bees. In the middle of each were two short-haired girls in silhouette, holding hands.

"It's called *The Beloved Girls*."

"Of course," said Catherine, her eye picking out the silhouetted details—the seven stars of the Plow, the hives, the handbells— among the brambles. "It's just right, Sylvia. It's us."

Sylvia simply nodded.

"I thought she might still be alive," Catherine said, her eyes ranging over the pattern, over and over again. She said it very quietly. "I think I see her too."

"Well, perhaps you do," said Sylvia.

She gestured to the corner of the room. There, in a small, wicker chair, which Catherine recognized from Vanes, sat a worn brown teddy bear. He had the pendant tied round his neck. His head was frayed and battered, one leg was half missing.

Catherine's eyes felt dry, she didn't blink. "Wellington Bear. That's Wellington Bear. How did he end up with you? He was with her...she took him..."

"I found him here one day. And that's all I know about it."

"Do you think—" Catherine put her hand on the mantelpiece, to steady herself. "My God, Sylvia. Did she bring him back to you? She must be—"

"I found him here. On the doorstep. And I don't want to know any more."

Catherine looked at her. She looked at the bear, who had seen more than Sylvia. She opened her mouth, and then realized Sylvia had said all she was going to.

In the small, warmly lit room there was a brief silence, and then Catherine stood up.

"I'm going to go."

"Do you want to stay the night?"

"No," Catherine said. "Thank you. But I'll—I'll just walk, if that's OK."

Sylvia didn't even try to persuade her. "My darling girl. Come back and see me, won't you? Joss won't be here in a few weeks. I'll be all alone, and happy as anything. I'd love to see you again—perhaps even your children." Her face was empty, hollow, suddenly. "I would like that."

Catherine stared at her. The idea that they'd come and visit, when Vanes was sold: stay in the village, or get an Airbnb. Introduce the children to Sylvia, eat fish and chips on the harbor wall as she had done...No. Suddenly the old feeling of terror washed over her. This seeming normality, the neat tidying up of what was wrong—there it was again. She did not know if she wanted it. She did not know if she'd ever be able to see Sylvia again, after this. But all she said was: "Yes. Yes, of course."

Impulsively, she crossed the room and touched the bear's soft head, feeling the worn and matted fur against her fingers. "Take care of her, will you," she told him, under her breath.

When she left, the noise from the engines was louder than ever, and a rusting creak, like an old swing but louder, had started up too. Catherine had no idea of the time now. She thought it must be very late. Above, the stars covered her, growing in number as she looked up, more pinpricks of light that were other suns, worlds, galaxies, the view deepening the longer she craned her neck, scanning the skies above her.

She glanced back at the little bell-shaped house, the light still on. "I'm working on a new version of the Girls at the moment. I'll carry on for a bit. I'm not tired," Sylvia had said at the door. "I want to make sure it's perfect, before I send it off next week."

Pebbles cut into her bare feet, as Catherine turned off the Vanes driveway and into the wood.

She took the footpath that cut across the edge of the Vanes woodland to come out onto the main path, only twenty meters from the chapel, and as she emerged she saw what the noise had been about. They were demolishing the chapel.

There were two trucks, and a digger. It had bright, diamond-sparkling headlamps, four in a row, fixed to the top of the digger, and it was hacking away at what remained of the ancient bricks. As she watched in horror, she saw to the east the faintest wavy line of light on the horizon, mottled from black to aqua-gray then silver, flooding the sky, turning it slowly into day. A man stood in front of the chapel, with a headlamp on. She realized why Joss had been so jumpy when she'd appeared. He'd thought she was a prying local, or more likely Merry had warned him she might turn up: Janey Lestrange, come back to ruin things one last time.

She should have cared—the lawyer in her should have been outraged, filming it on her phone, looking up precedent, making notes. She could hear the cracking of rock, as bit by bit the ancient place was destroyed. With a flash she remembered the crunch underfoot, the eerie stillness of the place, and remembered that the bees had long gone.

She sat on the edge of the pathway, leaning against the boundary wall of the old house, and watched as, bit by bit, the Reverend Diver's chapel was demolished. At some point, she must have fallen asleep for a while.

High up on the moor, daylight was fanning out across the sky, as Catherine walked down into the village. All around her trees, bushes, and hedgerows rang out with birdsong. Her feet were sore now, cut in places, smarting in others, but she didn't really notice. Something had vanished inside her. She felt different. Not lighter, just different. Perhaps it was seeing Sylvia. Perhaps it was speaking to Davide again. Perhaps it was that the chapel lay in ruins.

Her street at home was quiet in the mornings, before the drills started, and the cars, and the sound of London waking up. She had always loved this time best of all, a pause after dawn before the day began in earnest. She had often got up and made herself tea, slipping into her little study overlooking the neat grid of gardens. She would work there for a couple of hours before the children woke, getting ahead of herself, making lists, replying to emails, reading cases, calling up documents. Order. All she'd ever wanted was to work hard and do well, to provide for her family, to enjoy the time she had with them, with her husband. She kept thinking of Sylvia, of how she had submitted to the work of being a wife and mother, subsumed herself to survive. But Catherine had not. She had enjoyed it. She found small children interesting. She enjoyed drawing butterflies and playing games and tracing letters and reading books. She had loved feeding them, and cleaning up after them, marveling at their mess. Most of all, she had reveled in their utter absorption in the present, their inability to see the past, to judge or make assumptions.

She had no desire to leave a legacy, a trail of light behind her like a comet. She wasn't an interesting person, not like Kitty had been. She had been happiest at home with Davide and the children, and all those years she hadn't really ever seen it. And she saw it now: the gift her father had given her, the strength of his love, and that she carried it inside her, and had transmitted it to her children.

There, in the middle of the lane, facing east, Catherine spread her arms wide and encircled herself, squeezing herself tightly, then she rubbed her eyes vigorously, waking herself up.

"She rescued herself, Daddy," she said out loud, and then laughed. She shook her head, and carried on, toward the village.

Chapter Thirty-Five

By the time she reached Larcombe, the sun was up. There was the old harbor, where they'd gone to eat fish and chips and throw stones into the sea, and there was the Good Leper pub, scene of Giles's birthday. It was so small, a low building; in her memory it was vast, sprawling, crammed with tall, thick-haired boys who smelled of cigarettes and fermented beer. *Does Giles's son go there and drink at the holidays?* she wondered. Had anything changed?

She caught sight of her reflection in the scratched, cracked plastic of the bus shelter as she hovered at the edge of the village, not sure what to do next. She stopped and stared at herself, fascinated. Her hair was a mess, sticking out in a tangled halo around her head, and she was covered in mud, presumably from walking and falling at various points. Catherine Christophe was usually immaculate, checking her phone on the walk into chambers each morning to make sure there was no stray nose hair, no spot, twig in the hair, piece of spinach in the teeth. Now she had no shoes, and hadn't cleaned her teeth for two, possibly three days. She had stopped trying to be in control: she honestly didn't know what she would do next.

Once again the enormity of what she had now unleashed, the edge of the reality of it, swept over her. She was not well. Something had broken. And she was so tired. She leaned against the thought of going back to that small, quiet study, back to how it was before she'd tried to destroy it, back to concentrating her mind on something before the first joyous sounds of her children dragging themselves out of bed and yelling for her, even if it was to moan about the wrong cereal. She pictured it. It was warm, and safe. It was her home.

And the sound of Davide, as he began the long process of making the coffee. His hair, grizzled at the temples, the light caramel of his skin, the tips of his sensitive, long fingers, his quiet voice. His calmness. He was always calm. He loved her, but would he still when he knew the depth of her deception, the years that had been a lie?

My birthday isn't in August. It's in September. I'm eleven months older than you think. Every year I buy myself a present for my real birthday.

I took a place from someone at university.

I heard someone else tell me she caused the deaths of two people. And I was glad for her.

I left someone to die.

No one was around, just the clinking of boat masts and the call of one or two gulls. Strutting oystercatchers pecked around on the brown mud.

A van pulled up at the back of the pub; Catherine watched it, trying to regain her breath, trying to steady herself. A man got out and started unloading laundry.

Janey Lestrange, it's time to go home, she said to herself.

She watched as the man heaved a large white fabric basket of towels and sheets out onto the floor, opening the side door of the shuttered, dark pub with his own key. He slung the laundry in there, and then, going back to the van, he pulled out another basket. A gull swooped, he stumbled, and one or two plastic packages fell out.

After he'd locked up and driven away, Catherine walked toward the Good Leper, heart still thumping. She picked up one of the fallen plastic-wrapped items off the road. It was a pair of toweling slippers, the ones you get in hotels and B&Bs. "The Good Leper" was embroidered on it in gold thread, which made her smile. She tore open the packaging and put them on, and then went over to the harbor wall, where she sat until the hotel next door, a boutique affair with black-and-white prints on the walls and striped carpets, opened its doors. She went inside, and ate a hearty breakfast: porridge, granola, toast, coffee. She ordered a paper and worked steadily through the news. She was not mentioned. When the waiter glanced down at her feet, she smiled.

"My sneakers washed into the sea yesterday. Rather embarrassing."

Never over-explain; she knew this, from years of cross-examining or defending liars. The ones you never believed were the ones who tried to oversell their story.

So she was keeping going, keeping momentum, just like Daddy had always said she must. She paid cash, and went out onto the street. It was eight thirty. The post office was just opening up. Catherine went in, bought a pair of canvas beach shoes, explaining the circumstances of her shoelessness again to the lady behind the counter, who was kindly sympathetic. The door swung open.

"Morning, Kel."

"Morning, Sheila."

"You all right?"

"Not too bad. You heard what he's done, did you? In the night? They've demolished the chapel. Not a brick standing. John was one of them hired to do it. Says they were paid in cash, sworn to secrecy."

"Oh, that one." Sheila leaned on the counter. "Thinks he's bloody Mr. Grand Designs or something. Big ideas. It's nothing to him. What does Sam say about it?"

"My dad? He said the buyers wanted it gone before they'd exchange contracts. *Accidental demolition*. That's what they call it. Threatened to pull out otherwise. It's all about money with him, like with his dad, that's what Dad says. As if they're going to be able to keep something like that secret."

Catherine went and stood by the bus shelter and waited for the bus. Country busses didn't change. She had no idea when it would come. But it would come, at some point. And then it would take her to a town, and then to another town, then to a train station, then on a train, then perhaps even a cab from the station, and later today she could, if she wanted, be standing on her own front doorstep.

She closed her eyes, and saw her children, at Davide's birthday in March, in the pub just up the road from them, illuminated by candlelight, laughing, Tom's hand on his mother's arm, Carys, so like Simon Lestrange, so like him, hugging her father, their young faces smooth, their eyes huge in the dark. She pushed the image away, right away, and kept her eyes closed.

Suddenly, she heard a voice, talking to her. So clear it was as if it was behind her.

I will always be by your side; you don't even need to look for me. I'll always be there. And remember: "All shall be well, and all shall be well, and all manner of things shall be well."

Catherine opened her eyes.

Rising above the village was a winding lane, and as she looked up she saw a figure, coming in off the fields behind the houses and onto the lane. She was walking toward her. And Catherine knew who it was, without having to see her any closer.

She did not have to see the flushed pink cheeks.

She did not have to see the long, golden hair, framing the heart-shaped face.

She did not have to see the calm, swaying stride to know.

It was her. Catherine steadied herself against the bus stop. Salt wind stung her eyes, her cheeks.

The other woman smiled at her, blinking into the sun. Catherine looked down, at her own long shadow, wondering where the shadow of the other woman was. Where was it?

"Hello, Catherine."

"H-hello."

"So you went back."

"So did you."

"I wanted to be here when they pulled it down."

Catherine opened her mouth, then closed it. A middle-aged woman in a beige raincoat hurried past. She stared at Catherine, curiously. This gave Catherine more conviction.

"You're dead," she said, firmly. "You disappeared up by the Vane Stones. You died. Animals, whoever it was, they took your body. The beast of Exmoor, maybe, or the ghost of the Reverend Diver." She laughed wildly. "That's why they never found you."

"Ah," the woman opposite her said. She cracked her knuckles, slowly. "That's what happened, is it?"

"You knew you were dying. That's what I've realized. You left me to…I—I—I…" Catherine watched. The face, still pale, still solemn. Tendrils of Kitty's long hair fluttered as she breathed out. "I don't know."

"You don't *know*?"

And suddenly Catherine saw she knew the answer. "No. I don't know. But it doesn't matter. You were there. You told me to take it. You tricked me."

The other woman laughed. Her voice was soft, shimmering like a breeze, like wind chimes. "That's not true. Tell the truth. You lied. You didn't kill anyone, but you lied. You left me to die. You abandoned me, and I loved you so much. From the day we first met, when we were girls. I thought you'd be the one to save me."

Catherine screwed up her face, her eyes. "I had no other choice."

"You made me vanish." Kitty put her head on one side, looking at Catherine with those huge, curious bloodshot eyes. Catherine noticed new things about her, bargaining frantically to convince herself this meant she was real. She had on a bright yellow waterproof with a big hood, lined in striped white and blue fabric. Her boots were black, and old, and covered in fresh mud. These were real things—weren't they? Her fingers were pressed against the brown paper and one nail had a torn cuticle—it was red, and swollen, raw, like her own nails had been that summer.

Her chewed and sore fingernails—Kitty's shining hair, like a golden mane—Joss's guitar—Merry's chirpy gamboling across the fields—the smell of mushrooms frying for breakfast, and ratatouille—Wendy James's pale, sheer pink lipstick—the portrait of the Reverend Diver, gleaming in the dark paneled hallway— Sylvia, crushing lavender between her fingers, all the time—the *Neighbours* theme tune—the acid brightness of the day-glo clothes—the salt air, it came back to this fresh, strange air that she hadn't smelled since—suddenly, she was back there, as surely as if she had torn a hole in the fabric of the present and simply stepped through it, back thirty years. She could feel burned skin on her bony shoulders, the prickly-soft moss on the flagstones, the rush of the sea, the roar of the bees.

She looked up, and said clearly: "It wasn't my fault. It wasn't yours. I love you, you loved me. We wanted to save each other. I wish you well. I miss you. This isn't you." And Catherine took a step forward. "Go home, Kitty."

"I am home," said Kitty, but she seemed to back away.

"I want to go home now," said Catherine, in a small voice. She could feel Kitty's laugh, and felt the faintest flicker of hot air on her cheek. "Please."

Kitty folded her arms. "I'm here because of you. Come with me again, Janey. Come with me again."

Catherine's tired fingers fiddled with her rucksack straps, fumbling to do her checks again. The bus was trundling down the main coast road; she could see it now.

She didn't have to go home. She was good at this, she knew. She could get on the bus or she could carry on walking, up into the woods, through the combe, over onto the moor, trying to escape this, the voices, everything. She could just keep on walking, and never go back. What had Sylvia said? *You never belonged here.*

The doors opened, and she stared up at the bus driver.

"Where to, then?" he said. Catherine looked round but she couldn't see her.

"Kitty?" she said, and she blinked, and saw her again.

The bus driver was more patient than he would have been in London. "Hello, miss? Are you getting on?"

Catherine put her hand out toward her. She knew if she touched Kitty it would be over, because it would be real.

She raised her hand, slowly. Kitty raised hers. Their hands met.

Or so she thought. But then Catherine blinked and when she opened her eyes Kitty had vanished.

The bus driver shook his head. The doors closed. The fumes of the bus, distorting the early morning air, shimmered in the near distance.

Catherine stood back, looking around, out at the shingle of the beach. Carefully, unused to her new shoes, which caused her to stumble on the hard flat stones, she walked slowly out to shore. The closer she came to the sea, the wind caressed her face. Every few seconds she would stop, and look, but there was no sign of her. None at all.

And Catherine knew she was gone.

A trestle table and bench stood on the shore, resting at a slant amid the stones. Catherine sat down. She added it up, calculating that she hadn't slept more than eight hours in four days. She was still for a moment, and then she looked over toward the seafront, where someone had slammed a car door and was walking toward her.

She froze, eyes widening. Then she stood and began to move, walking at first, and then, when she got to the road, running. In case the car drove away. In case she missed him. In case this seam of unreality that had been ripped should open any further, could not be sewn back together.

She called, as loudly as she could: "Is that you?"

But her voice was too soft, her throat closed up.

"Is that you?"

And then, across the wind, she heard him.

"Where have you brought me to now, Catrine?" he was calling, across the empty parking lot, and she was laughing—it was not romantic, she was dirty, exhausted, in a parking lot, but she could not stop crying. Her body arched with the release of it, her face stretched, using muscles she had not used for days, weeks, months. She threw the backpack off her shoulders, kicking it out of her way.

When he reached her, he caught her in his arms. "You are a difficult person, Catrine," he said. "I have always said so." His face was creased, the pain of what she had done written all over it. He kissed her, and kept kissing her. "You smell of saltwater, my darling. I have missed you. But let me say again: you are very difficult."

"You have no idea," Catherine said. "I'm so sorry." And she buried her face in his chest. "I'm so sorry," she kept saying, over and over.

"But I am here now."

"How did you know? To come here?"

"Well, didn't you always say it was Larcombe? And that it was tiny? Why would I not come, when I knew you were here?" Davide said. He pronounced it Lar-cohm-buh. She stroked his face, his hair, the wonder of him. He was real. He was here. "Please, do not run off again. We can change—everything. We can move. You can stop working. Or not! Everything." She could see the shadows under his eyes. *I did this*, she told herself. *I have done this to him, to my children. I must mend it.*

"I didn't know what else to do. That is the truth of it."

"*Chérie*, you need to talk to someone." She nodded, mutely. "Someone who can help you. I cannot do it, I think. I always hoped that, one day, you would come to me and say it to me. Whatever it is. Whatever terrible thing you did."

"It wasn't so terrible, I don't think. Not anymore."

"What is the secret?"

She faltered. "Well, it's a long story. I'll tell you on the drive back."

"Come to my hotel, madam. I have a shower, and my breakfast is waiting. And afterward I can drive you back home. If you'd care to go."

He was here. It really was him. And she had chosen that life. She had chosen him. She had done the right things. She had done well.

Something fell past her shoulder onto her feet, and she looked down, smiling, hands locked around the firm, solid muscles of his arm.

It was a dead honeybee, golden body slightly curled, the light of the morning shining on its tiny folded wings. It lay at Catherine's feet. She braced herself, clutching Davide's hand, and looked around. But there was no one else. No one at all.

Catherine picked up the rucksack. She handed it to Davide. "I've been carrying this for too long. Can you take it?" she said.

"Of course." He slung it over his shoulder. "Now let's go. I am very hungry."

"Goodbye," she said, calling behind her as they walked away. "Goodbye, my friend."

But even as she spoke, she knew there would be no answer.

Acknowledgments

For help with research, thanks to Richard Danbury and Tamara Oppenheimer for legal information, to Roland Philipps and Seema Nahome-Burgess for bee chats, and to Andy Lavender for help with Oxbridge admissions. Thanks are also due to Fran Beauman, Sophie Linton, Rob Linton and Jo Langley. Thank you to Kirstie Smith for our weekly conversations about motherhood and life. I miss you and the wigs. I'm very grateful to Carola Hoyos for setting up the Writers' Zoom mid-lockdown. It saved my sanity and saved this book.

Thanks to all the team at Headline Publishing, especially Fergus "spoiled all other proofs for me" Edmondson, the one and only Becky Bader, Caitlin Raynor, Emily Patience, Joe Yule, Frances Doyle and everyone who worked on the book. I'm very lucky. Special thanks to Louise Swannell: I feel honored to have you on my side, Lou; to Rebecca F. Folland, doyenne of the rights community, Yeti Lambregts for her stunning cover, Eleanor Dryden for her gentle soul and brilliant blurb, Imogen Taylor for her immensely helpful edits and the cheering line notes on those edits, and the incredible Rosanna Hildyard, who I wish was in charge of everything. Most of all thanks to Mari Evans, whose grace, subtlety and wisdom infuse everything she does and who holds me to the highest of standards.

At Curtis Brown, huge thanks to Jonathan Lloyd for the conversation and everything else, plus Lucy Morris, Jodi Fabbri, Sophia MacAskill and especially Hannah Beer, and to Sarah Harvey for pitching my own book better than I ever could.

Thank you to everyone at Grand Central Publishing, most especially Beth de Guzman and Kirsiah McNamara. I am thrilled to be working with you.

I would just like to take the opportunity here to thank all NHS workers, everyone working in a care home, all supermarket and other front line workers, every single teacher on the planet (as I am now in awe of you more than ever), and everyone who, in the face of daunting odds, tried their best last year.

Finally thanks to Sam O'Reilly and Jake O'Reilly, to my mum, Linda Evans, for setting up the St. Mary's Cottage Homeschooling School for Wayward Girls, and most of all to Chris, Cora and Martha for making the past year full of joy when it could have been much bleaker than it was. As Madonna says, somehow I made it through.

I found the following books invaluable while writing *The Beloved Girls*:

Songs & Ballads of the West: A Collection Made from the Mouths of the People—Rev. S Baring-Gould & Rev. H. Fleetwood-Sheppard (Methuen, 1895)

The Laura Ashley Book of Home Decorating—Elizabeth Dickson & Margaret Colvin (Octopus, 1982)

A Year on Exmoor—Adam Burton (Frances Lincoln, 2010)

The Collins Beekeeper's Bible: Bees, Honey, Recipes & Other Home Uses—(William Collins, 2010)

A Beautiful Mind—Sylvia Nasar (Faber & Faber, 1998)

Naples '44: An Intelligence Officer in the Italian Labyrinth—Norman Lewis (Collins, 1978)

Stiff Upper Lip: Secrets, Crimes and the Schooling of a Ruling Class—Alex Renton (Weidenfeld & Nicholson, 2017)

The Hive: The Story of the Honeybee and Us—Bee Wilson (John Murray, 2004)

Reading Group Guide

Discussion Questions

1. Charles said "two...beloved girls" in the prologue, echoing the title. What is the significance or meaning of being "the beloved girls" in the story?

2. How does Catherine's job as a criminal justice attorney impact her character or personality?

3. Catherine is burdened by the ghosts of her past. Have you felt troubled by something that you find it hard to share with others?

4. Catherine's family wanted her to be "decorative, beautiful, compliant." How does this perspective impact women today?

5. Can you share one ritual or tradition you observe? Do you find this ritual or tradition reassuring or constricting?

6. What is Davide's role in Catherine's life? At the end, she shares her story with him. Had she chosen not to, what do you think would be different?

7. Can we free ourselves from the past, or is that impossible?

8. Kitty and Jane were able to form a quick but significant bond. What is the basis of their bond?

9. Catherine felt slightly out of place the first time she went to Vanes. Recall a time when you had to make a transition or experience a new place. How did you feel?

10. "Half for us and half for them, else the Devil take us all." The bees are central to the story, but what symbolic role do they play within the world of Vanes and the novel itself? What do they represent?

11. [Spoiler Alert] When did you start to figure out Catherine's real identity? How?

Questions for the Author

Q. What inspired this novel? Why bees?

A. I always start with an image that comes to me at some point when I'm writing the previous novel. I don't look for it. I saw, suddenly one day, this girl. She's lost her hair, she is about eighteen, and she has arrived at this house. It's a very remote, very beautiful, golden stone. A family is waiting for her on the terrace. They are glamorous, secretive, seemingly perfect. They greet her. She is an outsider, she desperately wants to be one of them. That was all I knew. I could feel this sense of something ominous about them, and why she'd come. I wanted to work it out.

As for the bees, I've always been fascinated by them. The way they work and exist as a colony, not an individual. How delicious honey is, how painful a sting is, all of that. And the noise, when you hear a swarm of bees, is unbelievable. Incredibly scary. I wanted the novel to be a bit scary!

Q. What are the challenges of writing alternating time-lines? Did you come up with the present-day story first or the events from the past?

A. I love writing in the past. I love building a world that the reader can step into and I really like pulling the rug out, starting again. I can't write novels where you only know about the characters in the present, not about their parents, their upbringing, their past... I wish I could! I want to go back and mine it all.

Q. Given that superstitious rituals were more common in the distant past, why did you set that fateful summer in the recent past?

A. I think it's important to show how things don't change as much as you think. It always annoys me when I'm watching a film set in 1961 and everything in the heroine's house is from exactly 1961. Look around the room you're in right now. What furniture is from this year? None mostly! It's the same with traditions and change. My mum grew up in the sixties and what I always find interesting is how people assume everyone was wild and swinging and everything was equal and traditions were shattered the moment the clock struck midnight on January 1, 1960. No way. It was a tiny group of people on the King's Road in Chelsea. The rest continued the same for at least the rest of that decade.

Q. What are some takeaways you hope your readers can gain upon finishing your novel?

A. That's a lovely question. I suppose the main thing is everyone has secrets and you don't know what their history is, so go gently with people. Most people are just trying their best even if you disagree profoundly with their political views or lifestyle choices. But mostly, I honestly just want people to lose themselves in the world of the book. What means the most to me about *The Beloved Girls* being published is when people keep saying they couldn't put it down and that they read it over a couple of days or stayed up late to finish it. I'm always looking for books like that and that is fantastic to hear.

Beloved Rituals

Harriet Evans

I was asked by my lovely publishers to write about rituals that have meaning for me and at first, I was at a slight loss. How could I connect the rituals I and my family have built up over the years—some big, some tiny jokey moments—with the Gothic, mysterious ritual at the heart of *The Beloved Girls?* The two aren't linked at all and my family is nothing like the Hunters (I hope no one's is...). This is a family that, for the last two centuries, has constructed an extraordinary series of events around the collection of honey at the end of the summer. They put on special clothes, they sing an ancient folk song they've adapted for their own purposes, they ring bells, and they process in a line away from the house toward the crumbling chapel on the edge of their land, where the bees have built combs and lived there, collecting nectar and making honey, for hundreds of years. They smash open the combs, take the honey, singing the song, and in this way in some way they affirm themselves again every year.

We put up a Christmas tree. It's not quite the same thing.

As a child I thought rituals were something other people imposed on you. I was head chorister of our local church choir (yes, I was single for most of my teenage years; why do you ask?), and I loved ritual and the mystical sense of performing the same actions and imbuing them with meaning. I loved decorating the cross at Easter with blue and yellow spring flowers. I loved the scent of pine we tied onto the choir stalls at Christmas. I thought those were the only rituals.

I found myself thinking about it some more, though, and I fell to considering what makes a family. How we give ourselves labels to try and fit in, feel at home. When I was in my twenties, living in London, having a fine old time, I had something called the Urban Family. We were there for each other. We got drunk together and helped each other get rid of mice, exes, mold. We had our own

Christmas dinner before going back to our biological families for Christmas. We had dance routines and we had badges printed (do you guys say pins? I think you do!). We were a family, anyway, and I owe them a lot, but we gained so much from the rituals of our friendship. The sense of belonging.

I've always been interested in large families, as my mother was one of four and they all married only children, which I find noteworthy, and my partner is one of four too. With the Hunters in *The Beloved Girls*, I wanted to write about this idea of how some people become entrenched in the idea of family, how preserving the status quo turns into an obsession. The Hunter family is so rigid. Charles Hunter has absolutely no identity beyond wanting to be the head of this family. When we see him in the past and realize who he is, he exists only as a kind of caricature, a paper-thin sleazy British toff whom it's obvious you can't trust. When we see him at home at Vanes, he absolutely revels in his power and position as head of this family. For him, the ritual is everything. I find this with lots of people, that they need to let you know they're mothers, or fathers, or brides-to-be, as if that is the most important thing about them, not what music they like or what kind of person they are.

And there's class, too. As I was writing about them, looking down on Janey, their poor abandoned young visitor who arrives one summer at their beautiful remote manor house, I came to realize that the Hunters are symbolic of a kind of rotten core at the heart of the British class system. This system sends children off to boarding school at the age of five, thinks conquering other countries and colonizing them is a good idea, brings up girls to display them to the queen and effectively auction them off to the right family, marrying only within the same class, and adheres to the same customs for years and years. Those are all rituals of the upper class.

When I met my other half, one of the first things I learned about him was that he was half American and, I may say, my lovely American readers, that that is one of the reasons I fell for him. I love the States, and always have, having made many trips there for work when I was still an editor working in publishing, and having lots of American friends. His dear mother, whose family can trace their ancestry back to the *Mayflower* and the building of the railroads, made sure when she married his father and moved to England, that her customs and traditions came with her. So all her children and grandchildren, including my daughters, celebrate Thanksgiving on the Saturday after the actual day, in their barn, with fifty or so other family members and neighbors. We dress the trestle tables with ancient dried ears of corn and squash, we get out the best silver, we spend hours chopping vegetables and peeling potatoes and making chess pie and ice cream. A fire is lit in the grate, and the windows steam up, and people who often see each other only once a year gather together in this picturesque corner of England and say what they are thankful for. There are bookshelves running along the back of the barn, filled with ancient paperbacks from the fifties, sixties, and seventies, and there you'll find the mixing of two countries—copies of Laura Ingalls Wilder, *New Yorker* short stories, and Peanuts cartoons jumbled together with Agatha Christies, Regency romances, and children's classics.

Our children are five and nine, and we are about to move yet again for I hope the final time, when we will establish our own home, the one we stay in. And that's so important to me, giving my girls a proper home. What I've learned, though, is that the most important rituals aren't the ones the Hunters are obsessed with, special though Thanksgiving and other occasions are to me. It's the little rituals. When we travel up to Scotland on holiday every year, as we cross into the place we stay, there's a cattle grid, and you're not truly on holiday until everyone in the car has made a rumbling sound in their throat as we rumble over the cattle grid.

When the UK had its third lockdown, in January 2021, and my children were off school again, every Saturday evening we would have a disco, then order fish and chips and eat them while watching *The Masked Singer.* And I saw how important smaller rituals are, to shape the days when time has no meaning and life seems scary. Each Sunday we have pancakes. My sister and I collect anything with flamingos on it and send them to each other, without comment. When it's January I make marmalade. My two best friends and I have to message each other every time we see a picture of a particular road sign that we think is hilariously rude but no one else would find funny. These are all rituals. They are perhaps more valuable than the ones we all set great store by. The rituals of taking care of yourself, of stopping to laugh at something, dancing to a song, being present for just a moment, they are the ones that matter. And the more I thought about it, the more I saw how necessary they are, how much we all need them, more than the ones we've been told are important.

About the Author

Harriet Evans has sold over a million copies of her books. She is the author of twelve bestselling novels, most recently the *Sunday Times* Top Ten bestseller *The Garden of Lost and Found*, which won *Good Housekeeping*'s Book of the Year, and *The Wildflowers*, which was a Richard & Judy Book Club selection. She used to work in publishing and now writes full-time, when she is not being distracted by her children, other books, crafting projects, puzzles, gardening, and her much-loved collection of jumpsuits. She lives in Bath, Somerset.